T0182610

the
WEDDING
Engagement

ZOE ALLISON

Berkley Romance

New York

BERKLEY ROMANCE
Published by Berkley
An imprint of Penguin Random House LLC
penguinrandomhouse.com

Copyright © 2024 by Zoe Allison Author Ltd.
Excerpt from *The Ex-Mas Holidays* by Zoe Allison copyright © 2023
by Zoe Allison Author Ltd.
Penguin Random House supports copyright. Copyright fuels creativity, encourages
diverse voices, promotes free speech, and creates a vibrant culture. Thank you for
buying an authorized edition of this book and for complying with copyright laws by
not reproducing, scanning, or distributing any part of it in any form without
permission. You are supporting writers and allowing Penguin Random
House to continue to publish books for every reader.

BERKLEY and the BERKLEY & B colophon are registered
trademarks of Penguin Random House LLC.

Library of Congress Cataloging-in-Publication Data

Names: Allison, Zoe, author.
Title: The wedding engagement / Zoe Allison.
Description: First Edition. | New York: Berkley Romance, 2024.
Identifiers: LCCN 2024004316 (print) | LCCN 2024004317 (ebook) |
ISBN 9780593550090 (trade paperback) | ISBN 9780593550106 (ebook)
Subjects: LCGFT: Romance fiction. | Novels.
Classification: LCC PR6101.L4577 W44 2024 (print) | LCC PR6101.L4577 (ebook) |
DDC 823/.92—dc23/eng/20240206
LC record available at https://lccn.loc.gov/2024004316
LC ebook record available at https://lccn.loc.gov/2024004317

First Edition: October 2024

Printed in the United States of America
1st Printing

For all the women who have been falsely taught that their

worth is tied to their staying quiet and compliant.

And for all the strong ones, who everyone leans

on but forgets to support in return.

The WEDDING Engagement

Chapter ONE

"**T**HAT'S IT, CATHERINE, LEG NICE AND STRAIGHT," LIV INstructed, reaching out to point at her young student's posture. "And, Josh, remember to keep your thumb outside your fist, not tucked inside. If you strike someone with your thumb tucked in, then you might break it."

"Yes, Sensei," Catherine and Josh said in unison, immediately correcting their errors.

"Good," Liv said, adjusting the black belt tied around her waist and moving on to the next pair of students. The kids in her class had really come along in the relatively short time she'd been teaching them. She was pleased that her own sensei had talked her into it. *"Who better to instruct them than a black belt who's already a qualified teacher?"*

She continued around all of the students, giving them constructive criticism along the way.

Returning to the front of the class, she folded her hands behind her back. "Yame!"

The students ceased their movements.

"Line up," she told them, and watched as they moved quickly

into position in front of her. "Excellent work today. Keep it up and we'll be right on track for the next grading." She bowed to signal the end of the class, and the kids followed suit, then filed out of the dojo to meet their parents.

Once she'd ensured that everyone had found and left with their parent or guardian, Liv went to the locker area to pull on her shoes. Just then, a buzzing noise sounded from her rucksack, and she lifted out her phone. It was a FaceTime from Arran.

Her insides did the familiar tumble at the sight of his name. *How long do we have to be friends before I stop feeling like a giddy schoolgirl whenever I see him?*

She connected the call and Arran's face appeared on-screen, causing her stupid heart to squeeze like an accordion playing a lovesick melody. His honey-colored eyes were unusually tight and he was frowning as he ran a hand over his dark hair.

"What's up?" she asked, picking up on the tension in his posture.

He sighed in a very un-Arran-like manner. "This is an SOS call. 'Help me, Obi-Wan Kenobi. You're my only hope.'"

She laughed. "I'll do my best. Though I have to warn you, my control of the Force is on the fritz."

He smiled; however, it was less bright than usual. "I've got a situation. I'm out of town getting some painting supplies. Jess called to say she can't pick Jayce up from his street-dance class as planned, and I can't get back in time to do it. Her parents are away for the weekend and I just called mine, but, as usual, their mobiles are turned off." He rolled his eyes. "What's the point of having a fucking mobile phone if it's permanently off?"

"My mum and Angus are the same," she told him. "They say they're 'saving the battery.'"

He huffed out a breath. "Parents."

Liv shot him a smile. "*You're* a parent, remember?"

He rubbed a hand over his dark stubble, and she experienced a strong craving to know what it felt like against her own fingers. Against her mouth. *Down, girl.*

"Oh yeah," he said absently. He flicked his eyes to meet hers. "But I'm way cooler."

"Sure you are," she said, giving him a wink. "Anyway, yes, I can pick up Jayce. Shall I take him home with me or bring him to yours?"

Arran hesitated for a second, glancing away from the screen. "Thank you. I'm really sorry to ask for your help." He swallowed, returning his gaze to hers. "Again."

"That's what friends are for," she said, waving her hand dismissively. "Don't sweat it."

The defeated look on his face made it clear that he *was* sweating it. Copiously. She'd never known anyone as proud and reluctant to ask for help as him. And it didn't escape her notice that he hated even voicing the question, which was why she had jumped in to say yes before he'd outright asked.

"I thought it might make sense to call you, because I knew you'd be nearby," he said, as if still trying to justify the very legitimate action of asking a close friend for a small favor.

"Arran, it's fine," she told him, her tone kind but firm. "It wouldn't matter if I wasn't nearby; I'd still be happy to help. I'll nip across the road to the dance studio now and fetch him."

Arran's shoulders sagged with relief. "Thank you. If you head over to mine, I'll meet you back there ASAP."

She gave him a two-fingered salute. "No problem. How come Jess couldn't pick him up anyway? I thought this weekend was hers."

"Yeah, so did I," he muttered, before clearing his throat. "I'll tell you later."

Liv grabbed her bag, heading for the door. "I'll take him for a milkshake first, give you time to reach home."

This time his smile was more relaxed. "You're a lifesaver. I owe you one."

"You can pay me back in scones," she told him, eliciting a laugh from his lovely, soft-looking lips. "Let the teacher know I'll be picking him up, so they don't think I'm trying to kidnap your adorable son."

"Will do." He raised his eyebrows and it made her heart skip a beat. "And by the way, we need to get your scone addiction under control. You, Maya, and Elise have a problem."

She shrugged. "There's no problem. I can give them up anytime I want."

He laughed. "Yeah, right."

They ended the call, and Liv pulled her purple-framed glasses out of her bag, taking out her hair tie so that her wavy dark locks fell free. Then she made her way over to the dance studio. She knew Jayce's class would be finishing in around ten minutes because sometimes she'd see Jayce leaving with either Arran or Jess.

Once inside the studio, she headed over to where the group of parents were waiting for their kids to exit, and she peered through the small window in the door to watch the class. The wee ones were having an absolute ball, performing moves that, in some cases, barely resembled what the teacher was doing. *So cute.*

A few minutes later, the class was dismissed. Liv kept watch for Jayce, hoping he wouldn't be disappointed that she was there instead of his mummy. Before long, his little face appeared behind a crowd of kids, big brown eyes wide and sandy curls bouncing. "Lib!"

"Hey, buddy!" she said, crouching down as he ran over and practically threw himself into her arms.

"Teacher said you were coming," he told her in an excited tone. "We going to play at your house?"

She ruffled his soft hair. "Not today, pal. I'm just picking you up as a favor to Mummy and Daddy."

He grasped her hand as she stood. "You taking me to Mummy's?"

She gave his hand a squeeze. "We're off to Dad's house. I think there's been a change of plan because Mummy's busy."

They exited onto the street. Jayce pointed down the road, toward the fifties-style diner. "Can we get milkshakes?"

"Wow. You read my mind," she said with a smile. "That was exactly my plan."

He threw his small fist into the air. "Yay!"

"AND THEN WHAT HAPPENED?" LIV ASKED, MAINTAINING A SERI-ous expression as Jayce carried on with his tall tale.

"And then I rescued everyone from the dragon and saved the day," he said from the back seat, a proud look on his face when she glanced in the rearview mirror.

She returned her eyes to the road as she navigated the last turn onto Arran's driveway. "Wow. And this was definitely real, not a dream?"

"Wasn't a dream," he scoffed. "It really happened."

"Okay," she told him. "I believe you." She pulled up outside the house and exited the car to get Jayce out of the car seat. She couldn't even remember when she'd started keeping Arran's spare seat in the back; it had happened at some point after the New Year.

Jayce scrambled out of the car before she could help him, running past the grassy area lined with yellow daffodils and purple crocuses and up to the doorway, where he banged his fist. When she reached the doorstep, Liv glanced back at the outdoor scenery, the green of the Highland hills making her optimistic that spring was just around the corner.

The door opened and Arran's smiling face appeared. He crouched down as Jayce barreled into him in his signature greeting. "Daddy! We had milkshakes."

"What? Without me?" Arran said, pouting his lips in an exaggerated manner that made her fantasize—again—about kissing him. "What flavor did you get?"

"Chocolate!" Jayce yelled, running off down the hallway.

Liv laughed as she crossed the threshold. Arran held out his hand and she gave him a side five. Despite the fact that they now performed this gesture pretty much every time they met, the touch of his hand still gave her goose bumps. *That's not how "just friends" is supposed to feel.*

"Have you got time for a cuppa?" he asked her.

"Sure. Always time for tea," Liv told him as she followed him down the hallway.

"Excellent. Walk this way," Arran said, performing a comical gait for her to imitate, which she did. It occurred to her that she had as many in-jokes and gestures with him as she did with her best friends, Maya and Elise. And yet up until the previous summer, while Arran had always been best friends with her twin brother, Sam, to her he'd merely been a casual acquaintance. A really hot acquaintance whom she'd harbored a crush on for the past decade or so. Not that he'd ever noticed.

Arran set about making them some tea. "Don't judge me," he said, glancing up to meet her eyes.

She frowned as she took off her coat, then the jacket from her karate uniform. "Judge you for what?"

For a moment he was silent, and when she looked up, he was eyeing her tank top–clad form with an odd expression. He shook his head slightly, as if bringing his thoughts back to the conversation. "For my inferior tea-making skills."

Liv smiled. She *was* renowned in their friend group for making the best cup of tea in the land. She blew on her fingernails, then pretended to polish them on her white top. "Well. One does try." She took a seat at the breakfast bar, looking behind her to where Jayce was sitting at his little red table, energetically drawing something that resembled a tiny stick figure battling a dragon. "What's the deal with Jess, then? Change of plan for this weekend?"

Arran glanced over at Jayce, then pushed a steaming mug toward her, leaning his elbows on the counter to bring himself closer. Liv's pulse rocketed as she inhaled his scent and struggled furiously to keep her eyes off how his biceps flexed under the close fit of his T-shirt.

"Yeah. She asked if I'd have him last night so she could go to this party with the boyfriend." Arran always referred to Rory as "the boyfriend," and Liv was sure it was because he still resented the fact that his ex-fiancée was dating anyone.

He lifted his mug. "The deal was that I'd drop Jayce at street dance, then she'd pick him up and have him the rest of the weekend. But then she called to say they'd overdone it last night and she was too hungover to drive."

"Ah," Liv said, sipping her tea. "And by that time, you'd already reached the paint shop?"

"Yep," he said on a sigh. "I'm behind schedule on this commission. There's a specific deadline because it's a present for a wedding anniversary."

He took a drink, eyes down in a rather dejected manner.

She touched his hand. "Why the long face? I thought you loved doing these new portraits."

"I do," he said, eyes still on his mug. "Problem is, I'm . . ." He paused, rubbing the side of his face.

"You're what?" she asked, studying him.

He cleared his throat. "I'm struggling. To manage it all." He met her gaze. "Don't get me wrong, I love having Jayce more often. But Jess keeps reneging on her weekends, and it's the only free time I get to paint."

She could tell admitting that was a big deal for him. "Are you in a position where you could give up your day job to concentrate on painting during the week?"

He shook his head with a wince. "Nah. Not yet. But I can't wait

for that day to come. Especially since no one in the office appreci-
ates my sense of humor."

"What did you do this time?" she asked.

He grinned. "I replaced everyone's desk photos with Leonardo
DiCaprio memes."

She sighed, trying to suppress the smile threatening to break
out over her face. "You're *so* immature."

He gave her a nudge. "I can see how desperately you want to
laugh at my hilarious joke, karate kid. Don't try to hide it."

The corner of her mouth quirked.

"We have the same sense of humor." He waggled his fingers.
"We are kindred spirits, you and I," he said in a mysterious tone.

That was the last straw, and she broke down laughing.

He joined in, but as the laughter died away, the tense expression made a reappearance on his normally relaxed face.

Liv watched him, hating seeing her lighthearted and playful
friend so stressed, and wondered what she could do to help. "I'll
babysit for you," she blurted out.

He frowned. "You'll what?"

"Babysit. On the Saturday that's meant to be Jess's. I'll come
over after karate to watch him for the afternoon while you paint. I
can stay into the evening too if you need it."

Arran stared at her, his jaw working. "No."

She waited for him to elaborate, but he stayed silent. "No?
That's all?"

He swallowed hard, lifting his mug to his lips. "No, thank you."

Liv huffed out a breath. "Why not?"

Arran shook his head, frowning. "This is my responsibility, so
I'll handle it. You've got your own life to deal with."

She shrugged. "I'm not busy."

"That's because you're the only one of us that has their shit together," he said, shooting her a smile.

"Yeah, right," she muttered under her breath.

He cocked his head. "Pardon?"

"Nothing."

They both fell silent, and she willed him to change his mind, wishing she were an actual Jedi with the power to sway people's intentions. But he just sipped his tea with a determined look on his face.

She sighed. "You're so stubborn and annoying."

He grinned. "You love me, really."

"Hmm," she said, keeping her eyes on her tea.

"Any plans for tomorrow?" he asked in an obvious effort to change the subject.

She decided it was best to let it go—for now. "Yeah. I'm meeting Elise at Maya and Sam's house tomorrow afternoon. Sam will be there too."

"Oh yeah?" he said. "What time? Sam's meant to be meeting me and Nico at Nico's sister's house tomorrow after lunch." He paused, seeming to ponder for a second. "Sam seemed pretty eager to catch up. When Nico asked for a rain check—because he was babysitting his sister's kids—Sam said no and that we'd just meet Nico there."

She frowned. "Not sure what that's all about. But our thing isn't until midafternoon, so he must be seeing you guys first, then coming to us."

Arran arched an eyebrow. "Curiouser and curiouser."

She smiled. "Yes, indeed. Anyway, we'll find out what the story is tomorrow."

"Yep." He lifted his mug, she clunked hers with his, and as she sipped her drink she reminded herself that no good could come of her attraction to one of her best friends.

Chapter
TWO

FINISHING OFF THE LAST FLICK OF THE CURLING IRON, LIV paused to check out her efforts. Hair curled—check. Smoky eye and winged eyeliner—check. Little black skater-style dress with best lacy underwear hidden underneath—check.

She purposely hadn't mentioned her blind date to Arran when she'd dropped Jayce off earlier on, feeling rather self-conscious about the whole thing. Luckily, he'd only asked what she was doing the next day, not that evening, so she hadn't needed to make something up. She sucked at lying and loathed doing it.

At first she'd resisted the idea when her friend Maya had told her about the new blind-date app—BlindLove—but then her resolve had crumbled when she'd pondered how long it had been since she'd been on a date. It would be fun to find something casual again, and it didn't need to progress to anything serious.

She'd admitted to Maya and their other best friend, Elise, that she was going on the date but had asked them not to mention it to anyone because she couldn't be bothered with the inevitable pressure to pursue a serious relationship. People really were obsessed with converting single women's relationship status to "coupled up."

Her phone buzzed, signaling that her taxi was approaching, so she hurried down the stairs to put on her black heels and biker-style jacket before heading out to the waiting car.

On the way to the bar, she opened the BlindLove app again. The app's algorithm wasn't based on information such as job status or hobbies, but matched people anonymously using themes such as values, character traits, and life goals. Her date's profile indicated that he liked physical/slapstick and wordplay-type humor (tick), liked kids (tick), and was just getting into dating again and not looking for anything serious (big tick). He valued honesty, integrity, family, and friends above any monetary or materialistic possessions. He also shared her dreams of taking some time to travel before coming back to Glenavie to settle down. Both felt that this town of theirs carried a central, special place in their hearts.

Her date's handle was GlenavieTimelord and she wouldn't discover his real name until they met in person.

Liv scanned the rest of their messages. Careful not to reveal any details that would unblind them, they'd discussed their mutual love of *Doctor Who* and eighties movies.

Liv popped the phone into her handbag, peering through the windshield to see if they were nearly there.

Once the taxi pulled up and she paid the driver, the nerves really set in. She glanced down at herself as she crossed the threshold, hoping that her date would like the way she looked. As she scanned the crowd, searching for a man also wearing a homemade badge with David Tennant's face on it (they had decided to opt for this as their call sign, both being Whovians and in agreement that David was all-round awesome), she hoped that in addition she would like the way *he* looked. And then perhaps the lacy underwear wouldn't have come out for nothing . . .

Her gaze landed on a badge sporting David Tennant's smiling face, attached to a dark T-shirt stretching over an appealingly toned chest. And upon raising her eyes to her date's face, she found herself staring straight into familiar honey-colored eyes.

ARRAN BLINKED AGAIN, ASSUMING THE ACTION WOULD WASH away the hallucination of Liv standing there, wearing a David Tennant pin, and looking absolutely fucking gorgeous.

For a moment the shock of her appearing as his blind date faded into the background as he was taken over by a thunderbolt of desire. Her black dress ended at mid-thigh, showing off smooth legs that seemed to go on for days and were complemented by high heels that accentuated the shapely curves of her calves. The bodice hugged her breasts, closely tracing the mouthwatering outline that had caught his eye earlier that same day—when she'd removed her karate jacket and he'd inadvertently taken in an eyeful of her chest.

"*Fuck*," he muttered under his breath. His heart hammered as she appeared to recover from the shock of seeing him, unfreezing and walking toward him. His eyes snagged on her shiny dark hair. An overwhelming temptation surfaced as he imagined lifting a hand and coiling his fingers into her ringlets while looking into the sultry spectacle of her eyes, then pulling her head back to bite the long line of her neck. He resisted the temptation—barely—as his fingers twitched at his side, dying to follow through on the idea.

"Well," she told him, coming to stand in front of him. She was a lot taller in heels but still only came up to chin height on him. For a moment he fantasized that she might jump up into his arms and wrap those lovely legs around his waist.

"This is a surprise," she continued, giving him a lopsided smile.

He cleared his throat because it felt like his own tongue was attempting to choke him. "You can say that again."

She let out a laugh that was a little higher pitched than usual. His mind raced as he tried to come to terms with the last few mind-blowingly confusing seconds. His blind date was Liv, his best friend's twin sister. The woman who helped him with childcare. The woman who would soon become his son's nursery school teacher. The woman he'd known since they were about five years old and he hadn't ever looked upon as anything other than a friend—until the last few months, when little snatches of heat began burning whenever she'd touched his hand, held his gaze, or took off her top layer to reveal tight-fitting clothing underneath.

Well, that heat was anything but a little snatch now. The sight of her this evening had been like pouring lighter fluid on a slowly burning barbecue. Boom.

Should he voice it?

"Come on," she said, taking his elbow and pulling him toward the bar while he continued to stare at her. Her lips were painted cherry red. Would they taste like cherries if he kissed her?

Something hard smacked into his front and he realized it was the bar. Dazed, he watched Liv signal the barman (who was very quick to give her his attention, gracing her with an appreciative look—the fucking bastard), and she ordered them both a bottle of beer. His favorite one.

Arran tried desperately to kick-start his brain into action, but it seemed to have turned to mush, melted by the sight of Olivia Holland sporting sultry eye makeup, cherry-red lipstick, a sexy little black dress, and heels. He couldn't remember seeing her dressed up before. He wished he'd been prepared so that he could at least have retained the power of speech in this situation.

Grasping the cold bottle of beer the barman presented, he didn't even have the wherewithal to get his wallet out before Liv.

She lifted her bottle toward his, and he managed to interpret her actions through the lust fog in his brain and clink his bottle with hers. His mind raced. He should say something. Tell her how beautiful she looked and how his feelings had been evolving and that now that they were here tonight perhaps it was a sign that they should take their relationship further—out of the platonic and into the more . . . intimate. The issues of their friendship and her relationship with his son faded into the background as he stared hungrily at her mouth. With a start, he realized that her lips were moving.

". . . so at least we're on the same page," she finished.

Fuck. What had she just said?

He gave his head a small shake in the hope that it might reboot his brain. "Sorry, mate." *Mate?! Wrong time to use that word!* "It's a bit loud in here and I didn't quite catch what you said."

She laughed. "You're too old to hear in pubs now?"

"Hey," he said, giving her arm a nudge. The touch of her bare skin sent a slug of lust through his veins, making the hairs on his arms stand on end. "We're the same age."

She gave him a wink, and his skin about set on fire.

Whatever she had been saying ended with "we're on the same page." So had she just said what he'd been thinking, that they should make a go of this? His stuttering brain sent a stream of consciousness right to his mouth and he started to speak at the same time as Liv. "I was thinking that we should—"

"I was saying that—" Liv stopped. "Sorry, what were you going to say?"

He shook his head, realizing his interruption. "No, sorry, you finish first, then I'll go."

She smiled, glancing down and brushing the toe of her stiletto over the floor. "I was saying that this is awkward. Neither of us was expecting to see the other tonight." Her smile became a little fixed. "I saw you swear under your breath when you clocked me, and I'm sorry for wasting your time."

Oh shit. "No, Liv, that's not—"

She held up a hand. "It's okay, Arran. I don't mind. I also said that I feel the same way, so at least we're on the same page."

His mouth went dry. "You feel the same way, as in . . ."

"That this is a bit mortifying, and I wish it hadn't happened."

Arran's heart thudded and sank like a stone. "Ah, I see." All the potential sexy scenarios running through his mind swirled and faded away as if being flushed down the toilet. Damn it. At least he hadn't run his mouth off and ended up embarrassing himself—and her. As the cold trickle of disappointment doused his emotions and his rational brain took over from his lust-driven one, he realized that even if Liv were interested in him in a romantic manner, there was no way he'd risk losing her friendship. He'd always been on friendly terms with Liv, but over the past several months, she had grown to become one of his closest friends. If he started something with her and it went south, like it had with Jess, then their relationship would be destroyed. And the idea of not having Liv in his life at all was too painful to contemplate. Plus it would drive a wedge between him and Sam.

She looked sad, her eyes down at her feet, and his protective instinct rose.

"Hey." He gave her another little nudge. "Don't sweat it. At least we get to hang out tonight, right?"

She lifted those beautiful big green eyes and gave him a smile. "Yeah. Good point." She clinked her bottle with his again and they both took a drink. Liv sighed. "And to think I wore my sexy black underwear for nothing."

Arran gripped his beer bottle so hard it was lucky the thing didn't smash in his hand. She was wearing sexy black underwear underneath that hot little black dress? Was it lacy? Sheer? The kind that he could touch and suck the sensitive parts of her through? Scanning her body, he imagined with impressive clarity what she would look like standing in front of him in her underwear. Unfortunately, the process gave him a semi—standing in a public bar, in front of his best friend. He surreptitiously tugged at the front of his jeans.

Liv seemed oblivious. "Where's Jayce, by the way?"

He took a deep breath. "With my parents."

"Cool." She shifted from one foot to the other.

He gave her a rueful smile. "In hindsight, I don't know why we didn't guess it was each other. The *Doctor Who* thing . . . the eighties-movies geeks thing."

She smiled. "I'm sure there are other people in Glenavie who like that stuff."

He pursed his lips, giving an exaggerated slow shake of his head. "Uh-uh. Those are our things."

She let out a laugh that tinkled with pleasure at his sentiment. "Anyway, there's no way I would've guessed it was you because I never thought you'd be on the app in a million years, Mr. I Don't Want to Date Ever Again."

He huffed out a breath. "Yeah, well. This just cements that sentiment."

Her face fell, and he kicked himself for, yet again, inadvertently making her think that he was in any way disappointed with her company. "Sorry, I didn't mean that the way it sounded."

She smiled again, but it contained a tinge of sadness, and he hated seeing her sad.

Arran grabbed his phone from his pocket, knowing what would cheer her up and make her more comfortable, plus take his mind off any more R-rated scenarios. "Wanna see some photos we took this afternoon of me and Jayce playing dress-up as Disney princesses?"

Her eyes widened. "Yes, please."

He grinned, putting his arm around his friend's shoulders and pulling her in to look at the screen, trying desperately to ignore the resulting temptation swamping him, which now seemed to be here to stay.

Chapter
THREE

"YOU'RE TALKING ABSOLUTE BOLLOCKS," MAYA SAID, GIVING LIV a hard stare across the kitchen table.

Liv raised her eyebrows in response. "I am *not*." It was rare for her to argue with someone, but this was a very important subject. "I'm telling you," she continued. "The jam should go on first, and *then* the cream." She lifted her scone and took a big jammy, creamy bite. "That's how they do it down in Cornwall."

"But in Devon, they do cream first," Maya replied, taking a bite of her own scone and getting jam on her nose in the process.

"Ha!" Liv pointed at her with a grin. "Your nose is jammed. The downside of the jam-on-top method."

Maya shot her a mock-stern look, then tried to lick the jam off her nose. But her tongue wouldn't reach so she sat there for a moment, stretching the tip of her tongue desperately toward her nose while Liv tried and then failed to hold in a snort of laughter. Maya gave up and, with a smile, wiped the jam off with her finger—licking it instead.

Elise gave them both a wry smile from the head of the table. "The real question is, how do we do it here in the Highlands?"

"Jam first!" Liv shouted, as Maya yelled, "Cream first!"

Pursing her lips, Elise sipped her tea. "This is a very important debate, which I fear shall not be settled today."

Maya sniffed, sipping the tea, then shot Liv a smile. "This isn't up to your usual standard—methinks you might be distracted by pining for a certain gentleman?"

"Shut it, you," Liv muttered as she lifted her cup. She studied Maya's delicate china, imagining she really was in an Austen novel, in an attempt to take her mind off this conversation.

"A certain gentleman?" Elise chimed in. "I assume you mean Arran."

"Yep," Maya said, doing a poor job of hiding her grin behind her teacup.

"Ugh," Liv muttered. "I wish you'd let this one go." This repetitive conversation was more painful and awkward than the time Liv had been on a date with a hot guy and she'd gone to push her glasses up her nose—staring at him while he spoke, mesmerized by his beautiful face. Except she hadn't actually been wearing her glasses. So, she'd ended up poking herself in the eye instead.

Elise was watching her over the rim of her cup. "Can't you just tell him how you feel?"

Liv bit her lip, avoiding Elise's gaze. "We're just friends. I don't want to make it awks." She fiddled with her cup, hoping to avoid scrutiny. "Anyway. He's always been very vocal about wanting to stay away from relationships after Jess broke it off with him."

She tried not to cringe as she remembered the sight of him cursing under his breath when he'd seen that it was her. It had made the whole thing even more mortifying. At her insistence, he'd agreed not to tell the others. Liv had pretended to Maya and Elise that the date had been a washout because the guy had a major belly-button-fluff fetish.

"You don't know for sure unless you address it," Elise said. She lifted a jammy dodger from the plate in the middle of the table and dunked it into her tea. "You're always protecting everyone else. Put your own feelings first for once. And if he doesn't feel the same way, then he'll have to deal with it and carry on, like a grown-up. It's hardly a trauma, having a gorgeous friend say that they fancy the pants off you."

Liv pondered her tangled emotions where Arran was concerned. "It's more complicated than that," she said, aware she was being deliberately vague.

Maya shrugged. "We always think these things are more complicated than they are."

Liv stirred her already well-stirred tea, imagining that the words she was attempting to carefully choose might suddenly whoosh up through the small brown whirlpool she was creating inside the china cup. "It *is* pretty complex. He's my brother's best friend, and, since he and Jess split, one of *my* closest friends. And I've got a real bond with Jayce. I don't want to do anything to upset the balance—between us, between his son and me, or among our friends."

Liv bit her bottom lip, trying to avoid both Maya's and Elise's gazes. She desperately wanted this conversation to be over.

"What else is complicating it?" Maya asked, her brow knitting.

Hesitating a beat, Liv searched for something to throw them off. She couldn't tell them that the idea of a serious committed relationship terrified her. And whatever she did tell them couldn't be a lie, because she was as shit at lying as Pinocchio. "The fact that Jayce is going to be starting in my nursery school class after Easter."

Maya wrinkled her nose. "That's not a major complication."

Liv decided to steer the conversation further onto Jayce and away from Arran. "I've actually offered to babysit Jayce regularly, for a few hours on a Saturday afternoon and evening."

Maya and Elise both raised their eyebrows, and there was a moment's silence before Elise broke it. "*Every* Saturday?"

Liv shook her head. "No. Just one per month, the one that is meant to be Jess's weekend. The demands on Arran's one free weekend are going up just as his portrait work has been taking off, and he needs that time to work."

Elise frowned. "Isn't there someone else who can babysit? His parents?"

Liv shook her head. "They already have him one day in the week; so does Jess's mum. Arran won't want to ask them for any more. And I'm the only one out of our friends who doesn't have a life." She shot them a grin.

Maya fake coughed, muttering, "Because you're too busy pining over him."

Liv shot Maya her hardest stare. But because she loved Maya to bits, the stare was only about as hard as butter. "I mean—you and Sam have each other, and Elise is busy with work and wee Jack. And Nico—"

"Is busy with all the women about town," Elise finished, arching a brow as she sipped her tea.

Liv frowned. "I was going to say running his own fitness empire, leading the local Scout group, and helping out with his nieces and nephews. But okay." She leaned back with a sigh. "Anyway, it doesn't matter. I suggested it, but Arran wasn't keen. Too proud to accept any help."

Maya leaned her chin on her hand to study Liv. "You know what? You need to stop doing stuff for everyone else and do something for yourself. Like go on a proper date. Not a blind one, but a knowing-what-you're-getting-yourself-into one."

A heavy feeling tugged at Liv's stomach. "With who?"

Had Maya finally gotten the message that Liv and Arran were a lost cause? But aiming her matchmaking sights on someone else was nearly as bad.

"What about Brodie?"

Liv paused to ponder that question. Brodie was handsome and friendly, plus good fun. There was no logical reason not to go on a date with him, if he was interested. But logic wasn't driving her at the moment. "I dunno."

"Come on. He's got those gorgeous baby blues, lovely dark hair." Maya winked. "Runs a ski shop, where you can get your best friend loads of discounted skiwear . . ."

A smile tugged at Liv's mouth. "I'll think about it."

"Good," Maya replied. "Because your last big relationship was with Dean when we were eighteen, and even then, it ended before six months."

Liv stiffened. "I *have* dated since then. You're making it sound like I've been celibate for the last nine years."

Maya waved a hand. "Casual dating doesn't count." She sighed. "I don't get it. You're such a catch. And the only one of us who has their shit together."

Liv bit her tongue. Why did people always assume that a woman who didn't have long-lasting relationships craved anything other than that? No one ever seemed to consider that it might be *her* avoiding anything serious. *Her* pushing the guy away, not vice versa. But at least it created a convenient distraction.

Playing the reluctant, terminally single woman was a good front and meant she could keep up her pretense of being "the only one who has their shit together." Little did her friends know that she didn't really feel that way.

The front door opened and shut, signaling Sam's arrival. "Sorry I'm late!" he called.

His footsteps sounded up the hallway, and as he entered the kitchen, Liv stood to give him a hug.

"All right, twinny?" she asked as he leaned down to kiss the top of her head.

"Yep," he said, releasing her with a grin as he went on to kiss

Elise's cheek. He then gave Maya a full-on kiss on the lips with borderline tongue, which made Liv feel as if she and Elise should de-
part the vicinity, posthaste.

Liv sat, clearing her throat. "I *would* tell you two to get a room,
but we're in your house."

Maya broke off, blowing her fringe out of her eyes. "Sorry. Got
overexcited."

Liv took in the blush on Maya's cheeks and the manner in
which Sam was shifting his weight from one foot to the other. She
narrowed her eyes. "Spill it."

Sam shot Maya a look. She grabbed his hand to tug him into the
seat next to her. "You can tell them," she said.

He shook his head. "I got to tell Arran and Nico. Your shot now."

The smile threatening Liv's mouth broke into a full-blown grin.
Oh my God. I know where this is going.

Maya swallowed. "We're getting married."

A starburst of joy erupted in Liv's chest, driving her to her feet
with a scream. She grabbed hold of Sam tightly before he could get
fully to his feet, eliciting a laugh from him. Then she dropped him
like a hot potato to grab hold of Maya. Even that wasn't enough, so
she took one under each arm in a three-way hug, with Elise joining
in, circling Maya and Sam, with Liv in the middle.

"Ahh." Liv sighed, closing her eyes. "Four-way hugs are awesome."

Another voice sounded from behind her, one that gave her
goose bumps and sent her heart rate up a notch. "Five-way hugs are
where it's at."

She turned her head, looking up to meet Arran's eyes as he took
hold of her from behind, pressing into her back to circle the group
with his arms and eliciting laughter from everyone. The memory
of lifting her gaze from his David Tennant badge up to his eyes the
previous evening surfaced, causing her cheeks to grow red-hot. Her
face nestled in his neck as he leaned in, and she breathed the deli-

THE WEDDING ENGAGEMENT   23

cious scent of him—sandalwood infused with orange blossom. The hard pressure of his chest against her shoulders sent her nerve endings zinging into a frenzy.

Sam stretched a hand over everyone's head to ruffle Arran's loose, coily hair. "What're you doing here? I only just left. Miss me?"

Arran grinned. "I wasn't ready to finish celebrating and Nico had to get on with his babysitting duties. There was a major incident involving his little niece Aurora and a projectile vomit, so I hotfooted it out of there."

Liv laughed. "Some friend you are."

He shrugged. "Not everyone can be as amazing a mate as you."

Heat rose in her face. Deciding to extricate herself before he noticed her blushing, she broke up the hug from the inside, dispersing everyone back to their seats, with Arran taking up residence in the chair next to her. She poured him and Sam some tea.

Arran raised an eyebrow as she passed him his cup. "Hey."

Liv glanced down and clocked that he was holding out his hand. She gave him a side five, then flexed her fingers in an attempt to dispel the tingling sensation left by his touch.

Sam lifted his cup, took a sip, then set it back down again. "Enough of this tea," he declared, getting to his feet and rummaging in the fridge. He lifted out a bottle of champagne and proceeded to pop the cork, resulting in a cheer from the group.

He brought the bottle over with some champagne flutes and filled everyone's glass for a toast. As they clinked them together, Arran slid his hand over the back of Liv's chair and brushed her shoulders with his arm. "Cheers."

"To the happy couple." Liv smiled, attempting to ignore the heat of Arran's arm, which was stirring up heat in other parts of her body too. She dashed a quick glance at Elise, worried that the announcement of a wedding would elicit painful memories for her friend, who had been widowed the previous year. But she was reassured by the smile on Elise's face and the matching sparkle in her blue eyes.

"Tell us everything," Elise said, leaning forward. "How did you propose?"

Maya and Sam gave each other a look that turned Liv's heart into a pool of warm mush. She loved the two of them to bits. How lucky was she, her twin brother and best mate getting together?

Sam ran a hand through his hair. "I feel I've let womankind down, because it really wasn't very romantic. We were out for dinner and started talking about the future. We both said we wanted to get married and it should be sooner rather than later." He gave Maya a smile. "So Maya said we should get engaged and set a date, and I agreed." His smile morphed into a grin. "And by agreed, I of course mean I nearly bit her hand off."

Sam tugged her into his chest and kissed her forehead.

"Right," Arran said, rubbing his hands together. "On to the most important part. What are we doing for the stag do?"

Liv raised her eyebrows. "Most important part?"

Elise laughed. "Yeah. Surely the *most* important part is the day our friends make a lifelong commitment to each other."

Grinning, Liv shook her head. "No. I mean the hen do is more important than the stag."

Arran laughed heartily, the sound of his low rumble creating a warmth in her chest. "Touché," he said.

"Not to worry," Sam said, smiling. "Those two events will be one and the same."

"A combined hen and stag party?" Liv asked, her eyes widening. "That would be cool."

Maya nodded. "We're going to have a weekend away, with all of us."

"Nice," said Arran, leaning back and lifting his fizz. He stroked his fingers down his stubble with a raised eyebrow. "Everything's more fun when the ladies are around."

Liv shot him a smile, which he reciprocated, and she found herself caught in it for a second, her heart flipping. Arran had the kind of smile that gave his eyes a glow, like a tumbler of whiskey sitting in the afternoon sun.

She turned toward Sam and Maya, who were on the other side of the table. "Pretty cool that I get to go on my bro's stag. Gotta find me some dollar bills to slide into the panties of the hot strippers."

Arran nearly spat out his mouthful of champagne, coughing in the process.

Liv turned to him, patting him on the back. "Oopsie. You're meant to drink that stuff, not inhale it, sweet cheeks."

He managed a laugh through his cough, wiping his mouth with the back of his hand as his gaze raked over her, giving her goose bumps. "The image of you stuffing cash into the underwear of naked dancing ladies distracted me."

Something about the way he dragged his hand across his mouth did it for her. But then again, everything about him did it for her. She shoved that thought deep down into the basement of her mind, locking the imaginary cast-iron door, padlocking it, and drawing down a wooden plank to barricade it.

She sniffed, pursing her lips at him. "Don't be such a prude."

Maya leaned on the table to address Liv and Elise. "There's something I need to ask you guys." She paused to take a breath, seeming a little self-conscious. "Would you two be my best women?"

Liv's mouth dropped open, joy rising in her chest. This day couldn't get any better. "I'd love that."

"Me too," Elise said, her eyes shining. "Thank you."

Sam nodded toward Arran. "I've already asked this arsehole to be my best man, along with Nico."

Arran raised his eyebrow, lifting his glass toward Sam. "Watch it, Holland. Or I might *accidentally* misplace the rings."

Sam grinned, giving Arran a wink. "We're evenly matched. Two best men, and two best women."

Liv leaned her forearms on the table, excitement infusing her. "What do you need us to do?"

Maya swirled her champagne. "If you guys could organize the weekend away, that would be awesome. We're hoping to have everything covered with planning the actual wedding; it'll only be small anyway."

Elise rummaged around in her handbag, bringing out a notebook with spring flowers and rainbows on the front. She flipped it open and pulled a sparkly pen from the elastic loop on the side. "Tell us your wish list and let's get organizing right now."

Liv laughed. "Did you have that notebook on standby? Your stationery addiction is getting out of hand."

A smile tugged at the corner of Elise's mouth. "You never know when a new notebook might come in handy."

Maya glanced at Sam. "I'm not sure we've got a wish list, as such."

"What destination are we thinking?" Arran said.

Sam rubbed his beard. "Not sure."

Raising his eyebrows, Arran smiled. "Are we talking Ibiza, or Inverness?"

"Scotland-based, I reckon," Maya said. She glanced at Sam. "Is that okay with you?"

"Definitely," Sam replied, shooting her a soft look that made Liv's already mushy heart melt a little further. "Save our money for the honeymoon."

Maya grinned. "Probably less chance of naked dancing ladies, though, in Scotland compared to the Balearics. That okay?"

Sam looked her up and down. "Unless I get a naked dance off you?"

Shrugging, Maya lifted her glass to take a sip. "Depends on how much you're paying."

Elise was scribbling more notes, clearly taking the organizational role very seriously.

Liv peered over her shoulder, curious to see whether she'd actually documented "no naked dancing ladies."

"When are we talking?" Elise asked.

"Perhaps April or May?" Maya said. "Because we're thinking of a June wedding."

"Blimey," Elise said, glancing up. "Only four months to plan a wedding. You two don't mess about, do you?"

Sam took Maya's hand. "Nope. There's already been too much messing about and delay. So, we're going for it."

Maya leaned over and kissed his cheek.

Liv spotted Elise exchanging a look with Arran at that point, and she suspected that the two people in the room who had actually planned a wedding in the past thought Maya and Sam naive in their underestimation of the task at hand.

Arran leaned back. "No time like the present, I suppose. Long engagements are a bad idea."

Liv glanced at him, trying to read any underlying emotion behind his neutral expression. He and Jess had been engaged for a number of years before they set their date.

"Any specifics apart from Scotland-based?" Elise asked.

Maya and Sam shook their heads.

"Right," Elise said. "We should probably pick a weekend first, then decide where we want to go. Then we can curate a list of venues and narrow it down, see what places have vacancies."

The doorbell rang.

Sam stood and left the kitchen, then shortly after they heard the sound of him opening the door and Nico's deep voice.

Liv noticed Elise burying her head in her notebook and starting to scribble as Nico entered the room.

"Manage to get out of the vomit cleanup?" Arran asked.

"Nah. I cleaned it up, but then my sister came home early so I figured I'd come join in the celebrations." Nico tugged off his black leather jacket, his muscles bulging under his tight-fitting long-sleeved shirt. Elise glanced over from her notebook, her gaze seeming to land on the swell of Nico's deltoid, then whipping away back onto her scribblings.

Nico leaned on the table, glancing at Elise as she jotted away. "Kowalski."

She gave him a nod in return.

"Right," he said to the group as he took a seat. "Where are we at?"

"Deciding on a date for the pre-wedding weekend away," Maya said. "We should probably find a couple of options, in case one of them doesn't work out."

Liv lifted out her phone to open the calendar, the others following suit. She glanced at Arran, who was frowning at his phone screen, his brow furrowed in an adorable manner. "When has Jess got Jayce?" she asked. "Let's use those weekends as a starter."

He nodded, giving a couple of dates to Elise, who noted them down. She lifted her gaze. "Not many going spare."

Arran winced. "Yeah. Jess has a lot of stuff on." He looked at Liv, and she registered just then how much he needed her support. She was going to make him accept it by hook or by crook.

"Either of those weekends is good for us," Sam said, slinging his arm around Maya's shoulders.

Elise nodded. "Fine by me too. Mum and Dad will manage one weekend with Jack, I'm sure. It doesn't matter which one it is."

Nico scrolled through his phone. "Good for me too. Where are we going?"

"I've had an idea about that," Arran said, leaning his elbows on the table.

"Me too," Liv said, mirroring him.

He gave her a wink that made her skin tingle. "Ladies first."

Smiling, she faced the others. "I think we should go to Skye. Remember that school trip—"

"We all went on in sixth year?" Arran finished for her. He grinned. "Exactly the same idea I had."

Liv met his gaze, something warm passing between them. She found that they were always on the same wavelength. Except where romantic feelings were concerned—but she reminded herself that it was for the best that he didn't reciprocate her feelings. Even though it hurt.

"Yes," Maya said, clapping her hands together.

Sam nodded. "I loved that trip. And we were talking about wanting to visit again."

"Great," Elise said, jotting down a couple of things. "Hotel? Cottage?"

Nico interjected. "Leave that to me. I've got a contact who owns a huge property on Skye, a holiday home. I'm sure it'll be free because she's working away at the moment."

"Brilliant," Maya said. "Thank you."

"She?" Elise said, shooting Nico a wry smile. "An ex-girlfriend?"

Nico met her gaze head-on. "Yes. I'm friends with all my exes." He hesitated for a beat. "Mostly."

"Let us know if you can get the property," Elise said, "and I'll search for some alternatives just in case you can't. When do you think you can get hold of her?"

Nico lifted his phone, tapping out a message. "Right now."

"We'll need to decide what activities we want to do," Liv said, pushing her glasses up her nose. She shot Maya a death stare. "Probably a massive hike, knowing you and your springtime program at the ski resort." Maya stuck her tongue out at her.

"Don't worry," Arran said, bumping her shoulder. "I'll give you a piggyback if your feet get blistered."

"Thanks." She smiled, trying to cover the fact that imagining being on Arran's back, even fully clothed, gave her goose bumps.

Elise leaned back. "I'm going to see if I can book a nice restaurant for the Saturday night." She glanced at Nico. "Where's your friend's cottage?"

"Portree," he replied, tossing a cookie in the air and catching it in his mouth.

Elise appeared to roll her eyes a little as she went back to her scribbling. "Right. I'll sort food, Nico will do accommodation. Liv, can you and Arran come up with some activities?"

Liv nodded her agreement.

Elise closed her notebook, glancing at Nico. "Text me with the answer about the cottage, and I'll sort something if we can't get it."

Nico shook his head, frowning. "I'll text you with the outcome. But if it falls through, *I'll* sort something."

Leaning back in her seat and folding her arms, Elise eyed him. "Don't trust me to find somewhere to your liking?"

"I do," he said, holding her gaze. "But you've got enough on your plate. So I'll sort it."

Elise seemed taken aback for a moment. Then she nodded. "Great."

Arran gave Liv a nudge as the others began talking among themselves. "We should meet up soon and get the activities sorted." He gave her another one of those sexy winks, causing a delicious shiver to lick up her spine.

"Yeah, let's do it. I've got a few ideas already about the activities."

"Same." He nudged her arm. "We'll compare notes. See who comes out on top."

Her cheeks burned at the thought of either of them being atop the other, so she moved her gaze away from his sparkling honey eyes. *Planning a wedding-related activity with the guy I've been crushing on for years. What could go wrong?*

Chapter

FOUR

LIV PLACED THE PLATE OF COOKIES SHE'D NOT LONG AGO TAKEN from the oven on the center of the kitchen table, inhaling their warm, scrummy scent. Eyeing the cookies, she tried to keep her hands, and mouth, off them. A glance at the clock confirmed that Arran should be there soon, eliciting a burst of butterflies in her tummy. She'd purposely made his favorite cookies for their weekend-away planning date. Not that it was a date, of course; their last and only one of those had not gone well at all.

Over the last couple of days, the thought of her brother's wedding and the gathering of family had unexpectedly brought unwelcome memories to the fore, of the day that their dad had fucked off to Jersey with another woman. That event had come after his lying to their mum about his cheating for ages. In the end, all Liv had felt was relief to have him gone. But she'd been devastated for her mum. And for Sam, who'd always had more of a relationship with their dad—if you could call what was between them a relationship. It was more that Dave held Sam in higher esteem, being the son. Like he was some sort of trophy, with Liv as the third—unwanted—wheel.

The doorbell rang, cutting into her dark thoughts, and Liv

shook her head in an effort to banish them. She headed to open the door, her pulse picking up at the sight of Arran in his soft, tan leather jacket. The color complemented the smooth, coppery tone of his sepia brown skin. He smiled, leaning in to perform their signature shake as he came into the house. "Hey, karate kid." The smell of leather combined with his sweet and spicy natural scent drove her heart rate up another notch.

"Have you been baking?" he asked, his eyes widening. "It smells awesome."

Liv raised an eyebrow, gesturing for him to follow her to the kitchen. "I have indeed."

Arran pulled off his jacket and Liv dragged her eyes from the flex of his arms. She lifted the teapot, raising her gaze to meet his. "Tea?"

"Yes, please," he said, taking a seat and pushing two of the cups over for her. He took the milk jug and poured the perfect splash into hers. *Just the way I like it.* A fuzzy feeling warmed her chest.

He glanced at the plate of cookies, running his tongue over his bottom lip. "Is it bad form to eat one before they've cooled?"

Liv dragged her eyes from his mouth to meet his eyes, trying to stop imagining how that tongue might feel on *her* lip. "Nah. I was thinking the same thing myself."

"Excellent." He rubbed his hands together and lifted two, passing her one of them. She pretended she couldn't feel the zap of electricity when his fingers brushed hers.

Liv munched on her cookie, concentrating on the sugary goodness in order to banish illicit Arran-related images from her mind. "Any thoughts on what we were discussing the other day, about babysitting?"

He took a bite of his biscuit and licked his lips. Fucking hell. She couldn't cope with all this lip licking. How come his performing such mundane activities was borderline pornographic to her? Never mind Christian Grey and his whips and chains; give her Arran Adebayo and a plate of crumbly cookies any day.

He ran a hand over his hair. "I know it was your idea, but I feel like I guilted you into suggesting it. I shouldn't have been moaning about getting these portraits done on time. It's a big commitment for you, even in the short term."

"It's only one day a month. Anyway, I wouldn't have suggested it if I didn't want to do it," she said, pushing her glasses up her nose. "I love spending time with Jayce, and I'd be delighted to help you get your portraits done."

When he met her gaze, the warm honey of his eyes penetrated deep into her chest. "I don't want to take advantage. Especially when you'll be looking after him every day at nursery school soon."

Liv opened her mouth to reply, but he held his hand up to silence her, a puzzled look on his face. "Did you hear that?" he asked.

Liv paused, listening. "What?"

"That noise," he said, frowning. "I think it was the sound of the lesser spotted haggis."

She arched an eyebrow. "The lesser spotted haggis?"

"Mmm." His face was serious as he lifted his mug to take a seat at the table. "Even less common than the, er, *more* spotted haggis."

She smiled affectionately at his asinine attempt to change the subject. She wished he'd stop being so reluctant to take on any help. Getting him to accept it sometimes felt like hitting one's head against a brick wall.

Granted, if she could convince him, she'd need to be wary. She could hardly cope with watching the poor guy eat baked goods.

Arran blew on his tea, eyeing her. "Are we definitely good, after the David Tennant rendezvous?"

Her cheeks only heated slightly this time, so that was an improvement. "Yeah. We're good."

He nodded, then glanced away as he sipped his drink. "By the way, I need to point out that it wasn't disappointment that made me swear when I saw you arrive."

She looked at him as he met her gaze again, something squeezing in her chest. "No?"

He shook his head. "I was just . . . surprised is all."

She smiled. "You and me both."

He returned her expression. "Surprised to see you, and then surprised at the fact that you can lip-read."

Liv laughed.

He ran a hand over his hair. "Seriously, though. I'd hate for you to think I'd ever be disappointed to see you, in any situation."

A flicker of something flashed in her mind as she tried to parse his meaning.

His gaze grew more intense as he seemed to struggle with what he wanted to say next. Then his voice came out a little thick. "You looked beautiful. I should have told you that at the time." He swallowed. "I mean, you look beautiful all the time, but particularly so that night. I don't think I've seen you all dressed up before."

Her heart was pulsing in her ears and she could swear that electricity was crackling in the small space between her and Arran. Was he trying to say that . . . he found her attractive? Her cheeks heated up to about a million degrees.

He glanced at her cheeks—no doubt because they must have been as red as a baboon's bottom—and gave her a reassuring smile. "Anyhow. My point is, you scrub up well, mate." He cleared his throat. "Right. Let's get down to weekend-away planning business."

Liv took a breath, disappointed and confused. She pushed her feelings aside and tried to focus. "I'm so glad Nico got that cottage."

"I know," Arran said, raising his eyebrows. "Proper posh. I thought a cottage on Skye would be all low ceilings and crumbling brick, not glass patios and sweeping terraces. But then Nico still mixes in all the big-shot-lawyer circles."

Liv shrugged, smiling. "Friends in high places, that's us."

"Too right," he replied, clinking his mug with hers. "Okay. Nico and Elise have done their part, and we get free rein on activity booking."

Her pulse fired with excitement as she opened her laptop. "I've found a couple of things I think they'd love."

Arran shifted his chair closer, his arm brushing hers and causing a tingling sensation to rush across her skin. She ignored it as she opened the web pages she'd bookmarked.

"I wonder if you've come up with the same stuff as me," Arran murmured. She loved the smooth, deep sound of his voice. "Here," she said, showing him what she'd come up with.

"I knew it." He grinned as he studied the images. "I really want to go to the Fairy Pools too."

A warm feeling soaked into her skin. "I figured we could take wet suits and have a swim." She flicked through the pictures of the scenic Isle of Skye. The clear, glittering pools sparkled invitingly from the screen, with multiple cascades of misty falls pouring into them from the rocky face behind. "Sam and Maya will love it."

"They will." His honey eyes seemed to glow as he chuckled. "Hey, remember when we went with school, and Nico stripped off and skinny-dipped in there?"

She laughed, remembering the berating Nico got from the teacher and the open-mouthed drooling he'd received from all the girls.

"I also thought we could go to Neist Point," Arran said, leaning over her to open a new page.

His scent filled her airways and she tried to ignore the resulting flip in her stomach. "Way ahead of you." She moved on to the next tab, where Neist Point, the most westerly part of Skye, was pictured. The narrow strip of green land fell off into sharp cliffs as it greeted the dark blue sea, a white lighthouse standing proudly at the edge of the last step of land, looking out over the Atlantic.

"Great minds," Arran said softly.

Chancing a glance, she allowed herself a long moment to get lost in the golden tone of his eyes. "Yep. We're dialed in to the same frequency."

He held her gaze for a moment, smiling. Then he cleared his throat and eased away. "I'll draw up an itinerary and email it to you."

"Cool," she replied, shifting in her seat and mourning the loss of his body heat. "Nico said we could borrow Alessia's minivan. We'll get all eight of us in there."

"Eight?" he said, sipping his tea. "I thought there were nine of us."

She shook her head. "Maya's uni mate Kirsty can't make it. She's got a nasty fracture dislocation of her thumb."

"Oof." He winced. "How'd she do that?"

Liv tried to keep a straight face. Kirsty's pain was no laughing matter. "Flushing the toilet."

Arran nearly spat out his tea. "*What*? Are you joking?"

A chuckle escaped Liv's lips. "Nope. She was pissed and went to press the button-flush mechanism with her thumb. But the drink must've affected her coordination because she hit it awkwardly."

Clearly trying to hold in his laughter, Arran kept a straight face. "Wow. She must have hit that thing hard. She was trying to rage against the latrine."

Another snort of laughter slipped out of her mouth. "Poor thing. Apparently, she appeared a little flushed afterward."

His straight face slipped into a grin. "She needed a superhero to come to her rescue. Maybe Flush Gordon."

At that point Liv let the giggles out, grabbing Arran's shoulder as he dissolved into laughter with her. Friends who shared her love of silliness were her favorite people.

Eventually the laughter died down and she realized she was still gripping his biceps. The sensation of the hard plane of muscle beneath her fingers caused the blood to rush faster through her veins, so she hastily dropped her hand.

Just then, Arran's phone began to ring.

He lifted it to answer. "Hey." There was a pause as he listened to whoever was on the other end, and his smile morphed into a frown. "Oh, right. Yeah. Yeah, I suppose so. Okay, that's fine. Drop him off on your way."

Liv fingered her cup, watching him with a slightly anxious feeling. "Bye," Arran said, hanging up. He leaned back, lifting his mug. "Jess needs me to have Jayce on Saturday. Something about a get-together at the boyfriend's brother's house." His brow remained furrowed, not an expression he often sported.

"What about completing the portrait you're working on?" Liv asked, her concern mounting.

He sighed, fiddling with his phone, whose lock screen displayed an adorable photo of him smiling with a grinning Jayce on his lap. "Maybe I can pull another all-nighter."

Liv gave him a hard stare. "I'm coming over to sit for Jayce this Saturday."

He opened his mouth to protest, but she lifted her hand, placing her index finger on his lips, then regretting it as a bolt of fire burst in her belly. "Shh. Fingers on lips," she said, using her best teacher voice. He smiled under her touch, his stubble gently scratching her finger and making her skin tingle.

She dropped her hand. "It's happening, Arran. So just go with it."

He was silent for a moment, the muscles in his jaw working, and she knew she'd won. "I'll pay you for it," he said, his voice a little gruff.

She raised her eyebrows. "No, you will not. Friends don't charge each other for favors."

"Feels like you're always the one doing me favors, not the other way around," he said quietly.

She shrugged. "You can return the gesture one day. Maybe I'll eventually have a kid for you to babysit."

His brow briefly furrowed, but then relaxed when he smiled. "Of course." He cleared his throat. "Is it definitely okay, with you becoming his teacher?"

She nodded. "It's fine. The nursery school is small enough that we often get kids we know or are even related to in the classes." It was apparent by the look on his face that she'd won him over. She lifted her mug to clink with his. "Do we have a deal?"

"Okay," he replied, clinking back. "Deal. Thank you. But this weekend only."

She smiled as she sipped her tea. *That's what you think.*

Chapter
FIVE

"COME ON, PAL. JUST A WEE BITE," ARRAN SAID IN A SINGSONG voice, as Jayce eyed the broccoli speared on the fork with suspicion.

"No. I don't like broccy, Daddy," Jayce said with a tone of disparagement.

Not one to give up that easily, Arran continued to cajole his son into taking a bite of something nutritious. Inevitably his mind wandered to Liv's pending arrival in a couple of hours, his thirst to lay eyes on her intensifying. His mind drifted to remember when she'd jokingly mentioned strippers the other day over at Sam's house, and an image of her as the naked dancing lady had crashed into his mind's eye like the meteor that had allegedly killed off the dinosaurs. It'd made him inhale his drink and nearly choke to death at Sam and Maya's kitchen table.

Death by champagne. What a middle-class way to go.

The doorbell sounded, bringing him out of his thoughts, and he eyed his watch. "Who's that?"

Wondering why pretty much every human in existence asked that question when an unexpected visitor called, despite the fact that no answer would be provided until the door was, in fact, answered, he left Jayce at the table for a second to jog down the hallway and open the door.

His heart nearly stopped when he found Liv standing there, wearing a cute fitted T-shirt that read "Teacher, Because Superhero Is Not an Official Title" with her faded jeans, biker jacket, and white Converse.

"Hey," she said, pushing her purple-framed glasses up her nose and brushing a wave of dark chestnut hair from her forehead.

For a moment, he was thrown. "You're early."

She smiled. "Yeah. I got changed at the dojo and came straight over. Thought I'd give you a head start on the painting."

The view of the green hills peeked out in the distance behind her, bringing out the green of her eyes. And the early afternoon sun caught her hair, creating a russet glow around the top of her head. *Like a halo.* Arran pictured exactly which paints in his studio he would mix to create the warm waves of her hair. His autumnal shades. And the hue of her eyes would come from the collection he thought of as his sea tones.

Liv raised an eyebrow. "So, am I allowed in, or is there a special password now?"

Clearing his throat, he shifted to allow her past him. Her scent filled his lungs as she moved, like sweet berries mixed with vanilla. He felt like one of those old-style cartoon characters, set adrift through the air as their nose followed the trail of a delicious smell. "That's so awesome of you," he finally managed to get out. "Thank you."

"No problem," she said, giving him a side five before moving down the hallway to the open-plan kitchen at the end. He squeezed his hand into a fist to dispel his awareness of the touch of her skin. The blind date had brought with it a sense of clarity, leading to the realization that his instigation of that greeting had been driven by an unconscious but powerful need to make physical contact with her.

Jayce spied her enter the kitchen and his face lit up. "Hiya, Lib!"

"Hey there, buddy," she said, heading over and kissing his chubby cheek. "How you doing? Broccoli! My favorite. How about we eat some of this scrummy stuff while Daddy goes painting?" She lifted the fork, sitting next to Jayce. "Here comes the choo-choo . . ." She made "chugga-chugga" noises and swooped the fork down, Jayce automatically opening his mouth and taking a bite while Liv whooped as his own personal cheerleader.

Smiling at their antics, Arran left for the studio, the sound of Liv and Jayce giggling following him down the hallway.

He opened the door that led from the hallway into his studio, which he had converted from the garage the year before. Closing it behind him, he leaned against it for a moment.

His escalating feelings for Liv were getting out of hand. She was his best friend's sister. They'd been in the same class at school. When they were ten, he'd pretended to the entire year group that she had nits and earned himself an uppercut to the gut from her, for God's sake.

There was also the fact that a romantic relationship with *anyone* was not what he needed right now. This time the previous year, he'd been in full-on wedding-planning mode, and when his ex had broken things off, he'd been blindsided. How on earth hadn't he realized that she no longer loved him? Was he that dense? He couldn't trust his own feelings, that was for sure. In fact—that must be it. His emotions were such a fucking mess that it was making him irrational over Liv.

Moving over to his latest canvas, he began preparing what he needed to continue. The act of mixing the paints was therapeutic, though this time it didn't fully banish the turmoil of his thoughts.

He'd been determined to concentrate on Jayce and his new business, and he'd been pleased with how he'd managed both those things. That was how it needed to stay. Jayce and painting were his top priorities, and there was no room for anything else. Not since Jess had left him anyway. She used to occupy the top spot too, alongside their little dude.

Anyway, Liv helped everyone, and she would have offered her assistance to any of her other friends who needed her. That was one of the things he loved about her. Well, one of the things he really liked about her anyway. Love was a bit extreme. He didn't *love* her. Just because she was his best friend who totally got him, and she was his favorite person in the world to spend time with apart from his son, *plus* he was off-the-charts attracted to her didn't mean he loved her.

He hadn't been able to resist clearing the air about their blind date because he couldn't leave her thinking he'd been disappointed to see her. Nor could he resist telling her how gorgeous she'd looked—he wanted her to hear what a smoke show she was. But he'd noticed the way she'd blushed hard, those pretty cheeks turning bright red, and so he'd changed the subject to spare her further embarrassment. Though up until that point he'd wondered whether there had been some interest flickering in her green eyes . . .

Making a decent start with his painting, he resolved to stop torturing himself with the unattainable what-ifs regarding his relationship with Liv.

"PERFECT," ARRAN MURMURED TO HIMSELF AS HE FINISHED THE final brushstroke and took a step back, wiping his hands on a cloth. The portrait work was turning out to be very lucrative, with customers keen to commission them for loved ones' birthdays and special occasions. Maybe one day soon, he'd be able to get shot of the office work he'd had to take up after his redundancy money had run dry. At least he'd gotten the studio well off the ground by the time that had occurred.

His pulse fired when he realized it was after Jayce's dinnertime. He'd gotten lost in his work and the day had slipped through his fingers like sand. Poor Liv would be desperate to leave.

Striding to the doorway, he opened it and went down the hall, past the living room and into the kitchen, but Liv and Jayce weren't around. A flash of color caught his eye through the patio window, and as he moved toward it, he spotted them. Liv was chasing Jayce across the garden, scooping him up and making him squeal with delight.

Warmth flooded his chest. Watching them together always gave him this comforting glow inside.

Liv caught his presence and gave him a wave, coming toward the patio door with Jayce chattering away on her hip.

Arran opened the door for them. "Hey, sorry I'm so late. I got carried away."

She came through the doorway and into the dining area, setting Jayce down, where he cried, "I'll get you, dragon!," then ran off to grab his toy sword and shield from the corner.

"Oof. He's getting so heavy," Liv said, rubbing her arms. "And no problem, we've been having fun. I hope you made good progress?"

Arran nodded, smiling. "I've finished it."

Her eyes widened. "That's brilliant. Can I have a look later?"

That was the other thing about Liv. She was so enthusiastic about his art, and really invested in his success. But, he reminded himself, she was the same with everybody. It didn't mean there was anything special about him.

"Course you can," he said, shoving his pesky feelings to one side. "I'd love your opinion. But don't you need to get away?"

She shrugged. "Nah. I figured I'd stay and fix Jayce his dinner while you clean up."

Guilt needled his chest as he ran a hand over his hair, watching Jayce attack one of the kitchen chairs with his sword. "I can't ask you to do that, when you've already given up your entire afternoon for me."

Arching an eyebrow, she gave him a mock-stern stare that borderline turned him on. "I wanted to do it because I like helping with Jayce. And now I'm offering to do this too. Because you're my friend."

Her friend. That's all. "That would be awesome, if you're sure."

She lifted her hand to rub his cheek and the sensation made his breath catch in his throat.

As she brought her hand away, silver paint residue was apparent on her fingers. Liv smiled. "I'm sure. Because you really need a wash."

Arran laughed, somewhat dispelling the fiery sensation that her touch had created on his skin. "Charming."

Grinning, Liv wiped her fingers on a piece of paper towel. "I'm surprised you have any paint left to go on the canvas, when there's always so much on you." She moved into the kitchen. "I've got something to heat for Jayce's tea, so you go wash up."

Jayce turned his attention to the next kitchen chair, apparently having vanquished the first "dragon" and now preparing to defeat number two.

Lingering by the doorway, Arran realized that even though Liv had been in his house for a few hours, he'd hardly seen her. And he didn't like that. Clearing his throat, he leaned against the doorframe, aware that he shouldn't suggest what he was about to but couldn't help himself. "Do you want to hang out for a bit before you go? It'd be nice to get a bit of chat in. You can teach me some karate-master mind control."

She laughed. "That's not a thing, Arran." She hesitated a beat, glancing at him as she warmed a pot on the hob. "But that would be great. I'd love to hang out." For a second her gaze seemed drawn to where his arms were folded. Then she looked back at the pot and stirred it.

Shifting from one foot to the other, he shoved his hands into his pockets. "Do you want to grab some food? I'll treat you to a takeaway."

"I'd love that," Liv said quickly. She paused, then stirred the pot more fervently. "Thanks."

"Cool," he replied, his heart lifting and pushing the corners of his mouth into a smile. This was fine. Two friends having dinner, nothing untoward. "Right. Better get cleaned up, after my friend told me I was stinky."

"Stinky Daddy," Jayce sang as he continued to battle invisible dragon number two, indicating that the sneaky blighter was always listening.

Liv laughed. "I only said you had paint on you. You still *smell* really good." Her smile faded and she bent toward the pot, fiddling with the heat.

Arran exited the room to let her get on. She was clearly trying to concentrate on what she was doing.

He headed into the master bedroom en suite, taking off his clothing and climbing into the shower. Normally he liked it hot, but for some reason he felt like he needed the cold today. He turned it down a couple of notches. Funny, because February in the Highlands wasn't very warm.

He quickly finished his shower, drying and dressing. As he pulled on a fresh shirt, the options for dinner ran through his mind. He had a hankering for pizza, and that was Liv's favorite. She liked pepperoni, and he a veggie supreme. They usually shared half and half whenever the group ordered pizza together. Thank goodness she didn't like Hawaiian; otherwise, he would've had to seriously reconsider their friendship. Fruit had no business on a pizza.

Jogging down the stairs, he smiled at the thought that there could, in reality, ever be a situation that would make him not want to be friends with Liv.

Shaking his head to clear his mind, he entered the kitchen, where Jayce was tucking into his dinner, encouraged by Liv. "Right," he said, pulling out his phone and opening the well-thumbed pizza-delivery app. "One pepperoni and one veggie?"

Liv groaned in delight. "You read my mind."

He grinned as he typed in the order. "See? Never say I don't know how to please a woman."

Liv helped Jayce with his spoon. "No danger."

A little color seemed to flush her cheeks, but she was turned away from him, so perhaps it was just the angle.

Arran shoved his phone back into his pocket. "Done!" He moved over to Liv, giving her a nudge. "Shift. You get your feet up before the pizza comes." He managed to displace her from the chair she was sitting on and slid onto it to take over the supervision of Jayce's dinnertime. Jayce banged his little cutlery on the table, singing "Old MacDonald Had a Farm."

She watched them for a moment. "Spoilsport. I like spending time with him."

Arran grinned. "Make yourself useful. Get some of your signature tea on."

Liv huffed out a breath. "Fine. Then I want to see your portrait." She turned and headed for the kettle, putting it on and making them a mug each.

Taking his steaming mug from her, he watched her settle into the seat next to him, absorbing the hue of her eyes. *Jade ground with sea glass.* His mind's eye drifted to his paints, and which tones he would select to do them justice.

He blinked hard in an attempt to concentrate on the here and now. His artistic brain was always getting distracted with these little thoughts. He sometimes found himself pausing to take in a scene on a walk, pondering how he'd replicate the blue of the sky and the manner in which it reflected off a loch, or admiring his friend's eyes and wondering how he'd bring out their sparkle on canvas. Though for some reason, Liv was the only friend he imagined painting.

"You okay?"

Arran sat straighter. She was eyeing him curiously. "Yeah, fine." He sipped his tea. "Why?"

She shrugged. "You seemed miles away."

Setting his mug down, he turned away to clean up Jayce (who was now giving an excellent rendition of "The Wheels on the Bus"), hoping she wouldn't register his discomfort at being caught daydreaming about her. He stood to unbuckle Jayce from his booster seat and lift him out, joining in with his singing and drawing a soft smile from Liv.

"Can I have a peek at the portrait now?" she asked, getting to her feet.

His chest swelled with pride that she was so keen. "Yep," he replied, placing Jayce on his hip and moving ahead of her.

"Can I bring my tea?" Liv asked.

"Yeah." He shot her a glance over his shoulder. "But don't spill it on my stuff or I shall have to chastise you."

She raised an eyebrow at him and desire exploded in his belly. Striding ahead, he opened the studio door and held it for her as she came past. Jayce was getting a bit wriggly, and letting him loose among the paints was not a good idea, so Arran placed him in the small play area he had cordoned off by the window. The wee one set to work building a brick tower, which Arran knew would be deliberately brought crashing down by his son in a few seconds' time.

"This is beautiful," Liv said, her voice laden with awe.

He turned to where she stood in front of the canvas, staring at the middle-aged woman with long, flowing, silvery hair that he had painstakingly rendered on it over the last several weeks.

Drawing level with Liv, he took in her expression. Her lips were parted and eyes wide as she took in his work. "You like it?" he asked, pride rising in his chest. Her opinion meant the world to him.

She kept her eyes on the painting. "I love it," she said softly. She placed her mug down and lifted her hand to touch the photo pinned next to the canvas, from which he had replicated the painting. "She's beautiful. I love how you've captured her eyes."

Arran cleared his throat. "The eyes are my favorite part."

Liv nodded, still mesmerized. "Did she commission it herself?"

"No. Her husband did. For their silver wedding anniversary," Arran replied, remembering the doting man who had personally visited to bring him the photograph.

"Oh yes. I remember you saying it was for an anniversary. That's so romantic," she murmured, fingering the photo again. Her face morphed into a frown.

Shifting closer, he touched her arm. "All right?"

She blinked, pushing her glasses up her nose with a smile and meeting his eyes. "Yep." She sighed. "Good work, Mr. Adebayo. You are a talented man."

Studying her for a moment, he wondered where her thoughts had been a few seconds ago.

"Me and Lib made a fort, Daddy!" Jayce said from inside his play area.

Liv placed her palm on her forehead. "I almost forgot! Jayce and I need to show you the fort we built in the living room."

He smiled as she went over to Jayce and lifted him out of the play area, taking his hand to walk over to the door. "Let's show Daddy."

Arran made for the door. But as he opened it for Liv, she placed a hand on his chest. His pulse spiked as she looked him in the eye.

"You wait here until I call you," she said, her familiar scent filling his lungs as she moved past with Jayce.

For a second, he was silent, trying to recover. "Why?"

Disappearing across the hall into the living room, she called over her shoulder, "We need to set up the moat."

The door closed behind them, and he laughed. He loved the random quirky stuff that came out of her mouth. The pale pink hue of her lips sprang into his mind as he shifted into the hallway. They always appeared so soft, kissable and . . .

"Ready!" she yelled from the living room.

He grasped the door handle, the curve of Liv's mouth on his mind. Opening it, he let out a laugh as he surveyed the scene. Blue and green blankets were draped over stacks of storage boxes that held Jayce's toys, creating a tent-shaped structure. There was shiny blue wrapping paper on the floor surrounding the perimeter, representing the glinting surface of a moat. A piece of cardboard leaned up over the opening where the edges of two blankets touched.

Liv's voice boomed out of the fort. "Who goes there?"

Jayce's giggles followed.

Arran cleared his throat, putting on a deep voice. "It is I, Sir Paints-a-Lot."

"Hmm. Sir Paints-a-Lot. Let me confer with my master. What say you, Lord Jayce?"

"No! No daddies allowed."

"Hey!" Arran said, moving closer and trying to peer between the blankets. "I want to be in the fort gang."

He still couldn't see Liv, but he heard her sigh. "I'll try to convince him. But my master is rather stubborn." She paused. "Master Jayce. Daddy Paints-a-Lot says please."

"Ah, okay. C'mon, Daddy!" Jayce piped up.

There was a rustling noise as Liv's voice sounded again. "You may enter."

The piece of cardboard was lowered to the floor, attached to a couple of pieces of string. Arran grinned as he got to his knees and crawled over it and through the curtain of the blankets. Pausing, he took in the cozy-looking den Liv had created inside. Fairy lights hung around the top, and the floor was covered in soft cushions, with a light blue fleecy throw on top. Shifting right inside, he sat next to Liv, who was grinning at him, clearly proud of her work. Jayce was brum-brumming a truck over the cushions next to her.

"Great job," he said, settling in next to her and leaning back against the wall.

"Why, thank you, good Sir Knight." She did a funny little half bow that drew a laugh from his lips.

Smiling, she leaned next to him. "What time's my pepperoni coming?"

He raised his eyebrows. "*Your* pepperoni? I assumed we'd be sharing again."

Pursing her lips, she gave him a withering stare. "Never *assume*, Mr. Adebayo. For then you make an ass of 'u' and me."

Giving her arm a nudge, he stuck out his bottom lip in a pout. She glanced down at his mouth for a moment, the smile fading from her face. Then she met his eyes again, her expression brightening. "Fine, then." She sniffed. "You and your emotional blackmail."

He pumped his fist, reveling in her smile. "It'll be here in about an hour. I wanted time to get Jayce bathed and into bed so we can munch in peace without toy trucks getting pushed through our pizza."

"Sounds like a plan." She smoothed down the dark waves of her hair and his eyes were dragged along with the movement of her hand. He imagined how he might capture the way her glossy hair curled softly, framing the creamy paleness of her skin. And the light dusting of freckles across her nose . . .

"Arran?" she said, frowning. "What's up?"

He cleared his throat, glancing away. "Nothing." Placing his hand on the soft throw beside him, he fiddled with a corner. "I'll go and get Jayce bathed. You can have a rest inside the comfiest fort in Scotland."

"Nah," she said, shifting next to him. "I'll help. I like bath time."

"Is it bath time?" Jayce asked, looking at them wide-eyed. He loved the bath. Mainly, Arran suspected, because he adored soaking everyone within a five-mile radius.

"C'mon, then, troops," Arran announced, crawling toward the exit. "Company, march!" Leaving the fort, he scooped Jayce up, then began a march out of the living room and up the stairs with Jayce laughing and Liv matching his steps from behind.

Setting Jayce down on the landing, he closed the stair gate and made for the bathroom, turning on the taps and squirting in some bubble bath. Liv appeared next to him, leading Jayce in by the hand and beginning to undress him, the two of them chatting away about the fort and how Jayce had defeated the dragon that tried to attack its defenses. She folded his clothes in a little pile on the floor while Arran tested the water with his elbow. *We make a good team.*

Lifting Jayce into the water, Arran attempted to wash him. It was a bit like cleaning a slippery octopus, with Jayce flailing around and seeming to sprout extra arms and legs. Plus he kept getting up and moving around, then sitting back down with a huge splash. Eventually he met Arran's eyes with a wide-eyed smile that signaled danger. But before Arran could issue a tsunami alert, Jayce launched himself down with a force that about emptied all the water from the bath. Arran ducked to avoid the worst of it, but unfortunately, Liv wasn't as quick, being less experienced in the watery perils of bath time. She blinked from behind her droplet-speckled glasses, drips falling from the soaked tendrils of her hair.

Arran snorted, hiding his mouth behind his hand.

"Oi, you," she said, giving him a shove. She grinned. "Don't laugh at me when I'm in the midst of being drowned."

"Sorry," he said, trailing off as he took in the fact that her T-shirt was soaked to the skin. The white fabric clung to the appealing swells of her breasts, the outline of her bra apparent. *Fuck.* He glanced away, clearing his throat. "He got your top good and proper."

Out of the corner of his eye he saw her glance down, clearly realizing how much was on display, because she hugged her arms around herself.

Reaching quickly for a towel, he passed it over, keeping his eyes off her. Once she'd wrapped it around her shoulders, he looked at her again. "You can go and change into something of mine, until your shirt dries off."

Liv stood, bringing the towel close around her, her cheeks streaked with pink. "Thanks. Which one should I borrow?"

"Anything you like," he told her, trying to banish the uncomfortably clear image of her shapely breasts from his mind. "They're in the second drawer down."

She disappeared out of the bathroom and Arran shoved aside the thought that Olivia Holland was in his bedroom right now, taking off her top and standing there in her bra as she rifled through his T-shirt drawer. He gritted his teeth as he emptied the bath. "Get a grip."

Lifting Jayce out, he dried him off and got him into his nightwear. How was it possible that he'd known Liv practically all his life—only seeing her as his friend's goofy sister—and then that had all changed?

Now he couldn't look at her without imagining how good it would feel to kiss her, to have her fingers dig into his hair, urging him on. So much for his earlier resolve to stop those kinds of thoughts. His own fault for asking her to stay for pizza.

He took Jayce through to the nursery, tucking him into his little bed. A movement at the door caught his eye, and as he glanced up, his heart rose into his throat.

Liv was wearing one of his favorite T-shirts—the green brought out her eyes, and there was no denying that seeing her in one of his shirts gave him a thrill. He liked that it was oversized on her petite form, as if some part of him was surrounding her. Protecting her.

"Is it okay if I borrow this one?" she asked, eyeing him and clearly misinterpreting his staring to mean he was displeased with her choice. Far from it.

"Of course," he said, flashing her a smile. "It's one of my faves. It suits you."

She smiled, holding the edges of the tee in a self-conscious manner. Then she crouched next to him. "Can I do his story?"

He nodded, his mouth dry.

"Cool," she said softly, stroking Jayce's hair. "I like doing the voices."

Grinning, Arran settled back. "Really? I'm staying, then. Gotta hear this."

Liv shrugged, seeming unperturbed by the thought of an audience. "We nursery school teachers have to be good at the voices. Otherwise, you don't get past the first round of interviews."

She lifted their well-thumbed copy of *The Gruffalo* and began to read. Each animal was read in a different accent and was a fair representation of the actors who played the parts in the animated version. He found himself mesmerized by her rendition, joining in with Jayce as they spoke aloud the repeated lines.

She was so good with Jayce, and the wee one adored her. Another reason to keep his hands off her. If he screwed up their friendship, then not only would he lose Liv, but it would also affect her relationship with his son. Making a move on her would be the height of selfishness.

The doorbell rang, signaling the pizza guy's arrival, and Arran found himself disappointed at having to leave them to go and answer it. He gave Jayce a kiss on the forehead, ruffling Liv's hair as he got up to leave, then regretting it when even that brief platonic gesture caused fire to crackle across his skin.

He reached the front door to accept the warm pizza boxes, gave the guy a tip, then took them into the kitchen and got some plates ready. On a whim, he decided that they should eat the pizza in the fort. So, he took the boxes in there along with the plates and a couple of glasses of water, plus a cup of tea for Liv because she was the only person he knew who had a hot drink with a hot meal. He smiled as he made it just the way she liked it, with a splash of milk.

Footsteps on the stairs announced Liv's descent, and he called through to alert her that he was in the living room.

"Are you in the fort?" she asked, poking her head into the area.

"Yep," he replied, patting the space next to him. "Come on in."

She settled in next to him, lifting a slice of each pizza onto her plate. "I cannot *wait* to scoff this." She bit into the first slice, and a string of cheese connected her mouth and the remainder of the slice. She caught it, breaking the string and sucking it from her finger.

Arran glanced away, shifting uncomfortably as his jeans suddenly began to feel too tight. Spending more time alone with her had been a bad idea. But it was too late to go back on it now. Anyway, he was a grown man. He could control his emotions and his physical urges.

They demolished every last bite, wiping their faces and hands on some napkins and tossing them into the boxes.

Arran adjusted the cushions behind them so they could lie back comfortably. "Ugh. I'm so full I think I might die of a cheese overdose."

Liv sighed. "A great way to go."

He shifted to the side a little to look at her. "Agreed."

Mirroring him, she smiled. "What would be another great way to go?"

"Hmm." He thought for a moment, trying not to get lost in her eyes. "A chocolate overdose?"

"Yeah, maybe." She pursed her lips and he had to work hard to keep his eyes off them. "But I might prefer a scone overdose. No wait, a tea and scone overdose."

He laughed. "You guys are so obsessed with scones."

"But they're so light and fluffy and tasty," she replied, widening her eyes in a manner that seemed to make them luminescent in the soft light.

"They are," he said, losing the battle to keep his eyes off her mouth.

"What about a non-food-related way?" She paused, biting her lower lip. "A love overdose."

Arran raised an eyebrow. "How would that work?" He hesitated, unable to stop his mind from wandering onto lust-related activities, especially when she was biting her lip like that. "You mean like having a heart attack after strenuous sex?"

She laughed hard, taking her glasses off to rub her eyes when they teared up. "Okay. I walked into that one."

Smiling, he admired how her pretty features looked the same and yet so different without her glasses on. He liked how she looked either way. He just liked how she looked, full stop. Lifting a hand, he brushed a wave of hair from her face. "What *did* you mean?"

Her gaze meshed with his and it sent his heart tripping. "I was thinking about the woman in your painting. About how much her husband must worship her to commission her portrait."

He smiled. "Yeah. He clearly doted on her. I could see it in his eyes when he described what he wanted."

Liv swallowed. "What if you lived your whole life with your true love. Then, one night, when you were both super old, you went to sleep together and never woke up?"

Arran frowned, studying the earnest look in her eyes. "Not gonna lie, that's a little more morbid than I thought we were going with this."

Smiling, she shook her head. "Sorry, I'm not explaining it properly. It's like the couple's souls are interlinked. And after a lifetime of so much love, death overcomes them simultaneously, so they pass peacefully, enveloped in their love like a warm blanket. And neither has to live on without the other."

Thrown by the sentiment, he got caught in the green of her eyes, his breath catching in his throat. Growing old with Jess was a gift he'd assumed was his, but it hadn't worked out that way. They'd gradually grown apart and he hadn't even noticed, until she called off the wedding and then quickly moved on. A new boyfriend, who she was clearly infatuated with, because they'd moved in together after only a few weeks. The hollow feeling the rejection had created in his chest was still there, though time had made it less cavernous, filled to some extent by the love of his family and friends.

"I'm sure I sound dumb," Liv said, putting her glasses back on.

"No," he replied softly. "It's not dumb at all. I get what you're saying. And yes, it would be a good way to go."

Her soft smile made his heart ache. He wanted to ask her more, but then Liv's phone buzzed and the moment was lost.

Lifting it, she studied the screen, her frown melting away into a smile. "Maya says they've booked a date for the wedding, at Glenavie Castle! There was a cancellation."

A bittersweet rush filled his chest. This time the previous year, it should've been him getting married. But his best mate's finding the love of his life made up for the sadness of that. "The castle? Brilliant. That's so lucky of them, by the way."

"I know, right?" she said, her smile lighting up her face. "The most coveted wedding venue in the area."

His own phone buzzed, and it was Sam with the same news. Arran added the date to his calendar, tapping out a message to Jess to say that particular weekend was off-limits for any changes to their arrangements for Jayce. He couldn't handle saying no when she asked, mostly because he jumped at the chance to have his son. But perhaps also because he didn't like saying no to Jess either.

Liv was eyeing him.

"What is it?" he asked.

Her voice was wary. "Are you okay with all this?"

He frowned, glancing around the fort. "With all *this*? I mean, fairy lights aren't normally my thing. But they really set the place off."

She laughed softly. "Not the fort decor. The wedding stuff. Does it make you sad?"

Arran hesitated. Nobody else had seemed to click that he harbored a little sadness. Not that he was sad in a big way; he wasn't going to be a dick about it. This was Sam and Maya's time and he wanted that for them. Plus, Elise's feelings were more important than his, because her husband had died last year. His being jilted by his fiancée was hardly a big deal in comparison. But still, it meant something to him that Liv had noticed. "A little. But I'm so happy for them that I don't really think about it much."

Nodding, she held his gaze for a beat, as if she wanted to say more. But then she glanced at her watch. "I'd better head out. I've been in your hair long enough."

She sat up, and he found himself disappointed that she was leaving. "I invited you into my hair," he told her. "And you can stay in there as long as you like."

Laughing, she crawled out of the fort and he had to avert his eyes to prevent his gaze from being drawn to the perfectly round shape of her arse. As he emerged behind her, she ruffled his hair. "It is nice and soft in there. But I'd better head home."

He followed her to the door, where she pulled on her jacket and Converse. She leaned in to kiss his cheek, sending an electric current down his spine.

"Thanks for your help today," he said. "I couldn't have gotten that portrait finished without you."

She gave him a salute. "No problem, Sir Paints-a-Lot. Happy to oblige."

Leaning against the doorframe as she exited, he eyed her. "When are we hanging out again?" He knew he shouldn't ask. But not knowing when he'd next see her felt uncomfortable.

"I'll text you." She gave him a wave and climbed into her car. Arran couldn't resist watching her right until she pulled off the driveway and out of his sight.

Arran eventually called it a night and got ready for bed. As he turned off the light and lay in the darkness, he wondered why his thoughts of Liv were intensifying. It was as if he could smell her scent in the air.

Glancing across the room, he realized her T-shirt was still there, drying on the radiator. *I really should take it off there. This isn't helping me any.*

He stared at it for a few seconds, willing himself to get out of bed and lift it from where it hung. But he couldn't bring himself to do it.

Inhaling a big breath, he let his mind wander into dreams of her as he fell asleep.

Chapter
SIX

THE TEAROOM DOOR GAVE ITS FAMILIAR JINGLE AS SHE OPENED it, then glanced around for Maya and Elise. She spotted them waving from their usual table in the back corner.

"Good morrow, Miss M and Miss E. How are you this fine evening?" She hung her jacket on the back of one of the tartan-clad French-style chairs and took a seat.

"We are very well, thank you, Miss O," Maya said, placing a scone on a plate and handing it over. "I'm afraid the tearoom is out of strawberry preserves; they have only raspberry available." Maya rolled the r in *raspberry* and popped her lips on the p, drawing a smile from Liv. Maya pursed her lips. "I'm afraid it *just* won't do."

Elise shook her head, smiling as she sipped her tea. She never joined in with their Austenesque routine, but it always made her smile. And making Elise smile was an extra-special thing these days.

The frilly-pinny-clad waitress didn't even bother coming to take their order nowadays; she practically had it ready for them prior to their arrival every Wednesday evening. A massive plateful of scones and a pot of Earl Grey. Milk for Liv and Maya, and lemon for Elise.

"Right," Maya said, pouring Liv a cup from the flowery teapot. "Down to business."

A flare of excitement fired through Liv's veins. This must be the moment when Maya was going to ask for assistance with the wedding planning.

Maya lifted her cup with an air of authority. "So. About you and Arran."

Liv's mouth fell open for a split second, then she clamped it shut again, her excitement fizzling out like the proverbial bonfire being pissed upon. "There is no business where that's concerned."

Elise raised her eyebrows. "Really? Even after the whole arrangement to cozy up every Saturday night?"

Liv scowled. "It's not *every* Saturday. And I only managed to get him to accept my help last weekend as a one-off."

Liv did her best to hide her inner turmoil over Arran from her best friends. There was no denying how she felt about him. She'd always found him attractive, but he'd been with Jess for years and prior to that had had a string of girlfriends, so there hadn't been anything she could've done about it. Now he was single but still hung up on his ex and had sworn off relationships.

But that suited her, didn't it? Just because she was attracted to him didn't mean she wanted anything to happen between them. Granted, her traitorous heart had leapt when he'd asked her to stay for dinner, and she wasn't convinced she'd done a good job of hiding that—she'd practically stirred the pot she'd been tending off the hob. How come the sight of a hot man leaning against a doorframe, arms folded, was enough to drive womankind into a frenzy? And when it was a man she'd admired for years, despite his oblivious nature, it made the heat all the more acute.

He'd only ever seen her as his best friend's sister. And nowadays, even though he might view her as a close friend in her own right, that was where the line was drawn. The memory of the intensity in his eyes when he'd told her how beautiful she'd looked on their blind date surfaced, and a seed of doubt sowed itself in the back of her mind.

She blinked. "Even so, there's nothing cozy about it. I don't see much of him because he's painting in the studio when I'm over there. Plus, he's always given me very strong 'we're just friends' vibes."

Elise spread some jam on her scone. "I have noticed that he talks a lot about wanting to be on his own."

"Precisely," Liv said, wielding her scone as a means of emphasis, then taking a bite. God, this scone was good. It almost went some way to consoling her malfunctioning, divided heart.

Maya was frowning from behind her cream-and-jam-laden scone. Liv eyed her choice of cream application prior to the jam through narrowed eyes. Everyone knew the jam went on first, for goodness' sake.

"If there's nothing cozy going on, then why are you wearing his T-shirt?" Maya asked, her tone decidedly smug.

Glancing down at the offending green T-shirt, Liv wasn't sure what to say. She shouldn't have continued to wear it after he'd lent it to her, but she hadn't been able to resist. Especially when it smelled of him. *For God's sake. I'm a living contradiction. I don't want to want him, but I do.* "How do you know it's his?"

Maya arched an eyebrow. "Apart from the fact that it's massive on you? Because it's his favorite one."

Liv shot her a dead eye.

Elise was wearing a wry smile, clearly not convinced either.

Liv sighed. "Anyway. There's a perfectly innocent explanation behind it. And one that cements the fact that he doesn't feel anything romantic toward me. Jayce soaked me when he was in the bath, so Arran lent me this shirt while mine dried. Then I forgot to change back."

"How does that cement anything?" Elise asked, passing Liv another scone.

"You should have seen Arran's face," Liv replied, heat rising in her cheeks as she remembered how repelled he'd seemed. "There I was, my top soaked to the point of transparency, and he wouldn't even look at me." She let out another sigh, hoping they'd see it as her being the poor pining woman, rather than the product of her being at odds with herself. "If he fancied me even a tiny bit, surely there would have been some brief glance of interest at that point." Perhaps like the glimpse of appreciation she'd seen when he'd told her she was beautiful? Unless she'd imagined it. He *had* been quick to change the subject, after all.

To take her mind off the situation, Liv topped her scone, *jam* first, then pointed at it with the knife in a passive-aggressive manner for Maya's benefit, who stuck her tongue out in defiance.

Elise studied her, a soft expression on her face. Liv could tell she was tuning in to her feelings using her doctor radar. "And you've continued to wear the shirt after the fact, because you like that it's his."

Liv's pulse picked up, and she broke eye contact. That was true. It was as much of him as she would allow herself to have. "Yeah. I know it's a bit sad and more than a tad stalkery."

Elise gave her arm a quick squeeze.

"No, it's not," Maya said, smiling. "Anyway, it suits you. Brings out your lovely eyes."

"Thanks." Liv took a massive bite of her scone so that she wouldn't have to speak again for a bit. It was apparent that both of her best friends had resigned themselves to the fact that she was some sort of lovelorn fool. She should try to explain how she really felt, but the problem with her and relationships was so complex that she couldn't even explain it to herself. *The throwback of having an arsehole father who abandoned us without a second thought.* In any case, burdening those around her with her negative thoughts and feelings wasn't fair.

Maya was giving her a sympathetic look. "This brings me back to my proposition."

Frowning, Liv met her eye. "Proposition?"

Maya nodded. "The Brodie proposition."

She'd forgotten all about Maya's suggestion from the previous week. Instinctively, she opened her mouth to say no. But then she hesitated.

Perhaps it would be a good idea. A casual date, to put her friends off all this matchmaking crap with Arran. And this time, she'd actually know whom she was meeting. She could go on a date with Brodie and have a laugh, and that'd be it. Perhaps it would turn into a casual fling; she could manage that. Her relationship with Dean had been her longest and most serious, but it still hadn't gotten past six months. That had been a couple of years after their dad had buggered off to Jersey without warning.

Remembering the hurtful words Dean had fired at her back then still made her wince. Nowadays she kept her relationships much shorter.

Her heart told her that she was ready for something more. And yet it also told her to be wary. It wasn't a conscious thing; it didn't even feel like that heart-versus-head thing that people banged on about. The opposing views were both emotional, not logical. They both came from her heart, hence her viewing that particular organ as divided and treacherous. It ached for Arran, and yet gave her palpitations of terror whenever she imagined the two of them being in any sort of relationship other than platonic.

Liv was jealous of people who'd found a relationship they could trust in forever. She wanted it, and yet she was terrified of it in equal measure, and she couldn't understand how anyone got past that fear. Hence her preoccupation with the beautiful portrait woman and her doting husband.

As much as she played up the jokes to their friends about being the terminally single one, and being on the lookout for her Mr. Darcy, the truth was that was a smoke screen. A committed relationship was something she had actively avoided up until now, and perhaps that was partly because the Hollands had a seriously shit record where relationships were concerned. Their mum had been with their emotionally abusive father for years before he finally did them all a favor and buggered off with a younger woman. In the end, none of them harbored any ill feeling toward his new girlfriend; they just felt sorry for her because the curtain was bound to lift at some point, and then the poor woman would realize what a royal twat the guy was.

Not long after their father left, Sam had taken up with a girlfriend who had, to all intents and purposes, turned out to be the female version of their arsehole father—something it took them all, Sam especially, a long time to figure out. All that familial trauma had well and truly put Liv off relationships, and she had avoided anything but casual dating.

In effect, she and her twin brother had opposite reactions to their abandonment issues. Sam had jumped right into a very long-term relationship, and Liv had avoided commitment entirely. That Sam's relationship had turned out to be with someone with personality flaws similar to their dad's had made Liv more determined that her way was the right way.

Fair enough, now their mum had Angus and Sam was with Maya and both of them were the best things to ever happen to her mum and her brother. But something deep down inside still held her back. Something that made her stomach churn whenever she contemplated a serious relationship.

An intrusive memory surfaced of her paternal grandmother, Agnes, talking to her when Liv was eight.

"Sammy is your mother's spitting image. But you're so much like your father, Livvy. You look just like him when he was your age! Same dark hair and green eyes. And you know what? You're exactly like him in temperament too."

Liv shuddered at the memory. It had been the first time that she could clearly remember her grandmother commenting on the resemblance, but certainly not the last. And every time it had made her stomach roil—even before she was old enough to realize why. She met Maya's eyes, realizing she needed to give a response about Brodie. She might as well say she was up for the idea, to get Maya off her back. "See what he thinks. And if he goes for the idea, then I'll ask him out."

A big grin spread across Maya's face and she performed a small, tearoom-appropriate fist pump. "Excellent."

"Anyway," Liv said, keen to get the heat off her love life. "What about the wedding stuff? How's it going?"

Maya winced. "You know what? It turns out there's a lot to organize."

Elise was smiling behind her cup.

"I know we said that we only needed help organizing the weekend away," Maya continued. "But there's so much to do in such a small amount of time. I thought we could just go with the bare minimum, but Mum and Dad are determined that we're going to have *all* of the frills."

Liv smiled. "Need some help?"

Maya looked like she was about to collapse with relief. "Would that be okay? I wondered whether we might contract out some of the jobs to our trusty band of best women and men."

"Of course," Elise said.

"Phew," Maya said. She wrinkled her nose. "I mean, who knew that wedding planning was so much work?"

Elise laughed. "Don't worry. We can help."

"Absolutely," Liv replied. "Just say the word, and we're on it."

Maya sighed contentedly. "Cool. I'll check with Sam and we'll see what needs delegating."

FOLDING ARRAN'S SHIRT, LIV MOURNED ITS IMPENDING LOSS. BUT she'd had it for more than a week and it was his favorite one; she couldn't hold on to it forever, and so she was reluctantly planning to drop it off to him. At least it was an excuse to see him. The doorbell rang and she headed down the hall to answer it, her mind full of thoughts of Arran. When she opened it and found the man himself standing on the other side, she about collapsed. He was doing that bloody sexy leaning-in-the-doorway-with-his-arms-folded thing again. For goodness' sake, did he not realize the aphrodisiac nature of that stance?

"Hey," he said, and the sound of that one syllable had electricity zipping up her spine.

"Hey yourself," she said, clearing her throat when her voice came out a little scratchy. "Come in." He passed by her into the hallway, giving her a lungful of his heavenly scent.

She closed the door and led him into the kitchen, gesturing for him to take a seat at the breakfast bar. "What brings you by?"

He obliged, removing his jacket. Liv's gaze traced the outline of the muscles contracting in his arms as he worked it off and hung it on the back of the chair.

"I just wanted to give you something," he told her.

"Oh?" she said, distracted by the biceps display.

He shot her a grin and for a moment she thought he'd caught

her ogling. Then he whipped something out of his jacket pocket, holding it out to her.

She grasped the rod-shaped object, trying to focus on it instead of Arran's arms. Her brain finally managed to compute what she was seeing, and she broke out into a grin. "Oh my God! A sonic screwdriver!"

He nodded, a satisfied expression on his face. "Yep."

Liv turned it over in her hands, taking in the silver body and bright blue light at the top. To be precise, it was the tenth Doctor's (aka David Tennant's) sonic screwdriver. "Awesome," she whispered.

During their blind date she'd confessed that she'd love one of the sonic screwdrivers. He'd told her that he'd get one for her birthday, but it wasn't even her birthday yet.

She blinked, moved by his gesture. It wasn't a high-value gift, but it meant something that he'd remembered and thought to get it for her. She threw her arms around his neck, hugging him on his stool.

He froze for a split second, then quickly reached his arms around her waist, pulling her between his legs and close to his chest. She pressed her face into his neck and allowed herself a deep breath, fueling a kick in her pulse.

Arran trailed a hand up her spine and she couldn't suppress a shudder of desire. His chest was hard against the softness of her breasts and his skin smooth where she rested her cheek upon it. The sensation of him created a thick, syrupy-sweet desire that heated her core and pooled low into her belly, making her lady parts tingle.

"Thank you," she said, reluctant to let him go. "But it isn't even my birthday yet."

She forced herself to draw back and rest her hands on his shoulders as she looked into the warmth of his gaze. His hands shifted onto her hips, electrifying every nerve ending along the way.

"I know," he said, giving her a loaded look. Loaded with what, she couldn't quite tell. The touch of his fingers tightened almost imperceptibly, and for a moment she imagined herself on top of him, his strong hands gripping her hips as she rode him, hard. Her breath caught in her throat as the blood rushed faster through her veins.

"I wanted to give it to you early, as a thank-you." he said, his eyes intense as he slowly circled his thumbs over her hip bones. Her skin prickled with delicious sensitivity, sending her nipples into hard peaks.

"A thank-you?" she managed to get out, her voice husky.

"Mmm," he said, his gaze dropping to her mouth for a split second. "For babysitting."

"It was my pleasure," she said, unintentionally drawing out the word *pleasure* as very pleasurable sensations thrummed from the touch of his fingers down into her core. She shifted, heat pulsing between her legs. In that moment she knew, with absolute certainty, that Arran would be amazing in bed. And she wanted him more than ever. *But this time it feels as if he wants me too.* She remembered the little seed of doubt she'd experienced the day before with Maya and Elise, when thinking that he saw her only as a friend. The little seed that had first been planted when he'd told her she was beautiful.

Arran's phoned buzzed loudly with a message, cutting into her reverie. She dropped her hands, taking a step back. Arran released his hold but didn't take his eyes off her.

"You can, er, you can get that if you want," she told him, feeling a little light-headed.

He swallowed. "I'll check it later."

Liv held her sonic screwdriver to her chest. "I love it. Thank you. But you didn't need to get me anything. I was happy to hang out with Jayce. And you."

"I know," he said, shooting her a soft smile. "But I like doing things for you. You're always there for everyone else. I want you to know you're appreciated."

Warmth flooded her chest, creeping up to heat her cheeks. She dragged her eyes from his perfect face and moved around the counter to grab his T-shirt from where she'd left it lying on the kitchen side. "Here you go. I was going to bring it over, but now you're here. So . . ."

He eyed it for a moment, wearing an odd expression. "Nah. I've decided you can keep it. It looks better on you."

Liv hesitated. She really wanted to keep it but didn't want to come across as really wanting to keep it. "You sure?"

Nodding, he glanced away, then smacked his palm onto his forehead. "Shit. I forgot to bring *your* shirt. It's still on my radiator." Another odd expression passed over his face. As if he felt guilty about something.

He rubbed his palms on his jeans-clad thighs. "Anyhow. You did me a solid with the babysitting gig, because the money from that portrait really boosted my savings pot."

"Oh yeah?" she said. "Saving for something in particular?"

"Yeah," he said, shooting her a self-conscious look. "I'm saving to go traveling."

Liv remembered the details from his BlindLove profile, that he was interested in travel. It wasn't something they'd discussed before. "That's brilliant!"

The self-conscious expression melted from his face as he smiled broadly. "I feel a bit dumb saying it, when so far the farthest I've traveled is a package holiday to Benidorm. But I really want to go to Japan."

"Oh God, yes," she said, eagerly leaning on the counter. "I want to go in May and see the blossoms."

His smile widened. "Me too. I'd love to paint them."

Liv's excitement about overflowed. "That would be amazing. You'd do such a brilliant job." She was so proud of his talent; he was genuinely gifted.

He ran a hand over his hair, an adorable blush about his cheeks. "I haven't mentioned it to many people, except Jess—because I'd like to take Jayce when the time comes. I felt like everyone would think it a pipe dream, or, worse, that I wouldn't be able to pull it off, and then I'd lose face." He winced. "I made the mistake of briefly mentioning the idea to my mum a few years back and she was like, 'Ach, yer total Dundee United. What do you need to go to Japan to look at blossoms for? Just plonk yer arse down in ma garden and paint ma cherry tree.'"

Liv chuckled. Arran did a pretty accurate impression of his mum. "Why did she call you a 'Dundee United'?"

"It's a Nigerian insult meaning idiot, which Mum enthusiastically embraced from Dad. Mainly to use on me." Arran rolled his eyes affectionately. "Apparently it came about after Dundee United Football Club had a disastrous tour in West Africa in the 1970s and ended up looking like complete fools."

Liv smiled. "I think I'm going to adopt it as my favorite insult too."

He brushed his fingers over the back of her hand, giving her goose bumps. "I knew you'd get it, about Japan and the May blossoms. You always do."

He held her gaze and she felt as if she might melt. Mesmerized by his eyes, she didn't really think properly before speaking. "Perhaps we can go together one day." Immediately, she regretted saying that. It was too forward.

But before she could take it back, Arran closed his hand around hers, giving her a squeeze. "I'd love that." He smiled. "We could see if we could find your mentor, Mr. Miyagi."

She laughed, then clutched her stomach when the brief action caused her abdominals to go into spasm. "Don't make me laugh. My abs are sore from my last karate class."

He shrugged, smiling. "It's an extra workout for us. Who needs crunches?"

"You don't need a workout. You've already got killer abs," she said before she could stop herself.

Raising an eyebrow, he studied her. "How do you know?"

She removed her hand from under his to push her glasses up her nose, heat rising in her face. "From last summer when you, Sam, and Nico were lugging the stuff for your studio conversion around with your tops off." *And also from just now when they were pressed against my stomach and I imagined scraping my nails down them.* She cleared her throat. "You bunch of posers."

"Hey. It was hot." He leaned back. "Anyway, you don't need the workout either. Some killer abs of your own there, karate kid."

Liv dipped her head to peer at him over the top of her glasses, covering the fact that her pulse was racing as a result of this conversation regarding each other's bodies. "And how, pray tell, would you know that? I for one do not parade around with my top off."

He seemed to swallow a little hard, opening his mouth to speak, then shutting it when his phone buzzed again. He lifted it to study the screen, his face falling.

Frowning, she eyed the shift in his demeanor. "What is it?"

With a sigh, he pocketed the phone again. "It's Jess. She was going to have Jayce this weekend, but she says something's come up."

She studied him. "You finished your painting. So doesn't that mean you can have the time with Jayce?"

He rubbed his forehead. "I got another project lined up. A big one, and I was banking on getting the hours in this weekend." He fiddled with his phone. "I don't like saying no to commissions when I'm still in the process of building my reputation."

"Ah. I see." She paused to look at him. "And you don't like saying no to time with Jayce, nor when Jess needs you."

An unreadable look passed over his face, and he nodded in confirmation.

The urge to offer to help was too strong to resist. "I'll come over again."

"No," he said, shaking his head. "Not two weekends in a row. You should be enjoying yourself. And last weekend was only meant to be a one-off."

"If I had something else on, then I wouldn't offer," she said. "I like spending time with Jayce." She grinned. "And I suppose you're okay too. In small doses, obvs."

Arran laughed. "You're not so bad yourself." His smile faded as he met her eyes. He hesitated for a few seconds, and she could see his mind working. His need not to let anyone down—Jayce, Jess, his clients—battling with his pride over accepting assistance. "Are you sure? I don't want to be the d-bag who takes advantage."

Rolling her eyes, she lifted her mug. "It's not taking advantage. Now, stop fussing and drink your tea."

He swallowed hard, then nodded, taking a silent sip.

Liv eyed him for a second. "Has Sam spoken to you?"

Arran glanced up. "About what?"

"Wedding stuff. Asking us to help with the planning."

He cleared his throat. "Yeah."

She hesitated. "You okay with it?"

He nodded. "Sure." But his voice didn't carry its usual carefree tone.

Liv touched his hand. "You don't have to take it on. I'll manage, with Elise and Nico's help."

Arran paused, then put down his mug, shaking his head. "Nah. Elise has got enough to worry about, and nobody wants Nico the wedding-phobe organizing anything. It'd be a quick exchange of vows at the local registry office, then everyone dismissed."

Liv laughed.

He shot her a genuine smile. "I'll be fine. I want to help. And in any case, if we do it together it'll be more fun."

Her heart warmed as she met his eyes. "Yeah. It will be."

He lifted his mug to clink with hers. "To our engagement."

She paused, eyebrows raised. "Engagement?"

He gave her a wink. "Yeah. Our engagement as wedding planners."

"Ah, I see," she replied, concentrating on her tea to stop her imagination from running wild with thoughts of the lucky woman who got to enjoy an actual engagement to Arran.

Chapter
SEVEN

THE LANDLINE RANG AS ARRAN PASSED THROUGH THE HALLWAY, signaling that either his elderly neighbor, Agnes, or a cold caller was on the phone. They were the only two people who used that line instead of his mobile.

He lifted the receiver. "Hello?"

Agnes's voice came through the phone. "Make sure you don't forget the kidney beans."

He laughed. "And when have I ever gotten your shopping list wrong?"

"Ach, well, there's a first time for everything," she replied, a smile in her voice.

"Never fear. I'll be there to deliver your groceries with bells on. Or should I say with kidney beans on. What do you use all those kidney beans for anyway?"

"They're good for the heart," she told him.

He grinned. "Not so good for your wind problem."

Agnes chuckled. "Cheeky. See you tomorrow."

Arran hung up and made his way to the kitchen to tend to the stove. The scent of tomato and spice infused the air as he stirred the pan, his stomach rumbling in appreciation and anticipation.

Liv's voice rang out from the hallway as the front door opened. "Honey, we're home!"

"In the kitchen," he called, pretending that he didn't love the sound of her saying that.

A shuffling noise, indicating that Liv was assisting Jayce in removing his shoes and jacket, was followed by the pounding of small-person footsteps.

"Daddy!" Jayce shouted as he entered the kitchen, and Arran scooped him up.

He kissed his son's soft brown curls. Jayce's scent stirred a contentment inside his soul. "Did you and Liv have a fun walk?"

"We saw some bunnies," Jayce said, his eyes wide with excitement.

Walking into the kitchen, Liv dropped her jacket onto the back of a chair. "There was a family of rabbits in the field. Must have been the Easter bunny."

"Is the Easter bunny going to bring me some chocolate eggs?" Jayce asked.

"That's right, buddy," Liv replied, stopping to take an exaggerated sniff of the air. "Oh my God, that smells *heavenly*."

"Yep," Arran said, shifting away from the pan so that Liv could have a nosy at it. "I'm making us some jollof rice and grilled chicken."

Stirring the pan and appearing as if she wanted to dive into the fragrant contents, she was more appealing than ever.

"It's my grandmother's recipe," he added. "Mum learned to make it when she married Dad because he's so utterly crap in the kitchen."

Liv laughed, reaching into the cupboard to get out some plates.

"And *you* always profess to be crap in the kitchen too. So how come you've got this recipe up your sleeve?"

Grinning, he set Jayce down because the kid was wriggling like a grass snake jacked up on energy drinks. "Part of my cover. If I pretend to be crap at cooking, then other people tend to do it for me." Jayce went off toward the living room, no doubt to play in the fort, which was now a permanent feature.

She raised her eyebrow at him, and it did nothing to aid his efforts to cool his libido. "You sneaky little git."

Laughing, he dug out some cutlery to set the table. "It works with other stuff too."

"Mm-hmm," she replied, getting out some glasses and filling them with water. "Like what? Teach me your underhanded ways."

There are plenty of things I want to teach you. "If you load the dishwasher wrongly, then someone else comes along to put it right. Then they elect to do it every time because they've deemed you incompetent."

Shaking her head, she shot him a withering look. But even that was sexy on her.

They plated up the food, and Arran organized a small portion for Jayce, which he'd made in a separate pan with less salt and seasoning. He went through to the living room to fetch a reluctant Jayce out of the fort and bring him to the table.

Liv took a bite of her food and groaned with pleasure. "This tastes amazing." Shooting him a frown, she gestured at him with her fork. "I can't believe you've never made this for me before. A year of friendship and not so much as a cup of soup."

He tried to ignore how the sound of her groaning made him feel. And the dirty scenarios it created in his mind's eye. He gave her his best pout, complete with puppy-dog eyes. "I was saving it for you. Because now you're my *best* friend." He squashed the thought that it was actually because, deep down, he wanted to impress her.

Raising her eyebrows, Liv munched another mouthful. "Don't let my brother hear you say that. He's got dibs on being your best mate."

He shrugged. "Maya's his best friend now, and that's all good with me. Anyway, I've known you as long as I've known him. We just didn't get close until . . ." He tailed off. They'd gotten close after Liv had been one of the people, along with Sam and Nico, who had come through for him when Jess called the wedding off. He'd known that Sam and Nico would; they were his rocks. But he and Liv hadn't been close before that. Yet now he couldn't imagine a time when they hadn't been. Plus, he didn't want to. The idea of Liv's friendship not being a big part of his world was unbearable.

She was giving him a soft look, clearly knowing where his tailed-off sentence had been going.

Just then Jayce cut through the silence with an excellent rendition of "If You're Happy and You Know It," distracting them both from the shared moment. They joined in with him as they ate their dinner, performing the actions with cutlery in hand.

Once they finished their food, he watched her as they cleared the plates together, acutely aware that although she had been one of his rocks over the past year, she had never leaned on him in return.

At first, he'd been convinced that was because Liv was the only one without relationship baggage, whether it be manipulative exes, rejection issues, dead husbands, or—in Nico's case—terminal commitment-phobia. But the more he got to know her, the more of a conundrum she became. Did she really have it all together? Or was she so determined to be there for everyone else that she kept her own issues to herself? There had been more than one occasion when she would say something mysterious, like that whole soul-mates-dying-in-unison thing. Or she'd retreat into her own thoughts the way she had when she'd been studying his latest portrait.

Arran eyed her as they loaded the dishwasher. The dark waves of her hair were partially obscuring her face. She was like an open and a closed book all at once.

A thought slid into the back of his mind. Liv spoke easily of Sam's rejection issues after their dad had abandoned the twins and their mum. And yet she never mentioned how it had affected her. It dawned on him that, more than anything, *he* wanted to be the one she confided in. The one she chose to lean on.

AFTER THEY'D GOTTEN JAYCE BATHED AND TO BED, WITH ARRAN making doubly sure that not a drop of water got splashed onto Liv's clothing during the bathing session, they settled into the fort in the living room. He was aware that he shouldn't utter the sentence on the tip of his tongue, but he was going to say it anyway. "Are you sure you don't want a beer? You can stay over and drive home in the morning. I can sleep on the couch."

"No, thanks," she said quickly. "I'd better head home."

He nodded, hiding his disappointment. "No worries." His phone started to ring so he pulled it from his pocket, frowning as he clocked Jess's name on the screen. He answered it. "Hey, Jess."

Her words were a little slurred. "How's Jayce?"

"Fine, thanks," he said slowly, with a spike of concern. *Is she okay?* "How's the party?"

She laughed, and he relaxed. "Awesome. Rory's pals are mental."

"Okay . . ." Was that a good thing? "Sounds great."

"I'm really sorry for asking you to have him again. Rory just didn't want us to miss this one, you know?"

For some reason, his heart didn't perform its usual sinking at the sound of Rory's name. "It's no problem. I love having him and"—he gave Liv a nudge—"I've got my trusty sidekick here to help me."

Liv flashed him a grin from where she was scrolling through her Insta. "Actually," she replied in a low voice. "I think you'll find you're *my* sidekick."

He chuckled. "No way, José. I'm Batman and you're Robin."

She kept her eyes on her phone screen, a smile still playing at the corner of her mouth. "Piss off."

"Arran?" Shit, he'd almost forgotten Jess was still on the line. "Who did you say was there with you?"

He watched Liv as she continued to scroll through her feed, the waves of her hair falling onto her forehead. "Liv. My trusty sidekick."

Liv dug him in the ribs. "*Not* a sidekick. I'm the frickin' super-hero, baby."

Jess was silent for a moment. "Liv's there again?"

Arran shot Liv a grin. "Yeah. Why?"

"You guys are spending a lot of time together."

He startled. Her tone sounded a little accusatory for someone who'd dumped him and was off partying with her new boyfriend. "Yeah, I know. We're mates." Liv looked up to shoot him a question-ing glance. He shook his head as if to say, "It's nothing."

"Is something going on between you two?"

His pulse picked up. *What's it got to do with you?* He hesitated, trying not to let his thoughts become his words. "Like I said, we're *friends.* Not that it's any of your business." Liv was giving him a wide-eyed look now, so he patted her arm in a reassuring manner then mimed swigging from a bottle to indicate that Jess was just drunk. Liv smiled, but it didn't reach her eyes.

"It is my business." Jess's tone was sharp. "If she's helping to care for my son."

"Okay," he said, his patience having run well and truly dry.

"You're drunk and belligerent. Liv's a nursery school teacher, soon to be Jayce's nursery school teacher. So who better to help? Bye, Jess. Have a great time."

He ended the call. "Sheesh. That woman is *not* a happy drunk." He threw Liv a smile, but she didn't return it, fiercely scrolling through her feed, wearing a stressed-out expression. "Hey," he said gently. "You okay?"

She cleared her throat, shooting him a glance. "I don't want to cause any trouble."

He laughed. "There's no trouble. She's just had one too many Bacardis, that's all."

Liv pushed her glasses up her nose. "Is she normally the jealous type?"

Arran was about to say no, when he paused to ponder. "Not since we broke up. But she did used to be a bit jealous when we were together." He frowned. "Since then, I suppose she's had nothing to be jealous about. Because I've not been involved with anyone, but moreover, because she dumped me at the frickin' altar. So, ya know . . ." He shrugged, making a "yikes" expression in the hope of bringing a smile to Liv's face.

It worked, and she laughed. "It wasn't at the altar. It was two weeks before, so think yourself lucky you weren't standing there like Adam Sandler in *The Wedding Singer*."

Laughing with her, he gave her a gentle shove. "Think myself lucky? Never mind *The Wedding Singer*; it felt more like that scene from *Indiana Jones and the Temple of Doom* where the guy had his heart pulled out of his chest."

She returned his shove, grinning widely. "Crybaby."

"For fuck's sake," he replied, still laughing. "Can't even get any sympathy from my best mate."

Liv gave him a soft smile that conveyed she was pleased he

thought of her that way. But did she think of him as her best friend? He hoped so. He studied her, wishing she'd reveal some of her secrets. "Anyway. Once Jess sleeps off her hangover tomorrow, she'll be as right as rain, I'm sure. And probably won't even remember that conversation."

She nodded, putting her phone down. "Yeah. Alcohol does weird things to our brains. One time when I was pissed, I stole a potted plant from the pub."

"*What?*" He laughed at the idea of good-as-gold Liv doing such a thing. "Olivia Agnes Holland. I am shocked and appalled at your thieving ways." He sniffed, snapping his head around to look straight ahead and folding his arms in mock disapproval. "I'm not sure I can hang out with you anymore, now I know you're a criminal mastermind."

"Stop," she said, covering her face in a cute manner. "I'm still embarrassed about it. In the morning I felt so guilty that I took it back and pretended it had fallen into my bag by accident."

Arran snorted. "I take back the mastermind part. That's the shittiest excuse ever. Did they buy it?"

"Nope," she said from behind her hands. "But they were too polite to say anything. The person I spoke to just smiled and said to pop it back onto the table."

"C'mere," he said, putting his arm across her shoulders, aware that he shouldn't be doing so when he was fast losing control of his emotions where she was concerned. "I forgive you, Agnes." She felt so good nestled against him.

"Stop taking the piss out of my middle name," she replied, looking up from where she was tucked into his side and making his heart pump harder.

"Sorry, Aggie," he said, absorbing the sparkle in her eyes. "Won't happen again."

"Shut up," she replied, leaning her head against his shoulder. "We can't all have cool middle names like you."

He shrugged. "Mine's just my dad's name. Unoriginal."

"Yeah, but it gives you the initials triple A. Arran Abeo Adebayo. That's frickin' cool."

He lifted his hand to dust his shoulder. "Yup. That's me all over."

Liv chuckled. He loved the sound of her laugh. It was sweet with a spicy edge.

He tightened his arm around her. "So where does the name Agnes come from? Someone in your family?"

"Yeah," she said, her breath tickling his neck. "My granny, on my dad's side. And Sam's is after our mum's dad."

"My neighbor's name is Agnes."

"The one you grocery shop for?"

"Yeah. She may be practically housebound, but she's a feisty one." He grinned. "Reminds me of you. Though she isn't a common pot-plant thief."

She gave him a playful nudge and he picked up her hand, running his thumb over her fingers and appreciating the flow of heat that the touch of her skin created. He wanted to get her to open up a little. She was always asking about him and he felt he needed to even up the balance—he craved a piece of her in return. "Can I ask you something?"

"Yeah," she said, resting her head on his chest. *God, that feels good.*

He took a breath. "Do you think about him much? Your dad, I mean."

Her hold on his fingers tightened almost imperceptibly. "Sometimes."

Arran leaned his head on hers, taking the opportunity to

breathe in her scent. She smelled comforting and yet exhilarating. "You don't talk about him."

"There's not much to say. He was a gaslighting, narcissistic arsehole."

He gave her a squeeze. "Do you ever hear from him?"

"Nope." She turned his hand over to trace the lines on his palm, sending fire crackling over his skin. "Not for ages. He used to message every now and again, I think because his girlfriend, Georgie, made him. But clearly her influence wore off because there's been nothing for a couple of years."

"I'm sorry," he said, pulling her closer. Being dumped by his fiancée was nothing compared to the pain of being dumped by a parent. Why hadn't he asked her about this stuff before? Too busy feeling all sorry for himself like the crybaby Liv had jokingly told him he was.

She shrugged against his side. "Don't feel sorry for me. Feel sorry for Georgie. She's the one who's got to live with the bastard. Mum always says the poor woman did us a favor." She sighed. "But I'm sure she's suffering in the exact same way he made Mum suffer. A narcissist never changes its spots."

A queasy feeling rose in his gut. "Sam told me he was a pathological liar."

"Oh yeah, and then some," she said quickly. "He'd argue the sky wasn't blue until he was blue in the face himself. He called Mum crazy, paranoid, jealous, you name it, when she found more and more evidence that he was cheating. And he never admitted it, not even when he packed his bags and left for Jersey with Georgie."

Arran swallowed, his mouth dry. This was more than Liv had divulged before. "He was some piece of work. It must have made you and Sam feel like shit."

"Yeah. Especially Sam; that was how he fell in with Catriona. She exploited all those vulnerabilities." She shivered. "Thank good-

ness Maya the great showed up in town and chased the nasty demon away."

There she went again, deflecting all the sympathy onto Sam.
He kissed the top of her head, appreciating the way she nestled into
his side in response. "It was just as hard for you, Liv. You're allowed
some sympathy too." She stayed silent, and he wondered if he'd
overstepped the mark. But he felt he had to have one last try. "It
might have affected you guys in different ways, but it still happened
to you. Maybe it was just more obvious with Sam, because he fell
into the same trap as your mum."

She still didn't answer, and Arran's heart rate picked up with
the fear that he'd upset her. Pushed her away.

Then she cleared her throat, her voice small. "Maybe."

He wanted to probe further, but he stopped himself. There was
a risk that he was doing it for his own benefit, from a place of selfish need for her to open up to him, and that wasn't fair to her. She
needed to confide in her own time. He kept his mouth shut.

Eventually, she spoke again. "If Jess asked you to get back with
her, would you say yes?"

The question caught him off guard. "If you'd asked me that last
year, or even a few months ago, I would have said yes."

"And now?"

He paused to rub his chest. "It's kind of confusing. I feel pretty
fed up about her skipping her time with Jayce, and . . . I miss her
being around. But it's like I miss the idea of her and how we used
to be a family with Jayce. I don't think I actually miss *her* anymore."
He paused. "I'm sure that makes no sense."

Liv shifted and he absorbed the delicious friction of her cheek
against his chest. It went some way to distract from the hollow feeling inside there, and he wished he could feel it without a layer of
cotton between them.

"I understand," she said.

She always understands. "I suppose everything would be easier if she came back, for me and for Jayce. But she's with . . . Rory now." He took a breath. "And I realize that it wasn't right between us. The relationship had moved on since we'd gotten engaged, and that's the risk when you have a long engagement so young. Sometimes you outgrow each other. So, really, you were right."

She lifted her head to meet his gaze and the green of her eyes was like jade in the soft light cast by the fairy lights inside the fort. "Right about what?"

He couldn't resist tucking a wave of hair behind her ear. "About it being a good job that Jess ended it when she did. Before the wedding was much better timing than after. Then we would've had a messy and expensive divorce to sort out. I just couldn't see that at the time because I was so hurt."

Liv gave him a soft smile that he felt might possibly heal all his ills. "I think that's a good way to look at it."

Arran kissed her forehead, appreciating the soft feel of her creamy skin beneath his lips, and fighting the urge to slide them down her cheek and onto her mouth. "Come here, Aggie." He pulled her into a cuddle. "It's you who helped me to look at it like that. Thank you."

She hugged him close and he breathed her in, appreciating the way her small form fit perfectly against him despite the fact that he was a good deal taller. Her soft hair spooled around his neck, tickling his skin, and he imagined it trailing down his naked body as she kissed her way down his torso. He tightened his arms around her, and she pressed her breasts against his chest—sending a jolt of electricity straight to his cock. He was almost sure he could feel the hardness of her nipples through her T-shirt.

His mind went back to the evening he'd stopped at her place to drop off her present and she'd questioned how he knew that she had killer abs. He'd been close to admitting that it was because he'd been staring at her body through her transparent T-shirt when Jayce had soaked her in the bathroom, and he'd liked what he'd seen. But his phone buzzing had interrupted them.

He remembered how it'd felt when she'd unexpectedly thrown her arms around him, and the heat between them. Did she feel it too? He was sure he caught glimpses that she felt the same. But something was holding her back. Was it that they'd known each other forever and she didn't fancy him enough to take it further? He didn't feel like that was the case; their connection was too strong. Perhaps it was that she was about to become his son's teacher, a conflict of interest. Or that she didn't want to risk their friendship when they were so close.

He couldn't help thinking there was more to it. Something she kept hidden. Something he wished she would confide in him.

All he could think about lately was her. But perhaps what he wanted and what he needed were two entirely different things. The fallout from his breakup with Jess had been huge, and it would be wrong of him to take a chance on ruining his close friendship with Liv if he wasn't emotionally ready—plus when he didn't know the full extent of what was holding her back.

The stakes were too high to lose Liv. She was far too important to him. If his time with Jess had taught him anything, it was that he had to be wary of high-stakes relationships. The mother of his child had moved on and left him. There was no way he could let the same thing happen with his best friend. Especially when Jayce would be affected.

He kissed the top of her head, absorbing the cute sigh she released against his chest, and wishing they could stay cuddled in this cozy fort forever. *Us against the world.*

Chapter
EIGHT

"HERE YOU GO, SWEETHEART," ANGUS SAID, POURING LIV SOME tea from a flowery teapot that seemed tiny in his large, calloused hands. The overtly feminine nature of the pot made Angus appear even more masculine, which was a difficult task when he was already a stocky, six-foot hulk of a bloke.

"Thanks," Liv said, pouring in a bit of milk and taking a sip. She shot him an impressed look. "Not bad. You're moving away from builder's tea to Olivia Holland tea very nicely."

Angus gave her a two-fingered salute. "Thank you, ma'am. I'm learning from the best."

Liv's mum joined them at the kitchen table, giving Angus a kiss on the cheek as she accepted her mug from him. "Thanks, love."

The doorbell rang and Angus left to answer it, and when he returned to the kitchen, he had Sam and Maya in tow. They exchanged hugs and kisses with her, Tara, and Angus, and all took a seat around the table with mugs of tea.

Liv took a moment to absorb the fact that the Holland unit of three had rapidly expanded to five over the course of a few months. And she loved it.

"Where are you at with the wedding planning?" Tara asked.

"The big things are done," Sam replied, glancing at Maya. "Wedding venue sorted. Reception booked. Registrar booked."

"We've still got a lot to do with all the other stuff, though," Maya said. "Band, photographer, cake, flowers . . ."

"What about your dress, Maya?" Tara asked. "And the outfits for Liv and Elise?"

"I wanted to ask you about that," Maya replied. "I've got an appointment booked at the place I want to buy our dresses. They'll be off-the-rack because time's too short for fittings and all that jazz. But anyway, I thought you and my mum could come too?"

Liv eyed the look of delight on her mother's face with a smile. "I would absolutely love that," Tara said. "Thank you, sweetheart."

Maya flopped her hand down in an "It's nothing" gesture. "Wouldn't be the same without you, Mama Holland."

Tara's eyes shone and Liv's heart was fit to burst. She squeezed Maya's knee, catching her eye and mouthing, *I love you*. Maya mouthed, *I love you too*, and made a heart shape with her fingers.

Sam caught them, a smile playing on his face. "You'd better not be trying to steal my fiancée, sis."

Liv shrugged, sipping her tea. "She was mine way before she was yours, dude."

Maya nodded in a solemn manner. "Olivia is correct, Samuel." Sam leaned in to nuzzle Maya's neck, making her let out an involuntary squeal. "Hey, that tickles."

Sam pulled Maya into his chest so that she was nestled under his chin as he addressed Liv. "How're the plans coming along for our trip?"

"Awesome, thank you, dear brother." She peered at him over the top of her glasses. "No fishing for details, now."

He shook his head, flashing her a grin. "Wouldn't dream of it. I love surprises."

Maya played with Sam's fingers. "I like good surprises. Like, surprise! Here's a cool present. Not—surprise! Here's a massive bill you forgot to pay."

Liv pursed her lips. "Arran and I are hardly going to organize you shitty surprises, now, are we?"

"Good point," Maya said, giving her a wink.

"By the way," Sam said, "how's Arran doing? I've been a bit worried about him helping organize stuff for our wedding when this time last year, I was helping him with his. He says he's fine when I ask him, but then he can hardly say, 'No, my fucking heart is breaking, you insensitive piece of shit.'"

Angus snorted with laughter across the table and Tara gave Sam a wry smile that clearly read "Language, Samuel."

"Sorry, Mother," he said, turning back to Liv. "Anyway. You guys are tight these days, so I figured he might've told you something."

Liv cleared her throat. "Yeah, we're good friends." She put an extra emphasis on the word *friends* as she shot Maya a look. "And I've asked him about it. Don't worry, he's cool. He's so happy for you guys it eclipses any residual sadness."

Sam sighed. "I love that dude." He glanced down at Maya. "If things ever go south for us, I'm definitely coupling up with Arran."

Maya frowned. "I don't think Nico would be very happy about that."

"Hmm, good point," Sam replied, rubbing his beard. "We might need to make it a house for three. Golden Girls–style."

"Golden Guys," Angus commented. "Can I join in and be Sophia?"

"Sure thing," Sam said, raising his mug to Angus and receiving a clink in return.

Tara shook her head. "It must have been so tough for Arran. Poor boy."

"Yeah." Sam tugged Maya a little closer. "He was in a bad way for a while. To be honest I've avoided Jess ever since, I was so mad with her."

That comment needled a sore point in Liv's psyche and her mouth started moving before she could bite her tongue. "What was she meant to do? Marry him knowing she didn't love him anymore, so they could both make each other miserable till the day they died?"

There was a beat of silence, and a stab of regret pierced her at having spoken her mind. Sam was watching her with a frown. "Well. When you put it like that."

Liv puffed out a breath, the need to speak up overriding her usual self-censorship. "I'm sick of everyone acting like a woman's place is to get dumped. Like, she mustn't dare be the one to end things, but to know her place and only be 'let out' of a relationship when the man decides. Jess had no control over her feelings; none of us do. It just happened to her and so she had to be true to herself for both their sakes. You didn't choose to love Maya, did you? It just happened."

The words had come pouring out like steam from a pressure cooker. An inevitable outcome, really, when she kept everything simmering inside until her thoughts reached the boiling point and then erupted like red-hot lava as soon as a tiny nudge cracked her facade and provided an outlet.

But as she surveyed the surprised expressions around the table, the stab of regret amplified into a painful guilt. The heaviness of it dragged at her insides, swelling in her stomach like a sickening bubble.

She met her mum's eyes, registering the inevitable disapproval there. "Watch your temper, Liv." A flash of anger singed her guilt to a crisp. As usual, her mother disapproved of Liv's expressing any kind of opinion that wasn't one hundred percent rainbows and unicorns. Whereas if her brother did the same, then that was fine—he was just being honest and truthful.

Liv pressed her lips together, burying any further retorts.

Maya saved her with a nod. "I agree with Liv." She shot Sam a smile. "Your little sister just owned you," she told him.

"You know what?" Sam said with a shrug. "I actually feel sorry for Jess. You're right that she couldn't help falling out of love with Arran. And now she can't help falling in love with a twat."

"What do you mean?" Liv asked, anxiety rising.

"He's the kind who'll boast to any guy he meets about how he plays around behind his girlfriend's back. Total small-dick-energy kind of deal. At least, that's how he always was in the past." He sipped his tea. "Though you never know. Maybe he'll be different with Jess."

Tara shook her head. "A leopard never changes its spots. That's a lesson I know Georgie will have learned."

Liv shuddered at the mention of anything related to their father. "Small-dick energy all over," she muttered. Maya shot her a sympathetic smile.

"Anyhow," Sam addressed Liv. "I'm glad you're looking after my best mate while I'm busy with the wedding stuff." Sam gave her a sly glance. "Is there anything *more* than friendship going on between you and Arran?"

Liv raised her eyebrow at Maya.

"Hey," Maya said, holding her hands up. "Don't look at me like that. I've said nothing."

Sam smiled. "You'd have my blessing, you know, if you want to get it on with my bestie. That's what I've done with yours. It's tit for tat." His smile spread into a grin. "So to speak."

"Ugh." Liv rolled her eyes. "Please shut the eff up."

Sam laughed. "You can swear in front of Mum and Angus, by the way. They already know all the four-letter words."

Liv tried to reach around Maya to punch Sam's arm, but he dodged out of the way too fast.

"You effing suck," she muttered, giving Sam her iciest death stare while simultaneously feeling guilty that she hadn't confided in her twin about her feelings for his best friend, nor the mixed-up reasons why she didn't want to act on those feelings. Especially with her recent promise to him to always tell him everything, after his awful ex Catriona had come between them for the past several years. But after such a long time of protecting Sam from her woes, old habits were proving to die hard.

She shot Maya a quick glance. Perhaps she should try to be honest with Maya about it, but it wasn't fair to ask Maya to keep secrets from her fiancé.

Tara cleared her throat. "While we're on the vague subject of your father, I want to ask whether you'd like to invite him to the wedding."

There was a few seconds' silence and Liv felt the blood drain from her face. She took in Sam's expression and knew, even without a mirror, that she must be wearing the exact same horrified look.

Sam's jaw was tight. "He's not our father. He gave up the right to be called that years ago."

"I just wanted to ask," Tara said, reaching over to squeeze Sam's hand. "It's up to you and Maya. You have my blessing either way."

Liv held her breath, wanting to speak up and say her piece—that there was no way that dickhead should be allowed anywhere near her brother's wedding. But then she glanced at her mother, remembering her stern words from earlier. *Watch your temper, Liv.* Instead, she crossed her fingers and willed Sam to say what she wanted to hear, suppressing the need to speak up until it created an almost painful pressure in her chest.

Sam swallowed. "That's thoughtful of you, Mum. But the only parents I want there are you and Angus, and Omar and Yvonne."

Liv let out a breath of relief, darting her gaze over to Angus, who was wearing a visibly moved expression.

"Of course, sweetheart. Whatever you want," Tara replied with a soft smile.

Maya leaned into Sam and kissed his cheek, and Liv eased back into her chair, thanking the heavens that Sam had vetoed that awful idea.

"So, Miss O," Maya said, giving her a nudge. "I've got the green light from Brodie about that date. What say you?"

Tension was infused back into Liv's shoulders. *Can't I get a bloody break?* But Maya meant well. And it was her own fault, really, for not being more honest about her feelings.

She tried to think of an excuse, but then it occurred to her: If she agreed to meet Brodie, not only would it get Maya off her back about the relationship thing; it would also enhance her smoke screen of being on the lookout for love. Plus, it'd stop everyone from going on about her and Arran all the time.

She could meet with Brodie, have a laugh, tell him she wasn't up for a relationship at the moment, and that would be that. Perhaps she could even spin it that Brodie wasn't interested in her and that she was disappointed about it. *Genius.* "Yeah, sounds great. Give me his number and I'll text him."

Maya gave her a satisfied smile and Liv was relieved that it might mean a bit of peace where her love life was concerned. "Back to wedding business," she told the happy couple. "You need to tell us all what tasks we're taking on so we can divide and conquer."

Maya appeared a little relieved. "Thank you. If you all don't mind, I thought we could give one task each to you all in pairs so that you aren't having to choose stuff on your own. Tara, would you and Angus be in charge of flowers if I tell you the color scheme and budget?"

Tara nodded. "We'd love it. And I have a good friend with an excellent florist business."

Maya grinned. "Awesome."

Sam reached around Maya to shove Liv's shoulder. "And we thought we'd get Nico and Elise to pick a photographer, and you and Arran the band."

Liv raised her eyebrows. "The band? I feel that's quite a big responsibility. Sure you don't mind me being in charge of that, bro?"

Sam shrugged. "Your taste in music is way better than mine anyway."

Liv straightened, a smile on her face. "Attention, everyone! Please note that my brother has finally admitted to my superior taste in music." She got to her feet as if making a solemn speech, hands clasped in front of her. "Let this historical moment go down in the Glenavie annals of time. Forever to be remembered on this day, and celebrated by adults and children alike—"

She was cut short as Sam stood to give her another playful shove, and then she shoved him back.

"Now, now," Maya said loudly, holding her hands up to them both. "That's quite enough. Play nicely, please."

Liv shot Sam a grin, which he returned, and they both sat down again.

"In all seriousness," Liv said, "I'd be delighted to sort out the music. And I'm sure Arran will be too."

Sam's grin fell a little. "Watch out for him, will you? I don't want to put him in any awkward positions or make him feel bad."

Liv shook her head. "Don't worry. I've got his back."

AGNES'S VOICE RANG OUT IN ANSWER TO ARRAN'S KNOCK. "WHO is it?"

"Your friendly neighborhood delivery guy," he called through the letterbox.

It was the same routine they went through every week, even when he always came round with her shopping on a Sunday evening. He kept telling her to get a key safe so that trusted people could be given a code to retrieve the key and let themselves in, but she was too stubborn to accept. It had taken him long enough to convince her to let him shop for her.

He could hear her shuffling on the other side of the door, undoing the battery of locks she had installed. He smiled fondly as he patiently waited for her to complete the task.

She opened the door a crack, the chain still on, and eyed him suspiciously through the gap. She never trusted fully that it was him until she laid her myopic eyes on him through the safety of the tiny gap in the door.

He gave her a wink and her face crinkled in a happy smile. The door closed, followed by the sound of the chain coming off before it opened to reveal Agnes's soft features. Her blue eyes twinkled. "Hi, son." She lifted her chin to offer him her cheek, which he pecked with a kiss.

"Hey, beautiful," he said, leaning back to lift the bags laden with shopping. "Let's get this stuff away."

She turned to grab hold of her wheeled trolley and shuffled down the hallway toward the kitchen, where she took a seat and dished out instructions regarding exactly where each item should be placed. And woe betide him if he made a mistake—she had a whip-smart tongue and no qualms about lashing him with if he disobeyed her orders.

He placed the last can in the cupboard and closed the door. "There we go."

"Good lad. Here's your payment." She slid a cup of tea and a plate of biscuits across the counter.

He leaned on the counter and took a biscuit, dunking it in his tea as Agnes sipped hers.

"So," she said, giving him a shrewd once-over. "Tell me your update."

Every week she liked to hear what had been going on in his life, though often she'd already know thanks to her not-so-clandestine hobby of spying on all the neighbors from behind her net curtain. He knew for a fact that she had a pair of binoculars sitting on her living room window ledge, which she pretended she used for bird-watching. Nosy bugger.

"Well, I'm helping to organize my friends' wedding now." Sam had called and asked whether he'd mind getting a band booked. Apparently, he and Liv would be completing the task together, which was music to his ears (pun intended).

Agnes's eyebrows knitted together. "I thought you were already doing that."

He shook his head. "It was just the pre-wedding weekend away before. Now it's actual wedding tasks."

"Hmm. And what else?" She raised a gray eyebrow. "What about your lovely brunette friend? Seen her again this week?"

"Liv?" He shot her a chastising look. "Yeah, she came round on Saturday. But don't pretend like you didn't know that already, Mrs. 'I'm a Bird Watcher, Honest.'"

She shrugged. "I happened to see her arrive while I was watching a great tit." The corner of her mouth ticked up.

A standoff ensued during which both of them attempted to suppress puerile laughter at the double entendre behind the innocent bird's name. There might have been sixty years between them, but their juvenile sense of humor was still aligned.

Arran gave in first with a snigger, while Agnes looked on, smiling behind her mug. "You like that lassie," she told him in a matter-of-fact tone. "And I mean *like* like, as you youngsters call it."

"Aye, well. Maybe I do. Doesn't matter, though, because I can't have her."

"Why not?"

He shook his head, sipping his tea. "I don't know if she likes me like that. Sometimes I'm sure she does, but it's hard to tell for sure what she's thinking."

She rolled her eyes. "Just ask her, then, you numpty."

"I can't."

"Why?"

He gave her an amused look. "Because it's complicated, you nosy old bugger."

Agnes lifted an eyebrow. "Less of the *old*, whippersnapper."

He grinned. "Agnes, you're eighty-eight. I hate to break it to you, but you're old."

"Pfft."

They eyed each other, smiles on their faces.

"Anyway," she said. "Just tell her how you feel. What's the worst that can happen?"

"Er, I ruin our friendship and then it's awkward forever because she's my best friend's sister, and she's also about to become my son's teacher."

Agnes just shrugged, as if none of that were important. "When you get to my age, you realize that the crap you worried about when you were young was just nonsense all along."

He shook his head. "Perhaps you can spy on her some more with those binoculars. See if you can decipher her feelings better than I can."

She smiled. "I have no idea what you mean."

Chapter
NINE

"ARE YOU READY FOR THIS, AGGIE?" ARRAN ASKED, RUBBING HIS hands together with a glint in his eye.

"I'm not sure, to be honest," Liv replied. "I've not been out on a weeknight since around 2015."

He laughed. "Same. That's why it's exciting."

Only a few days since their recruitment as wedding-band bookers, and they were about to scout out their first group.

She eyed the pub they were queuing outside. "Are we sure these guys are legit? I mean, what kind of wedding band plays the small-pub circuit?"

He shot her a grin. "Who knows? They were recommended by Shuggie."

"*Shuggie?*" This was not good news. "For fuck's sake. I didn't realize the friend who was mates with the wedding band was him. The guy skis naked. Plus he's been sacked from every job he's had for fornicating on the premises."

Arran laughed. "But he has good taste in music."

She drew her mouth into a disapproving line. "Good taste in

music to shag in the back room to is not the same as good music to play at my brother and both of our best mates' wedding."

He shot her a wink, which made her weak at the knees. "We'll soon find out."

She shook her head with a smile as they moved to the front of the queue. At least they were getting in for free. Their names had been left at the door by Sam and Arran's friend.

The temperature rose by at least ten degrees and by one hundred percent humidity as they crossed the threshold, and Liv removed her coat so as not to overheat and keel over.

The pub was situated in a nearby town and had a very rustic feel. In the adjacent room, which was an old converted barn, the band were setting up to play. To be fair, the place was pretty packed, so perhaps these guys were actually good—despite their dodgy recommendation.

Arran bought them a couple of pints at the bar and they made their way through the throng to a round table at the back of the gig area. It was the sort that was designed to stand at, so it had no seats. They put their beers down, and Liv shoved her coat underneath the table, Arran following suit with his leather jacket.

He ran a hand over his hair. "I haven't been to this place in years. I saw my first gig here."

"Nice," Liv said, taking a sip of her pint. "I had my first snog here."

Arran arched an eyebrow and it did funny things to her insides.

"Really?" He eyed her as he drank. "A situation you're planning on re-creating tonight?"

Liv held his gaze for a moment, trying to work out whether he was flirting with her or not.

He gestured behind them. "Any of these guys take your fancy?"

Okay. Not flirting, then. She craned her neck to look behind him. "Nope."

He let out a pained sigh. "Oh well. You'll just have to be single with me forever."

"I suppose so," she replied, performing her own dramatic sigh and placing the back of her hand on her forehead as they smiled at each other.

Arran cleared his throat. "Let's hope these guys are what we're looking for and we can give Sam and Maya the go-ahead to hire them."

Liv nodded, crossing her fingers under the table. Perhaps this would be a good find, despite the small, sweaty venue and the recommendation from the world's flakiest man.

"How much do wedding planners make, by the way?" Arran asked her with a grin. "We should invoice Sam and Maya for our time."

Liv laughed. "Are you saying that you need to be paid in order to spend time with me? Am I that much of a chore?"

His smile softened, and something flickered in his eyes. "Nah."

Her attention was drawn from him as the crowd began to cheer and move away from their table, toward the small stage. Four bearded men appeared from stage side to clamber up to the equipment. One headed to the back to sit behind the drums and the other three took up positions in front, one lifting a bass and the other a guitar. The fourth, clearly the front man, grabbed the mike. "Hey. We're Devil's Erection."

The crowd cheered loudly as Liv practically spat her drink across the table. "*Devil's Erection?*"

Arran was laughing so hard he couldn't speak. "Oh my fucking God," he finally managed to get out.

"Are you telling me you didn't know their name up until this point either?" Liv asked, her tone incredulous despite the smile threatening to crack her face in two. Though it only now occurred to her that she hadn't asked the name of the band either; they'd heretofore only referred to them as "the wedding band."

Arran shook his head, still laughing as the band did a sound check. "I can't believe we didn't notice that we didn't know their name."

"I know," Liv said, moving round the table to shout into his ear as the music started. "But I suppose it's easily done, like how no one noticed they didn't know Edward Norton's character's name in *Fight Club*, or Phoebe Waller-Bridge's name in *Fleabag*."

He nodded, jutting out his lower lip in an "it figures" kind of expression. His lip looked soft and bitable and Liv had to drag her eyes off it. "Anyhow," he said. "It isn't necessarily a measure of their music—"

"*Fuck you and your stupid fucking crock, if you don't like it, you can suck my cock!*" the front man half sang, half shouted down the mic to a tumultuous response from the die-hard fans in the mini mosh pit at the front.

Liv arched her eyebrow, giving Arran a sardonic look. His face was frozen, the last syllable of his cutoff sentence still on his lips. He met her gaze, closed his mouth, and swallowed. "Perhaps this isn't their wedding repertoire?"

She let out a laugh that was close to a snort and Arran joined in, the two of them dissolving in laughter until they both had to pretty much hold each other up.

Liv wiped her eyes with one hand as she gripped Arran's biceps with the other. "Can you imagine this playing in the function suite at Glenavie Castle?"

He gave her waist a squeeze as he grinned. "Yes. I think I'd fucking love it."

She shook her head, imagining the scene as people dressed in their wedding attire moshed their heads off, wedding hats and fascinators sent flying through the crowd. "As much as I love that scene, I think this is a nonstarter."

Arran nodded. "I think you're right." He took out his phone as the band started their second verse, this time imaginatively rhyming the words *fuck* and *Innsbruck*. "I'm defo texting Shuggie about this, though, before we leave."

"I mean," Liv said, checking out the manner in which the front man commanded the stage and the heavy yet surprisingly catchy melody, "they are talented. Just perhaps not what we're looking for on this particular occasion."

"Right?" he replied, looking at his phone screen. He glanced up, a glint in his eyes. "We'll keep them in mind, though, like if we're planning a children's birthday party or something."

Liv chuckled.

He glanced back at his phone screen. "Shuggie says their wedding repertoire is classic wedding songs. But with a metal twist."

She raised her eyebrows as he brought his gaze up to hers. "Metal twist, you say? Sounds like the perfect romantic ambience."

His smile grew wider, making his eyes shine. "We'll say no to this option this time but keep it in mind for the next one of us to get hitched."

"Excellent plan, Mr. Adebayo." She clinked her pint glass with his and they drained their drinks.

They reached under the table to grab their jackets and made their way toward the door, but then Arran grabbed her hand. As she turned back to look at him, he had a mischievous look on his face. "Fancy a go in the mosh pit before we leave?"

A smile spread over her face, as if his cheeky expression was contagious. "Let's do it."

They bunged their coats in a corner and Arran kept hold of her hand as they pressed through the crowd to the front, moving with the rest of the crowd to the music. The heavy bassline throbbed in Liv's chest, making her head nod on reflex.

Right at the front the crowd were pressed in tight, and Arran hauled her around in front of him to protect her from the throng. She realized that a person as tiny as herself could well get trampled, so having a tall bloke as her marker was fortuitous. And the fact that he was hot didn't hurt either.

They surged forward and back again, not in control of their movements but carried with the throng and simultaneously held up by it. They were shoved left, then right, then Liv found herself and Arran being dragged in different directions. But before she could reconcile herself to the fact that she was going to lose him and just have to deal with it, she felt the strength of his arm around her waist, hauling her to him and against his chest. She was facing the stage with her back pressed into his front, both of his arms wrapped tightly around her middle.

A tsunami of sensation enveloped her. The heat of his body against hers and the strength of his arms around her. The touch of his lips on her ear as he pressed in to shout, "Okay?" Every bit of her body that was in contact with him (which was a lot) was tingling and fizzing with excitement.

She managed a nod, her heart accelerating to near passing-out proportions.

Someone in front climbed up to the stage and then fell onto the crowd to surf the room. Liv turned her head and went onto her tiptoes to press her mouth to his ear. "I always wanted to try that but was scared 'cause I'm so little."

He smiled down at her. "Do it. I'll catch you."

Excitement pulsed through her. "Should I?"

His smile widened. "Trust me."

That was enough for Liv. She (somewhat reluctantly) extricated herself from his grasp, stepped forward through the front line of the crowd to the stage, and climbed up. The front man clocked her and gave her a wink as he sang/shouted into the mic.

The crowd was an undulating sea of faces in front of her, and it was kind of mesmerizing. As if enveloped in a cloud of unreality, she turned and fell back onto the crowd, hands underneath her holding her up as the ceiling moved overhead. She sensed she was moving away from where Arran had been standing. But just as she resolved that once back on her feet, she'd need to head back into the crowd to try to find him, a pair of hands grasped her around the waist, lifting her down. She knew it was him. It was funny how she'd already learned the feel of his touch.

He came into view as she was lowered into his arms, his head turned to the people who had been holding her up. "She's with me."

Something about that sentence made her feel warm and fuzzy. He held her gaze as he brought her against his chest. "How was that?"

Liv's feet made contact with the floor as she looked up at him. "It was awesome. I thought I'd lost you, though, and was a bit nervous about finding you again when I'm one of the smallest people here."

He shook his head, giving her a wink. "Nah. I was with you the whole time, waiting to get my hands on you."

Something pulsed between them and she could've sworn his pupils dilated slightly. But then he was taking her hand to lead her away toward where they'd stowed their jackets.

As they left the pub and headed out into the night air, the fun-filled heat of the pub gave way to the sting of cold. It was accompanied by a sense of disappointment that they hadn't solved the band issue.

"As much as I enjoyed that," she told Arran as they made for the bus stop, "we still don't have a band for Sam and Maya."

He was quiet for a moment as they walked the last few yards to the bus shelter. Then, upon reaching it, he leaned against the edge, an unusually pensive look on his face. "It's okay. I think I've got the answer."

She raised her eyebrows. "As long as Shuggie's not got anything to do with it. I don't want our next stop to be a gig by a band named Satan's Schlong."

He laughed. "Don't worry. This one will be different. What are you doing on Saturday night?"

LIV KEPT WATCH OUT OF HER LIVING ROOM WINDOW, WAITING FOR Arran's car to arrive. This time she had learned her lesson and refused to come along until he told her the name of the band. They were called Love to Love and that seemed like a good sign.

For some reason Arran had been ever so slightly subdued since he'd suggested them, though, which was weird, because surely if they were as good as he said, and also free on the date they wanted, then it was a win-win.

So why the long face? she thought as she spied him arriving.

She left the house and climbed into his car, shooting him a smile. "You sure you don't mind driving?"

He shook his head as he took them onto the main road out of town. "It'll be easier than getting the bus. And I don't fancy a drink anyway."

She eyed him as he drove. "But you said you'd drive from the get-go. How did you know a few days back you wouldn't fancy a drink tonight?"

Arran flashed her a smile. "Just a gut feeling."

He was hiding something, but Liv got the distinct impression that whatever it was, he didn't want to disclose it yet.

Their destination was a large hotel out in the countryside, between Glenavie and another town farther south. The band were playing a wedding (another good sign) and had told them they were welcome to pop in during the evening reception to listen to a couple of songs from the back of the room. Liv had been a little nervous about being seen as a gate-crasher, but Arran had assured her this was normal practice, he and Jess having done it when picking their wedding band.

Arran took them up a narrow, winding country road that eventually brought them onto the grounds of the hotel, and they parked at the front. It was an old converted stone building, with a large new extension at the rear that housed the function suite. The low pulse of music was apparent as they climbed out of the car and crunched across the gravel toward the main entrance.

Heartened by the fact that said music did not contain any expletives, she gave Arran a smile. He looked a little pensive again as they walked through the big oak doors and into the reception area.

"You know this is part of a chain of hotels?" she told him. "Apparently the sister one in Glasgow does the best afternoon tea *ever*. I'd love to go there one day."

Arran smiled at her. "You and your scone obsession."

"Yep," she replied. "Sorry not sorry."

They were directed through to the back of the hotel, where the music grew louder and Liv could already tell she was going to like the band. A gorgeous, soaring female voice was singing a cover of Stevie Wonder's "Superstition" with spot-on percussion, cool-as-fuck bass, and the backing of two male voices.

They walked through glass doors into a large conservatory, one wall lined with glass and overlooking the hills. "This is amazing," Liv said, casting her eye around the place. Arran still appeared ill at ease, and she tried to fathom what was wrong. This definitely wasn't the same venue he and Jess had booked for their canceled wedding, so it couldn't be that.

They bought a soft drink for Arran and a glass of wine for Liv and hung out by the bar. Liv smiled as she watched the happy wedding crowd, a few the worse for wear but in a joyful way as they danced and chatted and celebrated the wedding of their loved ones.

The two brides wore white, though very different styles, with one in a tightly fitting fishtail dress and the other in a long-sleeved bodice that gave way to a full pleated skirt.

"They look so beautiful and happy," Liv murmured, almost surprised when Arran agreed; she'd thought her voice had been too low to hear over the music. "And the band are brilliant," she added, eyeing the red-haired singer in her green velvet gown and nattily dressed male colleagues. "I mean, this is decided for me already."

He didn't comment.

She glanced over at him, and he was still watching the brides. "What say you, Mr. A?"

He blinked, then cleared his throat with a smile. "Agreed. I'll message Sam to say we should lock them down for the date."

"How did you hear about them?" she asked, watching the dancers again.

He hesitated for a beat. "I've heard them play before."

Glancing over, she raised her eyebrows. "Oh yeah? At a wedding?"

He swallowed. "Yeah. That's right."

Just as Liv was about to ask him what was up, the fishtail-dress bride popped up in front of them. "Hello! I don't think we've met. Are you friends of Sarah's?" She gestured toward her new wife.

"Oh no, sorry," Liv replied, feeling guilty. "I'm afraid we aren't on the guest list. The band said it was okay to pop in and listen to a quick couple of numbers because we're looking to book them for a wedding."

The bride's face lit up. "You two are getting married too? That's awesome!" Before Liv could correct her, she'd started waving madly at her spouse. "Sarah! Come here!"

Liv shot Arran an apologetic look, but he had a smile on his face. She turned back to the bride. "Sorry, I didn't mean—"

"These guys are getting married too!" Fishtail Bride said to Sarah, who gave them a shy smile.

"That's lovely," Sarah said. "Are you friends of Angela's?"

"No," Angela replied, clearly the more gregarious of the two. "They're here to see the band. They're going to book them for their wedding."

"When are you getting married?" Sarah asked.

"Oh, we aren't—" Liv began.

"June," Arran said, taking hold of her hand and stopping her in her tracks.

Angela squealed. "Not long to go! Bit last-minute, aren't you?"

Arran slung his arm around her shoulders and Liv thought she might drop down dead from a heart attack. "I know, right?" he said smoothly. "It's just that a cancellation came up for Glenavie Castle and we had our hearts set on it."

Liv swallowed against her dry throat. "Yes. Hearts set," she parroted.

"Well, we can definitely recommend these guys," Sarah said, gesturing toward the band. "The dance floor's been full all night. They really know how to get everyone up and partying."

"Thanks," Arran said. "We were just saying that we're going to lock them down because we liked what we heard."

Angela grabbed Liv's hand. "You should come and dance with us. That way you'll get a proper feel for them!"

Before Liv could comment, Angela was pulling her and Arran toward the floor, Sarah in tow. As soon as her feet touched the wooden dance floor, Angela began gyrating in time to the music, whirling Liv and Arran round to face her and grabbing Sarah to dance next to her so the four were in a circle.

Glancing across at Arran, Liv was relieved to see that he had finally relaxed and was performing on Angela's instruction, imitating her moves and adding one of his own to throw the dance baton back to her. Angela threw back her head and laughed in delight as Sarah smiled at the scene, her own moves more understated.

Liv grinned as Arran began to moonwalk across the floor between them, and Angela tried to imitate but ended up tripping on her tightly fitted fishtail and falling into her wife's arms. The two kissed as the band began to play Whitney Houston's "I Wanna Dance with Somebody," and Liv's heart turned to actual mush.

She turned away to let the happy couple dance in each other's arms and saw that Arran was moonwalking back toward her. He held his hand out with a grin and she took it, her skin tingling at his touch, as the opening bars of the song gave way to the first of the lyrics.

They moved in time with each other, his arm around her waist and her hand reaching up to take his shoulder, holding hands on the other side. Her senses were heightened by his proximity, as if she were aware of every microscopic nerve ending in contact with his body—and each one of them fizzed with excitement.

His face was fully open and relaxed for the first time that evening, and it made her heart soar. The chorus kicked in and he released her waist to spin her around, coming to meet her and lift her in the air as the spin ended.

She laughed in exhilaration, holding her arms out like Kate Winslet on the bow of the *Titanic* as he twirled them around, her trust in him to hold on to her and keep her safe unwavering. The room was still spinning a little as he lowered her to the ground, bringing her down against his body. *"With somebody who loves me,"* sang the lead singer as Liv's eyes met Arran's.

Her heart smacked against her rib cage at the intensity in his gaze. His pupils were large and dark, swallowing up all but a tiny rim of the honey color of his irises as his eyes dropped to her mouth. She held on to his neck and he held her waist, and for a second, Liv almost believed the two of them were the couple that Angela and Sarah mistakenly thought they were.

The last notes of the song played out and Arran eased forward to rest his forehead against hers. Liv's breath caught in her chest. As they swayed together, she gently let it out through parted lips, somehow afraid that any larger movements might break the spell between them. She closed her eyes, clinging to the moment, and wished with every fiber in her being that he would kiss her.

But the spell inevitably faded with the dying notes of the song and he shifted away from her, meeting her eyes for a second before giving her a sheepish smile and running his hand over the top of his head. "Good moves, Aggie."

She smiled, though it felt kind of wobbly on her face. "You too."

She blinked, and someone standing at the edge of the dance floor caught her eye, a man their age in a white shirt tucked into gray trousers. He appeared familiar and was looking at her. For a split second she didn't recognize him. Then her brain clicked and a heaviness dropped in her stomach, spoiling the magical feeling that dancing with Arran had created.

Liv tried to give the man a weak smile, but he just blinked and turned away. Her stomach churned.

She stepped toward Arran and took his hand. "Is it okay if we go now?"

He eyed her expression, frowning. "Course. Everything all right?"

Liv nodded as she turned and pulled him off the dance floor and toward the exit. He fell into step next to her, still holding her hand.

Arran grabbed the door to let her through, and she mourned the loss of his touch. "What's wrong?" he asked her as they walked through the hotel to the main exit.

She took a breath, attempting to quell her nausea. "Just saw an ex-boyfriend of mine."

He raised his eyebrows. "Anyone I know?"

"Yeah. Remember Dean?"

A look of recognition crossed his face. "The one you were with when we were eighteen?"

She nodded, stepping out into the night air and feeling grateful for the cool temperature. "That's the one."

He touched her arm as they crossed the gravel. "Was that the first time you've seen him since he broke up with you? That's tough."

"Mmm," Liv replied, not wanting to confirm or deny that statement. It was the first time she'd seen him, all right. But she didn't fancy discussing the "who broke up with whom" thing.

They got into Arran's car and he fired it up. "Wanna talk about it?"

She glanced over. "Not really, to be honest. It didn't end well and I haven't seen him since. I just got a bit of a shock when he was there tonight. He left Glenavie years back, so I didn't expect to see him again."

Arran nodded as he took them out of the car park and onto the windy road.

"Anyway. Apart from that, it was really fun," Liv said. "That's definitely the band for Sam and Maya. Did you text him to say?"

"Yeah. He's going to call them in the morning."

She sank back into her seat, content in the knowledge that they'd helped solve that issue. "Awesome."

He smiled gently as he drove.

Liv hesitated for a second, then pressed ahead with what she wanted to say. "I'm glad you enjoyed it. Because up until we met the brides, you seemed like you'd rather be anywhere but here."

He was silent, and for a moment she thought he wasn't going to answer. "I was just a little apprehensive, that's all." He paused. "Love to Love were the band that Jess and I had hired for our wedding."

Of course. That explained everything, and she didn't understand why she hadn't put two and two together before. She touched his hand. "I'm sorry."

Arran flashed her a smile. "It's fine." They drove silently for a couple of minutes, and Liv took hold of his fingers. He held hers back.

"I feel bad for not suggesting them earlier," he told her. "They're probably the best in the area, so I knew it was likely that the canceled wedding at the castle had them booked and now they'd be free." He sighed. "Fucking selfish of me not to say anything to Sam sooner."

She squeezed his fingers. "It's okay."

Arran glanced over to give her a smile.

"Was it as bad as you thought?"

"To be honest, no. It wasn't. Once we were there and started talking to the brides, I enjoyed myself and even forgot that they should've been my wedding band."

A sense of relief warmed her. "That's good. So you think you'll be okay on the day, when they're playing the evening reception?"

He nodded firmly. "Absolutely." They reached the junction and he let go of her to execute the turn. "You know what?"

"What?"

He gave her a warm smile. "Being there with you helped."

Her breath snagged like it had when he'd held her close on the dance floor. "I'm glad I was there."

She allowed herself to study him and the contented expression on his face for a few more seconds, before dragging her eyes away and onto the dark scenery ahead.

"By the way," Arran asked, "what do you want for your birthday?

Not long to go now until the twins' big day, and I already got you the sonic screwdriver."

"That's okay. You don't have to get me a present."

He pursed his lips and shook his head. "Oh, yes I do. We're best buds now. I get something for Sam, and so I'm getting something for you."

Liv laughed. "There's really nothing that I want."

He smiled knowingly. "I'll just have to go with my gut, then."

Chapter
TEN

CLIMBING THE STAIRS TO THE FIRST FLOOR, ARRAN CAST HIS gaze around the pub and settled on where the guests of honor were seated around a table with Maya, Elise, and Nico. His gaze did linger somewhat longer on the birthday girl in particular, though, his pulse firing a little more rapidly in response.

He made his way over, pleased to see that the one remaining seat was next to Liv. He placed a hand on her shoulder as he reached them, the heat from the contact driving up his arm and into his chest, zapping his heart. "Many happy returns, Aggie."

She gave him a show-stopping smile that electrified his skin, and when she got to her feet to lean up and kiss his cheek, it scrambled his brain.

Arran moved over to embrace Sam, trying to regain his bearings. "And happy birthday to you too, you complete tosser."

Sam grinned. "Thanks, pal."

Arran greeted the others, then took off his jacket and settled in the seat next to Liv. "So." He rubbed his hands together. "What did I miss?"

"An argument," Liv replied, raising her eyebrows.

"An *argument*?" He dropped his jaw in exaggerated surprise. "On the twins' sacred birthday?"

Liv sniffed, giving her twin a mock-stern stare. "Sam says Matt Smith was the best Doctor Who."

His jaw dropped for real, and Arran shot Sam a look of horror. "You're joking."

"Nope." Sam took a swig of his beer. "Matt's the best."

Liv glanced at Arran. "Everyone knows the best Doctor is—"

"David Tennant," Arran finished for her.

"*See*," Liv accused Sam. "You know nothing, Sam Holland. I hereby claim your best friend for myself because we are more attuned than you and he." She took hold of Arran's hand, the soft pads of her fingers burning into his skin and making the hairs on the back of his arm stand on end.

Sam shrugged. "You can borrow him for a bit. As I said the other night, tit for tat." He pulled Maya close.

"Pardon?" Arran asked, as Liv shot Sam a death stare.

"Nothing," Liv replied quickly, releasing his hand. "Sam was saying some crap about me becoming your bestie as recompense for him claiming Maya as his."

Arran's fingers reached out of their own accord, aching with the loss of her touch. "Pimping me out to your sister, Holland?" he said, catching a little blush appearing on Liv's cheeks.

Sam gave him a grin.

"Don't be so hasty," Nico chimed in. "I'll throw my hat into the ring for the best-friend stakes, Liv. You don't want Adebayo when you can have me."

Elise raised her eyebrows at Nico.

"I'm good anyway," Liv said. "I'm already in the lucky position of having two besties." She nodded toward Elise. "Dr. K has my back."

"I reckon Dr. Kowalski also needs my services," Nico said, looking at Elise with a smile playing on his lips.

Elise openly rolled her eyes.

"Okay," Liv said, smiling. "You versus Arran to be besties with Elise and me. But how will we decide?"

"Whoever got you the best birthday present," Nico said. "Speaking of which . . ." He lifted a couple of gift bags, handing one each over to the twins. "You'd better open them simultaneously, because it's the same thing."

As soon as he said that, both Liv and Sam tore into the tissue paper inside the bags, each clearly determined to be the first to brandish the present, which was a big bottle of something, judging by the shape of the bag. Despite their efforts, they both pulled the bottles out simultaneously—a magnum of champagne each.

"Wow," Liv said, eyeing the bottle with a sparkle in her eyes. "This is our favorite one. Thanks, Nico."

"Yeah, thanks, man," Sam added, holding his hand out above Maya's and Elise's heads for Nico to high-five.

Nico folded his arms, giving Arran the smuggest smile in the history of the universe. Arran raised an eyebrow in return, shooting Nico a look that said, "You're toast, Hadid."

"What're you countering with?" Elise asked Arran hopefully, seeming keen for him to trump Nico.

Arran shrugged and pulled a couple of envelopes out of his pocket. He silently passed one to Sam and one to Liv. "You don't need to perform synchronized present opening with these. They aren't the same." He absorbed the spark of excitement in Liv's eyes and the deadpan arching of an eyebrow from Nico.

Sam was fastest. "Awesome. A voucher for the ski shop." He gave Arran a fist bump.

Liv lifted the card out of her envelope, taking in the contents and looking up with wide eyes. The shining emotion on display in the sea of her gaze made his heart ache.

"Thank you," she said, quietly.

"Don't hold out on us," Maya said, bouncing in her chair. "What is it?"

Liv cleared her throat. "It's a voucher for afternoon tea for two at that posh hotel in Glasgow I was telling you about. It got a great write-up." She met Arran's eyes. "I told Arran about it recently."

"That's lovely, Arran," Elise said, shooting Nico a smug smile, which clearly conveyed that Arran had won the best-present competition, hands down.

Nico, unfazed, gave Elise a wink in return, which seemed to cause color to flush her cheeks, and she glanced away. He smiled at Arran. "You win, bro. So, Liv. Who's going to be the lucky person you take with you for your afternoon tea?"

Liv glanced between Maya and Elise. "I'm not sure. I don't want to cause any scone-based arguments." She leaned back, eyeing Arran. "I might have to choose you." She cleared her throat. "In order to avoid any fallout, I mean."

Arran dragged his eyes from the hypnotizing green hue of Liv's to check out Maya's and Elise's reactions. They appeared more than happy with the idea, judging by the slightly sappy smiles on their faces.

Turning back to Liv, he swallowed against the dry sensation in his throat, his pulse surging at the idea of accompanying her on something that could, possibly, in some sense of the definition, be classed as a date. A *real* date, as opposed to their blind-date fiasco. "I can't buy you a present and then use it for myself."

She shrugged. "Yeah, you can. My present, my choice." She gave him a defiant look that was more than a little sexy and stuck out her hand to shake on it. He grasped her hand and sealed the deal, trying to ignore the electrifying sensation caused by her skin grazing his. Every time he touched her was more intense than the last, and at some point soon he'd likely self-combust. Her eyes lingered on him and he was caught in her gaze for a couple of beats, his fingers slow to release hers. She seemed in no rush to let go either, and again he let himself wonder . . . Maybe she also felt the attraction between them.

Sam's voice cut into the moment. "I got a call from Dave today."

For a second, Arran had to think about who that was. And as he put two and two together his heart went from its dizzying going-on-a-kind-of-date-with-Liv heights right down to the soles of his boots. He shifted his eyes from Liv, her fingers slipping away. "Dave, as in . . ."

"Our shitty father, Douchebag Dave," Liv concluded, her expression clouded.

Arran shot her a look of concern before addressing Sam. "What the hell did *he* want?"

Nico and Elise were leaning in, the frowns on their faces mirrored all around the table, and from the tension in his brow Arran knew he must look the same.

Maya was circling Sam's shoulders as he continued. "Fuck knows. He called out of the blue. Said he'd heard from our uncle that I was getting married and was asking about it. I told him it wasn't any of his business."

Nico eyed Sam. "Stupid question, but could he have been calling out of genuine interest?"

Liv made a stifled noise that Arran could interpret as "not fucking likely."

Sam shook his head. "I ended the call. Then Georgie phoned Mum not too long after, to let her know she'd chucked him out. He's been playing her the way he did Mum, unsurprisingly. Had a string of affairs since they've been on Jersey and lied to her about them all."

Arran let out a slow breath. *Once a douchebag, always a douchebag.*

Elise was wearing a concerned expression. "So, you think he called you to try to wheedle his way back into the family, now that Georgie's given him the heave-ho?"

Sam sighed, and Maya kissed his cheek. "Maybe. I'm trying not to think about it."

"I'm sorry, man," Arran said, and Sam shot him a grateful smile.

Arran glanced at Liv, who appeared as if she had the weight of the world on her shoulders. They were slumped under an invisible ten-ton force.

Arran was about to ask her if she was okay, when Liv gave Sam a supportive smile. "Don't worry, Sam. It'll be okay."

The twins exchanged a look of solidarity and, yet again, it occurred to Arran that Liv always deflected any sympathy regarding the Dave situation onto her brother. In fact, she always shone a light on everyone else's struggles, yet he couldn't remember her seeking or accepting any attention for herself.

His phone began to ring before he could ponder the idea further, and he saw that it was Jess. She'd been calling more frequently of late, even when he didn't have Jayce. It was getting a little weird, but he still answered every time just in case she was calling because something was wrong with the wee one. He connected the call, mouthing, *Sorry, it's Jess,* to his friends.

"Hey," she said, her voice bright. "Are you out for Sam and Liv's birthday?"

He hesitated, confused. "Yep, that's right. Like I mentioned last time you called. What can I do you for? Is Jayce okay?"

"Yeah, yeah, fine. He's good. I just needed to ask whether you could have him an extra weekend."

He paused, unable to think that there were any weekends left for him to take from her, because he had pretty much all of them now. Apart from the two major ones—the weekend away and the wedding. But he'd told her about those. "Which weekend?"

She told him a date that he immediately recognized as the date of the Skye trip, and a sinking feeling dragged at his gut. He hated saying no, but he had to. "Sorry. No can do. That's the weekend I'm away, remember?"

Sam shot him a WTF look and Arran shook his head in reassurance.

Disappointment infused her tone. "But there's this party Rory wants us to go to. He says it'll be epic."

He took a breath, feeling guilty and resentful all at once. "Jess, I told you about that weekend already. It's off-limits. Ask your mum instead."

Her tone was short. "She's busy."

He swallowed. "Well, I'm sorry, but I can't help you. That weekend is iron-clad. Liv and I have got all the activities arranged, Elise has a restaurant booked, and Nico's got us accommodation."

She was silent for a moment and his jaw clenched at the idea that she could possibly be mad about this.

"Fine," Jess replied, in a tone suggesting that it was anything but. "By the way, did you get Sam a birthday present from me?"

Arran opened his mouth, then closed it again, unsure what to do with that question. Replying with "Why the holy fuck would I do that?" did seem rather impolite. "No. Why?"

"We used to always get joint presents for our best friends."

He lifted a hand to rub his forehead. *What's going on?* "That was when we were a couple, Jess. We aren't anymore." He closed his eyes briefly in discomfort. Being short wasn't like him, but she was really testing his patience of late.

"Right." She paused, and the uncomfortable moment's silence caused his pulse to spike. "Bye, then."

"Bye." He hung up, feeling decidedly nauseated.

Liv's eyebrows were knitted. "What was that all about?"

Arran let out a slow breath. "I have no idea." Everyone was looking at him with a mix of sympathy and puzzlement.

"Was she asking you to take Jayce when you're meant to be away with us?" Sam asked, his tone incredulous.

"Yeah," he replied, trying to fathom what had been going through Jess's head. It was an unreasonable request, but what made it worse was her having the audacity to be annoyed when he said no. And yet, he still felt guilty about it.

"For fuck's sake," Sam muttered. "You *told* her about that weekend."

Liv nudged Arran's arm. "What else did she say? Before you told her you weren't a couple anymore?"

He ran a hand over the top of his hair. "She asked me if I'd bought Sam a present from her. Because we always used to get our best friends presents from each other."

Liv nodded, clearly understanding why he'd answered Jess the way he had. "Do you think she's okay?" she asked Arran. "I mean, she's not usually possessive, is she?"

"Possessive" was a good way to describe Jess's current behavior. "Not since we split. But why would she be? We haven't been a couple for a year, and she was the one who ended it."

Liv was nodding, a frown on her face.

"Sounds like she's insecure, to me," Elise chimed in.

Liv and Maya were nodding in agreement, and Arran absorbed their sympathetic outlook. Maybe they were right.

The others began to talk among themselves, and Liv leaned in toward Arran. "I hope it's not me that's upset Jess."

He frowned, meeting her gaze. "What do you mean?"

Her eyes were wide with concern. "She was funny the other night on the phone, once she found out I was there. Now she's calling you when she knows you're out for our birthday and also trying to stop us being on the same weekend away together."

He opened his mouth to protest that it couldn't be the reason, because why would Jess care who he was socializing with? But then he closed it again, realizing that Jess's keeping tabs *had* begun after that day she'd called when Liv was round.

"I wonder," Liv continued, her head cocked to the side with a cute frown on her face, "whether Rory's putting pressure on her too."

Arran raised his eyebrows. "How do you mean?"

She pushed her glasses up her nose. "He's quite the party animal. Perhaps he's pressuring her to get you to have Jayce so they can go to all these parties together. It doesn't sound like he's the stay-in-and-play-happy-families sort." She paused. "It must be hard to devote enough time to a new relationship, especially with someone high-maintenance like him."

Arran hadn't really taken any time to consider all that from Jess's point of view before. He'd been distracted by his own hurt and had painted a mental picture of Jess and Rory running off hand in hand into an idyllic existence together.

Maya's voice brought him out of his ruminations. "Isn't it your date this weekend, Liv?"

It took a couple of seconds to process what Maya had said, and he snapped his gaze to Liv, his heart rate spiking. *What date?*

"Yeah," she said, glancing away. "That's right."

"Come on, then," Maya said, raising her eyebrows. "Give us the deets."

Liv laughed, but it sounded slightly high-pitched. "Not much to say, really. We're meeting for a drink."

"Where?" Elise asked. "Here?"

Liv shook her head. "The new cocktail bar on the high street."

Sam flashed her a grin. "Fancy."

Liv gave another of those high-pitched laughs. "Not really. I don't think anywhere in Glenavie could be described as fancy."

Arran listened, desperate to ask whom she was going on a date with. But he was trying to figure out how to interject in a polite manner, rather than going with his current instinct, which was to shout, "Who the fuck are you going on a date with?"

"Who's the lucky guy?" Nico asked, rescuing him from his dilemma.

"Brodie, Maya and Sam's friend," Liv said, glancing at Arran, then away again quickly.

"Oh yeah, he's a cool guy," Nico said. "I've got a date this Saturday too. Maybe we'll see each other." He flashed Liv a grin. "A double date."

She laughed again; this time the pitch sounded more normal. "We can rescue each other if it goes wrong."

If it goes wrong, I want to be the one to rescue her. Arran realized that he was *hoping* it would go wrong, and a wave of guilt washed over him. He lifted his beer and took a long sip, trying to douse the hot jealousy consuming his insides.

Chapter
ELEVEN

LIV DROPPED A PACKET OF BISCUITS INTO HER BASKET AND headed toward the canned goods section. Her phone started to ring in her pocket, so she lifted it out as she walked.

Elise's voice was a little panicked. "Liv. We've got a bit of a situation."

She paused next to the tinned tuna. "What situation? Are you okay?"

"Oh, yes, sorry. I'm fine. It's a wedding-planning-related situation."

"What is it?"

"You know how Nico and I were meant to meet with that photographer this afternoon?"

"Yeah?" She reached out to take a pack of cans from the shelf.

"We can't make it."

Liv dropped the tuna into her basket. "Neither of you?"

"No. Jack's got a fever, so I don't want to leave him with Mum. And Nico's got a vomiting bug."

"Blimey. Everyone's under the weather."

"Yeah. Though Nico's is probably a hangover."

Liv smiled at Elise's signature negativity wherever Nico was concerned. "I don't think so. He wouldn't have been out on the lash the night before his big date." He'd mentioned having a date the same night she did, and hers was tonight. That thought sent a feeling of dread to her gut. "Anyhow. No need to panic. I can meet with the photographer and still have plenty of time to get ready for my date tonight."

Elise let out a sigh. "Thank you so much. I owe you one."

"No problem. Just text me the details."

They ended the call and Liv grabbed a couple more things from the shelf, just as her phone started to ring again. "Shit," she said, then glanced over to meet the disapproving eyes of an elderly lady across the aisle. She gave the woman a weak smile as she juggled the goods in her hands and the basket in order to answer the phone, not taking in who was calling. "Hello?"

"Hey, Aggie. I need to recruit you for a mission."

Arran's voice caused a delicious tingle to lick up her spine, prickling her skin with goose bumps. "Really? Well, I'm afraid I've already accepted a mission for today."

"Has Elise called you?"

"Yeah. Why?" Liv managed to get her stuff into the basket.

"Aha. Nico called me."

"So it's the same mission?"

"Indeed it is. I figured two heads are better than one? Although it'll actually be three heads. Well, perhaps two and a half, because the third is small."

A smile spread across her face. "Jayce is coming with us?"

"Yeah. That okay?"

"Perfect," she said, heading toward the tills.

"Excellent. We'll pick you up at one p.m."

THEY PULLED UP ON THE DRIVEWAY AT THE ADDRESS SUPPLIED BY Elise, and Liv turned round to Jayce. "Here we go, buddy. Ready to look at some photos?"

Jayce looked at her with those big brown eyes. "I want to play."

"Sure we can, pal." Liv thought she felt Arran's gaze on her, but as she turned her head he looked away. They exited the car and she got Jayce out of the back, taking his hand to walk up the drive.

As they headed for the front door, Arran put his hand out to take Jayce from her, but the wee one grasped her hand with both of his, pressing his face into her arm. "I want to hold Lib's hand."

"Charming," Arran said in a mock-hurt voice, but there was a soft smile on his face.

Arran rang the doorbell, and a tall silver-haired man answered. He was smartly dressed in checked trousers, a long-sleeved shirt, and a waistcoat. "Hello there. You must be Elise and Nico."

Liv shook her head. "I'm afraid we're stand-ins. Both of them are unwell today."

"I see," he replied, casting an eye over the three of them with an air of interest.

"I'm Arran," Arran told him, holding his hand out for a shake. "And this is Liv, and Jayce."

"I'm *Lord* Jayce, of the fort," Jayce piped up, a serious expression on his little face.

"And I'm Henry," the man replied with a smile. "Delighted to meet you. Please do come in."

Henry had a refined kind of voice and Liv imagined it was because he mixed in cultured circles. As he took them down the bright, white-walled hallway, her eyes were drawn to the beautiful photographs of Highland scenery lining the walls.

"Wow," Arran said, his voice full of awe. "Are these all your work?"

"Yes," Henry replied. "The scenic shots are my other passion, outside of my wedding photography business."

"Have you taken any pictures of dragons?" Jayce asked, eyeing the photos with an air of disappointment.

"I'm afraid not, young man," Henry said with a smile in his voice. "They are indeed very difficult to capture on camera." He opened a doorway at the end of the hallway and showed them into a large modern extension that housed his studio. There was a comfy sitting area to the left as they walked in, where they settled in while he prepared some coffees from a machine sitting between the squashy leather sofas.

Liv admired the large white-walled studio beyond, with camera equipment set up between them and the space. A big skylight cast a soft, natural light over the area. "This is amazing. Have you had the studio for long?"

"A few years," Henry said. "I had the extension built so that I could enhance my business with portrait work."

Jayce wriggled on Liv's lap, keen to get down. She let him onto his feet and kept an eagle eye while he investigated the leather-bound folders on the coffee table in front of them. She didn't quite have the heart to tell him that there would, more than likely, be a paucity of dragons in the folders too.

"Feel free to look through those," Henry said. "They're examples of weddings I've done."

Arran lifted a folder and Liv scooted up next to him so that they could both leaf through the shots, Jayce opening another folder on the table and scouring it with a determined look on his face.

"These are beautiful," Liv murmured, taking in various shots displaying natural poses between smartly kilted grooms and beautifully gowned brides. Henry had captured the background scenery in each one perfectly—rolling hills and glassy lochs.

"Yes," Arran replied, eyeing the book. "And the aspect of these is spectacular." He glanced up to where Henry was depositing their coffee cups on the table. "Did you use a drone for some of them?"

Henry smiled. "That's right. I started using it fairly recently. It provides some fantastic aerial shots."

Jayce flipped his folder shut. "Urgh. These people are kissing." He stuck his tongue out in a gag.

"Yes," Henry said with a patient nod. "These wedding couples are a darned nuisance, kissing all the time."

"Kissing is stupid," Jayce said, wandering over to play with one of the cushions.

"I love this one," Arran told Henry as he pointed to a picture. "I painted this loch recently."

Henry's eyes lit up. "You're an artist?"

Arran nodded, a modest smile on his face. "I set up my own business last year."

Henry began to ask Arran various questions about his enterprise, offering sage advice along the way. Liv moved over to follow Jayce, whose eye had been caught by the white space across from them.

Arran glanced up from his conversation with Henry, making to get to his feet when he realized Jayce was straying toward the studio space and a pile of off-white beanbags.

"That's okay," Henry said. "He can play on those. I use them during my family shoots."

"Thanks," Arran said, walking toward her and Jayce as if to supervise Jayce's play.

Liv touched his arm. "You chat to Henry some more. I'll play with Jayce."

His eyes were soft. "Are you sure?"

"Of course." Liv took Jayce's hand and they headed for the beanbags; Jayce launched himself onto one of them, laughing as he made his soft landing. Liv took the opportunity to remove his shoes, just in case they sullied Henry's stuff.

Arran and Henry's conversation moved on to Sam and Maya and the kind of shots they wanted.

"They love this kind of outdoor scenery," Arran was telling him. "These backdrops are right up their street. And the views from the castle will look amazing."

"I have some shots at the castle here," Henry said, lifting another book.

Liv tickled Jayce as he lay in the beanbag, the wee one letting out a squeal.

Arran and Henry looked at more photos together, Arran describing the couple's wish to have photos from the evening reception as well as daytime, preferably with some outdoor nighttime shots because Maya loved the moon and stars. It occurred to Liv how it was fortuitous that Arran was here even though that hadn't been the original intention, because his artist's brain was perfectly placed to relay to Henry exactly what the brief was. She felt a strong sense of pride at his handling of the situation, and with a start she realized that it was the kind of pride someone might feel about a partner, rather than a friend.

She tried to tune out of their conversation as she and Jayce played on the beanbags, taking it in turns to fall onto them in a variety of comical ways and make each other laugh. Then Liv got kind of stuck in a beanbag and couldn't get out, Jayce giggling and clambering on top of her.

She became aware that the conversation at the other end of the room had ceased and that Henry and Arran were on their feet by one of the cameras, Henry showing Arran the equipment as he trained it on Liv and Jayce. Henry smiled. "Is it okay to take some shots of you and the wee one? You're both naturals."

"Fine by me," Liv replied, glancing at Arran.

He smiled. "Me too."

Henry began clicking away as Liv and Jayce played, every now and again giving a small suggestion for a shot but largely shooting organically. Eventually he shifted back to speak to Arran. "Can we get some with you in as well?"

"Sure," Arran said, coming over to the two of them. He joined in their game with aplomb, launching himself onto the beanbags and making both her and Jayce laugh out loud. Then he pulled Liv down next to him and grabbed Jayce, tickling him until the room filled with the delightful tinkle of childish giggles.

Henry snapped away.

The beanbags shifted under them and Liv found herself lying right up against Arran's side, looking into his eyes as Jayce cuddled into his chest. For a moment she forgot that Henry was there as she breathed Arran's warm scent and admired the shape of his mouth, turned up at the corners in a soft smile that traveled right up to his eyes and infused them with a sparkle.

Her heart flipped as he glanced down at her lips and she realized that her want of him had evolved even further over the past few weeks. It felt . . . more than physical.

Henry's voice cut into the moment, almost making her jump. "You really are the most photogenic family. I don't normally herd visitors into a photo shoot, but I'm afraid I just couldn't resist."

"No problem," Arran murmured in a distracted tone, his eyes still on her. She vaguely registered that Henry had referred to them as a family but was too consumed by these new thoughts of Arran to process it.

"I'll send you some of these shots in case you like any of them," Henry continued. "Free of charge, of course, because I corralled you into it!"

"We can't accept that," Arran said, finally glancing up away from Liv. "I'll give you something for them."

"No, no, I insist," Henry said, busying himself with dismantling the camera.

Arran turned back to where she was still burrowed against his side, paralyzed by the warm feeling of being cuddled with him and his gorgeous son. "Here," he said quietly. "I'll help you up." He shifted away and got to his feet holding Jayce, extending a hand and pulling her up next to him. He slid his arm around her shoulders as if it was the most natural thing in the world.

"I think he's definitely our guy," Arran murmured as he set Jayce down. "Do you?"

She nodded, her heart still tripping. "Absolutely."

"Thanks, Henry," Arran said more loudly so that Henry could hear. "For the visit, the coffee, the advice, the photo shoot, and of course for signing up to shoot our friends' wedding."

Henry smiled as he came over to shake each of their hands in turn. "Delighted."

Arran bent down to get Jayce's shoes back on.

Henry took down Liv's email address to send on the photos.

"We really do need to give you something for them," Liv told him.

"I'll tell you what," Henry said. "How about we say no charge, but instead I ask for your permission to display a couple of the shots in my folder of family portraits? I think having you three in there will really enhance that portfolio. As long as that meets with your approval, of course."

Flattered, Liv felt heat rising in her cheeks. But she finally connected the dots that Henry mistakenly thought she and Arran were a couple and that she was Jayce's mother. "That's fine by me as long as it is with Arran," she told him. "But I should probably point out that we aren't actually a family. Just good friends."

Arran stood up next to her, holding the hand of a freshly shoed Jayce. "Yeah we're BFFs," he said, slinging his arm around her shoulders again. "And Jayce is my son with my ex."

Henry's eyes widened a little. "I do apologize. How presumptuous of me."

Liv waved her hand. "Oh no, that's okay. We didn't introduce ourselves properly."

Henry smiled as he showed them to the door. "Funny, because I find I'm very intuitive about these things and I was convinced you were a couple. You clearly have a very special bond."

Liv's heart thumped in her chest.

"We do," Arran replied as Henry opened the front door for them. "To be honest, I don't know what I'd do without her."

She glanced up to give him a shy smile as they said their good-byes, something new blooming in her chest. Henry gave them a wave as they got Jayce into the car, and then Arran took them in the direction of Liv's house.

"I'll call Sam once I get in," Liv told him, "and tell him to lock Henry down."

"Excellent," Arran replied. "It's all coming together." He paused, then cleared his throat, his voice coming out a little stiff. "So. Tonight's the night."

"Why, what's tonight?" she asked, still feeling a little breathless from all these thoughts and recovering from the sensation of being tucked up against him.

He glanced over quickly. "Your date."

Her heart sank as his meaning became clear. "Oh yeah. I nearly forgot." She didn't want to go on a date with anyone except Arran.

Arran was silent for a second. "You meeting him there or is he picking you up?"

The conversation felt a bit stilted and wooden, very unlike their usual banter. "Meeting him there," she said, aware that her speech was flat.

"Cool." He shot her a brief smile. "I hope it goes well."

For some reason that comment put her on a downer. If Arran

had a date, she wouldn't want it to go well. She didn't want him going on any dates at all.

"Thanks," she said quietly, sinking down into her seat and staying silent for the rest of the short journey home.

"YOU'RE KIDDING," LIV SAID, STARING AT BRODIE OPEN-MOUTHED. "There's no way anyone could be that dense."

He shook his head as he sipped his espresso martini. "Nope. True story. I told her that her ski jacket wasn't from our chain of stores, so unfortunately, I couldn't give her a refund. She put in a formal complaint about me."

"That is absolutely mental," Liv said, shaking her head. "The audacity."

He nodded, a solemn expression on his face. "The barefaced, brazen audacity."

Something about his tone tickled her and she couldn't stop laughing, drawing Brodie in with her.

He shook his head. "That's the service industry for you. There're plenty of unreasonable types around."

"Yeah, same," she replied, leaning forward. "We get a load of nonsense from some of the parents we deal with."

Brodie rolled his eyes. "Ugh. I can imagine. All teachers deserve a pay rise, in my opinion. And a huge fuck-off medal."

She laughed. "Excellent idea. You should run for first minister. I'd vote for you."

He winked. "Thank you. Maybe I will."

Being around Brodie was really easy; no wonder Maya and Sam were such good friends with him. It would have been unfortunate that there was no chemistry if she'd actually been interested in this as a "real" date. But as she wasn't, the fact that there was only friendship blossoming between them was perfect. She lifted her glass, taking a sip of her French martini. "Does Glenavie feel like home for you now? Hasn't it been around eighteen months?"

"That's right. And yes, I love it, thanks. The turning point was getting involved with skiing and meeting Maya, and Sam." He grinned. "After I backed off from Maya and Sam realized I wasn't a threat, that is."

Liv laughed. "Sorry about that. He was going through a bit of a tough patch back then."

"So I heard. I had nothing but sympathy when he explained it all." Brodie smiled. "Anyway, it's not your place to apologize for him. He did that himself."

She shrugged. "I know. It's just a twin tendency."

"I'm glad the two of them worked things out. It's apparent to anyone that they belong together."

Her heart warmed a few degrees. "Totally. I always knew there was something between them."

He raised an eyebrow. "Twin tendency."

Liv winked. "Precisely."

He fiddled with the stem of his cocktail glass. "Speaking of breakups et cetera, how's Ben doing? I heard he and Derek split."

Liv nodded. "Sam and Maya say he's okay, just a little grumpy to work under at the ski resort. Apparently it had been in the cards for a while, but it's difficult to get used to being on your own after a long relationship." She said that like she knew the feeling, even though she had no idea what coming out of a long relationship was like. She would have to have been involved in something for more than two minutes to appreciate that. *Nico Hadid, eat your heart out.*

Brodie cleared his throat. "Listen, I feel like I need to say something at this stage. I'm really enjoying this, and I hope you and I can be friends. But—"

Liv held up her hand. "Say no more. I agree. We get along well, but there's no chemistry."

Brodie's face relaxed into a smile. "We're on the same wavelength."

Liv lifted her glass to clink it with his. "That we are, my friend."

He sipped his cocktail, then eyed her carefully before leaning in. "I haven't told anyone this yet, but there's someone I'm interested in. I think that's kind of why I'm not really on the lookout for anyone else at the moment."

She arched a brow. "Intriguing. Tell me more. Who is she?"

Brodie laughed. "Well." He cleared his throat. "It's actually a guy."

She nodded, taking a sip of her drink. "And who's the lucky chap?"

He eyed her for a moment, eyebrows raised. "I knew I had a good feeling about telling you. Most people would say, 'Oh, I didn't know you were gay,' at this stage, as if bisexuals don't even exist."

Liv frowned. "Really?"

"Yep. I haven't told anyone here yet because of the mixed reaction I got back in Glasgow. One friend used to ask me on a regular basis, 'So, are you still bi?'"

Liv coughed on her drink. "What? Were they straight?"

He nodded.

"And do you message them regularly to ask if they're still hetero?" she asked with a grin.

Brodie laughed, smacking his palms gently on the table. "No, but now I'm totally going to do that." He lifted his glass to clink with hers again. "To be honest, I even got microaggressions from some of my gay friends."

She shook her head. "That's shit."

"Right?" He gave her a smile. "So is there anyone else you're interested in? Male or female or otherwise?"

Liv shook her head. "I think I prefer to be alone." She paused to take a drink, aware that she had spoken unfiltered. Then the image of being cuddled against Arran came to mind. Somehow, being with him made her question her solitary instinct.

Brodie was giving her a quizzical look, but her phone pinged with a message before he could speak.

She lifted the phone from the table and her stomach turned to ice as she clocked the name on the screen. Her horror caused her to speak without processing her thoughts properly. "Shit. It's from Dave."

He raised his eyebrows. "Who's Dave?"

Liv stared at the message, hovering her finger over the phone as she attempted to decide whether to open it. "Dave is the man whose genetic material makes up fifty percent of mine."

Understanding melted the frown from Brodie's face. "Ah. I'm guessing this is a man whom you don't wish to refer to as a father, which speaks volumes."

She swallowed, her mouth dry. "Indeed."

"I take it you don't really hear from him?"

"Nope," she replied, still eyeing the name on her phone screen— *Douchebag Dave.* "On account of him being a total scumbag."

He shot her a sympathetic look. "You can read the message. I won't ask for any details."

She tried to put the phone down; after all, this had been a really cool and fun evening so far. But she'd only worry about what the text said; then the night would be ruined anyway. *Why didn't I block him? Oh yeah, that's right. Because deep down, I always held out that naive hope that one day he'd call and act like he actually gave a shit about my life.*

Liv took a breath and opened the message, unable to stop herself from telling Brodie the contents. He was too easy to talk to, and he'd already confided something personal. "For fuck's sake. He's asking why I didn't tell him about Sam's wedding." She glanced up to meet Brodie's gaze. "And that's it. Not a word about me. I could be maimed or in prison for all he knows."

He smiled. "I can't imagine you going to prison for anything."

Liv grabbed her cocktail and took an aggressive sip, which nearly caused the contents to slosh out of the glass and drench her in tasty French martini. "I dunno. Maybe father-icide."

He reached over to give her arm a brief squeeze. "Please do tell me to fuck off and mind my own business, but is your dad the reason you said that you'd rather be on your own?"

Glancing up to meet his gaze, she realized she didn't have the energy to suppress it or lie about it. Maybe it was the alcohol, or the unexpected jolt of emotion at hearing from Dave. Or perhaps it was because Brodie was a safe, objective ear. She didn't need to worry that confiding her feelings would upset him the way she constantly had to with everyone else. "Maybe."

He gave her a soft smile. "Is that because you worry that all men will turn out to be like your dad—I mean, like Dave?"

Liv returned his smile, appreciating his correction. She paused to assess her tangled mess of emotions. It was like the viper's nest of cables that she hid behind her TV stand. "I'm not sure." Dean, her ex, floated into her mind. *"For fuck's sake, Liv. You're just like your dad."* A wave of nausea washed over her, driving her heart rate up a notch. *"Just like your dad."* She closed her eyes, Dean's voice morphing into her grandmother's. And then her mother's.

She cleared her throat. "Anyway. I'm not interested in a serious relationship."

He nodded, studying her face. "You only do short-term, casual stuff?"

"Yeah." She took a breath. "Everyone thinks I'm lonely and forlorn and looking for love. When really, I'm lonely and forlorn and actively avoiding it."

Brodie laughed gently. "Sounds like self-preservation."

Except that she didn't feel very well preserved. "Mm-hmm."

"What if you chose someone you know well? Then it's safer."

Arran's handsome face appeared in her mind, with his soft coily hair and warm whiskey eyes—calming her inner turmoil. "But if I choose someone I know and care about, then when it goes wrong, I'll have lost something important and precious." Despite having said those words aloud, she wasn't sure whether they were for Brodie's benefit or her own.

In any case, it was clear to her that there was unfinished business between Arran and Jess. That was why Jess had been calling all the time, keeping tabs on him. She must mistakenly think there was something going on between Liv and Arran, and it was bringing out her jealous streak. And no way did Liv want to play the third wheel there.

She absorbed the understanding in Brodie's eyes, a little surprised that he wasn't staring at her with his mouth agape. Would this be the way her loved ones would react if she confided in them? She imagined her mum looking at her with disapproval. *"Don't be negative, Liv."*

She shook her head. Everyone had their own shit going on. It wasn't fair to moan to them about her problems.

"I get it," he said. "Have you had any therapy?" He winced. "Shit, sorry. I didn't mean for that to sound blunt."

She smiled. "That's okay. Kind of, a few years back. Just a bit of counseling. It helped me let go of Dave a bit, to realize his actions weren't my fault. But I haven't explored this relationship stuff in therapy."

He nudged her hand. "Why not?"

She bit her lip. "I don't know if I'm ready."

He smiled. "Maybe one day you will be. Until then, I'll keep your secret if you keep mine."

"Thank you." She let out a breath, a little nervous that she'd said more than she intended, but somewhat reassured that they were mutual secret holders. "By the way, this might be a small town, but it's not small-minded. You can be yourself here. Especially with our friends."

His smile broadened, lighting up his blue eyes. "Thank you. I'll get there, sooner rather than later."

Liv drained her drink and pointed to their glasses, and he nodded to indicate they should get another round. She gestured to the waitress that they wanted the same again, turning back to Brodie. "You should definitely tell Maya. She's totally cool."

"I know. It's just that confiding in people I don't know is somehow easier than confiding in those I do." He gave her a meaningful look.

Liv smiled. "I'm with you on that one. And it was a bit hypocritical of me to advise that, when I haven't ever told her as much as I've just told you."

Brodie raised his empty glass. "Pending our refills, here's a toast to new friends."

Liv grinned. "New friends, and keepers of secrets."

Chapter

TWELVE

THE HOTEL WAS MODERN AND OPULENT, ALL GLASS SURFACES and shiny floors. The room they'd been ushered into for afternoon tea was like something from an upscale Scottish stately home—mahogany tables and gray tartan chairs spiced with colorful cozy throws. Arran glanced across the table at his beautiful "date" and wished that this was a real date.

He bit his lip, wondering for the millionth time that week how Liv's actual date with Brodie had been. This was their first meeting since then, and a few times he'd started to compose a text asking her how it'd gone but then had deleted it every time. He wanted to know, and yet he didn't want to know. Plus he was aware of the need to play down his interest in the subject so as not to reveal his jealousy. He'd bide his time and find a way to bring it up in conversation.

He couldn't stop thinking about that last outing to the photographer's studio and how it'd felt to have her in his arms along with his son. They'd been in that position before, in the fort, but this time it had felt different, as if they were a real family, and he couldn't help thinking she felt it too. He was sure Liv found him attractive and that they had real, intense chemistry, plus something more.

Something special. And yet he still felt her keeping him at arm's length. Why? And she'd gone on that date with Brodie. Had she been able to let *him* in where she wouldn't allow Arran?

Her green eyes were narrowed through the windows of her cute black-framed glasses as she watched him apply jam and cream to his scone, and for a moment, he was concerned that she knew what he was thinking.

"Why're you looking at me like that?" he asked.

Liv's face broke out into a smile, and it made his breath catch. "You put the jam on first. Thank God. Now we can be *best* best friends."

He laughed, feeling relieved. "That's your criterion for a best mate, Aggie? How they apply the condiments to their scone?"

She sniffed, lifting her cup. "Of course. 'Tis a most important test, Mr. Adebayo. Ms. Bashir has failed on multiple occasions, and now you shall take her place."

He grinned as he took a bite, licking the crumbs from his lips and catching her gaze being drawn to his mouth. "Excellent. Glad to take on the mantle." He wiped his fingers on his serviette. "So you're telling me Maya puts the *cream* on first?"

Liv nodded, a sage expression on her face. "I am."

He pretended to gag. "That is appalling. No wonder you've ousted her."

"Right?" she replied. "It really is disgraceful."

He took out his phone. "I've got an idea." He opened Google and began typing.

Liv leaned forward in an attempt to spy what he was doing across the table. "What is it?"

"You'll see." The results of his search popped up and he grinned. "Aha! Got it."

She clearly couldn't wait for him to elaborate because she got to her feet to come around their low table. He took the opportunity to grab another gander at her gorgeous legs, feeling as if he was burning up inside. She was wearing a black above-the-knee pencil skirt with a white button-down shirt tucked in and black suspenders, which accentuated the curve of her breasts. The ensemble was completed with a black bow at the neckline. She looked like a sexy librarian.

Suddenly the thought of a secret tryst between the bookshelves slammed into his mind—her legs wrapped around his waist and him covering her mouth with his hand so the library patrons didn't hear her cries of passion and point angrily at the "Shh! Quiet, Please" sign. His heart pumped harder in response to the tangibly clear image, blood rushing straight to his groin.

She settled in next to him on the two-seater chaise-style sofa, her petite form fitting snugly beside him, and her scent exacerbating his inappropriately sexy thoughts. "What is it?"

He cleared his throat, shifting in his seat. "See? The late Queen Elizabeth the second used to apply the jam first. So if it was good enough for Queenie . . ."

Liv took hold of the phone, her hand covering his and sending hot pulses over his skin. He shifted uncomfortably, trying to keep his thoughts on the former Queen of England and away from the sexy library fantasy.

"Good old Liz, God rest her," Liv said, releasing his hand and giving him a grin. "Just wait until I tell Maya about this. She'll be livid."

Arran gave her a wink and admired the way her cheeks flushed in response. *She's so gorgeous.*

His phone vibrated on the table and Jess's name flashed up, killing his buzz. He could tell Liv had spotted it from the way she immediately put some distance between them on the sofa. Grabbing the phone to check that everything was okay, he read the message, which was a photo of Jayce waving. Jess had taken him back early so that he and Liv could come to Glasgow for their Sunday afternoon tea. Though she'd asked quite a few questions about the outing.

"How's Jess doing?" Liv asked, reaching across the table to pick up her teacup.

A weird feeling infiltrated his stomach at the sound of Liv saying his ex's name. He'd been infinitely confused since Jess had started her calling-all-the-time-to-keep-tabs routine. "She's okay, I think."

Liv sipped her tea. "Has she still been calling you as much?"

He ran a hand over the top of his hair. "Yeah. She gave me a bit of a grilling about today, actually. I just changed the subject in the end."

Liv eyed him for a second, seeming to be thinking about what she wanted to say. "I know how hard the breakup has been for you. But it must be really hard for her too."

He frowned. "How do you mean?" It hadn't seemed too hard for her when she'd told him the wedding was off and then promptly taken up with Rory, moving in with him only a few weeks later. He rubbed at the hollowness the memory left in his chest.

She gave him a soft smile, reaching over to touch the back of his hand. "I'm not taking away from your hurt. I just feel she's insecure, like Elise said the other night. Perhaps she's always had that tendency, but it must be worse now that she's with Rory. Sam says he's a major player without much integrity." She glanced away for a moment. "Maybe Jess is missing the trust she used to have with you."

His heart seemed to thud a little more forcefully in his chest. She was missing him? Could that be true? It hadn't seemed like it thus far. "Really? She's seemed pretty infatuated with Rory from the word go."

She nodded, bringing her gaze back to him. There was an odd look in her green eyes, but what was it? Sadness? "Sometimes people need a frame of reference in order to realize what they're missing. I wonder whether Rory's example has provided that, and now it's dawning on Jess that she doesn't like what she sees."

A few months ago, he would've been delighted to hear someone express that opinion. But now it made him feel uncomfortable and sad. "You think she's unhappy?"

She winced. "Sorry, I didn't mean to make you worry about her. I just think that you need to open yourself up to the idea that she might want to rekindle things. I mean, I don't want you to get your hopes up and then it not come to anything, but if the opportunity arises, you should have a conversation about it."

Get his hopes up? He hoped for nothing of the sort. He'd tried to seek a reconciliation when they'd first broken up, and she hadn't been interested. And now that ship had long sailed. He eyed Liv, feeling their connection and his deep, "want her to the depths of my soul" attraction. "I can't do that."

She shifted a little closer, her scent distracting him. "Arran. Don't let your pride get in the way. If there's any chance of a rekindling and you still love her, you can't let it slip through your fingers."

Love her? He didn't love Jess. Not anymore. But before he could say that out loud, a couple of women walked past the back of their two-seater sofa, and Liv leaned in. "You see those two ladies?" she asked softly.

He nodded, even though he didn't. He'd been distracted by Liv and for all he knew it could've been a couple of wild beasts wandering past the area. Though that was probably unlikely in a five-star city hotel.

Liv smiled. "I overheard them before saying that you look like Regé-Jean Page."

Arran frowned. "Who?"

"You know." She leaned closer, bringing her mouth close to his ear. If his playing dumb brought her into this proximity, then he'd pretend to never understand anything ever again.

"The Duke of Hastings," she finished, pulling back to give him a knowing look.

He gave her a bemused smile in return. "Who?"

Liv rolled her eyes. "He's an actor. He played the Duke of Hastings on the first season of *Bridgerton*."

"I have no idea what any of that means," he replied, loving the exasperated expression on her face.

She grabbed his phone and fiddled with it, passing it back with an image on-screen. Arran studied the photo of a handsome dude in a smart fitted emerald-green suit, a matching waistcoat under his jacket. "Nice. My suit's darker, though, and my waistcoat isn't in a matching material."

Liv laughed, bumping his shoulder. "Not your *outfit*. Your face, dumbass."

He smiled. "I suppose I'll take that. The guy is good-looking."

"And hot," Liv said, her eyes widening as she finished the last syllable and her face staining pink again.

He couldn't help his smile morphing into a grin. "As in, *he's* hot, or I am?"

She cleared her throat and he found himself enjoying her discomfort. Recovering, she flicked a wave of dark hair from her face, her chin raised in defiance. "Both of you."

He held her gaze, his pulse ramping up. She was looking at him like she'd been having her own sexy fantasies. But could that be right when only a couple of minutes ago she had been telling him he should consider getting back together with his ex?

Her phone buzzed and her whole body jolted, eyes wide with what looked like fear.

"Whoa there," he said, touching her hand in concern. "It's just a message."

She was staring at her phone on the table as if it were a poisonous snake.

An anxious feeling circled his gut at the wide-eyed look on her face. "Liv? What's up?" He shifted closer as she leaned over to lift the phone.

Shuddering, she shook her head. "It's . . ." Ducking her head, she glanced around. "It's *fucking* Dave."

Arran couldn't help but smile that she'd checked the coast was clear before swearing in public, though this place was pretty posh and they probably didn't get that many expletive-shouting patrons. His smile quickly fell away when he registered the name she'd mentioned. "Your dad? What the hell does *he* want?"

She lifted the phone between them and they huddled round it, Arran absorbing the privilege that she was allowing him to read it with her.

DOUCHEBAG DAVE

Why haven't you replied? I'm your father,
Olivia. Show some fucking respect.

Normally the fact that Liv had her dad in her phone as "Douchebag Dave" would've tickled him, but the nasty words on-screen left him cold and nauseated. He clenched his fist. "What's he talking about?"

She sighed and crumpled against him, as if she were deflating, and he put his arm around her. "He messaged before, last weekend. And I deleted it."

Lifting a hand, he tucked her hair behind her ear. This was a big deal. Dave never contacted the twins, and now he was messaging Liv multiple times after recently speaking to Sam? "What did it say?"

She shrugged. "Asking about Sam's wedding."

Frowning, he lifted her chin to meet her eyes. "That's it? Nothing about you?"

Something shifted in her gaze and he could tell he'd tuned in to an important point. "Nope," she replied. "Not a sausage."

"Douchebag," Arran said under his breath.

"Yeah." She nestled into his side. "Hence the handle I've given him in my phone."

Arran allowed himself a gentle laugh, giving her a squeeze.

She played with one of the buttons on his waistcoat. "I mean, it's no surprise. Well, him contacting us is. But him not asking about me isn't. He was never interested in me at all. Not that he showed Sam much more attention, but he kind of saw him as a reflection of himself. When he was forced into taking on a parenting role such as a lift to our clubs, he'd always say he'd take Sam to his and Mum could take me to mine. Said he couldn't relate to me because I was a girl." She took a breath. "I always felt like the third, unwanted, wheel."

Arran stiffened. "What a dick." If he was ever lucky enough to have a daughter, there would be no way he'd behave like that. He drew Liv closer. "He was privileged to have you as his daughter. I'm sorry he fucked it up."

Her voice was so quiet that he had to strain to hear her words. "And fucked *me* up. At least when he left, I didn't truly feel like I lost anything. Because I never really had a dad in the first place."

An icy knife dug into his heart, and he grasped her hand.

She gave him a squeeze. "It was worse for Sam, really. Because they'd had some semblance of a relationship before Dave buggered off."

"There you go again," he said, rubbing his thumb over the back of her hand. "Putting everyone else's feelings before your own. It was just as bad for you as it was for Sam. You deserve support too, Liv."

She stayed silent, so he didn't push it any further.

He kissed the top of her head, his heart aching for her. "Come

on, Aggie. Let's finish the scones and tea, then I'll buy you something stronger before we catch the train home."

LIV COLLAPSED INTO THE SEAT BY THE TRAIN WINDOW AS HE
placed their takeaway coffee cups on the table. "Blimey," she said,
blowing a wave of hair away from her glasses. "That last cocktail
has totally gone to my head."

He grinned, sitting down next to her. "Are you sure it was the
last one, and not the two prior to it?"

She pursed her lips and it made him want to kiss them. "No. It
was defo the last one."

"Okay. Whatever you say, Aggie," he said, taking off his jacket.

She removed her coat and stretched. Arran toiled to keep his
eyes off how her breasts strained against the white fabric of her
shirt. It was such hard work that it had him questioning why he
was so determined to keep his hands off her. With his inhibitions
somewhat eroded by the alcohol, he was thinking that maybe he
should stop being cautious and go for it. Lay it all on the line and
then if it all went wrong, surely they were grown up enough to still
be friends. *Surely, with the way we gel, it wouldn't ever go wrong . . .*

"Arran. I have had the most wonderful day with you out and
about town." Her words were slightly slurred, and with a cold dous-
ing of his feelings, he figured now wasn't the time to voice his
thoughts. He needed her to be sober and of sound mind first.

Arran tipped an imaginary cap. "You are welcome. I'll take you
out on the town anytime."

Liv smiled. "Thanks for listening to my woes."

Warmth filled his heart. "You are, again, very welcome. I like
that you can talk to me." *I love it, actually.*

"Me too." She sighed. "I seem to be quite the motormouth
lately. Moaning to you today, and even with Brodie last weekend."

Ice formed in his veins, freezing him in his seat. It had finally come up in conversation, and this was the bombshell—she'd confided in Brodie? When she hardly knew the guy? His heart clenched and a fiery jealousy consumed the warm, privileged feeling he'd gotten when he'd thought that he was the only one Liv had opened up to. The date must have gone well if Liv had poured her heart out to him. He rubbed at his chest, the hollow sensation feeling deeper than usual.

Arran fiddled with his coffee cup as the train began to move, suppressing the urge to ask her what was going on with Brodie because he couldn't trust himself to do it in a socially appropriate manner. He wanted to get home, track Brodie down, pin him against a wall, and tell him to keep away from Liv.

He took a breath, his voice tight. "Sounds like you two got along well."

"Yeah, brilliant," she said, settling into her seat. "He's really cool. I'm glad he's coming on the Skye trip. Hopefully you can get to know him better too, because I reckon you'll get along great."

Arran clenched his jaw. *Get along great? If that involves me whupping his ass, then yeah. We'll get along great.* "I'm sure we will."

Hold on, why did Liv *want* him to "get along great" with Brodie? Because she wanted Arran, as her new "best friend," to make pals with her new love interest? His heart plummeted into his gut. That must be why she had been trying to get him to rekindle with Jess. She wanted her best friend paired off in the same way that she was pairing off.

Fuck fuck fuck. Typical. The moment the idea of voicing his feelings for Liv crossed his mind, this happened. He'd been right when he'd told Agnes next door that it was a bad idea.

"Speaking of the weekend away," she continued, seemingly oblivious to his emotional turmoil, "I think we've got it all organized now."

He swallowed, trying to get hold of himself. "Yeah. The transport is arranged, accommodation and dinner booked, and"—he managed a wink—"the most important part, the itinerary, is set."

"By the A team," Liv said, holding out her palm for a low five, which he took. She then settled back into her seat and snuggled against his shoulder. Arran took a couple of breaths, trying to compose the words to ask her how serious this thing with Brodie was, but he struggled to find a casual enough manner in which to phrase it. Why him? *Why not me?*

When he eventually opened his mouth to stutter the start of a sentence, her eyes were closed and her breathing even as she slept on his shoulder.

Arran grabbed his jacket, lifting it to cover her as he put his arm around her. He glanced up, catching an older couple across the carriage giving them a soft smile—clearly laboring under the misapprehension that they were a couple. Something that seemed to happen often nowadays. First with Angela and Sarah, the two brides at the evening reception they'd visited. And then with Henry the photographer. Clearly people were seeing something that wasn't there, because Liv was going out with someone else.

He'd honestly felt that he and Liv had been coming together, slotting right into a position that was meant to be. But now events were taking them in a different direction. Pulling them apart.

He tried to settle into his seat, feeling her chest rise and fall against him and mourning the fact that she was slipping through his fingers. But he wanted her to be happy, so if she had made the choice to pursue someone else, then he had to respect that. And yet his stupid heart still had trouble with the idea of letting her go.

Perhaps her getting with Brodie had come at the right time—when he had been close to telling her that he liked her as more than a friend. When he'd been close to asking if he could kiss her. Because his getting involved with anyone again was a bad idea, and that person being his best friend was a *seriously* bad one. Especially since said friend was about to become his son's nursery school teacher. Even more imperative that he didn't fuck up their relationship by trying something romantic that might end up going south. He couldn't let his relationship status affect his son. Perhaps this was for the best, then. He just needed to come to terms with that. And part of that objective would involve not discussing Liv's relationship with Brodie until he could trust himself not to burst into a fiery ball of jealous rage.

He glanced down at her beautiful sleeping features. The only way he could think of to successfully extricate himself emotionally was to put a bit of distance between them. He'd get her home safely and into bed, then he'd keep away from her for a bit. Just until he could be sure that he wasn't going to ruin her happiness.

Chapter

THIRTEEN

L IV STARED AT THE TWO-DAY-OLD MESSAGE SHE'D SENT TO
Arran.

> Hey, do you and Lord Jayce fancy
> accompanying me to Sam and Maya's
> Easter egg rolling thing at the ski resort
> this weekend?

It was marked as read, but not a sausage in return. He must
have been too busy to reply. She hovered her thumb over the key-
pad, wondering whether to prompt him or not. In the end she decided she might as well; the event was only a couple of days away,
so she'd need to get them some tickets if they were going.

> Any thoughts on the egg rolling thing? I
> might even treat you to a chocolate egg . . .

She put the phone down on the coffee table and went back to
reading her e-book, but she couldn't concentrate. Why did she have

the feeling that Arran had been avoiding her since their afternoon tea? It had been lovely, and the first time they'd had a whole day just the two of them. He'd seemed to enjoy it too but then had gone uncharacteristically silent all week. Normally they'd text most days with daft stuff to make each other laugh. But while she'd kept up her end of that bargain, Arran had been slow to reply to half the messages and the other half had gone entirely unanswered.

Looking up from her book, she frowned at the wall. She hadn't said anything dumb when she'd been pissed on the journey home from the afternoon tea, had she? Her blood ran cold at the thought that she might've done something stupid in her inebriated state, like tell him that she'd had a crush on him for years (and now it felt like more than a crush) or try to kiss him. But she hadn't been that drunk that she couldn't remember stuff. Just tipsy; then she'd slept on the journey home, and Arran had dropped her off at hers in their shared taxi before taking it back to his. Although . . . had he been a bit quiet at that point too?

The phone buzzed with a message and she lifted it, her heart rising as she took in his name on the screen.

> Sorry for the delay. Been busy. Jayce has been asking for you and he'd love to do the egg thing so we'll meet you there.

She tapped out a quick reply, aware that her immediate response would give away that she'd been desperate to hear from him.

> I can pick you guys up if you like?

Contrary to his recent slow reply style of the previous week, the three dots appeared straightaway, followed by:

> That's okay thanks. Got stuff on that
> morning so we'll meet you there.

Letting her hand drop into her lap, she paused to think. Arran wasn't the sort to be moody. He just had a load on his plate. That's all it'd be.

THE HILLS WERE LUSH AND GREEN AND THE AIR CRISP AS LIV craned her neck toward the terrace at the back of the resort center, watching for Arran and Jayce. She sighed. No sign yet. Whatever they'd had on earlier must've run over.

There was a tug on her sleeve and she turned to find Maya holding Elise's one-year-old son, Jack.

Liv gave Maya a hug, then leaned in to kiss Jack's cheek. "Hey there, handsome. Sorry your mum couldn't make it."

Maya smiled. "But he's got the next best thing, his auntie Maya."

"Indeed." Liv smiled at him, placing her hands over her face to begin a game of peekaboo with Jack. "Where's Sam?" she asked, as Jack giggled at her antics.

"Over there." Maya nodded toward where Sam was chatting to his colleagues as they finished setting up what normally served as the baby ski slope for the race. The contestants would go to the top and roll their eggs down the grass.

"Where's your egg?" Liv asked Maya.

Maya brandished a vibrant-looking hard-boiled egg from her pocket, the shell painted in bright colors by Jack's hand. "Here he is. We call him Egg Sheeran."

Liv snorted, realizing why the top of the shell was colored orange, to represent the mop of red hair sported by the egg's human pop-sensation equivalent.

Maya snatched Egg Sheeran away as if Liv were trying to grab it. "Hey. No trying to *poach* him, now." She winked at Liv, clearly pleased with her own egg-related pun.

Liv raised her eyebrow, bringing out her glitter-adorned egg. "Don't need to. He's no match for Scarlett Yolk-hansson."

Maya chuckled. "Nice." She shifted Jack on her hip. "Shall we go and take our places?"

Liv's heart sank. "Arran and Jayce aren't here yet. I hope they're still coming."

Maya gestured over Liv's shoulder. "That's them coming now."

Her pulse spiking, Liv turned to see Arran holding Jayce's hand as they came through the ski center's back entrance. She lifted her hand to wave, a smile on her face, but before she managed to catch Arran's eye someone grabbed her from behind and lifted her up.

"Hey, ladies." Brodie's voice sounded behind her.

He set her down again and Liv turned to flash him a smile. He hugged her, then Maya. "Hope you guys don't think you're going to beat me," he told them, brandishing his egg, which was painted in an abstract manner.

"Nice," Liv said, bumping his shoulder. She lifted her head to see if Arran was on his way over but was disappointed to find that he was nowhere in sight.

Brodie slid his arm around her shoulders. "Come on. Let's get our places at the starting line."

They started walking up the hill, Maya and Jack next to them. Brodie glanced at Maya. "Is Ben here today?" he asked, scanning the crowd.

"Yeah, somewhere," Maya replied. "He's been stomping around like a grumpy git, criticizing everything." She rolled her eyes. "We need to find him a new boyfriend, stat."

Brodie's eyes seemed to widen for a moment, then he smiled. "Maybe a bit of egg rolling will cheer him up."

"Hope so," Maya muttered, as they neared where Sam stood chatting to said grumpy Big Boss Ben.

Ben was running a hand through his dark, silver-streaked hair as Sam placed his hand on his shoulder to give it a squeeze.

"Hey, dudes," Maya said, reaching them first. She kissed Sam's cheek, then nudged Ben's arm. "All right, Triple B?"

Ben huffed out a breath and Sam surreptitiously shot them a "yikes" expression.

"I will be, when this thing is over," Ben told them, his mouth drawn into a tight line.

"'S'up?" Liv asked him. "Not a fan of Easter-themed activities?"

"Nope," Ben replied, folding his arms. "This whole thing has been a pain in the arse to organize."

"Okay," Sam said in a slow breath, putting an arm around Ben's shoulders. "Why don't you go get a coffee, and I'll sort all of this out. No need to worry."

Ben scanned the large crowd. "Don't you need my help?"

Maya handed Jack to Sam, stepping closer to Ben. "Look into my eyes . . ." She gestured around her face, then snapped her fingers, as if hypnotizing Ben. "And you're under. You're no longer a stressed-out boss, but a happy chappie off to enjoy a coffee in the café . . ." She snapped her fingers again. "And you're back in the room."

A smile was tugging hard at Ben's mouth.

Maya turned him around to face down the hill and gave him a gentle push. "Now, off you pop! Only one shot, though—can't have you jacked up too high on caffeine."

Shaking his head, Ben started out down the slope toward the café, and Liv was sure she heard a low chuckle escape his lips as he went. When she glanced back at the others, Brodie was watching Ben go.

"Right," Sam said. "Let's get this show on the road." He set Jack down with Liv and Maya, then went to grab his megaphone.

"Good afternoon, everybody! Welcome to the first annual Glenavie egg-rolling event. Please take your places at the starting line."

The crowd jostled a little for position, and Liv placed her Scarlett Yolk-hansson egg in between Egg Sheeran and Brodie's abstract egg. As she glanced down the line, she spotted Arran and Jayce, her heart lifting as she gave them a wave. Jayce's wee face lit up as he noticed her, and he waved back in an overenthusiastic manner. Liv's heart swelled as she realized how she'd missed seeing him for a couple of weeks. *Aw, he's so gorgeous. I love him to bits.*

Arran looked up as he took in the direction of Jayce's gaze, the sight of his warm honey eyes giving her heart a jolt. He smiled softly and lifted his hand in a wave. Then he darted his eyes to where Brodie was crouching next to her and looked away again. Sam lifted his megaphone. "On your marks. Get set. Roll!"

Liv gave Scarlett an almighty flick and she tumbled down the hill after Egg Sheeran and Brodie's abstract affair. They all jumped to their feet to cheer on their hard-boiled eggs, some of which ended up felled by large tufts of grass; others sustained race-related injuries such as cracked shells.

The winner was declared—sadly, none of them. But happily, it was a little girl who was absolutely delighted, and even more so when Sam went down the hill to present her with the biggest chocolate Easter egg Liv had ever seen.

The crowd moved down the hill toward the post-race activities, including a bouncy castle for the kids and various stalls featuring the wares of local artisanal food outlets and crafts.

Liv stood next to Maya and Sam, scanning the crowd for Arran and Jayce. Brodie leaned in to tug on her sleeve. "I'm going to get a coffee from the café. Want anything?"

"No, thanks," she said absently, still on her mission to detect a hot, honey-eyed local artist and his adorable curly-haired son. Brodie moved off and she continued to scan the periphery of the crowd, as Maya and Sam chatted with Jack.

A figure at the edge of the crowd caught her eye. A solitary form who stood at the tree line a little way from everyone else. She frowned, wondering why the guy was so removed from all the activity. *Perhaps he's waiting for someone.*

A weird feeling stirred in the bottom of her stomach as she shifted her gaze. Something about that man bothered her. Made her unsettled and uneasy. She looked back at him. Perhaps it was that he was standing so still? And that he was staring into the crowd. The weird feeling developed spikes and rose further into her chest. Was he up to no good?

Squinting at him, she felt like he was familiar somehow. As if he looked like someone she knew from the past, albeit ten years older and softer in the middle.

The spiky feeling in her chest exploded, sending shards of ice into her veins. She grabbed Sam's arm as the hairs on the back of her neck stood on end, her heart thumping.

Sam glanced down at her. "What's up?"

For a moment, she couldn't answer, the icy shards seeming to have cut her vocal cords.

Sam shifted his head to follow her gaze, landing on the man. He stiffened under her hand. "Holy shit."

Maya looked up from where she'd been tickling Jack. "Language, Samuel. There are children present."

Liv turned her head to look at them both. Sam was still staring ahead, and Maya's face fell as she took in their expressions. Liv knew she must be as white as a sheet because she'd felt the blood drain from her face as soon as she'd realized who was standing at the tree line, watching them.

Maya lifted Jack. "What's wrong?"

Sam nodded toward the man. "Dave's here."

"*What?*" Maya replied, whipping her head around.

Sam made to move forward. "You two wait here. I'll go and see what he wants."

Liv gripped his arm, Maya grabbing his other side in unison.

"You're not going over there without me," Liv told him, her jaw set.

"Or me," Maya said, her tone uncharacteristically firm.

Sam covered Maya's hand on his arm, giving her a squeeze. "You need to stay here with Jack."

"I'll get Ben to watch him," Maya said, glancing around.

Sam's tone was imploring. "Please, Maya. I don't want him knowing who you are. He doesn't get to have a piece of my relationship with you; it's too important to me."

Maya's face softened as she looked him in the eyes. Her expression seemed conflicted, but then she nodded and leaned up to kiss his cheek. "Okay."

Liv let out a breath, relieved that Sam had insisted. They couldn't have the poison that was Dave seeping anywhere near the good things in the lives they'd created without him. "I'm still coming, however," she told him, putting her arm through his and registering the relief in his eyes.

They started to move through the crowd as Maya called after them, "I'm keeping watch, though. And my threshold for calling the cops is very low!"

Liv brought herself close in to her brother's side as they left the edge of the crowd and closed the gap between them. Pressing closer, she felt like the two of them conjoined might act as some kind of emotional shield.

His features came sharply into focus as they approached. Softer around the edges and with more wrinkles, but the same self-satisfied aura. *And the same green eyes and dark hair as me.* Nausea swirled in her gut, forcing up her heart rate and making blood whoosh in her ears.

They came to a standstill in front of him. He didn't speak, just surveyed them with an air of condescension, though Liv didn't miss the fact that she merely received a token glance while most of Dave's appraisal rested on Sam.

She felt Sam shift next to her. "What are you doing here?"

Dave surveyed him coolly. "What do you think?"

Sam let out an exasperated breath. "How the fuck should I know? I'm not psychic."

Liv gave his arm a squeeze, attempting to convey to him to play it cool.

"I'm here," Dave said, his voice dripping with superiority, "because neither of you saw fit to answer your own father when he messaged you."

"For fuck's sake," Sam muttered. "Why would we?"

Dave's brow furrowed into a tight line. "Because, Samuel, I am your father. And I command a little respect."

Liv couldn't help the tiny snort of laughter that escaped her lips. Respect? The man deserved zero respect from anyone. The words *I am your father* reverberated in her brain, morphing into Darth Vader's voice. *How fitting.*

Dave darted his gaze briefly to her, then back to Sam. "When my son is planning to get married, I expect not only my approval to be sought, but to be consulted on the arrangements. What if I'm busy on the date you've booked? It'll have to be rescheduled."

Liv's mouth dropped open. All these years, and the audacity of the man still hit like a ten-ton truck. A glance at Sam confirmed that he was mute with shock at that ridiculous statement.

She decided to take over for her brother. "We will do no such thing. You have zero rights here, so check your privilege. You aren't welcome at Sam's wedding. Or anywhere near us, for that matter."

She earned herself a two-second glance that time, before he looked back at Sam, as if his daughter was invisible. "Well?" he said to Sam. "What have you got to say for yourself?"

For fuck's sake. I'm clearly inaudible as well as invisible. No change there, then.

Sam took a step forward, speaking through gritted teeth. "The same as Liv just said. So stop pretending you can't hear her, you complete twat."

Dave's eyes widened, and he stepped forward so that the two men were only inches apart. "How dare you speak to me like that."

"I'll speak to you how the hell I want," Sam shot back, and Liv realized he was taller and a lot more muscular than their father.

Something flickered in Dave's eyes, and he shifted back slightly.

Sensing that it was time to retreat, Liv tugged on Sam's arm. "Come on. We need to get you back to your event."

Sam stayed put for a second, so she pulled a little harder. He began to shift backward with her. "Piss off, Dave," he said. "You aren't welcome at my resort. Or in our town." He turned to walk with Liv, and neither of them looked back as he put his arm around her to move back into the crowd.

A sense of emptiness filled her chest, replacing the previous spiky feeling. All these years she'd assumed that a showdown with Dave would mean she'd get to say her piece and have him listen. That it might leave her with some sort of closure. But achieving that was impossible when the guy acted as if she didn't even exist.

Shifting through the throng, they spotted Maya standing with Brodie, the two of them watching with anxious expressions.

Sam ran a hand through his hair. "Fuck. He still gets me so riled up." He squeezed Liv's arm. "Are you okay?"

She briefly considered an attempt at explaining how she felt— not riled up, but hollow. However, that would be selfish when Sam was so agitated by their father. She gave him a soft smile. "I'm all right. I'm sorry he was such a dick to you."

He tugged her in to kiss her forehead as they reached Maya and Brodie. Maya reached out to give her a hug, and then turned to fold herself into Sam's chest. He held her tightly, closing his eyes and resting his chin on his fiancée's head as if he was absorbing her essence in order to heal his soul.

Liv watched the two of them wistfully for a second. Then a new, odd feeling overcame her. As if she were the third wheel with her brother and best friend—a sensation she'd never experienced around them before.

Confused, she shifted to the side, and Brodie slid his arm around her shoulders to give her a squeeze. "I hope you don't mind, but Maya told me that was Dave."

She shook her head, feeling a little light-headed. "I don't mind." Plastering a smile onto her face, she met his eyes. "Has he gone? I don't want to give him the satisfaction of looking back."

Brodie craned his neck to peer through the crowd. "Yep. Gone."

Liv's shoulders sagged as the invisible weight lifted, and then she spotted Arran coming toward them holding Jayce, with a look of concern on his handsome features.

The edge of her turmoil was softened with his arrival and the soothing sound of his voice. "Are you guys okay? Was that your *dad*?" He glanced from Liv to Sam, then back again, taking a step toward her but then stopping as his gaze fell to where Brodie's arm was still slung over her shoulders.

"Hiya, Lib," Jayce said, looking a little sleepy-eyed as he reached out for her. Her heart thrummed as she took him from Arran, kissing his soft curls and inhaling his comforting scent. Jayce snuggled into her shoulder and she rested her chin on his head, meeting Arran's eyes as something warm passed between them. He blinked, his body language slightly awkward as he opened and clenched his hands. He eyed Brodie, who was giving her shoulders another squeeze.

"Yeah," Liv told Arran, aching for him to hug her. "It was him."

Arran ran a hand over the top of his hair. "Shit. What did he want?"

"To throw his weight around," Sam said, his jaw set. "So nothing's changed in the last decade."

Arran let out a big breath, darting his eyes back to Liv. "What right has he to throw his weight around?"

"None," she replied, squeezing Jayce gently. "It's just his over-inflated sense of self talking. Hopefully that'll be the last we'll hear from him." She looked at Sam. "I think he was a bit scared of you. You're a lot bigger than when you were a teenager."

Sam managed a small smile as Maya lifted her head from his chest to kiss his cheek.

"Not like me," Liv continued, smiling back. "I'm still tiny."

Sam shook his head. "Tiny but deadly. It's you he should've been scared of."

Arran swallowed, still looking at her. His body language was a little off and he didn't seem to know what to do with his hands. She met his eyes, feeling their connection. She wished it was his arm around her shoulders.

"Okay," Sam said with a sigh. "Let's forget about him. We've got an Easter egg-stravaganza to enjoy and I won't have him tainting it."

Maya released him, glancing over to Jack, who was on the bouncy castle, being supervised by Ben. "Let's get mingling." She smiled at Jayce, still in Liv's arms. "Want to come bounce with me and Jack?"

Jayce nodded, his sleepy eyes brightening, and Liv set him down for Maya to take his hand. Brodie released Liv in order to walk over to the bouncy castle with Maya and Jayce, toward where Ben was watching Jack.

Sam shifted over to Arran, who took him into a hug and rubbed his back. "Thanks, man," Sam said as he pulled away, giving Arran a smile. He turned to Liv. "Don't leave without me. I want to see you into your car."

She rolled her eyes. "Who's the black belt here, me or you?"

He let out a laugh and gave them both a wave as he departed.

Liv waited for Arran to dish out her hug too. But he didn't.

He rubbed the side of his face. "Are you sure you're okay?"

She nodded, feeling somehow a lot colder than she had a few minutes before. "Yes, thanks. It was more Sam who was het up."

Something shifted in his gaze and he began to lift his hand; then he stopped and used it to run over the top of his hair. "As long as you're sure."

Why did it feel like there was a chasm between them? She opened her mouth with the intent to somehow voice that question, but then his phone rang.

Arran let out a frustrated breath and lifted it from his pocket. "Sorry. I need to take this. It's Jess." He answered it, moving out of earshot. Liv waited for a minute, wondering if he'd come back to speak to her once the call was over. But whatever the conversation was seemed quite animated and was taking a while, so she left the area for the bouncy castle before he clocked her staring at him like an idiot.

The calls from Jess were clearly still a frequent occurrence, and she could feel in her bones that Jess was having regrets about leaving him. It was only a matter of time before they got back together. She knew she should feel happy about that because it would make Arran happy. Yet she didn't feel that way at all. The idea made her miserable. And what kind of a horrible person felt miserable about their best friend piecing his family back together?

Chapter
FOURTEEN

RESTING HIS HEAD BACK ON THE CUSHIONS, ARRAN STARED UP at the fairy lights adorning the inside of the fort. Being in there felt like he was surrounded by Liv, and yet she seemed to have moved so far beyond his reach.

The events of the day scrolled through his mind and he squeezed his eyes shut in discomfort as he recalled the sickening feeling of looking at her while she was distressed, another man's arm around her shoulders. He'd been desperate to hug her, but he'd had to physically restrain himself because her new love interest had been hanging off her like a commemorative plaque, one that read "In Memory of Arran Adebayo's Heart, Which I Broke in Half and Tossed in the Trash."

She'd been deflecting again, talking about how seeing Dave had been tougher on Sam, and yet he could see it in her eyes, the hurt displayed there in a language he'd recently learned how to read, one he wanted to become fluent in.

He sighed, sinking farther into the cushions. The worst thing was, she and Brodie had looked good together. And Arran wanted to see her happy. He just wished he could be the one achieving that for her.

The Skye trip was the following weekend, and he'd have to redouble his efforts to keep his distance and not do anything dumb to spoil her burgeoning relationship. Nor spoil the new relationship between Liv and his son, as teacher and pupil. They had a visit to the nursery school planned the next day, when he and Jayce could look around with the other parents and pupils before the term began midweek.

He'd been intending not to see her until then, but then he'd caved and agreed to go to the egg-rolling event when Jayce had asked for her. At least that was what he was telling himself, rather than admitting that he too had caved—in his desperation to lay eyes on her again. The reality was that Jayce asking for her should've been a signal to bolster his intentions to keep her at arm's length. If she was getting into a serious relationship, then she'd have less time for both of them.

Shuffling down a little, he turned his face into the cushions, hoping that there'd still be a trace of her scent buried in there somewhere.

ARRAN SQUEEZED JAYCE'S HAND AS THEY REACHED THE FRONT door of the nursery school. "Okay, pal?"

Jayce was admiring the little playground in the front garden, complete with an adventure playset. "I want to play on that, Daddy."

"Sure, we will. We just need to go and see Miss Holland first, okay?"

"Miss Lib," Jayce said, completely undermining the conversation Arran had had with him about the need to call Liv by her formal title at work.

Arran pressed the doorbell, and an older lady with her gray hair tied back appeared and opened the door. "Morning!" she said in a tone so bright it blew the cobwebs from Arran's brain. "And who is this?"

She opened the door to allow them into the foyer, where rows of pegs with children's names lined the walls.

"My name's Jayce," Jayce replied, wandering over to inspect the pegs.

"Well, hello, Jayce. I'm Mrs. MacKay. Whose class are you in?"

"Miss Lib's!" Jayce exclaimed happily, turning back toward them and clapping his hands.

Arran coughed. "He means Miss Holland, don't ya, buddy?"

Jayce pursed his lips. "No. I mean Miss Lib."

Mrs. MacKay raised an eyebrow, and it felt very much like a chastisement. "Follow me," she said in her overly bright voice, and led them down the corridor toward a doorway where the sound of children chatting was apparent.

Jayce bounded round the corner ahead of them, and as Arran followed, Jayce was running up to Liv where she stood speaking to a male parent. Her eyes lit up when she spotted Jayce, who flung himself at her as she crouched down to give him a hug.

"Hey, buddy," she said. "Want to have a look around our classroom?"

"Yeah!" Jayce said.

As Arran approached, Liv stood and finished her conversation with the parent standing with her. She turned and met his gaze, something shifting in her eyes, and the all-too-familiar want he felt whenever he was near her gathered within him.

"Hey," he said, the desire to hug her tugging strongly. But he suppressed it.

"Morning," she said, fiddling with the arm of her glasses. "Let me show you two around."

"Thanks," he replied, taking in the fact that the guy she'd been speaking to wasn't drifting away but rather hanging around and looking at Liv in a way he didn't like. Arran eyed him for a second as Liv led Jayce away, glancing down at the man's wedding ring then back up to give him the deadliest dead eye in the history of dead eyes. Then he turned to follow Liv and Jayce.

The classroom was bright and airy, with colorful paintings and pictures plastering the walls. Liv showed them the craft area, the free-play area, and the little library corner, where colorful books lined the walls. Then they moved into an adjacent room where there was a messy play area and a door that led back out into the front playground.

"Want to have a little play in here with Emily and Charlie?" Liv asked Jayce, pointing to a table nearby where two kids were getting involved in some water-based activities, each in a wee apron.

Jayce's eyes lit up. Making a mess was right up his street. Arran smiled as Liv got him an apron and introduced him to the other kids. The three began happily chatting and playing together.

Liv came over to stand with Arran as they watched them. "Is he looking forward to his first day?"

"Totally. I think knowing he's in your class has made the idea a piece of cake."

A little color rose in her cheeks, and it was so cute. "I'll look out for him, but I'm sure he won't need it. He'll be grand."

Despite her proximity to him, it felt as if she was a world away. Out of his reach. But he reminded himself that the main thing was that she was there for Jayce. Even if her new relationship put a damper on her spending time with him, Jayce would still get to see her for a few hours every day at nursery school. At least there was some comfort in that thought. Though it didn't appease the hollow feeling in his chest.

"You sure you're okay after Douchebag Dave's reappearance?"

he asked her quietly. He'd messaged her to ask the same thing and she'd replied to say she was fine. But he didn't believe it.

Her expression clouded. "I'm fine, thanks. All good."

"Miss Lib!" Jayce shouted from the play area, and Arran winced.

"Sorry," he told Liv with a pained expression. "I tried to tell him he needed to call you Miss Holland while he's at nursery school, but he's having trouble with the concept."

She laughed, and he admired the way her green eyes sparkled. He could watch her smile and laugh all day. "That's okay. I like it. Perhaps I'll get them all to call me Miss Liv."

"I'm not sure Mrs. MacKay would approve," Arran said, remembering the chastising arched eyebrow.

"Ach, don't worry about her. She's just a stickler for old-style rules," Liv said.

Creepy Married Dad appeared in the doorway, eyeing Liv again and making Arran all the more determined to hog her time. It made him think of Brodie, which in turn caused his heart to sink. "Looking forward to the weekend?" he asked her, his jaw clenching.

Her eyes lit up. "Yeah. It's going to be a good laugh."

He nodded, resolving to back off and let her get plenty of time with her new love interest when the time came.

AGNES'S CORNFLOWER-BLUE EYE PEERED AT HIM THROUGH THE gap in the door. "Hi, son."

She let him in and he dutifully followed her down the hallway, carrying the shopping bags. Wordlessly, he began the process of putting everything in its proper place, not even bothering to give Agnes any lip back when she criticized him for putting a can of baked beans with the kidney beans.

She surveyed him through narrowed eyes. "What's wrong? Why's your face tripping you?"

He glanced over as he closed the last cupboard. "Nothing." He took the tea she pushed toward him, lifting it to blow on the surface.

"Hmm. Looks like you're lovesick to me."

He managed a weak smile. Lovesick felt like a good description, given that he felt nauseated whenever he thought of Liv and Brodie together.

Agnes graced him with a sympathetic look. "Aw, son. What's happened?"

He ran a hand over his hair, letting out a breath. "She's dating someone else."

She nodded slowly. "I see. And this is despite you telling her that you liked her?"

He shook his head. "I haven't told her."

Agnes frowned. "Well, that's where you've gone wrong. I'm sure she wouldn't be seeing someone else if she knew you liked her. I've seen the way that lassie looks at you."

He raised his eyebrows. "Really? You mean through your *bird-watching* binoculars?"

She sipped her tea silently, a smile on her face. "Listen to me. Stop being a numpty and be honest with her. You don't know how she really feels about either of you unless you have a conversation about it."

Arran fiddled with his mug. "I don't want to spoil things for her."

"Nonsense. You're just trying to save face."

He opted to stay silent because there might have been a kernel of truth in that remark.

She sighed. "You youngsters. Wasting time over barriers you've created in your own minds."

A change of subject was called for. "What'll you be doing while I'm away to Skye? Raving it up?"

"None of your cheek." But her smile indicated that she enjoyed his cheek. "My friend Nancy's coming to take me to the tearoom for an afternoon tea."

"Very nice." Nancy was Agnes's slightly younger friend who had a car that was high enough that Agnes could comfortably get in and out. "Well, you girls enjoy yourself. Don't do anything I wouldn't do."

She pointed her finger at him. "And you do something I *would* do. Stop being a fool and tell your sweetheart how you really feel."

"I'll think about it."

Chapter
FIFTEEN

LIV GLANCED OVER HER SHOULDER, TRYING TO CATCH ARRAN'S eye in the row of seats behind her. He was across the vehicle, next to Maya and Sam. It seemed as if he was avoiding her gaze.

She turned back and smiled at Brodie, who was next to her, Ben on his other side. She'd tried to engineer the situation to sit next to Arran, but he'd hung back when everyone had climbed into Nico's sister's car, and the two of them had gotten separated.

Looking over at Brodie chatting with Ben, Liv took in the way Brodie kept glancing away and smiling whenever Ben made consistent eye contact.

"Okay," Nico called from the driver's seat. "Toilet break."

Elise looked across at him from the passenger seat. "Again? We're only half an hour away now. Can't you hold it in, like a big boy?"

"Nope," Nico replied, pulling into the rest stop. "I had that coffee, remember?"

Elise shook her head. "I think you need to get your prostate checked."

He raised an eyebrow at her. "Is that an offer?"

Elise muttered something under her breath.

Nico parked and everyone clambered out, some heading for the facilities and some stretching their legs. Arran legged it with Nico and Ben to the loo before Liv had a chance to engage him in conversation.

She went over to Brodie and bumped his shoulder. "Hey."

He smiled. "Hey yourself."

"So. Brodie. This guy you like . . ." She glanced around, double-checking that Sam and Maya were still out of earshot and confirming that they were indeed still canoodling between the large supply of windshield wiper fluid and the bank of trashy "news"-papers. Elise was in the shop perusing the healthy snack aisle.

She turned back to Brodie. "He wouldn't happen to be a dark-haired-with-a-tinge-of-silver, blue-eyed, handsome chap named Ben, would he?"

A smile tugged at his face as he scuffed his foot on the ground. "Maybe."

"Aha!" she said loudly, before catching herself and glancing around furtively. "I *knew* it. All those puppy-dog-eyed looks you were giving him." She fanned herself with her hand. "Swoon."

Brodie laughed. "Shh. Maya and Sam'll hear."

"So what if they do?" she replied with a shrug. "In fact, we should tell them, because they'll be able to get you guys set up."

He shook his head. "I'd rather wait. I want to suss out Ben a bit more first; he's only just broken up with Derek, so I don't want to be too full on."

"No worries." She tapped the side of her nose. "Your secret's safe with me."

"By the way," he said, shooting her a smile. "What's the deal with Arran? Whenever I've met him before, he's been dead chatty. But today, he's kind of giving out these 'fuck off' vibes."

She pursed her lips. "I don't know. But you're right, he is acting pretty out of character. I feel like he's avoiding me."

Brodie glanced toward the shop. "Have you had an argument?"

"No. Not that I can remember, anyway," she said, a dragging sensation in her chest. "He started being aloof after we went for afternoon tea, and at first I wondered if I'd said something to upset him, because I did get a bit tipsy. But I honestly can't remember anything untoward."

The others came out of the rest stop, so they started heading back to the car as they chatted. "Why don't you ask him?" Brodie said.

He took her hand to help her into the car, and as she lifted her gaze it meshed with Arran's across the car park, sending a bolt of electricity into her chest. "If I can get him to have an actual conversation with me, then I will."

THE "COTTAGE" WAS IN FACT A STUNNING, MODERN, DETACHED house right by the water, and the living room wall was entirely made of glass so they could look out over Loch Portree.

"Nice one, Nico," Liv said as she gazed at the scene. The water was flat and calm in the still air, with the lush green of the opposite bank reflected perfectly on the surface.

"What can I say?" Nico answered from the kitchen. "I've got the contacts."

She glanced across the open-plan area, where the five guys were bustling around the kitchen, preparing dinner for everyone. Sam had insisted because he said it was in order to counteract the cliché of the men sitting on their arses while the women prepared dinner. Then the three women had been "forced" to sit and have a glass of wine while the blokes got on with it. Liv had, of course, made the obligatory Five Guys joke and asked if the five of them were making burgers and fries. It had resulted in much groaning and eye-rolling, which really was rather rude when it was a top-quality quip.

Elise had planned the sustenance to her signature nth degree, not only booking the meal out the following evening but arranging for a shopping delivery shortly after their arrival.

"It's a shame your sister was too heavily pregnant to come," Elise said to Maya.

"I know," Maya replied. "But I figured you were off duty and wouldn't be keen on delivering any babies."

Elise sipped her wine. "God, no. I've not delivered a baby in years. Not much call for that in general practice."

"How's work going?" Maya asked.

"Okay," Elise said. "But I'm still only doing one day a week at your dad's surgery because Mum can't handle more than a day looking after Jack. It's tough for her with her joints. That's why I arranged to leave him with Harry's sister in Edinburgh this weekend."

"What about a nursery place?" Liv asked. "Then you could work a bit more."

Elise hesitated. "I'm a bit reluctant for that yet. I know it's silly, but I don't feel like I'm ready to leave him with strangers. I'm sure I'd feel differently if Harry were still around."

A prickle of cold ran down Liv's spine. Every decision in Elise's life was tainted by Harry's death, and there was no escaping it. His sister was too far away to be of regular assistance, and his parents had been a lot older than everyone else's—both having sadly passed away a couple of years before Harry himself. "I understand. I wish I could help, but it's no use when I work full-time." A thought popped into her head. "Unless I could take him at the weekend, for you to do out-of-hours shifts like Maya's dad does?"

Elise smiled. "That's very kind. But I'm trying to keep work in-hours for now. Plus I can't have you giving up your weekends for me. You work hard and need the time to relax. Especially when you're already helping with other childcare." Elise darted a meaningful glance over to where Arran was busy with the others in the kitchen.

A heavy weight hung in Liv's chest. "I haven't been doing much of that lately."

Her gaze settled on Arran as he smiled at something Nico said. Her eyes seemed to get stuck on his handsome face and she had trouble prizing them away. Then he glanced over and caught her staring, and she dragged her eyes off him to furiously study a random vase across the room.

"Okay, ladies," Nico called. "Dinner is served."

Brodie and Ben had the table set, and Nico and Sam were putting down plates of spaghetti and meatballs at each place, as Arran poured wine into all the glasses.

Maya led them over to the table. "Well, gentlemen. This is rather fabulous. I'm thinking it should be a weekly event, yes?"

Elise nodded as they took their seats. "Every Friday night we get dinner cooked for us by the men? Sounds good to me."

Nico settled into the seat opposite Elise. "Dr. Kowalski, I would be delighted to give you the pleasure of my company every weekend."

Liv was sure Elise's cheeks colored a little as she shot him a withering look.

Somewhat predictably, Arran had positioned himself at the other side of the large table and Liv was no longer able to hold on to the vain hope that things were normal between them. *What have I done to upset him?*

Brodie leaned in from beside her to whisper in her ear. "Arran's definitely being off with me, and I get the feeling it's because of you."

She turned her head toward him, her pulse picking up. "Me?"

"Yep," he murmured into her ear.

Liv concentrated on keeping her voice low. "Why do you think that?"

"Because my experiment has worked."

She frowned at him. "What experiment?"

"The one where I sit next to you and whisper in your ear. He's giving me the evil eye."

Liv's heart thudded as she briefly raised her eyes and clocked Arran watching them, though he glanced away and nodded at what Sam was saying when she caught him. "I don't understand."

"I do. Did you tell him we went out?"

"Yeah, but he's just a friend," she said, watching Arran surreptitiously as she spoke and trying to ignore how hot he looked with his hair pulled up into a small topknot. "Why would he mind?"

"He's clearly jealous. Does he know we decided to just be mates?"

"Yes." Hold on, did they discuss that part? "No, wait . . . I can't remember if I specifically told him that bit."

Brodie leaned away, a knowing look in his eyes and a smile playing on his face.

She raised her eyebrows. "Are you enjoying this?"

"Kind of," he said. "I seem to have a penchant in this friendship group for creating unnecessary jealousy. I think I like it." He lifted his wineglass and sipped, pinkie sticking out and lips pursed as if he was an evil villain. Liv couldn't help but laugh, and when she chanced another quick glance at Arran, he was watching them again, his face set in a frown.

She brought her eyes down to pay attention to her food, taking a mouthful. "Mmm, this is delicious."

Brodie nodded. "Nico said his mum's Italian? It's her recipe."

"Yeah, she's an amazing cook."

"Anyway. Stop changing the subject. Do you like Arran?"

Her mouth went dry, so she lifted her wineglass to take a sip. "Course I do. We're friends."

He rolled his eyes. "You know what I mean."

She took another mouthful, staying silent as she chewed and

weighed up her response. She kept her voice low. "Yeah. I like him. But it's complicated."

"Perhaps it doesn't have to be," he said softly.

Emotion pricked at her eyes and constricted her throat as she considered Arran back together with Jess. Why did the idea hurt so much, when she'd managed to cope with the reality of his being with her in the past? She blinked hard, then gave Brodie a weak smile, unable to get any words out.

Brodie touched the back of her hand with a reassuring smile, glancing at Arran briefly, before topping up their wineglasses.

Chapter

SIXTEEN

THE SPRINGTIME SUN WARMED LIV'S FACE AS SHE SAT AT THE edge of the Fairy Pools with Brodie, Ben, and Elise. Closing her eyes for a moment, she tuned in to the gentle sound of the waterfalls cascading into the far end of the pool.

Liv rubbed a towel over her wet hair, then wrapped it around her wet-suit-clad form. "Are you sure you don't want to go in, Elise? It's really refreshing."

Elise glanced at the clear pool next to them, the stones and pebbles at the bottom perfectly visible—as if the water were glass. "It does look lovely," she said. "But I'm such a wimp when it comes to cold water. My bad circulation goes mental and last time I tried open-water swimming the pain in my hands and feet made me faint." She screwed her face up. "But don't you guys tell anyone that; I'm still really embarrassed about it."

Ben laughed. "Don't worry, Elise. I'm with you, and I don't even have bad circulation. I just hate being cold."

Brodie nudged Ben's shoulder, smiling. "But you work at a ski resort."

Ben grinned. "Yeah, but I'm all cozy with a coffee inside the center, not out on the slopes like Sam and Maya."

Brodie laughed, his blue eyes lighting up. Liv secretly rooted for him in her head. *Come on, Ben. Fall in love with Brodie, you know you want to.*

Brodie stretched in his wet suit, and Liv was sure she caught Ben's eye being drawn to the flex of Brodie's biceps. *Yas.*

A splash in the pool caused her to turn her head toward where Sam and Maya had been left swimming alone, after she and Brodie had gotten out. The splash had resulted from Arran jumping in from a ledge just above the pools. He surfaced, laughing as he ran a hand over the wet tendrils of his hair, the water running down his beautiful face. His eyes sparkled as he turned to Nico. "Come on in, mate! The water's fine."

Nico shot him a smile. He was the only other one, apart from Elise and Ben, who wasn't wearing a wet suit and was still dressed in his shorts, T-shirt, and hoodie. "Not yet. I'm biding my time."

"What for?" Arran asked, sculling through the water on his back.

Nico glanced over at the only other group left at this particular pool, who had just gotten out of the water and were toweling off. "You'll see."

Distracted, Liv couldn't tear her eyes off Arran as he glided through the water, his long limbs effortlessly graceful in his strokes. She was grateful for the opportunity to watch him from their side of the pool—safely out of his eyeline.

Then, as he reached the shallower edge, he stood, droplets of water flowing down his wet suit and accentuating the way it hugged his lean and muscular form. Liv's eyes patrolled every ridge and contour, tracing the outlines and imprinting them on her brain so that whenever she closed her eyes, the image of his tight body would be right there behind her eyelids. Then her gaze was drawn lower, to where the fabric defined the bulge between his legs. Fire erupted in her belly, rippling out in hot waves that made her core pulse and her nipples tighten. The water was cold; therefore, logic would dictate that anything on display would be smaller than it might normally appear. So, the fact that that bulge already looked pretty big meant that under normal circumstances . . . *blimey*.

Arran picked that very moment, just while she was having inappropriate thoughts about his endowment, to glance up and into her eyes. Her mouth went dry.

"Oh, for fuck's sake," Elise muttered from next to her.

"What is it?" Liv asked, guiltily snatching her eyes off Arran.

Elise had her hand placed against the side of her face, shielding her vision from the pools. "Nico's at it again."

Liv turned back to look at the ledge Nico had been sitting on and did a double take. He was now fully naked, muscles rippling, one large hand cupping between his legs to keep the show from being X-rated. The arm in use for his self-censorship was the one housing a full sleeve of ink, with a tattoo running from the ball of his shoulder right down to his wrist.

"Please tell me that other group has gone," Elise whispered, her voice pained.

Liv looked over and confirmed that to be the case. "It's okay. We're the only ones here."

Elise sighed with relief.

Nico jumped in with an almighty splash, finally alerting Arran to what had been going on behind him, as Nico grabbed his legs and dunked him under.

Arran surfaced, laughing as he clocked Nico's nakedness. "Old habits die hard."

Nico grinned, running a hand through his wet hair, the tattooed muscles of his arm flexing under his inked sleeve. Liv could swear she could see Elise peeking out at him between her fingers.

"Well, that's quite the spectacle," Ben said in an approving tone.

"I wouldn't know," Elise replied in a prim voice. "I'm not looking."

"I am," said Ben with a smile.

"Me too," said Brodie, earning him a curious glance from Ben. And perhaps one tinged with a little jealousy?

Liv laughed. "Well, you're about to see more. Because it's time for them to get out." She leaned over to call to the four friends in the pool. "Guys, it's time to head back if we want to get ready for dinner."

"Okay, thanks," Maya replied from where she was holding on to Sam's shoulders as he pulled her around the pool.

Nico went to hoist himself up onto the side, Arran following. Liv could tell that Nico's perfectly formed gluteals were on display from the murmurs of appreciation from Ben and Brodie and the stony silence from Elise, though she couldn't tell by sight because her gaze was too distracted by Arran as he pushed himself up onto the ledge, water droplets clinging to the skintight fabric that hugged the stretch and flex of his muscles. In one lithe movement he swung his legs up to stand, the sight of his appealingly taut arse delighting her vision. She imagined herself sinking her teeth into it, then shook her head to chastise that thought out of her head.

Arran must have had some psychic way of knowing when she was having dirty thoughts about him because he chose that moment to turn and look over his shoulder into her eyes, sending a shock wave throughout her entire body. For a second she thought he gave her the tiniest of smiles, but then Nico threw a towel at him and he caught it, breaking both their gaze and the moment.

"CAN YOU PASS ME MY MAKEUP BAG?" MAYA CALLED TO LIV.

Liv tossed it across the room and Maya caught it with one hand.

"Nice catch, Miss M," Liv said, impressed at her friend's reflexes.

"Why, thank you, Miss O." Maya turned to appraise her, giving a low whistle. "Wow. Looking gorgeous."

Liv gave her a wink. "I can scrub up when I want to." Her little black dress served her well, being dressy enough for a nice meal but casual enough that she didn't appear overdressed. The length trod a very fine line regarding what was decent in terms of tomorrow's washing being on display, but as long as it wasn't too windy out and she avoided bending too far, then it was all good. Tonight she would pair it with red heels and her red coat, which she thought of as her Little Red Riding Hood coat.

Maya winked back. "You're a sexy mofo, so you are. Have you got your contacts in? Your eyes look even bigger than usual. They're beautiful. I feel like you're hypnotizing me with your green-goddess eyeballs."

Liv laughed. "That sounds weird. Like I've got an eyeball on the end of a string and I'm swinging it like one of those hypnotizing pocket watches."

"Ew," Maya said, screwing up her face. "Not quite as sexy a sentiment."

"Indeed," Liv replied as she climbed onto the bed and lifted her Kindle to continue reading her romance novel, allowing Maya to get back to applying her makeup.

"Thanks for letting me get ready in your room, guys," Maya said. "When Arran and Nico turned up with that hip flask full of whiskey at my and Sam's door, I figured the environment would not be conducive to the application of eyeliner."

Elise emerged from their en suite. "No problem." She settled into a seat at the desk to do her hair. "This is lovely. It reminds me of us getting ready together before we went out to the pub when we were teenagers."

Maya was pulling the universal open-mouthed application-of-eyeliner face. "Ah yes. When Elise used to buy drinks for the under-age Liv and Maya. It was cool having an older friend."

Liv smiled as she flicked the page on her e-book. "Those were the days."

Elise glanced at her in the mirror. "What're you reading?"

"A romance," Liv told her. "It's about a couple who hate each other."

Elise frowned. "How is it a romance if they hate each other?"

Liv grinned. "It's a trope called enemies to lovers, and it's the best one ever."

Shaking her head, Elise took out her hair curler. "That makes no sense."

"Course it does. I'm going to buy you some reading material so you can do some *research*."

Elise laughed. "Okay, then. I'm normally into cozy crime, but I'll give it a try. Aren't they a little unrealistic, though?"

Liv raised her eyebrows. "And you think your whodunnit crime novels are realistic? Dead bodies all over a small town until there's no population left, and the little old lady who owns the local café solves all the murders? Anyway, if I want realism, I'll watch the news. Plus, men written by women are far superior to most real-life men."

Maya raised her hand. "Except Sam."

Liv pointed toward Maya. "Exception noted." She paused. "And Arran."

"And Harry," Elise said, quietly.

An icy needle dug into Liv's heart. "And Harry," she added softly.

Elise shot her a smile in the mirror, then went back to adding some curls to her shiny blond hair. "That's all the exceptions, though, as far as I can work out."

"Nico too," Maya said as she capped her eyeliner.

"Yeah," Liv replied, at the same time that Elise said, "Nope."

Maya laughed. "Come on, Elise. He's a lovely guy. What's your beef with him?"

Elise shrugged, sliding the tongs over her hair until a curl bounced up into place. "He's a total pain in the arse. When we were at school everything fell into his lap with zero effort, while I had to work extra hard to be recognized for all the school prizes, which he still stole from me half the time."

Liv raised her eyebrows. "Jealous rivalry between head girl and head boy?"

"You could say that." Elise sighed. "But the problem is, the bar is lower for men. We're held up to a higher standard so we have to work twice as hard for the same accolades. It's not fair. One time we were paired on a science project and I had to cover for him when he didn't turn in his fair share because he'd ditched study time for a hot date." She rolled her eyes. "And he's the same now, jacking in law to open a gym, where he no doubt swans around all day checking out the ladies. And only ever having short-term, no-strings relationships." Her voice wobbled a little. "He doesn't know what it's like to have to juggle work and a child as a single parent."

Liv's heart squeezed painfully. She hadn't quite put two and two together that for Elise, Nico represented all her struggles in life. The man who used to be her high school rival now had the "easy" life Elise wished desperately she could have. Though of course she wouldn't change the fact that she was mother to wee Jack for the world. "I get that," she told her gently.

Maya was nodding, a soft look on her face, and Liv could tell the penny had dropped for her too. "I'm sorry, Elise," Maya said. She paused, seeming to tread carefully. "I think, though, from having gotten to know Nico pretty well now, that his life isn't as easy as he makes out."

Elise darted her gaze over to Maya and back again. "Oh yeah?"

Maya nodded. Elise opened her mouth as if to ask more; then she appeared to catch herself and closed it again, concentrating instead on creating more shiny blond curls. "He certainly seemed pretty easygoing today, when he stripped naked to jump into the Fairy Pools." She huffed out a breath. "*Again*. So those antics haven't changed since school. At least the teachers weren't there to witness it this time."

Liv grinned. "Hope you averted your eyes during the stripping-off part, and the emerging-from-the-water-naked part, like Maya and I did."

Maya shrugged, her face deadpan. "Maybe I did, maybe I didn't."

Liv eyed Elise for a moment, watching her cheeks stain pink and imagining her as the perfect heroine in an enemies-to-lovers romance. Starring opposite Nico. *Ha! That'd really piss Elise off.*

Elise cleared her throat. "When did Nico get that sleeve tattoo? It's huge."

"A few years back," Liv replied, a smile playing on her face. "But I thought you weren't looking."

Elise's cheeks were practically glowing now, and she fell silent, concentrating on her hair. Liv decided that her friend had likely had enough teasing for one day and went back to her book.

"Liv?" Elise asked.

She glanced up, now feeling guilty about ribbing Elise and worried that she'd hurt her friend's feelings. "Yeah?" she said, about to apologize.

"Are you feeling okay?" Elise asked softly, looking at her via the reflection in the mirror. "After your dad showed up last weekend?"

"Yeah. I'm good," she said quickly, trying to cover her discomfort. "We've not heard from him again, so hopefully he's fucked off somewhere." Probably back to hell to hang out with his best mate, the devil. She took a breath, blinking. "Anyway. I assume I don't need to remind you both about the first rule of the sten weekend?"

Maya and Elise glanced at each other before saying in unison, "We don't talk about Dave."

Liv nodded, forcing a smile onto her face. "And the second rule?"

The two of them smiled back. "We don't talk about Dave."

"Excellent," Liv said, shifting her eyes back onto her book and trying to get Dave out of her mind.

There were a couple of seconds' silence before Maya broke it. "Thanks again for organizing this. I've loved everything about it so far."

Elise set down her hair equipment and ran her fingers through her freshly curled hair. Liv almost wanted to cross the room and join in, the blond tendrils looked so temptingly soft.

"I hope you like the restaurant," Elise said as she got to her feet. "I'll feel terrible otherwise." She was wearing skintight shiny black trousers and a sparkly silver tank top, with little black ankle boots.

Maya stood to join her, and Liv put down her book, slipped on her red heels, and moved around the bed to follow the two of them out of the room.

"Of course I'll love it," Maya told Elise, linking arms with her. "You've got excellent foodie taste. In any case, with this company I'd love it if we went to McDonald's." She led them out of the room, her soft black jumpsuit swishing around her stilettoed feet.

"Aw, man," Liv replied as her tummy rumbled. "I could really go for a Big Mac right now."

Elise laughed, turning her head to flash her a smile as they headed toward the stairs. "I'm afraid this place doesn't do Big Macs."

"Why is it even called a Big Mac?" Maya asked as they descended the stairs. "It's *Mc*Donald's, not *Mac*Donald's. So really, it should be a Big Mc."

Liv chuckled. "Good point, Miss M." She glanced down as she stepped onto the landing behind Maya and Elise. "Bloody hell, Elise. Are you wearing space pants?"

Elise shot her a puzzled look. "Space pants?"

"Yeah." Liv grinned. "Because your arse is out of this world."

Maya broke down laughing as they rounded the corner to where the blokes were sitting having a drink in the living room. Elise joined in and Liv's chest warmed as she took in how Elise's eyes lit up. It was something she observed much more rarely in her friend since Harry's death.

Sam was studying them curiously, a smile on his face, and the warmth in Liv's heart swelled at the look of adoration he gave Maya as he appraised her evening ensemble. She signaled to the women to take a drink and Maya nodded, as Sam stood to kiss her cheek.

Elise turned and said, "Yes, please," then started after Liv as if coming to help, but Liv shook her head and shooed her away to go sit and relax.

As Liv glanced up before heading to the kitchen area, she was sure she caught Nico doing a double take as his gaze was drawn to Elise's out-of-this-world arse. Suppressing a laugh, she kept her head down as she rounded the kitchen island and grabbed three glasses.

She poured prosecco into the glasses and placed the bottle in the fridge. Then, smiling to herself, she took hold of the full glasses and looked up—straight into the honey color of Arran's eyes. He was unabashedly staring at her from the living area.

For a second, she was thrown. His hair was loose and he was wearing a pair of slim-fit dark gray checked trousers paired with a soft wool charcoal jumper. The dark tones of his outfit seemed to reflect the brooding expression on his face, and all in all, the spectacle of him was heart-racingly, panty-meltingly sexy.

Her mouth dry and her heart pumping, she continued to lift the glasses and attempted to control her trembling fingers as she walked toward the sitting area, waiting for him to hurriedly break eye contact the way he'd been doing all weekend. But he didn't. Instead, he ran his eyes leisurely down her little-black-dress-clad body all the way to her red-stilettoed feet, seeming to linger for a moment on the line of her legs. It was as if his gaze had a direct effect on her body—each place his eyes traveled burned with waves of liquid heat, all convening in a tsunami between her legs and making her core clench. He took a slow blink and met her eyes again, giving her a megawatt smile that nearly caused her to stumble.

Her pulse rocketed and she managed a quick smile back before she lost her nerve and dragged her eyes away, handing Elise a glass where she was sitting in an armchair, then crossing the room and passing one to Maya, who was on Sam's lap. As she bent to deposit the glass in Maya's hand, she realized that she had her back to Arran, who was on the adjacent two-seater with Nico, and that the view of tomorrow's washing was right on the cusp.

She straightened again and chanced a glance over. Arran was watching her, his lips parted and a heated look in his eyes, which made her fingers tremble even harder as she held her glass. Nico was chatting to Brodie, who was sitting in a love seat next to them.

Sipping her drink to steady herself, she eyed the options for seats, realizing that they were all taken. She glanced over at the table, deciding that she could bring one of the dining chairs over.

But before she could execute that plan, Brodie met her eye and crooked his finger to beckon her.

She crossed over to him and he scooted right over to let her squeeze in on the small two-seater; she took a seat, facing Arran and Nico.

Their arms were quite constricted in the small seat, and so Brodie stretched his arm behind her, holding his beer in the other hand as he chatted to Nico and they included Liv in their conversation.

Smiling at something Nico was saying, she let her gaze drift over to Arran, and the smile dropped from her face as a shiver licked up her spine. His eyes were on her, dark and brooding, with his clenched fist resting against his mouth as he darted his gaze to Brodie's arm about her shoulders. Her breath caught, and she couldn't look away.

Arran slid his eyes down to her legs, and it was as if his gaze were his touch, his fingers caressing her bare skin and leaving gooseflesh in their wake. She crossed her legs, trying to adjust to the heat pooling between them. His jaw tightened as he watched the movement.

This was the dress she'd worn to their blind date. The one that he'd told her she looked beautiful in. She'd known that when she'd packed it, but being under the heat of his gaze was something else—something achingly good that she hadn't experienced that first night. Or perhaps she had but hadn't noticed—not being aware his appreciation existed until that day in her kitchen when he'd confessed it and when, for the first time, she'd felt an inkling that he might be attracted to her. Well, it was more than an inkling now. And it was *red-hot*. No man had ever made her feel like this with just his eyes. Being under Arran's lingering gaze was like a sensual caress.

Nico turned to Arran to ask him something, and he dragged his eyes off her, dropping his hand and nodding in response to Nico. He returned his gaze to look her right in the eyes, electricity arcing between them.

"Okay, guys," Elise said, cutting into the moment. "Drink up. We need to head out to make our reservation."

Liv had to take a second before she stood, her legs feeling weakened from the impact of Arran's gaze. She sank the rest of her drink in an attempt to douse her molten hot insides. Everyone hustled to get their coats on, and Liv slipped her arm through Elise's as they left the house, feeling that she needed the support for her wobbly legs. They'd decided to walk to the restaurant because it was only five minutes away.

Her red coat was cozy in the chill of the air, and she cuddled into Elise's fur jacket as they walked together, chatting about the Fairy Pools and what was on the menu at the restaurant as Liv tried to calm her lust-filled thoughts.

She glanced ahead to where Sam and Maya were walking in front, and with a jolt she realized that so far she'd been subconsciously gravitating toward Elise and the others in order to stay away from Sam and Maya. The uneasy third-wheel complex seemed to have taken up residence in her psyche ever since the anticlimax of her confrontation with her father.

Liv had noticed that Nico had hung back to walk behind them with Arran, and she had a sneaking suspicion that it might have something to do with the rear-end view of Elise's sexy pants—her fur jacket was short enough that the display was still in full effect.

Chapter

SEVENTEEN

THE RESTAURANT LOOKED OUT OVER THE HILL ONTO THE opposite shoreline of Loch Portree, toward a row of pastel-colored terraced houses lining the bank on the other side—soft pink, baby blue, mint green, and lemon yellow. Like pieces of candy lined up along the edge of a mirror.

The food was delicious and Liv took the opportunity to gorge herself. At the beginning of the meal, Elise had leaned in to ask her whether she was going to go for a starter or a dessert with her main course and Liv had given her a look of disbelief. "Elise. There is no *or*. There is only *and*."

She'd gotten the feeling that Arran's previous avoidance of her was no longer deliberate but that he'd been angling to sit near her at the meal; however, he'd been thwarted by Maya, Elise, and Sam, who'd all gotten there first. Arran wasn't in the seat farthest from her, but he was at enough of a distance that they'd hardly shared any conversation by the time the meal ended. But every time their eyes met, fireworks erupted in her chest.

On the way home, they decided to stop by a pub that they'd

passed on the way to the restaurant and have some more drinks before returning to the house.

The pub was cozy and the rest of the clientele were dressed casually, mostly in walking gear. A couple of them seemed to raise an eyebrow at their formal attire. Though on second thought, Liv realized it was a couple of men raising their eyebrows at the women's attire. *Space pants strike again.*

Maya clinked her glass with Liv's, then Elise's. "Thank you, my wonderful besties, for an awesome weekend."

Liv sipped the champagne that Nico had treated them all to, savoring the fizz of the bubbles on her tongue. "It's not over yet. Don't forget that Arran and I have a trip to Neist Point planned for tomorrow morning before we head home." Even saying his name did things to her now. Each syllable on her tongue was like tasting him. At least, what she imagined he might taste like—and she was desperate to know for real. She chanced a glance over at where he was chatting to Ben and Nico. He appeared relaxed and she wondered if he was having thoughts similar to hers.

Maya smiled. "I love Neist Point; it's so romantic. Thank you."

Liv lifted her glass toward her. "No problem, Miss M."

"And thanks for organizing a lovely dinner," Maya told Elise.

Elise leaned in to kiss Maya's cheek, simultaneously sliding an arm around Liv's waist. Maya lifted her arms around them both too, creating a three-way hug. Liv cuddled in and both of them gave her a squeeze. She could tell it was their way of silently conveying to her that they were there for her after the trauma of Douchebag Dave's showing up the week before, without their breaking either rule one or rule two of the sten weekend.

She smiled to herself, the affection of her friends creating a fuzzy warmth in her chest.

Glancing up from the cocoon of her best-friend snuggle, she thought she caught one of the raised-eyebrow men from their entrance looking away. They mustn't have been expecting dressed-up people. It was a casual pub, after all.

Once the champagne was drained, there were noises about going back to the house, started mainly by Sam and Maya. Liv had the sneaking suspicion that they wanted some alone time, which was fair enough.

Everyone gathered their coats, and as they got to the door, Liv's bladder complained loudly. She decided that she'd need to visit the ladies' room prior to departure. "You guys start walking; I'll only be a sec," she told Elise.

"I'll wait for you," Elise replied, pausing at the exit.

"It's fine, I'll catch up. I just don't think I can hold it until we get back," Liv said, holding her belly and doing a little full-bladder dance.

Elise laughed. "No worries. We'll walk slowly."

Liv nipped past the bar to use the restroom. She washed up quickly and headed to the front door, opening it and stepping out.

Something grasped her wrist out of the darkness, nearly yanking her shoulder out and making her wobble on her heels. She snapped her head around and took in the raised-eyebrow man from inside the pub, lurking next to the doorway and holding on to her wrist tightly.

Steadying herself, she glanced down at his hand on her wrist, then back at his sneering face. Anger spiked her chest. "Let go."

"Where are you off to?" he asked, not loosening his grip.

She stiffened. "None of your business."

His grip tightened. "Why don't you come with me instead, darling?"

She gritted her teeth. "No, thanks."

He shifted closer, his fingers pressing painfully into the soft underside of her wrist. "I'm staying just around the corner."

Liv took a deep breath. "This is your final warning. Let go of me."

He let out a snigger and gave her a leery smirk, which set off a hot burst of anger in her gut. He didn't loosen his grasp.

In a fluid movement, she stepped back with her right foot and yanked her wrist down and out of his grip, simultaneously smashing her other hand onto his forearm in an open-hand strike. As the twat let out a yelp and went to grab his arm, she crashed the heel of her hand into his face, causing him to recoil and stumble back as he lifted his hands to his nose.

He took his hands away briefly, glancing at the blood streaking them. "You fucking bitch."

In the split second that it took her to slip out of her heels, ready to grab them and run, something whooshed past her and slammed into the man.

Liv grasped her shoes and was about to begin her sprint when she realized the whooshing thing was a person. Someone whose honey-colored eyes appeared black and menacing in the moonlight.

"Stay the hell away from her, or I will fucking *end* you," Arran said to the twat through gritted teeth. "Do you understand me?"

The twat let out a whimper and held his hands up, and Arran dragged him away from the wall, practically throwing him along the street, at which point he started to run in the opposite direction, holding his nose.

Arran turned back to Liv and took her shoes from her, the dark look in his eyes melting away to soft concern. "Are you all right?"

She nodded, trying to catch her breath.

He crouched to place her shoes back on her feet. "You can't walk without shoes on. There's some broken glass farther down the street."

She lifted each foot in silence, the warm sensation of his grasp on her calf in order to place each shoe rapidly evaporating the adrenaline of the fight.

Arran stood to meet her gaze, holding out his hand. She took it, sliding her fingers between his. He held her firmly with just the right amount of pressure, instilling a sense of safety and protection while simultaneously stoking the ever-burning desire deep in her belly. They began to walk and he rubbed his thumb over the back of her hand in a slow, soothing circle. His touch was comforting yet sensual, making her recall her instinctual thoughts that he would be amazing in bed. She ached to have him touch her in a sexual way.

He gave her hand a squeeze. "I would say sorry that I didn't get here sooner, but you clearly had the whole thing under control." He glanced down. "So, instead, sorry for adding in my twopence worth. I know you didn't need it. It was for my own benefit."

She gave him a quizzical look. "Your own benefit?"

He swallowed. "Yeah. My own basic need to smash the guy in the face. I saw the way he was looking at you in the pub and I didn't like it. So I hung back to wait for you down the street. When it took a little longer than anticipated for you to appear, I walked back a bit and saw the two of you." He took a breath. "Nice moves. You're awesome, Aggie."

She smiled. "Thank you."

The tension in his face dissipated, replaced with a smile. "Remind me never to get on the wrong side of you. You're a total badass."

Liv laughed. "I reserve my moves for douchebags. Hence, you're safe."

"Good to know." His smile faded, and his jaw tightened. "I so wanted to flatten that guy, by the way."

Her breath seemed to get stuck in her chest. "I know. But best to leave it at that and report him to the police."

He gave her a look of concern. "Do you want to call them when we get home?"

"Yeah. Just in case he gets any ideas in the meantime about trying the same thing with a woman who *doesn't* happen to be a black belt in karate."

He nodded. "I'll stay up with you until it's sorted. At least he won't be in any fit state to try anything else tonight, what with the bloody nose you gave him."

She laughed. "Yep. Also, it makes him easier for the police to recognize. Probably not too many others going around town with a flattened nose."

Arran shook his head, grinning. "You're a mastermind as well as a badass."

Liv bit her lip, studying him as they walked. The need to have him closer, to extend their touch, was too great. She let go of his hand, sliding her arm around his waist. He immediately responded by circling her shoulders. And it felt *so good.*

"Thanks, though," she said, absorbing the warmth of having him pressed against her side. "For noticing the twat and hanging around."

Arran squeezed her shoulders in response.

She cleared her throat, trying to keep her mind on their conversation because his proximity was short-circuiting her brain. "How come you clocked him, by the way? I don't think anyone else did. And I misinterpreted his attention as being due to us appearing overdressed for the pub."

A dark expression slid over his features, and his jaw clenched. "He noticed the way you were dressed all right. He kept staring at you when you were chatting to the girls. And not in a surreptitious, admiring kind of way, but in a predatory, sleazy way. It fucked me off."

Liv snuggled further into his side and felt the tension leave his body in response.

He took a deep breath, his tone becoming a little unsteady. "And to answer your question, the reason I clocked it is that I've not been able to take my eyes off you all night."

Her heart flipped, her breath getting caught in her throat.

His voice thrummed into her body as she pressed into his side.

"I've not been able to take my eyes off you for a long time, if I'm honest. And I don't just mean this weekend."

Her head began to spin. This felt dangerously close to him admitting what she wanted to hear. Would he take things further than he had the evening he'd stopped by after their blind date and told her she was beautiful? Anticipation made her heart beat so hard that blood whooshed in her ears.

"And I've been feeling more than a little jealous about you and Brodie." He sighed. "I know that makes me a dick."

She swallowed in an attempt to halt her palpitations, and stopped walking, placing her other arm around his waist to bring him in to face her. With her heels on, she could look him in the eye with a tip of her head. "You're not a dick."

Keeping his arm around her shoulders, he lifted his other hand to graze his fingers against her cheek. Her skin ached under his touch, filling her with an intense craving to feel it all over her body.

"I am," he said gruffly. "It's none of my business who you date."

"True," she said, eliciting a smile from him. "But Brodie and I aren't dating. We both decided on our first date that there was no chemistry."

He hesitated, searching her eyes. "But you guys seem . . . close."

"Yeah, he's become a friend. But that's all we are. He likes someone else." *And so do I.*

Arran nodded, some weight seeming to drift from his posture. "I just thought . . . because he was so tactile with you . . ."

She recalled how Brodie had whispered in her ear at dinner on Friday night and admitted he was testing to see if it got a rise out of Arran. Then her eyes widened as she connected the dots regarding his invitation to join him on the love seat. Had it been a little more than his being considerate? Had he purposely done it to make Arran jealous for her benefit? *The sneaky sneak.* "He's a tactile person. But I'm afraid to say I think he was overdoing it for your benefit."

He raised his eyebrows. "*My* benefit?"

Well. This was embarrassing. As much as she loved Brodie, she'd be giving him a swift kick up the arse when she next saw him. "He . . . told me he thought that you, er, liked me and were jealous. So he was playing up to it."

She was worried that might make him cross, but a smile tugged at the corner of his mouth. "He was, was he?"

Arran was so close that she was enveloped in his intoxicating scent. Each breath of it drove up her heart rate, making her head soft and fuzzy. "He didn't mean anything by it. He's a good guy."

"I know he is. I like him." He traced his fingers along her cheekbone, his voice turning husky. "I just don't like him touching you."

A sweet thrill coursed through her veins. *This is new. And I think I like it.*

"Last weekend. After you and Sam . . . spoke to Dave." He paused, swallowing hard. "I wanted to hold you. Comfort you. But Brodie had his arm around you and I thought . . ."

She went onto her tiptoes to touch her forehead to his, to comfort him, and he dipped his head to meet her. "You thought it was because we were a couple," she said softly, feeling terrible that she'd inadvertently given him the wrong idea and caused him pain.

He nodded, taking a shaky breath. "And not being able to hug you felt like shit."

Her voice came out in some sort of scratchy state. "I wanted you to hug me."

Arran lifted his chin, bringing his lips softly to her forehead and making her skin come alive. "I could tell you weren't okay. You might've fooled everyone else, but not me."

The heat was burning through every nerve ending, making her pulse throb. Making her want him closer still.

"I tried," he said, his voice hoarse. "I really did. To keep away from you. Give you and him some space. But I couldn't do it, Liv. Not when you needed me last week. And not when I saw that twat grabbing hold of you"—a hard edge coated his words—"and calling you a fucking bitch."

She pulled him closer, wanting to comfort him fully. She kissed his cheek and let her lips graze his stubble. "That's why you've been avoiding me?"

He nodded, his breath hitching as she pressed her lips to his jaw. "I'm sorry," he said.

"It's okay," she breathed against his skin, resting her face against his cheek.

They both stayed perfectly still, the cool night air stretching out in silence around them, with only the sound of their breathing audible. He lifted her chin to mesh her gaze with his, tracing her jaw with his fingers. She wanted his fingers all over her. "Your eyes are amazing." He drifted his gaze down. "I love that dress. You look beautiful." He looked back into her eyes. "I've been wanting to tell you that all night."

Her mouth was too dry to answer him, so she ended up nodding and uttering some kind of squeaky sound.

"And I love your red heels, and your red coat." He lifted the soft, spacious hood to cover her head, holding on to the sides to pull her impossibly closer. "Little Red Riding Hood," he whispered, making her pulse spike.

Her voice trembled. "That's how I think of it too. Little Red Riding Hood."

He smiled softly, and she became caught in it, like a small animal dazzled in the headlights. "I love your smile," she said, before she could stop herself.

He gently brushed the tip of his nose against hers. "Thank you."

Her brain fused. "You have nice teeth." *What?*

Arran didn't miss a beat. "All the better to eat you with."

Liquid fire flooded her veins and she grasped the back of his jacket tightly, unable to hold back any longer. "Arran."

He searched her eyes. "Yes?"

"I want . . ." She swallowed, her palpitations returning with a fierce intensity.

"What do you want, Aggie?" he whispered.

"I want you to kiss me."

The words were finally out there after years of thinking them. Her heart raced so hard she thought she might pass out.

He rubbed a thumb across her cheek, drawing a shaky breath as he glanced down at her mouth. "Thank fuck. Because I've wanted to kiss you for months."

Fireworks erupted in her chest.

He fixed her with those honey eyes and gently brought her face to his, closing the minuscule gap that remained between them. Somehow those two seconds seemed to last for hours. But when he brushed his lips against hers, an intense starburst of desire exploded inside her, sending a trail of fire down into her belly.

Arran moved his mouth over hers, the gentle grazing sensation of his stubble contrasting with the softness of his lips and intensifying the fire, pooling it lower and lower until her core clenched and her legs felt like jelly.

She held on to him tightly, breathing him in as he kissed her, the terror that she was forevermore spoiling their beautiful, tender friendship being scorched away by the intense desire rushing through her veins. Arran teased the seam of her lips with his tongue and she opened for him, reaching her arms up and around his neck, pressing her breasts against his chest. He swept his tongue into her mouth and she met him with hers, lifting herself onto her tiptoes to gain deeper contact and dragging her taut nipples against the fabric between them. The silk of his tongue slid against hers with an achingly intimate give-and-take that stirred up intense sensations she'd only ever experienced before during sex. When Arran looked at her it felt as if he were kissing and caressing her. When he kissed her it felt as if he were already inside her. So the idea of having sex with him blew her mind. He broke off for a split second to breathe her name and she gripped him more tightly, pressing her fingers into his scalp to bring his mouth down hard onto hers.

Footsteps sounded around the corner and they sprang apart, both breathing significantly more heavily than they had been a few moments before.

"Liv?" Elise's worried tone rang out as she rounded the corner, Nico in tow. "Oh, thank goodness," she said, stopping in her tracks and placing a hand over her heart. "I was worried when you didn't catch up, but I see Arran found you." She smiled at them both and Liv straightened a little, trying desperately to stop giving off the "we were totally just making out" vibe as she brought her hood back down.

"I'm fine, thanks," she said breathlessly, meeting Arran's blown-out pupils with a thunderbolt of lust. "I had a slight altercation with a pub patron on my way out, but then I broke his nose and Arran found me, so all good."

Rattled, she started walking toward the house before she gave anything away.

Elise shot her a panicked expression as she walked next to her. "*What?* Oh my God, Liv. Are you okay?"

The others fell into step as they went around the corner toward the house's sweeping driveway. Liv tried to drive down the intense feelings and sensations swarming inside her, hoping that the others wouldn't notice.

"Course she is," Nico said from behind. "Liv is the baddest ass among us. I've seen her in action at the gym."

Liv managed to throw him a smile over her shoulder, accidentally (or maybe not so accidentally) meeting the intense heat of Arran's eyes as she turned back again. He was looking at her like he wanted to devour her. *Yes please, Mr. Wolf.*

Elise flashed Nico a frown. "That's not the point, Nico. I know she can handle herself. But she shouldn't have to, especially when innocently enjoying a night out with friends." She took Liv's hand as they approached the front door. "Are you anxious about it? We can call the police with you."

She squeezed her friend's hand. "Thank you. That'd be great." She'd pretty much forgotten about the broken-nosed twat, such was the strength of the distraction Arran caused. However, as they crossed the threshold into the house, a sense of unease gathered at the back of her mind, making her stomach start to churn. Gently at first, but then harder as they took off their shoes and jackets and convened in the living area.

Liv took a seat, hoping that taking the weight off would help. "Maya and Sam aren't still up, are they? I'd rather not tell them until the morning." That would definitely be a selfish, third-wheel move.

"Nope," Nico replied with a smile. "They headed upstairs for some *shut-eye* as soon as we got home. Brodie and Ben have retired too."

Liv managed a smile, hoping they'd retired in the same manner as Sam and Maya. Score to Brodie, if so. Although he'd still be getting an ass whupping from her in the morning regarding his little stunts.

"I stayed up because I could tell the good Dr. Kowalski was worried," Nico continued.

"You needn't have," Elise informed him. "I told you I could go and search for her alone."

"And I told *you* that Arran had stayed back to walk with her. Therefore, you would've been the only one out there alone, and that's why I insisted on coming with you." Nico gave Elise a patient look, which only served to heighten her annoyance, judging by the thin-lipped expression she gave him in return. She clearly hated it when he was right.

"Anyway," Arran said, slicing through the tension. "We'd better call the police and get it reported." He took her hand and gave it a squeeze, making her shiver in response. "Shall I make some tea while you talk to them?"

Ah, a man after my own heart. She closed her eyes briefly as said heart began spasming in hefty palpitations, a panicky feeling infusing her gut. "Yes, please."

What is wrong with me? She took a deep breath. Perhaps her altercation had rattled her more than she thought. She tried to assess her emotions, remembering the sneer on the twat's face and then the crunch as she'd slammed her hand into his face.

"Watch your temper, Liv."

She took another breath.

"You're just like your father, Liv."

She shuddered. Had she been wrong to defend herself? Was guilt driving her unease?

Arran made them all tea and Liv watched him, taking deep breaths to stem her rapidly firing pulse and mounting nausea.

ARRAN TOOK HOLD OF LIV'S HAND AS THEY SAT ACROSS THE DINing table from the two policewomen, studying her face as she spoke. She answered their questions calmly and eloquently and he was so proud of her.

He'd pushed the memory of that kiss down in order to concentrate on the task at hand. But it had taken some willpower. It kept threatening to burst into the fore every time he looked at her.

When it was his turn to speak, he told the policewomen his part, albeit through gritted teeth because he was still so enraged at the twat.

He'd been waiting farther down the hill from the pub, just out of sight, when he'd heard Liv's voice. He'd doubled back to take a look and spotted the guy gripping her arm, then Liv karate chopping the sleazebag. So he'd started to run the few yards back to the pub, arriving right as Liv flattened the guy's nose.

Arran might've managed to control his temper and merely shout and lead Liv away, had he not heard him call her a fucking bitch. His temper had exploded and he'd slammed the dickhead into the wall.

He tried hard to sound as calm as Liv when he spoke, to keep the anger out of his voice, though he wasn't sure he'd succeeded. The policewomen gave them both sympathetic looks and noises as they took down the information.

When they finished, he and Liv saw the police out, past where Elise and Nico were sitting in the living area. They said that the guy shouldn't be hard to find and that they'd keep in touch. Luckily, there would also be CCTV footage from the area outside the pub.

Arran closed the door behind them, turning to gently take Liv's shoulders. "Okay?"

She nodded quickly, giving him a look that set his blood on fire, but then blinking with a worried expression and looking away.

"I'm fine," she said, not looking at him. "Just tired. Think I need to go to bed."

"Come on," he said. "Let's get you upstairs." He put his arm around her to go back into the living room. She collapsed against him like she had when they'd walked home, before they had kissed. But this time he sensed a new tension in her.

Elise stood as they entered the room. "How're you doing, Liv?"

Liv gave her a weak smile. "Just knackered."

"I'll come up to bed with you," Elise said, crossing over to take Liv's hand.

Arran's heart sank. He'd wanted to be the one to accompany her upstairs. Not because he wanted anything further to happen between them. Well, he did. But not tonight. He just had this inexplicable need to see her safely tucked up in bed. Ideally, he wanted to lie there with her and hold her all night.

But she was sharing a room with Elise, and suggesting otherwise felt inappropriate. Reluctantly, he let his arm slide off her shoulders as Liv took Elise's hand. She glanced back as the two of them neared the stairs, and he met her gaze with a spike in his pulse.

"Night, Arran," she said.

His voice was hoarse. "Night."

Liv dragged her eyes off him onto where Nico was coming to stand next to him. "Night, Nico."

"See you in the morning," Nico said. Arran could feel Nico's eyes on him as he continued to watch Liv and Elise climb the stairs, until they disappeared onto the upstairs landing.

Nico nudged his shoulder. "Are *you* okay? You seem pretty rattled too."

Arran swallowed, trying to decide whether witnessing Liv being harassed by that twat or the heat of their kiss was the thing rattling him the most. "Yeah. It's been an eventful night."

Nico put his arm around his shoulders and gave him a squeeze. "You get off to bed too. I'll tidy down here and lock up."

Arran nodded, giving him a grateful smile. "Thanks, man."

Nico ruffled his hair, then departed toward the table to clear away the mugs.

Arran climbed the stairs, his gait slowing as he passed Liv and Elise's door, before he continued to his and Nico's room.

Tomorrow, at Neist Point. It was time to speak to Liv about this thing between them.

Chapter
EIGHTEEN

ARRAN EYED LIV AS SHE SAT NEXT TO HIM, STARING OUT THE window of the van, and tried to fathom what she was thinking.

There was a new tension between them. There had, of course, been tension so far on the weekend—though that had been down to him and his jealousy. However, the situation had now evolved into something altogether more intense, and yet yesterday, he wouldn't have thought that possible.

All morning he'd been orbiting around her, feeling like she was too precious to let out of his sight. Ridiculous, when she didn't need him to protect her at all. But he'd felt like she'd still welcomed his backing her up, and that had given him the best feeling.

Since breakfast, though, he'd had to battle Sam for the role of protector. Once Liv's twin had discovered what had happened the previous evening, he'd been distraught that nobody had come to wake him to support his sister. So now he was trying to make up for it by hovering around her constantly. Nico had managed to elicit a smile from Sam when he'd commented that they all knew he and Maya hadn't been sleeping during the night's events, and there had been no way anyone had wanted to knock on their door and interrupt their shenanigans for fear of being traumatized for life.

Arran glanced over again at where Liv was still staring out the car window on the drive to Neist Point. He wished desperately that he could get inside her head. He needed some time alone with her to talk things through.

Holy shit. That kiss.

He'd known that kissing her would be good, but he hadn't anticipated just how mind-blowing it would be. The intensity of it had knocked the breath right out of his body and projected tangibly detailed images into his mind of what he wanted to do to her.

His determination to keep his distance had already been wearing thin as he'd watched Brodie being affectionate with her over the weekend. But then the sight of that twat gripping her arm outside the pub had exploded any remaining willpower he had over keeping his feelings to himself.

She was still turned away from him, and he wanted to hold her hand but didn't want to overstep the mark in front of the others. He'd been getting strong vibes that she didn't want the rest of the group to know what was happening between the two of them. Shit, *he* didn't even know what was happening between them. But he knew what he wanted to happen. Did she want that too? Last night he had been certain that she did.

Once they arrived at the car park and climbed out, he noticed that Liv was trying to walk apart from him.

Touché. That's what he'd been doing all weekend, and now the tables had turned. But why? *His* previous avoidance had been born from a wish to give her space when he'd thought she was involved with Brodie. Plus, if he were honest, it was an instinct to protect himself from his escalating feelings for her. But then he hadn't been able to hold back after the adrenaline spike of seeing her in danger, and he was glad he hadn't. If he'd only listened to Agnes's advice and spoken to Liv sooner rather than acting like a jealous fool, he would've discovered sooner that she and Brodie were just friends. Not that he'd be telling Agnes that anytime soon; the nosy bugger would be insufferable if he admitted she'd been right.

So why was she distancing herself now? She'd seemed the previous night as if she'd wanted him close. What had changed this morning?

Arran bided his time on the two-kilometer walk to the lighthouse at Neist Point. He'd keep his distance, then take the first opportunity to speak to her alone. But perhaps he'd need to recruit reinforcements to achieve that.

The view from Neist Point was spectacular, the most westerly edge of Skye looking out to the Outer Hebrides. It was a clear day, and the deep blue of the ocean stretched out to meet the bright baby blue of the sky, the salty sea breeze adding a crisp sting to their faces.

They were at the front of the lighthouse in the field of stone towers built by walkers. Sam and Maya were flanking Liv, as they had been for the whole walk. He roamed his gaze around for an ally and spotted Nico chatting to Brodie. Time to enlist some support.

Making his way over, he gave the men a nod. "Gentlemen. I need your assistance."

Nico raised his eyebrows. "Oh?"

Arran stuffed his hands in his pockets. "I need to speak to Liv. As in, speak to her alone. But I'm being inadvertently foiled by Sam and Maya."

Brodie grinned. "You're going to go for it, then?"

Arran flashed him a smile. "Yeah. Thanks for the push."

Brodie gave him a wink.

Nico laughed. "Thank fuck for that. Everyone's been waiting months for you to make a move, you total pussy."

Arran rolled his eyes, still smiling. "Fuck you. Are you going to help me out or not?"

Nico looked at Brodie. "I'm in."

Brodie shifted his lips into a determined line, nodding. "Let's do this."

Nico smiled. "I'll take Sam. You get Maya."

They both turned and walked away from Arran, sidling up to the trio of Sam, Maya, and Liv.

Nico slid an arm around Sam's shoulders and gestured at something nearer the lighthouse, and Brodie took Maya's elbow to whisper something in her ear. She nodded and followed him a few yards away.

Arran didn't waste any time. He closed the gap between him and the now solitary Liv. "Hey."

She startled, her voice hesitant. "Hi."

His confidence wavered. "Can we talk?"

Liv opened her mouth, pausing for a second before any sound came out. "Sure."

Taking her hand, he led her a little way back, away from the other groups of people. "How're you feeling after we gave the statements?"

She nodded. "Okay, thanks. I'm glad the police are involved and can sort it before the guy does any actual harm."

"Good. You can talk to me, though, you know? If you feel anxious about anything."

She smiled, her green eyes lighting up, and for a second, he was lost at sea.

"I appreciate that," she said. "You're a great friend."

"Yeah. About that." He took a breath, feeling like he was climbing out on a limb, where the cliffs fell away beyond the lighthouse. In his mind's eye the wind buffeted him, and sharp rocks and rough seas lay below. He rubbed his chest. "Friends don't kiss each other the way we did last night."

"I know," she said quickly, and for a moment, his heart lifted, pushing away the hollow feeling in his chest. Was she going to say what he hoped? But before she could continue, his phone began to ring in his pocket. And he knew it would be Jess. *Fuck.*

Liv looked him in the eyes, and he could tell she knew it too. "You'd better answer," she told him. "It might be something about Jayce."

He pulled the phone out, also concerned that might be the case, but suspecting it was more likely to be one of Jess's newfound, but very regular, check-ins. He answered it, taking hold of Liv's hand when she looked as if she were about to move away and shaking his head. *Stay*, he mouthed at her.

He quickly answered Jess's usual questions, about what he was doing and whom he was with. Then he made an excuse and ended the call.

He took a breath. "You were saying. About the kiss."

She studied him for a few seconds, blinking as she searched his face. She was trembling a little and worry mounted in his heart. She opened her mouth, then glanced down at where his phone was still in his hand and closed it again. After another couple of seconds, her voice came out strained. "I don't really know what to say, to be honest." She blinked, her eyes wet.

His heart rate spiked. "Hey, it's okay." He held out his arms to invite her in but gave her the space to decide whether to take him up on it, rather than going in to touch her. She immediately came to him, letting him envelop her in a hug, nestling against his front. "What's wrong? Did I do something to hurt you?"

"No, no, not at all," she said quickly, shaking her head against his chest. "Everything I said was true and I wanted to kiss you so badly. But then when we got back to the house I just felt so sick and panicky and . . . I just . . . I don't know what's wrong with me."

He stroked her hair, wishing he could make it all better for her.

"Is it that guy from last night? It was a really traumatic event. And then giving the statement must have been hard."

"Yeah, maybe." Her voice was small. "But I feel like it's something else too. I've felt like this before when I . . ." Her voice trailed off.

"When what, Aggie?"

She sighed. "It doesn't matter."

He hesitated, wanting to help her but not wanting to push too hard. "Is it anything to do with you becoming Jayce's teacher? I don't want to cross any boundaries you aren't comfortable with."

"No, it's not that." She fell silent, and he didn't know what to say for the best. All his instincts said there was something she was hiding, a secret she kept to herself. But perhaps it was something unconscious, rather than an issue she was able to put into words. He didn't want to push her before she was ready to try.

"It's okay, sweetheart. I'm here for you, whenever you feel ready and able to talk about it."

She squeezed him tight. "Thank you. That means so much to me." He felt her swallow hard against his chest. "I'm sorry for being fucked-up. I shouldn't have kissed you when I'm such a mess."

Arran pulled back and lifted her chin to meet his eyes. "You don't have to apologize to me. You're always there for me and everyone else, and I need you to know that I want the privilege of doing the same for you."

Her chin wobbled, her eyes welling up. "I'm so glad I've got you as a friend." She blinked a few times, clearly struggling to keep the tears in, and it wrecked him. "I don't want to lose that with you. Please tell me I haven't spoiled it."

He shook his head gently, stroking her cheek in an attempt to comfort her. "Never."

She gave him a wobbly smile. His beautiful, brave girl. He would wait for her to be ready to talk to him, as long as it took.

Chapter
NINETEEN

ARRAN WILLED HIMSELF TO START PAINTING, BUT THEN HE SET down the brush with a sigh, folding his arms and staring into the distance. He hadn't been able to concentrate since returning home from the sten weekend for worrying about Liv. Every time he messaged her, she said she was fine, glossing over everything. He was desperate to see her in person because he knew he'd be able to read her better face-to-face.

But she had been busy with work, and his painting workload had steadied so he hadn't needed any weekend help with Jayce. Not that he'd feel right asking Liv at the moment anyway; she needed his support—not to be in his service.

Standing abruptly, he decided he needed some fresh Highland air.

He left the studio, getting on his fur-lined leather jacket and trainers and heading out into the late afternoon sun to his car.

When he parked at the Tavern pub and exited the vehicle, the crispness of the spring air that little bit higher in the hills seemed to cleanse his mind. He struck out for the tree line, heading through the woodland path that led out to a clearing and across the field. He stopped at the point where the field was fenced, beyond which the grass gave way to a rocky descent into the valley.

Leaning on the fence, he looked out over blue skies dotted with little puffs of white cloud. The gray, still snow-topped peaks of the Glenavie Mountains jutted into the blue, then dipped down into the green valley below. On impulse, he took out his phone and snapped a photo.

He'd painted this view before, as a night scene. Sam had taken the picture for him and it had turned out to be one of Sam and Maya's favorite stargazing spots.

He glanced at the lush green of the grass, and Liv's eyes came to mind. But thinking about them brought a tinge of pain and frustration—at himself for failing to help her. Especially when she had never failed to come through for him in the past.

Something nudged his arm, and he came out of his thoughts to see a cute Highland cow giving him a curious look through its long, shaggy brown hair as it stood beside him at the fencing.

"Hey, pal," he said, giving the creature a gentle rub behind the ear.

Someone wolf whistled behind him, and when he turned, Sam was there, flashing him a grin. "You look like you're posing for a catalog. Fur-lined leather, gazing ponderously into the valley while leaning on a fence."

Arran managed a laugh.

Sam joined him at the fence, glancing at the cow. "And you've got a new friend too."

The cow moved its gaze onto Sam, then turned its back on them and shuffled off.

Arran shot Sam a look. "I don't think he likes you."

Sam stuck out his bottom lip. "How dare he. I'm fucking de-lightful."

"Dunno about that," Arran muttered with a smile.

Sam gave his arm a gentle shove, then leaned on the wooden perimeter next to him.

Arran eyed him. "Now it's a double catalog pose."

Sam furrowed his brow, leaning his bearded chin on his thumb and index finger as he adopted a rather good catalog pose. Arran snorted, shifting his phone to snap a shot of him. "That's going right onto my Insta."

Smiling, Sam relaxed again.

Arran stuffed his phone back into his pocket. "What're you doing here anyway? I thought you preferred it here at night."

Sam nodded. "Doing a little recce for the wedding venue."

Arran smiled. "Still going with the outdoor idea for the ceremony?"

"Yep." Sam gestured behind them. "We'll have a gazebo in case we get kiboshed by the weather. Then onto the castle for the reception."

"Cool. Hope my new pal Hamish can make it," Arran said, gesturing at the cow, which was heading down the hill.

Sam smiled. "You've named him already?"

"Yeah," Arran said. "I think we're kindred spirits. And he looks like a Hamish—Hamish the Highland cow."

Sam laughed. "I'll invite him. I heard he looks awesome in a kilt."

Arran took in the genuine excitement in Sam's eyes and assumed it was related to getting married rather than to the idea of having a Highland cow in a kilt at his wedding. "I'm looking forward to it," he told his friend.

"Me too," Sam said, giving him a side glance. Then he shifted over to nudge Arran's shoulder with his own. "What's up?"

Arran ran a hand over his hair. "Why would anything be up?"

"You've been giving off a very subdued and decidedly un-Arran-like vibe of late."

He swallowed, avoiding his friend's gaze. "No, I haven't."

"Hmm."

Arran chanced a glance over at Sam, who was studying him rather intently. "Stop staring at me, dude."

A smile playing on his lips, Sam shifted his gaze back out over the valley. "Sorry. You're just so damned handsome, ya know?"

Arran let out a soft laugh.

Sam cleared his throat. "Is this about Liv?"

Arran's pulse picked up, his mouth awfully dry all of a sudden. "I don't know what you mean."

Sam sighed. "Come on, man. I've been waiting for you to talk to me about it, but it seems as if I'll be waiting until we're ninety and sitting next to each other in our armchairs at the nursing home. So, I'm bringing it up."

Shit. Why hadn't he at least anticipated this conversation? If things had gone the way he'd wanted, then it would've involved telling Sam at some point. "It's . . . kind of complicated. And I didn't want to upset you."

Sam met his gaze, raising his eyebrows. "You're not seriously thinking I'd be pissed off?"

He didn't know what to say. "Well, yeah. Kind of."

Sam shook his head. "Fuck, dude. I'm not the sort of guy who doesn't want his sister to have a love life."

Arran sucked in a breath. "I know, man. I'm not saying that."

Sam eyed him. "And if she's with my best friend, the coolest guy on the planet, then that's amazing."

His heart swelled, and for a second Arran wasn't sure what to say. Sam smiled. "And it might have escaped your notice, but I'm with *Liv's* best friend. So it'd be pretty hypocritical of me to object."

"Good point," Arran said, his tension easing a little. "But before you get too excited, I've stumbled at the first hurdle. Something happened between us, but now she's backed off."

Sam frowned, nodding. "Something happened on Skye?"

"Yeah, just a kiss." Although it had felt more significant than "just a kiss." He tried to swallow down the pain in his chest. "How did you know something happened?"

"A feeling. The way you've both been acting since."

Arran snapped his gaze onto Sam, concerned. "She's been acting different?"

"Yeah. Kind of subdued." Sam smiled. "Kind of like you. Hence, I took two, added another two, and hey presto. We have a four."

Arran wondered for a moment why the saying was "put two and two together." Surely putting one and one together was even simpler. Though not when it came to him and Liv.

He wasn't sure how much to tell Sam. The little Liv had confessed was in confidence, plus he didn't want to upset Sam and make him worry about his sister. Especially when he was shouldering a lot of wedding-planning-related stress. Arran knew from experience that though it was a happy time, it was also a full-on one.

Sam pursed his lips. "Weird that she's backed off. Because I had definite vibes that she fancied you. And when I asked her about it, she didn't deny it. Plus, Maya intimated that Liv had confided in her about it."

Arran nodded. He didn't doubt Liv was attracted to him; he believed her when she'd said she'd wanted to kiss him, and he'd felt it too. Their connection was intense. "I don't think it's lack of interest. I'm just . . . not sure what's going on with her." He opted not to say anything further, to protect both Liv's and Sam's interests.

Sam raised an eyebrow. "So basically, in summary, you kissed her and now she doesn't want anything to do with you?" He grinned. "Maybe you're just a really bad kisser."

Arran couldn't help laughing. "Watch it, Holland. I'll have you know my kissing skills are top-notch."

Sam was grinning. "Don't worry, I know. I heard all about it from Chloe Reid in sixth year."

"Really?" Arran said, raising his eyebrows.

"Yep. She was singing your praises to anyone who'd listen."

Arran smiled. "Nice."

"I'll bet if you got a bit of time alone with Liv, you'd discover what's gone wrong." Sam rubbed his beard. "She's so shit at lying, you'd be able to figure out what's up."

"Maybe," Arran said, aware that he'd been thinking the very same thing before he'd left the house—that if he could just see her face-to-face, and one-on-one, he'd be able to help her figure stuff out.

"I'm telling you," Sam continued. "She was the first to realize Santa wasn't real and did a really crappy job at hiding it from me."

Arran dropped his jaw in mock affront. "Santa isn't real? What the fuck, dude?"

Sam laughed.

"I'd love to get some quality time with her," Arran said. "I wouldn't push it; just be there with her and give her some space."

Sam gave him a soft smile. "I tell you what," he said, leaning back to stuff his hands into his pockets. "There's something I've been thinking about. Something I wanted to get Liv for our birthday but I didn't get around to it because of wedding brain. And it might help your cause."

Intrigued, Arran took his arms off the fence to face him. "What is it?"

Sam took a breath. "She loves your portraits. I want to commission one of her."

Immediately, his sea-tones palette came to mind as he imagined capturing Liv's eyes, his autumnal shades tracing the shiny tendrils of her hair. *I would love that.*

"You can take the commission and see what happens," Sam

soothed. "No pressure. It's just you and Liv, like always. And if something happens, well." He shrugged, then put on a singsong voice. "Bo-nus."

Arran smiled. He'd finally get to do what he'd been daydreaming about: paint the gorgeous loveliness that was Olivia Agnes Holland.

PICKING UP JAYCE'S COPY OF *THE GRUFFALO*, ARRAN GOT HIM SET-tled in his bed and began to read.

He looked up when Jayce didn't join in as usual. "What's up, buddy?"

Jayce blinked. "I want Lib."

A cavern of ice opened up in his chest. *You and me both.* "I know," he told his son in a soothing tone.

"Lib does the voices," Jayce said, gesturing at the book.

Arran raised his eyebrows as if affronted. "Are you saying Daddy isn't as good at the voices?"

Jayce looked at him silently, casting his preschooler judgment.

Arran let out a breath. "Wow. That cuts me deep, little dude."

He began reading again, this time channeling his inner Liv and trying to do the different voices for all the characters. Jayce seemed a bit happier with his efforts, but Arran knew it was a poor substitute for Liv.

When the book was finished, Arran kissed his son's soft curls, pausing for a second to breathe him in.

He said good night and left the room, leaning against the door as he paused on the upstairs landing. Liv had infiltrated their lives over the past year, filling in all the gaps that needed filling. As much as Arran had said he'd wanted to avoid commitment, he hadn't even noticed that he'd been making a big commitment with his close friend, and she'd done the same with Jayce.

He cursed himself for (a) being so slow on the uptake when it came to his attraction to Liv that it had taken him more than a decade to realize she was right under his nose—what a dick; and (b) not going out on a limb that night on their blind date and telling her he wanted her, even though he was worried she didn't feel the same way. What had he to lose? Just his stupid goddamn pride.

He had to make up for lost time and show her he was there for her. For her sake, his, and Jayce's.

Chapter
TWENTY

LIV CLIMBED OUT OF THE CAR AND TOOK A DEEP BREATH. "COME on. You can do this. You're just a normal girl, coming to sit for her portrait. Not someone who can't kiss the guy she desperately wants without having some kind of mental breakdown." She looked around, double-checking that none of the neighbors had witnessed that little pep talk. Ironically it wouldn't have helped her case in proving that she wasn't having a breakdown. For a moment she could've sworn she saw the net curtains twitch in the house next door to Arran's.

Once she rang the doorbell, she waited anxiously for him to answer. When he did, she had to reach out and hold the doorframe for support because, oh my God, if the guy hadn't become an extra fifty percent sexier since the last time she'd seen him. How was that even possible when he'd already been one hundred percent sexy?

Arran Adebayo. One hundred and fifty percent sexy.

He smiled as she leaned against the doorframe, staring at him, trying to stand upright on her wobbly knees.

She cleared her throat. "Hi."

Arran's smile widened, making his eyes twinkle, and she thought she might drop down dead. "Want to come in, or should I paint you on my doorstep?"

She straightened, managing to walk into the house and not outwardly react to his evocative scent. The memory of him grasping her red hood and pulling her close surfaced. *"All the better to eat you with."* A shiver ran down her spine.

"Liv?"

"Mm-hmm?"

"Did you hear me?"

She paused in the hallway. "Er, no. Sorry. What did you say?"

He was still wearing an amused smile. "Do you want some tea before we start?"

"Oh, yes, please." She removed her jacket and shoes and followed him into the kitchen, where she helped him make two mugs of tea, which they took into the studio. "Can I have a quick nosy?" she asked him. There were a few new pieces since she was last there.

"Be my guest." He busied himself with getting some paints prepared, and it occurred to her that he was acting very naturally. Not like he thought she was unhinged and was keen to run a mile. She relaxed a little, remembering his comforting words at Neist Point. The studio lights were bright in the Saturday evening dusk, casting illumination onto the sofa where she would sit to be painted.

Moving over to it, she took a seat. "It was so cool of Sam and Maya to commission my portrait." She sipped her tea. "Though a bit weird that I'll have a picture of myself hanging on the wall."

He smiled. "It'll look beautiful."

Her breath caught in her throat. He kept telling her that she was beautiful, and he made her believe it. Arran Abeo Adebayo was a very charming man. She sighed internally. He was also hot as fuckity-fuck. "At first I assumed you'd be painting me from a photo."

He shook his head. "It's better to have a live sitting. I only do it the other way when the person wouldn't be available to sit for long enough."

She settled back into the sofa, watching him prep. "How long will it take?"

Arran paused what he was doing to run a hand over his hair. "Depends on how it goes. I've usually got a deadline to work to, so I ramp up my schedule to meet it. But if it's not needed by a certain date, then maybe about six weeks."

She sipped her tea. "Good thing I have no social life, then."

He smiled gently. "I'm ready when you are."

LIV TRIED TO STOP LAUGHING BUT IT WAS DIFFICULT. "SORRY. I'M doing not well at sitting still."

A smile tugged at the corner of his mouth. "That's okay. I love seeing you laugh."

Her heart rate picked up. "Thank you."

There was silence for a few moments while he frowned in concentration at the canvas. It made him look sexy. *For goodness' sake. I think everything he does is sexy. I even thought it was hot when he knocked that paint over earlier.*

She cleared her throat. "To be fair, it is *you* who's been making me laugh. So . . ."

He slid his gaze over to hers, eliciting an adrenaline spike. "So . . . it's my own fault?"

"Precisely." She shot him a grin.

Arran smiled as he continued what he was doing.

Liv fidgeted in her seat. "When can I see?"

"In a minute." He checked his watch. "We'll stop shortly. Four hours is long enough for today."

"Four hours? Wow." Liv glanced at her own watch, feeling the need to confirm the timing. "It only felt like thirty minutes."

He looked up at her below furrowed eyebrows. "Because I've been keeping you entertained with my sparkling wit?"

"Yes." She held his gaze for a moment and her heart felt as if it was about to beat out of her chest. *Why am I not jumping his bones again? Oh yeah. Because I'm an emotional hot mess.*

"Okay," he said, putting down his brush and wiping his hands on a cloth. "You can have a peek. But remember there's a ways to go."

Liv practically jumped out of her chair in her hurry to cross the room. She leaned on his shoulder to take in the canvas. There were lines sketching the outline of her hair and shoulders, and her hair was blocked out in a dark mass of waves. The proportions of her face were sketched in.

She opened her mouth in awe. "Wow. It looks like me already."

He gestured at the canvas. "Next, I'll start painting in the light and shade of your face, then the tones in your hair. After that I'll refine your face a little more and paint in the upper body. I like to save the eyes for last." He glanced into her eyes for a second, then away again quickly, clearing his throat. "Do you need to head off straightaway or have you got time for another cup of tea?"

"Tea always wins out for me." She helped him tidy away his equipment, then followed him to the kitchen. "Do I need to wear the same top each time I come?"

He smiled. "No, it's not essential. We can just select what color you want it painted in."

They made the tea and sat at the breakfast bar together, chatting. She pondered the fact that he'd been very calm today, joking around less than usual. At first she'd worried it was because she'd upset him, but as time had gone on, she'd realized that he was giving her space. And that turned her heart to mush. She just wished she could find the words to explain what was going on in her head—and her heart. But after years of suppressing her negative emotions it was proving difficult to express them.

Her gaze snagged on his mouth as he sipped his tea. The sensation of having his lips pressed against hers was seared into her memory. Absently, she lifted a hand to touch her bottom lip.

"Okay?" he asked, eyeing her attentively.

She dropped her hand. "Yes, thanks."

He smiled and she recalled him doing so on the night of the kiss, and then her blurting out that he had nice teeth. *Cringe.*

Despite that embarrassing moment, every time she thought about it, that same delicious heat pooled between her legs, making her squirm in an attempt to relieve the ache. Nobody had made her feel that way with just a kiss before.

She fiddled with her mug. She longed to kiss him again. But every time she considered voicing that desire, the idea of what would come next came to mind. They would no longer be "just friends." She'd never had a relationship, sexual or otherwise, with someone she was so close to emotionally. She wanted it, but whenever she considered it, a deep, breath-stealing anxiety took hold. She shivered, trying to even out her breathing.

"Are you sure you're okay?" he asked, frowning.

"Absolutely," she replied, closing her eyes briefly as she sipped her tea.

He was watching her quietly. "Can you come back again tomorrow afternoon? Jess will be dropping Jayce off after lunch, but we can do a bit more during his nap."

She nodded. "That would be great. Then I get to see Jayce too, when he wakes up."

The corner of his mouth quirked. "If you're sure you won't get bored doing this two days in a row."

She managed a smile. "In your company? I very much doubt it."

He gave her a soft smile, which made her feel like she'd won the lottery.

Chapter
TWENTY-ONE

ARRAN NARROWED HIS EYES AS HE CONCENTRATED ON THE canvas. "Mountains or beach?"

"That's an easy one," Liv replied. "Mountains."

He smiled. "Same. Your turn."

Liv thought for a moment. "Okay . . . when you're out at a restaurant, is it starter or dessert?"

He slowly lifted his gaze from the canvas in mock disapproval. "That's not an *or* situation. I'd want both."

She grinned, pointing her finger at him. "Correct. It was a trick question, and you passed. Your turn."

Smiling, he went back to the painting. "Scones or cake?"

She huffed out a breath in mock exasperation. "That, Mr. Adebayo, is a silly question."

He met her eyes. "But what about those wee cakes we had at our afternoon tea? Surely some of those rivaled the scones."

She pursed her lips. "Nothing can rival scones." Her phone buzzed in her pocket, signaling a message, but she ignored it. "Scones rule." Her phone buzzed again twice in succession. *I'm popular today.*

"Fair enough," he replied.

"What about . . . Han Solo or Luke Skywalker?" Her phone buzzed yet again, and this time her curiosity won out and she reached into her pocket to retrieve it.

"Luke," Arran replied, continuing to paint. "The Force is strong with that one. Plus the poor guy had major daddy issues."

Smiling, Liv unlocked her phone. But the expression froze on her face as she registered the sender of the messages.

"What's up?" Arran asked, looking at her with a frown.

She ran her eye down the stream of texts, her blood freezing in her veins and the hairs on the back of her neck standing on end. For a moment she couldn't speak.

He put his brush down and came to sit next to her, wiping his hands on a cloth as he went. "It's not him, is it?"

She nodded, her mouth dry. It was impossible to read the messages out loud, because just glancing through them made her feel sick. So she showed him the screen. He closed his warm hand around hers, and they held the phone together as they read through.

I'm sick of your disrespectful attitude.

It disgusts me. Ignoring my needs
constantly. It's so selfish.

When I message you I expect a prompt
reply. You can't be that busy with work.

You're only a glorified baby sitter after all.
Not much brain power needed for that.

I want to know the date for your brother's
wedding and I expect an answer from you. Today.

Arran slid his arm around her shoulders, bringing her close and kissing the top of her head. She closed her eyes to counteract the burning sensation within them, her hand with the phone flopping into Arran's lap, where his hand closed over hers.

"I'm sorry," he said quietly.

She turned her face into his chest, trying to swallow the painful lump in her throat. "I should've blocked him."

He lifted his other arm to circle her, pulling her right into him and holding her tightly. "Shall we block him now?"

She attempted to summon the power of logic. "Yeah. Could you do it for me, please? I don't want to look at it again."

His voice was soft. "Sure." He kept an arm around her as he took the phone and quickly tapped the screen. A few seconds later, he placed it next to him on the couch, then wrapped his arm around her again.

They stayed silent for a moment, Arran stroking her hair as she pressed her face against his chest. Maybe, if she pressed hard enough, it'd squeeze the painful thoughts from her mind.

"I deleted the messages too," he said, the vibration thrumming soothingly against her cheek.

Her throat felt tight. "Thank you."

The bass of his voice was calming. "Do you think he's still in town?"

The idea somehow seemed less scary when Arran was holding her. "I don't think so. It's been a few weeks. Hopefully Sam saw him off last time."

He kissed the top of her head again, then eased her away, meeting her eyes and tucking her hair behind her ear. "You sit here for a minute. I'm going to bring us some tea."

She managed a weak smile. "That sounds great."

Arran paused, brushing his thumb over her cheek, and it

seemed as if he wanted to say something more. But then he pressed his lips quickly to her forehead and got up.

When he came back, it seemed as if he'd only just left the room, and Liv realized she'd been sitting and staring at the wall with a blank mind the whole time he'd been in the kitchen.

She accepted a warm mug of tea as he sat down, slipping his arm around her. "How're you doing?" he asked.

She sighed. "Trying not to think about it."

He squeezed her shoulder. "Hopefully you won't hear from him again now that he's blocked."

Blinking, she took a deep breath. "I should've blocked him years ago. I should've known that if I did ever hear from him, then it wouldn't be because he was actually interested in me."

He ducked his head to look at her, and she turned hers to meet his eyes, leaning back against the heat of his arm. "There's nothing wrong in that, Liv. It was only natural that you'd hold out that hope."

She took a deep breath. "Natural, or naive?"

He smiled. "Perhaps a little of both. But naivety isn't a sin. It's a reflection of being a good person at heart."

A jolt of anxiety pierced her chest, and nausea circled her stomach. "Do you think that we're in charge of the goodness of our hearts? Or is it something printed from birth? Like, as in . . . genetically determined?"

He frowned, studying her face. "I think it's complex. A bit of nature and nurture. Like most things."

She nodded, the nausea intensifying and making her a little breathless. What if it was more nature than nurture?

"What is it?" Arran asked, his eyes shining with concern.

Dean's voice cut through her thoughts. *"For fuck's sake, Liv. You're just like your dad."*

She swallowed. "Nothing." She sipped her tea. "You know, Mum told us these stories about how he behaved when they first got together. He seemed like this huge romantic. Showering her with affection, making these grand gestures. One time he got on-stage at a gig they'd gone to, grabbed the mic, and told the crowd he was in love with her." She took a breath, noticing that Arran was listening intently. "And when he proposed to her, he hired one of those small aircraft pulling a banner that read 'Marry Me Tara.'"

"Wow," Arran said, his brow deeply furrowed. "That's intense."

She nodded. "I've read up on it. It's called love bombing, and it's what narcissists do to tether their . . . victim to them, emotionally."

"Shit," he said softly. "That's sick."

"Yeah." She took a deep breath. "Catriona was the same with Sam. She wasn't as showy, but she used the same tactic. Stealthily creating scenarios where he'd end up hurt, then comforting him like his savior. Overboard on the public displays of affection, acting like she was running around after his every need at home."

He nodded. "I remember all that. I'm sorry to say that I thought she was just madly in love with him. So I guess I was love bombed by association."

Liv shook her head. "It's not your fault. None of us spotted it at first. And the only person to blame was her." She pushed her glasses up her nose, letting out a shaky breath. "The gestures of 'love' get withdrawn, with their victim believing if only they could behave in just the right way, then they'd get it back again." Her voice was starting to wobble, so she stopped and sipped her drink quietly.

"It sounds like you've read a lot about it," he said, tucking a wave of hair behind her ear. "Is that because of what happened to your mum and Sam?"

She hesitated, her mouth going dry. "Yeah, I suppose so."

He was studying her again. She could almost hear the click and whir of his brain.

"I'm sorry," she told him, closing her eyes in discomfort.

He raised his eyebrows. "What for?"

Liv opened her eyes to meet his. "For off-loading on you. Sam's your best mate, so hearing all this is upsetting."

Hesitating for a moment, he placed his mug on the floor, followed by hers, then took her shoulders. "Liv, you don't need to apologize to me. I want you to tell me stuff because I'm your friend. I told you that before. And it applies to everything, not just that scumbag we had to report to the police at the time." He gave her a soft smile. "I feel like you always hold back from leaning on me. Or anyone else. I think you're too consumed by protecting everyone's feelings."

Her pulse was tripping along—because every word rang true.

"The only thing that does upset me," he said slowly, "is that everything you've just said was about your mum and Sam. Not you." His gaze was warm but intense. "Dave's behavior affected you too, Liv. Just as much as Sam. You deserve to tell *your* side of the story. You deserve empathy in return for the shiploads of stuff you dish out to everyone else. You can tell me anything you want, and you don't need to worry that I won't be able to hear it. I'm your friend and I want to be there for you."

She was starting to feel a little dizzy now. Overwhelmed. His words soothed her psyche, and she remembered Sam giving her a similar sentiment at Christmas, trying to encourage her to open up. And yet she still hadn't been able to confide in him properly either. *"Don't be negative, Liv."*

She nodded, tears pricking at her eyes. "Thank you."

Arran smiled, and she wrapped her arms around him in a hug, trying to convey her appreciation through her body rather than the words that were failing her.

The baby monitor on Arran's desk crackled to life with the sound of Jayce waking from his afternoon nap.

Liv lifted her head from Arran's chest. "Can I fetch him? I've not had a Jayce cuddle in ages and I'm getting withdrawal symptoms."

He had a soft look on his face. "Course. I'll come with you."

They stood and left the studio for the stairs, Liv going ahead so that she could be the first into the nursery to surprise Jayce. Her heart was tripping with excitement by the time she neared the top of the stairs. Seeing him in a classful of kids at nursery school wasn't the same as being one-on-one with him at home.

She cracked open the door, waiting for him to spot her. He was sitting up in his cot bed, facing away from her. She let the door open a little farther, the creak of it causing Jayce to turn his head. The wide smile that spread over his face as he spotted her swelled her heart so big it seemed to push all thoughts of Douchebag Dave out of her mind.

Jayce sat up straight in bed. "Miss Lib!"

She entered the room, grinning. "Hey, buddy!" Reaching out, she lifted him into her arms, cuddling him close and absorbing the adorable squishiness. Jayce leaned back to finger her glasses and she rubbed her nose against his.

There was another creak at the door, and she lifted her gaze to see Arran doing the devastating leaning-against-the-doorframe-with-folded-arms pose, giving her a hot, fuzzy feeling. He smiled at her with a kind of wistful longing that she didn't know what to do with but really liked nonetheless.

Chapter
TWENTY-TWO

THE NURSERY SCHOOL KIDS LOOKED A LITTLE BORED TO ARRAN. It was career day in Miss Holland's class and the ensemble were currently listening to Creepy Married Dad Guy go on about how important his work as an orthopedic surgeon was. Every so often the guy would glance over at Liv, clearly attempting to gauge whether she was impressed. The bloke was good-looking, and his patter no doubt usually got him a lot of attention. Despite the silver wedding ring on his left ring finger.

Dickhead.

Although so far, Liv didn't look very impressed at all. A smile tugged at Arran's mouth.

The knowledge that Liv had opened up to him at their last portrait sitting went some way toward encouraging him that they would be okay. She'd let him be there for her. Leaned on him a little. And it had felt good.

Clearly there was much more to her story. But he was in this for the long game and happy to wait to hear it.

Liv sidled up to him and went onto her tiptoes to whisper in his ear, as Creepy Married Dad Guy kept droning on. "You ready for your presentation?"

He nodded, breathing in her sweet scent with an acceleration in his heart rate. "Yeah, but mine's a bit more interactive than this dude's."

"Thank goodness," she whispered, giving a small shudder, which drew a chuckle from his lips.

He turned his head to speak right into her ear, keeping his voice low. His lips grazed her skin, sparking temptation within him. "If his work is so important, how come he's always hanging around at the nursery school like a bad smell?"

He felt her convulse slightly as she suppressed a laugh, the bare skin of her arm brushing against his. She had goose bumps.

"Apparently," she said in a low voice, "according to a local source, he's been suspended from work for a bit. Got caught shagging one of the nursing staff in a broom cupboard when he was meant to be performing an operation."

Arran arched an eyebrow in his best Mrs. MacKay impression. "Very important work indeed."

Liv shot him a grin.

Broom-Cupboard Shagger kept droning on, something about intramedullary nails, whatever they fuck they were. Arran suppressed a yawn. What kind of twat used medical terminology in a talk for four-year-olds? This kind, obviously.

Liv clapped her hands together loudly, cutting the guy off. "Thank you so much to Charlie's daddy! What a wonderful talk, wasn't it, everybody?"

The kids were chatting among themselves and pretty much ignoring the speaker. The man himself seemed oblivious, clearly laboring under the misapprehension that Liv's enthusiastic outburst was a sign of true admiration rather than a tactic to get the fucker to shut the hell up.

"Okay, class," Liv said, commanding the kids' attention with just the tone of her voice. Arran's heart swelled with admiration. "Time for us to move over into the painting corner for Jayce's daddy's talk. And then Emily's mummy will speak to us in the messy play area."

There was much excited chatter as the children came over to where Arran had set up some small easels for everyone. Arran went around the group handing out aprons, and Liv helped the kids get them on. Cupboard Shagger was standing to one side eyeing them all, with Mrs. Mackay standing quite close next to him. Perhaps hoping to snag herself a shot in the supply cupboard later.

"Okay," Arran said, rubbing his hands together. "Who likes to paint?"

"Me!" the whole class shouted, most of them shoving their hand right up in the air in an enthusiastic display.

"Excellent," he said, taking a seat by his own easel. "Because painting is what I do for a living."

There was a murmur of awe from the class at the idea that something they saw as a fun activity could be an actual job.

"I want to be a painter," a wee girl said.

"Me too," said the boy next to her.

"I'm going to be a painter like my daddy," Jayce said proudly, and it made Arran's heart soar. He glanced over at Liv, who was sitting among the kids, and she was looking at him with a soft smile on her face.

"Right. Down to business!" Arran said. "Each of you has a little mirror pinned to your easel. We're going to have a go at self-portraits. That's where you paint yourself. So have look in the mirror, and try to paint what you see onto your paper."

There was more excited chatter as the children took up their brushes and began dipping them in the paints, splashing color onto their paper.

Arran did a quick representation of himself on his own paper, then got up to go around the class and praise each one in turn.

Every now and again Arran would look up from whomever he was chatting to, to find Liv watching him with that same soft look. And it made him all the more determined to be there for anything she needed from him.

"COME ON, THEN. TELL ME WHAT'S HAPPENING," BRODIE TOLD her, his blue eyes sparkling through the phone screen.

Liv set the phone on the table, leaning it against her mug, while she shoved a few things into her bag. "Nothing's happening. He's just painting my portrait."

Brodie rolled his eyes. "You're telling me that after all my jealousy-inducing hard work on the sten, nothing happened with you guys?"

"Well . . ." She paused. "It did. But only one kiss."

He huffed out a breath. "For goodness' sake, woman. Just jump the guy already."

Liv zipped her bag, lifting the phone again and choosing to ignore that statement. "Enough about me. I want the deets about you and Ben. Did something happen with you guys? I noticed you both disappeared up to bed around the same time. But the next day we were all too distracted with the police for me to ask you about it."

Brodie frowned. "Are you okay, by the way? After all that?"

"Fine," she told him, suppressing the weird, guilty feeling that surfaced whenever she remembered the guy's bloody nose. "They've got it in hand. Now, stop changing the subject. What happened with Ben?"

A broad smile broke out over Brodie's face. "A gentleman never tells."

"Aha!" she said, pointing at the screen. "That says everything."

Brodie just continued to smile at her.

She shook her head. "Anyway. I need to head to Arran's now. We've got another sitting for my portrait."

He raised his eyebrows. "Sounds like a lovely way to spend a Sunday afternoon. By the way, is this a life portrait? As in, a nude?"

Liv let out a snort of laughter. "Yeah, right."

He shrugged. "Don't rule the idea out. That's all I'm saying."

"Okay. I'm going now," she told him, wanting to draw a line under his teasing. "Hope things go to plan with Ben."

"Thanks. I'm working up to asking him to go to the wedding with me."

Liv grinned. "Nice."

"Is Jayce going to be there today?"

"No. He's with Jess."

He gave her a knowing smile. "Bye, Liv." He winked. "Hope your clothes don't fall off during your sitting."

LIV SAT QUIETLY, COMFORTABLE IN THE SILENCE AS SHE WATCHED Arran make his concentration face. He bit his lip, dabbing delicately at the canvas with a fine brush. Watching him created a sense of calm within her.

As he glanced over to look at her, as he frequently did during the sittings, something had shifted in his expression. She kept quiet, looking away, not wanting to disturb him when he was on a roll. She could read it now—when he became fully immersed.

It was almost a shock when he spoke. "Your eyes are so beautiful." She glanced up quickly, and he was watching her, his brush no longer on the canvas. He swallowed. "I've often thought about how I'd capture your eyes."

Her heart lifted into her throat, making her voice catch. "You have?"

He nodded.

Her spirits lowered again. "Though I suppose . . . that's only normal for an artist."

He hesitated, fiddling with the brush. "To be honest, I've only ever done that with you." He held her gaze for a few seconds and Liv thought her heart might explode.

Clearing his throat, he ran a hand over his hair. "Do you want a drink?"

She didn't want him to leave for the kitchen. She didn't want anything to interrupt this conversation when he was saying these lovely things and making her feel like this. "No, thanks, I don't need a drink just now." *Olivia Holland turning down a cup of tea? Red alert!* She bit her lip. "How come you only think about painting *my* eyes?"

He seemed conflicted. "Yours are the most beautiful shade I've ever seen. I think of them as sea tones."

She studied him as her pulse raced, peaking when he stood and came over to nestle onto the couch beside her. He took her hand silently, and she gave him a squeeze.

"That's a lovely compliment," she told him softly. "Thank you."

Arran rested his head on the back of the couch, continuing to look at her and keeping hold of her hand. "It's true."

As he gazed into her eyes, all the feelings from that night on Skye resurfaced. The image of him grasping her red hood and holding her close. *"All the better to eat you with."* She shivered with desire at the memory.

He frowned, shifting closer. "Are you cold?"

She shook her head, goose bumps erupting along her arm as he brushed against her.

His gaze penetrated hers, and it felt like he could read her thoughts. "What is it?"

Liv swallowed. "Just a bit . . . confused."

He gave her a soft look, then squeezed her hand. "You know, Sam kind of engineered this portrait thing to get us some time together." He paused to assess her reaction. "He was thinking of commissioning it anyway, but it brought the whole idea forward."

She raised an eyebrow, the corner of her mouth lifting too. "He did, did he?"

He smiled, leaning a little closer. "I totally jumped at the chance. To spend time with you, and also to paint you."

Instinctively, she lifted a hand to stroke his face, absorbing the manner in which he shifted into her touch, closing his eyes for a moment. Then he opened them to look directly into hers. "Liv—"

Just then her phone sounded with the tones of Avicii's "Hey Brother."

Arran smiled weakly. "I take it that's your ringtone for Sam?"

She nodded, unable to tear her eyes off him. "Just let it go to voice mail."

The phone rang off, then immediately began to ring again. A heavy dread dragged in her stomach. Something was wrong. She exchanged a look of concern with Arran as she shifted away to pull her phone out of her pocket. "Sam?"

"Liv." He sounded breathless. "I'm sorry to interrupt your sitting, but we've got a situation."

A lead weight thudded in her chest. "What is it?"

"Dave's here. He turned up at Mum and Angus's and demanded to speak to me. I'm on my way there now."

Spiky shards of ice infiltrated her veins. "Shit."

Arran was looking at her with concern in his eyes.

"I'm coming too," she told her brother.

"You don't have to. I'll handle it."

She clenched her jaw. "There's no way I'm leaving you and Mum with him, without me there."

Arran raised his eyebrows, clearly putting two and two together.

"Angus is there. It'll be fine."

She tightened her grip on the phone. "I'm setting off now. I'll be there ASAP."

He sighed. "Okay. Drive carefully. Love you."

"Love you too," she said, hanging up and meeting Arran's concerned eyes. "Dave has turned up at Mum's. He wants to speak to Sam."

"Shit," Arran said, running a hand over his hair.

She bit her lip as she got to her feet, a million thoughts running through her mind, the most prominent of which being *I hope Mum is okay.*

Arran got up too, grabbing her hand and leading her out of the studio and down the hallway, where he passed her her jacket and began pulling on his own.

Liv frowned as she shoved on her Converse. "What're you doing?"

Arran looked up from where he was dealing with his own footwear, his jaw set. "If you think I'm letting you go there on your own, then you're very mistaken."

A warm feeling gathered in her stomach, starting to melt the lump of ice that Sam's phone call had created. "You don't have to do that."

He took her hand as they exited the house and he guided her toward his car. "I know that. But I want to. And I'm driving."

He opened his car and they climbed in. Liv didn't try to protest about taking her car instead, because the way her mind was whizzing, she'd prefer not to have to concentrate on the road.

They made the drive over to her mum's mostly in silence, with Arran reaching over to squeeze her hand every so often, and she was so grateful that he hadn't listened to her when she'd told him not to come.

They pulled up outside the house, and her reflex compulsion to hesitate and delay seeing her toxic father again was knocked out of the park by her need to ensure that her mum and brother were okay. Liv hurried out of the car, Arran by her side, and they went to ring the doorbell.

The few seconds it took for an answer felt like hours. It was Angus who opened it, and he immediately folded her into a hug. "It's okay, love. Everyone's fine."

Immediately soothed by Angus's ever-calming presence, she felt her shoulders relax a little. "Is he still here?"

Angus nodded. "Let him say his piece and then it'll be over."

Liv moved past him, not bothering to take off her jacket or shoes. Angus gave Arran a smile as he brought up the rear. "Hi, son. Thanks for bringing her over."

Arran shot Angus a smile in return. "No problem."

Liv instinctively reached out to take Arran's hand as they walked down the hallway to the kitchen, where the voices were by no means raised but the tension was thick.

He was sitting at the table as if he owned the place, lounging with one arm over the back of the chair. Liv ignored him, going straight over to where Tara was standing at the kitchen counter with Sam and giving each of them a hug.

Angus was the only one who sat at the table with Dave, and it didn't escape Liv's notice that he had positioned himself between Dave and the rest of them. Another tiny bolt of warmth fired into the iceberg in her chest.

Dave eyed her with a haughty air. "No hug for your old man?"

Liv met his gaze. "Nope."

Arran shifted closer, putting his arm around her.

Dave narrowed his eyes a little. "Who the fuck's this?" he asked, nodding toward Arran.

"You should probably know the answer to that, seeing as he's been your son's best friend his entire life," Liv shot back, sliding her arm around Arran's waist.

Dave blinked, then shifted his gaze back onto Sam, as if forgetting that Liv even existed. "I asked you to bring your fiancée to meet me. It's beyond rude that she hasn't come."

Sam rolled his eyes. "You don't get to make demands."

"You haven't even told me her name," Dave said.

"That's because it's none of your concern," Sam shot back.

Dave smirked, lifting the mug of tea that someone must have made him. What a waste of perfectly good tea. "I suppose I'll get to meet her at the wedding."

Sam laughed bitterly. "There's no way you're coming."

Dave smacked his mug down onto the table. "I'm your father. I have a right to be there."

Sam sighed. "Why are you even bothered? You don't give a shit about any of us."

Dave clenched his jaw. "I'm the father of the groom and I am entitled to be present."

"Entitled my arse," Liv muttered.

Dave snapped his gaze back onto her. "That's enough of your insolence, missy. You need to learn your place."

Arran made a move forward, his face stony and his fists clenched at his sides. But she squeezed his waist, holding him back.

Tara stepped behind Angus, placing a hand on his shoulder, and he reached up to hold it. Her voice was firm. "I won't have you speaking to my daughter like that, David. Especially not in my house."

Dave eyed Tara, then Angus. He muttered something incomprehensible before lifting his mug again. Liv glanced at Sam and took in the hard set of his jaw. *We need to get Dave out of here.*

Dave put his mug down again. "Perhaps if you hadn't poisoned my own children against me, we wouldn't be in this situation."

Tara let out a laugh devoid of any humor. "I didn't need to do any poisoning. You did that yourself."

Dave sat straighter. "You drove me away. You were an incompetent wife, never putting my needs first."

"Okay," Angus said, rising from his chair to reveal his full, stocky height. "This conversation isn't going anywhere constructive. David, it's time for you to leave."

Dave lounged in his chair a few seconds longer, clearly not wanting to give Angus the satisfaction of doing what he'd asked. Then he got to his feet. "I need to head off now anyway." He gave Sam a pointed look. "I'll be in touch."

"Please don't be," Sam muttered.

Dave turned and left the kitchen as if he hadn't heard what Sam had said, and Angus followed him to the door.

A prickly feeling filled her gut, and Liv instinctively moved away from Arran and followed the feeling, and the two men, down the hallway. She sensed Arran right behind her and heard Sam's and Tara's footsteps behind him.

Opening the door, Dave turned to stare past Angus, toward them. "I'll be at that wedding, by the way."

He stepped out of the front door and Liv's pulse spiked.

"I'll escort him to his car," Angus muttered, following.

Her spider senses escalated as she watched Dave let Angus overtake him on the driveway. Quickly, she stepped out, hurrying to catch up and ignoring her mum and Sam calling after her.

Just as she closed the gap between her and the two men, Dave aggressively yanked back his arm, making to strike Angus from behind.

Her pulse rocketed, immediately galvanizing her reflexes, and she threw herself into a rugby tackle, bringing Dave crashing down before his fist connected with Angus.

As they landed, she scrambled to get on top of his back, her adrenaline peaking with rage as she pinned him down and ground his face into the driveway.

All of her father's crimes pulsed through her mind in a river of rage. The pain her mum had gone through at the hands of this scumbag. How Sam had suffered because of his ex, a relationship he'd fallen into because of the trauma Dave had left in his wake. And now, tainting the happy occasion of Sam and Maya's wedding. *How he ignored me my entire life, making me feel insignificant and unwanted.*

All of it pushed her heart rate higher, infusing her muscles with boiling-hot blood and the strength of the enraged.

She pinned his arm behind his back, using her weight to keep him down and prevent him from hurting Angus or any of the rest of her family.

Liv was aware of her family's and Arran's urgent voices in the background, beyond the sound of the blood whooshing in her ears. Their sounds merged into an incomprehensible babble and she was vaguely aware of touches to her back as her family attempted to encourage her to back off.

No chance.

"Get off me, Sam," Dave shouted.

Liv leaned in, speaking through gritted teeth. "It's *me*."

She twisted his arm, causing him to yelp.

Crouching lower, she whispered in his ear. "Don't you *dare* try to attack Angus from behind, you fucking coward."

He sucked in a breath. "*I'm* your father, not him."

"Like hell you are," she shot back. "He's more of a father than you ever were."

She leaned even closer, spitting out her words. "Don't underestimate me again, *Dave*. If you do as I say, then I won't snap your arm in two."

He tried to wriggle, but she pressed him farther into the ground, halting his movements.

"Listen to me. When I let you up, you fuck off. Keep fucking off until you're outside the town limits. Then fuck off some more until you're so far away, none of us ever have to see your fucking face ever again. And if you even *think* of mentioning my brother's wedding one more time, I will pound you into the actual ground." She paused to let that sink in. "Deal?"

He didn't answer. So she twisted his arm a little more, eliciting another yelp. "Make the deal," she said through gritted teeth. "Or I'll tell everyone that you got beaten up by your own daughter."

Dave's voice was hoarse. "Deal."

Liv released her hold and stood, watching him through narrowed eyes as he rose. He avoided her gaze as he rubbed his shoulder, quickly walking away down the driveway and around the corner. She clenched her fists. *Couldn't ignore that, could you, dickhead? That's what you get.*

Someone grabbed her from behind, squeezing her into a hug. *Mum.*

"Sweetheart, are you okay?" Tara said, her voice wobbly.

"I'm fine," she said, the adrenaline calming, giving way to a hollow feeling in her chest.

Angus rubbed her back as Sam grabbed her from their mum to envelop her in another hug. She smiled weakly against his chest. "Bro. I said I'm fine." She could hear his heart thumping.

Sam released her, leaning down to press his lips against her forehead.

"Hey. Your beard is tickling my nose," she told him in an effort to calm his anxious demeanor.

He smiled, sliding an arm around her as the two of them headed back into the house, flanked by Tara and Angus. Liv glanced behind and met Arran's eyes, taking in his wide-eyed expression with a spike of guilt and giving him a reassuring smile.

She was placed at the table with a cup of tea, Sam on one side and her mum on the other, each holding a hand, and Angus fussing around them all.

Eventually, she told them she couldn't drink her tea because she had no hands left, and they both released her. Liv kept her eyes on Arran, who was sitting across from her, and sipped her drink. The warmth in his eyes sustained her through everyone else's concerned chatter. Comforting hands kept touching her shoulder and rubbing her back, and every time she was asked whether she was okay, she'd reply, "I'm fine" with a smile, all the while keeping her eyes on Arran, who was watching her silently across the table. And she *was* fine. If fine meant a hollow nothingness in her chest. An abyss devoid of any guilt or regret. A vacuum sporting the absence of any kind of anxiety about having just tackled her own father to the ground and very nearly broken his arm.

The conversation turned to the audacity of Dave and the fact that they'd never seen him with his tail between his legs before.

"I'm telling you," Sam said. "Never in a million years did I think I'd see him scurry off without a second glance. That was fucking awesome, sis."

Angus nodded in agreement. "I had no idea he was trying to attack me."

Then her mum frowned, and Liv knew what was coming. "You could have handled it yourself, though, Angus. Liv didn't need to get involved."

Her heart rate accelerated, but she held her tongue.

Angus's brow knitted. "It would have been hard to counter when he came at me from behind. He would have had me on the ground before I could do anything about it."

"Well, Sam could've intervened, then," Tara said, nodding toward her son.

Sam appeared bemused. "No, I couldn't have. Not in time. I hadn't even noticed what was happening." He shot Liv a grin. "Not like this one, sensing danger like frickin' Spider-Man."

Tara folded her arms. "It's best not to sink to his level."

Liv's stomach bottomed out.

Sam frowned, holding his palms up in confusion. "So it would be fine for me or Angus to take him on, but not Liv? Despite her being the only one of us who's a trained fighter?"

Tara stayed silent, and that said it all.

Liv stood. "Arran and I have to head out now. I need to fetch my car from his." She sent him a pleading look, and immediately he was on his feet, rounding the table to stand next to her, take her hand, and lead her down the hallway.

The others followed them, saying goodbye and not seeming to notice that final conversation had rattled her way more than the fight with her dad had. Arran tucked her under his arm and held her close as they made their way down the short driveway to his car.

Once they climbed in, he took hold of her in a tight hug. "Sorry. Been waiting a while to do this. I didn't want to intrude on the family fussing."

Liv managed a small laugh. "Hug gratefully received."

He let her go with a smile and started the car.

Arran must've correctly sensed that she wasn't ready to talk, because the return trip was as silent as the outward journey, punctuated by the same intermittent hand squeezes.

Once they arrived, he killed the engine, watching her.

Liv took a breath. "Can I come back in? I'd like us to finish a little more of the painting, if you don't mind. I don't see why Douchebag Dave should get to interfere with its progress, and at least we're both off tomorrow for the bank holiday."

He nodded. "No problem."

SHE'D BEEN SITTING THERE FOR A WHILE, STARING INTO SPACE while Arran painted, before it occurred to her that since they'd arrived home and he'd fixed them something to eat, he still hadn't pressed her to divulge how she was feeling. A refreshing change from her family's constant requests to know the answer to that question. Especially since she knew that she was required to censor her answer, in order not to be too negative or assertive or whatever else. Well, that was what her mum required anyway.

Maya had texted asking the same thing, and Liv had replied with **I'm fine, I'll speak to you and Elise about it tomorrow at the tearoom x**.

"Thank you," she told Arran.

He shifted his gaze from the canvas. "What for?"

She took a breath. "For coming with me to Mum's. For being there for me." She smiled weakly. "For not pestering me about my feelings like everyone else did."

Arran returned her expression. "Anytime." He lifted his brush to the canvas again. "By the way, you were spot on when you dubbed him Douchebag Dave."

She managed a soft laugh. "Right? I think we need to change his name by deed poll."

The sound of his chuckle soothed her ragged nerves. It was like warm honey, the same as his eyes.

"I really wanted to punch him in the face, though," Arran said, his voice tight despite the recent chuckle.

"I know you did."

He shot her a soft look over the top of the canvas.

They settled into comfortable silence again as he recommenced painting. Liv shifted a little on the couch, noticing that her left knee was tender. She rolled up her jeans to reveal a big purple bruise on her kneecap. It must've been acquired during that rugby tackle.

She tried to roll it back down before Arran saw, but she wasn't quick enough.

"Oof, that looks sore," he said, doing a double take.

Liv hurriedly covered it up. "It's okay. Not that painful."

Arran held her gaze for a moment. "Your knee, or the situation?"

The instinct to put on a front surfaced. But she was so sick and tired of hiding. Plus, the pull to confide in him was too great after he'd been there for her during Dave's barrage of toxic messages and after his steady, comforting presence this evening. "Both, to be honest." She took a deep breath, overwhelmed by her emotions. "Can I ask you something?"

"Of course," he said, leaning his forearms on his knees.

Her pulse gathered pace. "What does it mean that I don't feel anything about attacking my dad?"

He met her eyes steadily, as if willing her to continue.

The all-too-familiar sickening feeling swelled in her stomach. "I slammed my father onto the ground. I hurt him. And when I realized I'd hurt him, I didn't care. I just hurt him some more." She paused to search his face. "And still, I don't care."

Arran clattered his brush onto the desk, leaving his chair to come and sit with her. "I think it means you have closure." He took her hand. "Why? What do you think it means?"

Tightness swelled in her throat, and for a moment she couldn't squeeze her voice out. "I, ah . . ." She took a breath, and during the pregnant pause that followed, she tried to formulate the jumbled thoughts in her mind into some sort of coherent sentence. Surely translating her thoughts and feelings into words shouldn't be this hard. But she'd never tried before, not when it came to this.

He didn't hurry her, but held her hand gently while she battled to find her words. "What if it means, deep down, that I'm . . . a bit like him?" Her voice broke as she uttered the last syllable, tears spilling out onto her face. Tears that she felt she'd been holding in all her life.

Arran brought her closer, lifting a hand to wipe the moisture from her cheeks. "Sweetheart. Why on earth would you think you're anything like him?"

Her breathing felt shaky. "When we were growing up, everyone would go on about how Sam was the spit of Mum and I was Dad's double."

"That's only appearance, Liv," he said gently. "It's just DNA. Nothing else."

Her palpitations increased, making her breathless. "But there's more to it than that. DNA affects personality as well as looks."

He gathered her into a tight cuddle. "I promise you're nothing like him. He's a selfish prick who thinks of no one but himself. You think about *everyone*, Liv. You put everyone first. To the point that I worry you don't take care of your own needs."

Something broke inside her, and the tears flowed more freely. She cried them silently onto Arran's T-shirt, feeling guilty that she was soaking the poor man in the process. Pickling him in salt water.

Eventually, she managed to speak again, to continue saying what she'd never been able to tell anybody, including her twin brother and best friends. "You remember Dean?"

"Your ex who we saw at Angela and Sarah's wedding?"

"Yeah. He was my longest relationship, but still only about six months. Everyone thinks he dumped me, but the truth is, I dumped *him*."

He stroked her hair. "You're allowed to break up with someone, Liv. You can't stay with them if it's not right." He lifted her chin to smile at her. "Even I know that, and I've been on the receiving end, big-time."

She searched his face. "What did you say to Jess? When she told you. Did you shout at her?"

He frowned. "No, of course not. She was upset and crying. She wasn't trying to hurt me. I mean, I was shocked and my pride was hurt, so I didn't say too much. Then when we next spoke I asked her a lot of questions. But it was a discussion, not a shouting match." He paused, running his thumb over her cheek. "Why? Did Dean have a go at you?"

She swallowed. "I didn't know how to end it without upsetting him. I hadn't been feeling it for a few weeks, but he still seemed into me. So I . . . kind of ghosted him." She winced, remembering how immature and unkind it'd been. "Then when he asked me about it, I pretended I'd just been busy and had phone problems. I made out it was in his head."

Nausea swelled inside her, and her breathing became more labored. "I gaslighted him, Arran. Then, when he backed me into a corner and demanded to know what was going on, I finished it." Her chest was constricted and her head was spinning. "He—he told me I was just like my dad." Her voice gave out and Arran pulled her into him again. "He knew about the way Dad used to act, because I'd told him everything."

She took a breath, trying to stop her words from coming out in a broken staccato. "I never told anyone what I did because I was so ashamed. So I made out Dean had finished it. Everyone believed it, and when it got around that we'd broken up, I noticed he didn't correct anyone. I think it suited him to pretend he'd been the one to end it."

Arran's voice rumbled through his chest, soothing into her bones. "It was just his pride, sweetheart. That's all. His ego was dented, so he lashed out." He sighed. "I think a lot of dudes can be like that."

An invisible weight drifted from her shoulders. Arran hadn't thought she was irrational so far. Nor was he telling her she was an evil person. "But I pretended his observations and his hurt weren't valid. That he'd imagined it. Just like Dad did to Mum and Cat did to Sam."

"It's not the same. You cared about his feelings and you were trying to protect them. Perhaps you went about it in the wrong way, but you were only young, and your dad had just left a couple of years before, don't forget. The trauma of it was still pretty raw." He kissed the top of her head. "Also, I reckon no matter how you'd broken up with him, the reaction would've been the same. He sounds like the sort of guy who was always going to lash out when his pride was hurt. And, what's more, he knew exactly how to do it. What your weak spot was." He gave her a squeeze. "*He* was the bad guy, Liv. Not you."

She swallowed, relief at his support spurring her on. "Ever since I was little, my grandmother, Dad's mum, would tell me how much like my dad I was. In both looks and temperament. And then . . ." She tailed off.

"And then, what?" he asked, softly.

She sat back to face him again. "Mum was always on at me about speaking my mind. Insinuating I should censor myself and not express too much negative emotion or be too loud or disagreeable. My doing so used to cause arguments with Dad and she would say we were too similar, that's why we butted heads. She wanted me to put up and shut up to keep the peace."

Arran was listening intently, holding her hand with a gentle, reassuring pressure.

"Then one time I got into a fight at school. Some guy had been bullying my friend Olly and I stood up for them."

"Shit, I remember that," he told her. "Didn't you floor the bully by sweeping his feet?"

She nodded, half expecting to be chastised.

Arran held out his hand for a low five, and after a moment's surprise, she obliged him.

"That was awesome," he said, his eyes wide. "Everyone at school was talking about it and I was like, yeah, that's my best friend's sister." He had a proud look on his face and she loved him for it. "Hold on," he said, putting two and two together. "Did your mum bawl you out for that?"

She nodded.

"No way," he said slowly. "Why? That dude was a notorious dickhead. Didn't he have your friend by the throat at one point?"

"Yeah." She sighed. "I had to intervene before he choked Olly out. But when Mum found out, she wouldn't listen to my reasons. Just told me that I had trouble controlling my temper and was just like my father."

Arran was silent for a moment. "A bit like earlier, when she was critical of you defending Angus."

Liv nodded, a painful lump constricting her throat.

"Come here," he told her softly.

She about collapsed onto him, burying her face in his T-shirt. He smelled so good. "I think that was why I started reading up on it," she told him. "Narcissism, I mean. Perhaps I was trying to convince myself I wasn't the same." She swallowed. "But maybe emotionally charged thoughts carry more weight than logical ones, and deep down it still drives me? I don't really know."

"It's okay," he soothed. "I understand."

Her being felt lighter, as if speaking her most private thoughts had banished an inner demon. But it had sucked all the energy from her, leaving her physically and emotionally drained. "I'm so tired," she sighed into his chest.

He rubbed her back. "I can drive you home, in your car. I'll get a taxi back again."

She shook her head against his chest, then lifted it to meet his gaze. "Please can I stay here?"

He wiped the final smears of moisture from her cheeks, a soft expression on his face as he nodded. "Of course you can. Anything you want."

She searched his eyes. "Will you stay with me? I don't want to sleep alone."

His voice was gentle as he held her gaze. "I will."

He stood and lifted her to her feet, but her legs buckled. Everything felt like it had turned to jelly, and suddenly the bedroom seemed awfully far away.

Arran scooped her into his arms and carried her out of the studio and up the stairs into his room, where he gently deposited her on the bed. Then he got out a T-shirt and a pair of shorts for her to wear.

He left for the bathroom to change and brush his teeth, knocking on the door before he came back out, to make sure she'd finished changing.

Liv vaguely registered that he was wearing black boxer briefs and a dark T-shirt, before half stumbling into the bathroom to wash her face and use some mouthwash. She could have sworn she completed the walk from the en suite back to the bed already asleep.

Arran turned off the bedside lamp and cuddled her. His torso felt firm and defined through his soft T-shirt, and she snuggled in tightly. "I never told anyone that stuff before," she said, her eyes already closed.

"I know, Aggie," he whispered. "I'm glad you told me."

"Me too," she breathed, her consciousness drifting away.

Chapter
TWENTY-THREE

HE COULD SMELL HER AGAIN. WHY WAS THAT? THROUGH THE sleepy haze he tried to recall if he still had Liv's T-shirt on his radiator.

Opening his eyes, he was greeted by the beautiful sight of her sleeping, her face only inches away and the heat of her hand wrapped with his.

Arran lifted his head and very gently touched his lips to the tip of her nose. The feeling was still there, the one that had been swelling for months, then snowballing acutely for the past few weeks. The need to protect her. To support and nourish her.

Now that she'd confided in him, he couldn't believe he hadn't worked it out before. Deep down, she was terrified of being like her father. Despite the fact that Liv and her empathetic ways were the polar opposite of dickhead Dave, it kind of didn't surprise him that she was worried about that. Not because she was anything like her dad, but because it was typical of her to worry about everyone's feelings, how the way she acted affected them, to agonize and punish herself over how others felt. And that would be why she hadn't told anyone before. Too afraid of upsetting her loved ones. And it didn't help that her mum fueled Liv's instinct to keep any negative thoughts to herself and chastised her for assertive behavior.

Liv was so strong and put together that everyone forgot to look out for her. A meme he'd seen online came to mind—*Remember to check on your strong friend.*

She stirred, and when she opened her eyes, she gave him the most beautiful smile, which melted his heart.

"Morning." She stretched, keeping her hand entwined with his. "Thanks for letting me stay over. And allowing me to nick half the bed."

Arran grinned, feeling like he hadn't smiled properly in weeks. "Delighted to have you."

Shuffling a little closer, she lifted their hands to kiss the back of his, and the feel of her soft lips on his skin sent a red-hot thrill right into his belly. "I feel so much better for having told you all that."

He lifted his other hand to brush her hair from her face, letting his fingers settle in her soft curls. "I do too. Thank you for telling me."

Liv smiled. "I was worried you might think I was unhinged or an evil bitch, and not want to be my friend anymore."

He laughed. "You could tell me you'd murdered someone and I'd still be your friend. I'd even volunteer to help you bury the body."

She joined in his laughter, and the sound of it was like the sun shining on him. "Don't worry, whoever I murdered would deserve it." She arched a brow and he knew exactly whom she was referring to. Then her smile fell slightly. "Can I tell you something else?"

He nodded, the warm privileged feeling that she was trusting him settling like a cocoon around his heart. He rubbed his thumb across her cheek and let his fingers rest in her hair.

"I wonder if that's why I've kept away from serious relationships. Because I don't want to be hurt or hurt anyone the way Dad did Mum. Or Cat did Sam." She paused. "Or how I hurt Dean."

It killed him that she was still beating herself up about that. Good job that fucker Dean had left town years back, otherwise Arran would've hunted the twat down and kicked his arse all the way to John O'Groats and into the North Sea. *Get in the sea, dickhead.*

"You know now that's not true, right?" he asked her, searching her face. "Your intentions were good with Dean, and he was a dick who exploited your emotional vulnerabilities. You could never hurt someone the way Dave did. You're the total opposite." He smiled. "The anti-Dave."

She laughed softly. "I like the sound of that. But I suppose it's something I need to work on. I think I'm jaded about relationships in general, after witnessing both Mum's and Sam's trauma." She swallowed. "Every time I get too close to someone romantically, I get these horrible palpitations and this sickening feeling. But instead of facing it and trying to fathom it, I buried it, and for years I let everyone think I was this unlucky-in-love, desperate-for-a-relationship person. But really, I was actively avoiding commitment." She raised her eyebrows. "I'm like Nico, by stealth."

Arran laughed. "I never thought there'd be a scenario where we'd be grouping you in with Hadid."

She pulled his hand closer, pressing her lips to his skin again, and the heat pooling in his belly sent a ripple lower, making his morning glory strain hard against his boxers. He shifted his hips backward lest Liv accidentally brushed against it and it had her running for the hills, traumatized by her best mate's erection.

"I think that's why I backed off after we kissed," she told him tentatively. "That horrible feeling came over me, exacerbated by the altercation with that guy. I had this twisted sense of guilt about defending myself. Must be a throwback to Mum telling me that standing up for myself means I have a bad temper like my dad."

He pulled her close to kiss her forehead.

She snuggled in further, giving him a shy look. "I think what made it worse this time is that, I, ah . . . I *really* like you."

A burst of joy caught fire in his chest, and it really didn't do anything to help the tent situation in his underwear.

She was looking at him with that same intensity, the way she'd done when he'd nearly kissed her on the sofa the previous evening, before they'd been interrupted by Sam's SOS call. The way she'd looked at him that night on Skye. *But this time it's a million times hotter.*

"I wanted more to happen between us," Liv said, her voice scratchy. "I just got scared." She cleared her throat. "Because you mean so much to me."

He gave her a smile, his heart fit to burst. "Well, shit. And here was me thinking I was the tortured, brooding, relationship-averse one. When all along it was you."

Liv let out a laugh. "Brooding? You?" She gave his chest a little nudge. "You're a total sweetheart." She grinned. "However, that'll teach you to go in for gender stereotypes."

He chuckled. "Yep."

"I need to admit something else," she told him, her voice soft.

"What's that?" he asked, mesmerized by her eyes.

She swallowed. "I've kind of been wearing your green T-shirt to bed."

The idea of that was as hot as a volcano. "Kind of?"

She smiled. "Well, not kind of. Totally. Every night."

He let out a gentle laugh, pushing his fingers farther into her hair, then trailing them through her dark waves. "Not gonna lie. I fucking love that." He bent his head to drop a feather-soft kiss at the corner of her mouth, and she shivered in response. "I like the idea of something of mine being wrapped around you while you sleep." Her breath hitched, and his eyes were drawn to her mouth as he remembered the feel of her lips against his. His gaze dropped lower. The T-shirt she was wearing was a *Doctor Who* design and sported a big picture of a Dalek on it. The material was pretty threadbare and, unless he was mistaken and Daleks had nipples he hadn't been aware of, he could see the stiff outline of Liv's. Never mind exterminate; he was about to spontaneously combust. "I also need to confess some things," he told her, his voice thick.

"Oh yeah?" she whispered.

"Mm-hmm." He dropped another light kiss, this time at the opposite corner of her mouth. No sense in leaving things uneven. Plus he loved the way she shivered whenever he did that. "I also want more to happen between us. I also really like you, and"—he leaned to brush his lips against the shell of her ear, sensing goose bumps erupting on her skin in response—"I also sleep with your T-shirt."

He leaned back to take in her puzzled expression.

"But it would never fit you," she said.

He smiled and lifted his top pillow to reveal her T-shirt spread out between it and the pillow below. "I can neither confirm nor deny the rumor that I smell it every night before I go to sleep."

She looked at the T-shirt, then back at him, her green eyes luminescent with desire. She tugged him back in, and he dropped the pillow back into place to oblige.

Holding her close, he studied every fleck of green and gold in her irises, feeling like he could look at her forever. He ran his gaze over the delicious curve of her cheek, dropping a kiss there, then on the other cheek. She began to tremble in his arms, and he stroked a hand down her back to soothe her. Then his eyes caught on her mouth. Her lips were so plump and pink. *So soft.* He brushed the tip of his thumb across her bottom lip, remembering how she'd tasted, and realizing this was a dangerous game with regard to the ever-evolving underwear-tent situation.

Then she bit the tip of his thumb, steadily meeting his gaze, and he was lost. *Oh God.*

"Arran," she whispered.

For a second, he forgot every word in his vocabulary. Then, when his voice did emerge, it was hoarse. "Yeah?"

Her eyes were so big and wide. "Can I kiss you?"

His brain ground to a complete halt. He managed to utter another "yeah" before she leaned in to brush those soft, plump lips against his, closing down all logical thought processes. Including the one that was telling him to keep his hard-on away from her, because he let her press right against him as she dipped her tongue into his mouth and ramped his heart rate out of control.

The feel of her mouth on his was so achingly good. He'd been craving more of it ever since that kiss on Skye. And the scent of her, God, it drove him crazy.

A desperate need pooled low in his belly. But he wanted everything to be on her terms. She'd come so far in being this open with him, disclosing deep vulnerabilities that must have left her feeling raw and exposed.

So he let her take control, let her guide him where she wanted. He slid his tongue against hers as she pushed her hands into his hair and ground her hips into his, making him groan with need. Then she rolled on top of him and he surrendered himself to her as she lifted his arms above his head, removing his T-shirt and then entwining her fingers with his, all the while torturing him with her soft, hot mouth. He wanted that mouth all over his body.

Her kiss left him breathless, and every time she broke away, he hungrily searched for her again, ravaging her with his tongue when she came back to him. Until, eventually, she broke off and sat up, straddling his hips and breathing heavily.

For a desperate moment he thought she was going to stop. But instead, she grasped the bottom of her T-shirt—his T-shirt—and by God, if Olivia Holland lifting his shirt over her head wasn't the sexiest thing he'd witnessed in his entire life.

He was paralyzed—staring as her luscious breasts were revealed and she dropped the shirt onto the floor. His hands moved instinctively, almost of their own accord, sliding up the smooth skin of her stomach to cup her softness with both hands as she came back down to kiss him again, his thumbs grazing the hard peaks of her nipples. For a moment a weird thought entered his mind that he wished he'd moisturized his hands in case they were too rough for such delicate, soft skin.

She felt so good. Tasted so good. And now she was sliding off her shorts and kissing her way down his abdomen. *Holy fuck.*

Liv tugged the cotton of his underwear to slide it over his legs and off, and the way she was looking up at him was something else. Like all she ever wanted to look at was him.

"You're so hot," she whispered, and it blew his mind. Then she bent down to take him into her mouth and the bolt of pleasure made him jerk his hips off the bed with a groan.

He slipped his fingers into her hair as she pumped him in and out, the soft heat of her mouth making him ache. "Liv," he said, unable to believe this was really happening. That the woman he'd wanted for what felt like an eternity had him at her mercy, laid out bare and desperate for more.

He wanted to make her moan.

Twisting his fingers into her hair, he used the gentle traction to lift her head. "Come here," he said, his voice sounding more like the growl of a wild animal than his own. She obeyed, crawling up him, her smooth skin brushing against his in the most exquisite manner. She lay on top of him as he ran his hands all over her naked body.

He felt like she was made to be under his hands. Designed to fit against him and surround him. He cupped her delectable arse, grinding into her as he kissed and gently bit the soft skin of her neck.

Her breathing was already ragged, and the sound of it was so fucking hot. When he slipped his fingers between her legs and began to tease her, they slid easily through her folds. His desire ramped up impossibly further as he realized how ready for him she already was.

She was moaning his name against his mouth and he didn't want her to stop. He pushed her harder, tuning in to how to touch her in order to tease out more of her delicious sounds.

Liv began to buckle against his fingers, so he slid them inside, eliciting a sweet gasp. He gave her some languid rubs of his thumb in tandem with the push and pull of his fingers until her heat clenched around him. He kept up his movements, the roll of her climax moving over his fingers as he shifted his open-mouthed kisses over her face.

Eventually, she stilled on top of him, her skin slick against his, breathing heavily.

Arran paused for a few seconds, holding her head against his neck. Then he gently rolled them over, securing her with his weight. He waited until she opened her eyes, staring into them as he kissed her.

She smiled, lifting one hand into his hair and grabbing his arse with the other. She squeezed, pushing him more intimately, until his tip was teasing her entrance.

"Wait," he said, catching her chin in his fingers and looking into her eyes, needing to know this was okay so soon after her emotional unloading. "Are you sure?"

"Are you joking?" she replied, her eyes widening. "If this doesn't happen in the next couple of seconds I'm pretty sure I'm going to die."

He chuckled softly, knowing exactly what she meant but choosing to delay a little longer, to intensify the sensations. "Really? As in, death by cock?"

"No," she deadpanned. "Death by *lack of* cock."

"A serious affliction," he murmured against her neck. "Just let me grab a condom."

Reaching into the bedside drawer, he took one out, dealing hastily with the wrapper and sliding it on.

Liv was pulling him in again, and that was as much delay as he could stand.

He paused for a second to hold her beautiful face, then drove into her, groaning at how her heat surrounded him so tightly, how she gripped him as he thrust in and out.

It was as if all his life's choices had brought him to this one moment. The heartbreak he'd felt last year was a memory so distant that it seemed like someone else's. Everything that had happened had been meant to be, a path that had led him into Liv's arms, and now he was where he belonged—inside Olivia Holland not only physically but emotionally. She'd let him into her head, to places no one else had been allowed. And he hoped she'd let him into her heart too.

She was calling his name again and it was so hot, he couldn't stand it. Then she began to tighten around him as her second orgasm crested, and it was all he could do to hold on through her climax before he came himself.

The intensity of it stole the breath from his body. It wasn't just that this was the best he'd ever had; there was something more to it. Something deeper. A connection that only strengthened the more she let him in, the more vulnerable they were with each other.

He kept his eyes on hers, trying to anchor himself in the moment, getting lost in the sea of her eyes. Wave after wave of warm ocean washed over him, leaving him drowning in pleasure and sweet emotion.

Then the words crashed into his brain. *I love you.*

For a moment he thought he'd said it out loud, then realized his thoughts were just distorted in his mind, as if he'd detached a little from reality. The words drifted away as the fierce intensity of his climax ripped through his consciousness, so that he almost forgot what had been going through his head.

He allowed himself to slump a little on top of her, holding back some of his weight in case he was too heavy.

But she tugged him down, collapsing him onto her. "I don't want to hurt you," he told her.

"It's okay," she said, breathless. "I like feeling the weight of you. I like that you're so much bigger than me." A smile played on her lips. "I can still fell you, though, with my karate skills. So you'd better watch yourself."

He smiled as he rested his forehead on hers. "In that case, I don't think I will watch myself. Because the idea of you pinning me down is a huge turn-on."

Those three little words resurfaced, and free of his climax-rattled brain, the thought fully hit home. *I love her. I'm in love with Olivia Agnes Holland.*

It was the cliché to end all clichés—but he'd never felt this way before. It was almost as if the physical act had tethered a little piece of his soul to her. He was connected in a way he hadn't been before, to her or anyone else who'd come before. Did she feel it too?

He could've easily uttered all of it aloud, but something stopped him. The same thing that stopped him from telling her how long he'd dreamed of this. How long he'd wanted her to look at him the way she was doing right now. How much he wanted them to be together.

He didn't want to rush her, to scare her off. Not when she'd only just managed to let him in.

She was stroking his hair. "Can I ask you something?"

"Anything," he said.

Her eyes were wide. "Do you really think Dean said that shit to me because he was proud? Not because he thought it was true?"

He managed to bring his thoughts back to some kind of clarity. "Of course, sweetheart," he murmured, brushing his nose against hers.

She searched his face. "But you never said anything nasty to Jess. And you're really proud too." She arched an eyebrow. "I've never known anyone as reluctant to ask for or accept help as you."

"I guess I don't have the ego to match," he replied, lifting his head to grin at her. "Though I really should, being such a sex god and all."

She laughed, and he absorbed the warmth of it through his chest. "I can't argue with you there." She kissed him, then whispered against his mouth. "I always knew you'd be superhot in bed."

"Why, thank you Aggie," he said, peppering her face with kisses. "The same goes for you." *And then some.*

Her smile softened. "I like that you're using that nickname again. You hadn't called me it in a little while and I felt like I'd lost a bit of you."

Lifting a hand, he trailed his fingers down her face. "You'll never lose me." That was the most he allowed himself to say to indicate the depth of his feelings, keeping the rest buried.

When she's ready. Then I'll tell her everything.

Chapter
TWENTY-FOUR

THE HOT WATER RAN OVER HER SKIN, BUT DESPITE THE FACT that Liv liked her shower temperature high, the heat of the flow was nothing compared to the flush she felt from Arran's touch.

It had been the sexiest encounter she'd ever had in her life. She never came the first time being with someone because she felt too closed off to let go. And twice? That was unheard-of.

But he'd made her feel comfortable as well as turned-on. She felt safe with him, nurtured and secure.

She brushed her fingers over her lips, remembering the feel of his kiss, then trailed them down her body—tracing the places he'd seared his touch on her skin.

The connection they'd shared had been deep and intense, like nothing she'd ever experienced before. But this time she hadn't been scared, and she attributed that to having trusted him with her complicated jumble of emotions.

She left the shower to towel off and dress. She couldn't stop thinking about him, nor stop craving his touch. Was this a normal way to feel when one had sex with a person one cared about deeply? Because she had no frame of reference, what with her avoidance of anyone who might've been relationship material. What was she even supposed to call the tangled mess of emotion she was feeling anyway?

It had been rather difficult to leave Arran that morning, but she'd wanted a fresh change of clothes before heading back for another sitting. He'd asked her if she could return to get some more hours in, and she had of course been delighted to oblige.

Once she arrived back at his place, the butterflies were so intense that she had to take a few deep breaths, standing at his front door and feeling like a fish out of water. "Calm down," she told her inner tangle of emotion.

No sooner had she pressed the doorbell than he answered, giving her the sweet feeling that he'd been looking out for her.

The sight of him enveloped her in a rush—the usual surge in adrenaline and joy, but this time an additional element of shyness that she hadn't quite expected.

She wanted Arran to hug her, but instead he ushered her in with a smile and ran his hand over his hair as if he wasn't quite sure how he should greet her. "I know this sounds dumb when we only saw each other a few hours ago, but it's great to see you."

The small needle of worry at his lack of physical contact melted in the face of that adorable statement. Liv relaxed a little.

She followed him into the studio and settled into her seat. "This sofa has definitely got a Liv-arse-shaped dent in it now."

He glanced up to waggle his eyebrows at her. "Fine by me."

She laughed, lifting her legs onto the couch to sit cross-legged.

He cleared his throat as he began to work. "Feeling okay, after earlier?"

Her cheeks heated up a couple of degrees and she shot him a smile. "More than okay."

His face flushed, and he seemed as if he wanted to say something else, but then he turned back to the canvas and didn't pass any more comment.

The time went a lot more slowly than usual, and it was clearly because of the sexual tension building in the room. Every time she looked at him, little snatches of the morning's *events* flashed in her mind's eye. The sensation of his hands all over her. The scent of his skin. The way he'd moaned her name and the expression of rapture on his face.

All those thoughts were heating her body and causing her to shift uncomfortably in her seat. It was even worse when he made eye contact. Was he going to make a move?

Time dragged on, with Arran staying zeroed in on the task at hand, and something Brodie had said recently caused an idea to formulate in her mind. Perhaps there was a way to encourage Arran to make a move. It wasn't like she had a problem with doing it, but she *had* been the one to instigate it earlier, and she had to admit that his lack of tactile gestures since she'd arrived did have her feeling a little insecure.

She cleared her throat. "Are you nearly where you wanted to get to for today?"

He snapped his gaze from the canvas. "Yeah . . . I guess I am." His features settled into a look of concern, and she hoped that was because he didn't want her to leave yet.

She kept her voice casual. "Cool. Because I wondered . . . whether you'd do a quick charcoal sketch of me."

His face immediately relaxed. "I'd love to." He started gathering a sketch pad and a pencil, and Liv seized the moment to unveil her master plan—literally. She removed her glasses and began unbuttoning her shirt.

Arran lifted his head to glance at her, pencil and pad in hand. His eyes widened and he fumbled the pencil, partially catching and dropping it a couple more times before finally grasping it in his fist. "Ah . . . what're you doing?"

She blinked, keeping her face neutral and tone nonchalant as she dropped the shirt to the floor and stood to unzip her jeans. "Didn't I mention this was a nude?"

His eyes locked in on where she was sliding off her jeans. "That's . . . that's . . . er . . ." He seemed to lose the power of speech altogether for a few seconds, until the jeans joined her shirt on the floor. His voice came back hoarse. "That's awesome."

She gave him a smile as she unhooked her bra and held it out to the side, dropping it to join her little pool of clothing. His jaw was twitching now, as he stared at her topless form and shifted uncomfortably in his seat—as if his boxers were suddenly too tight. *Aha! Gotcha, Mr. Adebayo.*

She dipped down to slide off her underwear, and when she straightened, the guy looked as if he was about to swallow his tongue. He took a shuddering breath.

Liv arranged herself on the sofa, bringing her legs up to stretch out along it. "Okay," she said with a casual sigh. "I'm ready."

He hesitated a couple more seconds, gripping the pencil so hard she thought it might snap in two. Then he took another deep breath and shifted in his seat, dragging his eyes off her and onto the paper, where he began scratching out some lines.

She tried hard not to smile as he drew. "Have you done a nude before, by the way?"

He kept his eyes on the pad. "Yeah. I went to a life drawing class for a bit. But I have to say that sketching naked middle-aged men is by *far* a different experience to this." He raised his eyes to shoot her a look of molten heat.

Glancing at where his overalls hugged his crotch, she took in the shape of something that she sincerely hoped had not been present at his life drawing class. "I can see that."

Catching the direction of her gaze, he broke out into a slow smile, which pushed her temperature up another couple of notches. *My master plan is working. I'm a frickin' genius. Well, Brodie is anyway.*

Settling into silence, apart from the soft sound of pencil on paper, she watched him sketch. As time went on it became apparent which parts of her he was drawing, because his eye movements would get kind of rapid, glancing quickly from her to the paper a few times in quick succession before settling. Then he'd draw with his lips slightly parted, a slight flush on his skin.

She grinned. "Do you feel like him off *Titanic*?"

He paused what he was doing to laugh. "*That* is the perfect analogy." Smiling, he went back to the pad. "I hope that doesn't mean I'm going to die by the end of the day."

She shrugged. "Nah. I'd let you climb on my door."

His smile turned wicked. "Is that a double entendre?"

Liv shook her head. "It's a poor one if so." The corner of her mouth twitched. "But the sentiment is appreciated. If you know what I mean."

"Aha." He pointed his pencil. "*That* one was definitely an innuendo."

She grinned. "Don't point that pencil at me."

"Aw, man." He laughed. "Don't use a pencil innuendo. I'll get an inferiority complex."

She arched an eyebrow. "You've got nothing to worry about."

He shot her a grin, holding her gaze for a few seconds before he shifted his eyes over her body. The smile slipped and for a moment he looked as if he was about to get up and come over. But then he ran a hand over his hair and went back to drawing.

Dammit, how long did a sketch take anyway?

She settled back, trying to bide her time. Though she had to admit she hadn't anticipated he'd hold out this long. The ache between her legs was beginning to feel uncomfortable.

Eventually, he leaned back, tossing the pencil onto his desk. "Okay. That's about as much as I can manage with a raging hard-on."

She broke down laughing, with relief more than anything that he'd finally voiced that he was turned-on. She lifted the throw from the couch against her front. "Let's see it."

He gave her a heated look. "The sketch or the hard-on?"

Her pulse throbbed in her veins, sending a bolt of desire down into her core. "Hmm. Sketch first, please."

He leaned to pass it over.

"Nope," she said, raising her eyebrows at him. "You bring it here."

He immediately got to his feet and nearly tripped over them in his hurry to close the few steps between them. She shifted her feet down to the floor, still holding the throw over her front, and he sat close beside her so their sides were touching.

Arran passed her the sketch, and her intention to have a token glance went out the window, her heart swelling. "Wow, you've made me look beautiful."

The way he'd shaded the dark and the light gave her this kind of ethereal quality, gazing into the distance as if she were finding solutions to the universe's unanswerable questions.

He lifted a hand to her cheek. "I didn't *make* you look beautiful. You just are."

Her breath caught as the honey tone of his eyes glowed with reverence. She studied him for a few seconds. "What're you thinking?"

His gaze skidded downward. "That I'm really glad I bought a throw with a very open weave."

The corner of her mouth tugged up and she lifted a hand to stroke his face. He held her gaze a couple of seconds longer, then gently pulled the throw from where she was grasping it against her chest. He shifted it down her breasts, then let it fall to the floor before leaning in to kiss her neck. "You taste so good," he told her, gently biting her skin and making her shiver.

The softness of his lips and the graze of his stubble made her skin tingle with sensitivity, and each time he shifted his mouth lower, the new patch of skin was even more sensitive than the previous. By the time his lips touched her breasts, the sensation was exquisite, making her nipples harden and peak before he even took them into his mouth.

Arran broke contact to lean back and lift her legs onto the couch, lying between them in order to carry on his journey, to where the temperatures were at the boiling point and the season very wet indeed.

He gently licked her folds, making her grip his head in desperation. She needed more. "Please," she told him.

His eyes darkened and he buried his face between her legs, the electric sensation making her legs twitch. She let out a low moan.

He paused. "Is this okay?"

"God, yes," she said, pushing her fingers into his hair and driving his head back down because that mere second's broken contact was agony. She could feel him let out a low chuckle between her legs, which turned into a groan when she pressed him further in.

He darted his tongue inside her and her hips reared off the sofa.

"I'm glad to find that you found the whole nude-sketch thing as much of a turn-on as me," he said, his voice throaty and low. "I feel like I'm in some kind of montage of Leonardo DiCaprio films. First *Titanic*, and now *Inception* because this is an absolute dream."

Liv half laughed and half moaned as he did an awesome swirly kind of thing with his tongue. He lifted her legs over his shoulders and ramped up his movements, responding each time she moaned by pushing her harder and harder, until the sensations pooling and pulsating between her legs and into her belly intensified to the point that the huge tidal wave of pleasure broke and she gripped his head, calling out his name.

She had no idea how much time passed. It could have been seconds or hours. It was as if she were adrift on some kind of pleasure cloud.

He stayed between her legs, dropping gentle kisses onto the insides of her thighs and making her shiver. Then he gently took her legs from his shoulders to lay them down on the sofa, and released the clips of his overalls.

He shuffled them off and climbed up to lie on top of her in his T-shirt and boxers. "I didn't want the clips to catch your skin," he murmured as he kissed her.

She smiled against his mouth. "You'd better take the rest off too."

His breath hitched. "Your wish is my command."

With one hand, he gripped the back of his T-shirt and pulled it right over his head and off, dropping it onto the floor and continuing to kiss her while he slid off the boxers. She helped him by catching them with her foot and kicking them away.

Arran settled his weight on top of her, and she appreciated the hardness of his body against the softness of hers. Lifting her hands, she ran her fingers over his torso, absorbing the feel of lean ridges of muscle and the contrast of smooth skin against the graze of his chest hair. She concentrated on imprinting the sensations onto her brain. "That T-shirt move was hot," she told him.

"Thank you." He smiled. "I saw it on TikTok."

She laughed, holding his head as he leaned down to bury it in her neck.

He sighed. "You smell so good."

Need filled her body and she shifted under him, positioning him where she wanted.

"Wait," he said, lifting his head. "I need to go upstairs for a condom." He raised his eyebrows. "I don't normally need them in the studio."

She kissed his face gently. "It's okay, I'm on the injection, and clean. So I'm good to go if you are."

"Same," he said, teasing her skin with his teeth and making her shiver. "Well, clean anyway," he quipped. "Not on contraception."

He lifted a hand to hold her face for a few seconds, meeting her gaze as he shifted his hips between her legs. It was more than apparent that he could have driven right in easily, but for some reason he seemed to be holding back.

Gradually, inch by inch, he eased inside her, moving more deliberately than last time and stroking her face as he looked into her eyes. He used his other hand to grip her hip as he began to thrust, as if trying to anchor himself and his rhythm. His movements were slow and intense, his pupils blown out with pleasure.

Something squeezed hard in her chest, something that told her if this ended, she'd be irrevocably broken. Liv searched his eyes, feeling like her emotions were mirrored in them. *He must feel the same way . . . mustn't he?*

Her conscious mind drifted away, until there was only sensation left. The exquisite friction of his skin against hers. The softness of his lips and the hardness he was rhythmically driving inside her. Then the soothing thrum of his voice as he began murmuring her name.

His movements became more erratic as pleasure derailed his rhythm and his head lolled forward, his forehead touching hers. She wrapped her arms around his head to bury it in her neck as he came hard, his body shuddering.

She wasn't sure how long they lay in silence, she stroking his hair and he intermittently letting out an adorable sigh and kissing her neck. But still, he didn't voice anything about what this meant. Did he find it as profound as she did? Or was it only physical for him? He hadn't been with anyone for a year, as far as she was aware. So perhaps this was just the result of him getting really horny.

Eventually, he lifted his head to meet her gaze and she held her breath in anticipation.

He let out a big sigh. "I think I deserve a place in the Guinness book of records."

She frowned, hesitating. Not what she'd expected him to say. "How come?"

He stroked her hair. "For the longest time sitting with a boner hidden inside painting overalls. I don't know how I got that sketch done without exploding in my pants."

Her disappointment at him not uttering something more profound was still palpable, but her laughter went a little way to taking the edge off. "You could be right. But I reckon that'd have to go in the adult version of the publication."

Arran smiled as he brushed his lips across her cheek. "Can I ask you something?"

She nodded, stroking a hand over his hair.

He propped himself up on one elbow. "Do you ever regret staying in Glenavie? After Maya and Elise went off to university and then set up elsewhere, I mean."

"No. I've always loved it here. Though I have to admit that Dad leaving and Sam being with Cat affected my decisions at the time. I didn't want to leave Mum on her own or leave Sam in Cat's hands without me being around to keep an eye on him." She gave him a smile. "I know that Sam had similar reasons for staying around, wanting to keep watch over me and Mum. I didn't tell him until recently that I was also secretly looking out for him in return."

Arran smiled. "That doesn't surprise me. You're always there for everyone."

"I never regretted my decision, though; I wouldn't want to live anywhere else. What about you? Do you regret staying here?"

"Nope. I love it. I love that Jayce gets to grow up among the mountains. But I still want to travel a bit. I would have done it a little earlier, but then Jayce came along, so we delayed the plan for a while."

"You and Jess were going to travel?"

"Yeah. She wasn't too bothered, but said she'd come along for the ride." He paused, tracing his fingers across her cheek. "I would still like a travel buddy, though. Someone who's as enthusiastic about the adventure as I am." For a moment it seemed as though he was going to say something more, but then he closed his mouth and let his fingers slide onto her neck. "Oh shit," he said, lifting his hand.

She frowned. "What?"

He shot her a "yikes" expression. "I've got paint on you. Sorry, I should've washed up first."

She lifted a hand to her neck, and there was a little green residue on her fingers. A glance downward confirmed a few little streaks of it on her breasts, hips, and round onto her arse. *Everywhere his hands have been.* "That's all right. It's kind of sexy."

Arran kissed her. "Probably be sexier if I wash it all off for you."

A thrill coursed through her. "Sounds good to me."

He eased off, taking her hand to help her to her feet, then led her up to his en suite, where he turned on the shower.

His eyes were on her as she stepped inside. She could feel his gaze stroking over every inch of her skin as the water washed over her, before he finally stepped in behind her and closed the door.

He moved his hands over her, soaping up a lather and removing all traces of paint. Then he held her from behind, paying some more attention to rubbing the soapy bubbles over her breasts.

She smiled. "I think they're clean now, Arran."

"Just to be sure," he murmured against her neck.

The slickness of his skin slid over her back, contrasting with the graze of his chest hair and the hardness of his arousal. "Better call the Guinness book of records, because I can feel your prize-winning pencil again."

He chuckled against her, the rich sound thrumming into her being. "I told you not to call it a pencil."

"Sorry." She smiled as she bent her head further to the side, allowing him more access to kiss and bite her neck. "Prizewinning . . . very thick branch?"

"That's better." He took hold of her and spun her around to press her against the shower wall, sliding his hand between her legs and making her gasp. "Just one more time."

No way a girl could refuse that offer. She had a brief thought that it might take her a while to get there, with this being her third orgasm of the day. No, wait—was it her fourth? But Arran clearly *was* some sort of sex god because it was an embarrassingly short number of minutes before her orgasm was rolling over his fingers and she collapsed onto him as he held her up.

When he stepped back as if to turn off the shower, she dropped to her knees and took him into her mouth, enjoying his gasp of surprise, which turned into a groan of pleasure.

Once they did finally emerge, she felt as if all her bones were soft and her brain had turned into a relaxed mush. It went some way to quieting the little voice of doubt telling her that Arran still hadn't uttered a word about what any of this meant to him.

They toweled off and she watched him throw on some clean clothes, before he led her back down in her towel to get her things back on. Whenever she looked up, he was watching her, and he didn't try to conceal it.

As soon as she was clothed, he grabbed her into a hug, and for a moment, she thought he was going to voice something meaningful. But then he released her with a kiss to the cheek.

Arran smiled. "Best day ever."

I suppose that's something. She flashed him a smile back, suppressing her disappointment, then checked her watch. Time to meet Maya and Elise at the tearoom. "I need to head out."

He nodded, following her to the front door, where she stuffed on her shoes and put on her jacket.

"See you at the weekend?" he asked, a hopeful tone tingeing his words.

"Yeah." She kissed him. Then she reluctantly eased away. But he grasped her jacket, pulling her back into his kiss with a thrilling force and then pressing her against the wall.

He kissed her hard at first, his movements untamed, making her heart beat hard in her chest and white heat rush through her veins. Then he broke off to brush the tip of his nose against hers, and when his lips met hers again, he tempered his pace. His kiss became assiduous. Unhurried. As if he wanted to savor her. As if he needed to imprint her on his being.

Then, slowly, he eased back to bite her lower lip, making her tremble against him.

Once he eventually broke off, her breathing was pretty heavy for what had already been a four-orgasm day.

He lifted a hand to stroke her face, staying silent, his eyes dark and intense.

She cleared her throat. "See you soon."

Arran nodded, his voice hoarse. "Yeah."

She left the house and climbed into her car, and he stood watching her until she was out of sight.

One thing was for sure: The sexual chemistry was spot-on between them. But was there anything more to it than that for Arran? She dragged her mind back over everything he'd said from the night of their first kiss on Skye up to the present day. He'd indicated he wanted more from her physically, but had he alluded to anything deeper than that? Not that she could put her finger on.

But Arran wasn't the sort to hide how he was feeling. He'd been very vocal over the past year about not wanting another relation-ship. He'd been as clear as he possibly could have been. And al-though it was obvious he cared about her—they were such close friends—it didn't mean that he wanted an exclusive relationship. Navigating the way into a serious relationship was so alien to her, especially when the idea of it had given her palpitations and made her physically sick in the past. She didn't feel comfortable starting that conversation with him, nor was she equipped with the skills to do so.

She parked near the tearoom and wandered down the street, lost in her thoughts as the door jangled at her entrance.

Maya and Elise waved from their table and Liv gave them a smile as she approached and dished out hugs.

She took a seat and shrugged off her jacket.

"Tea and scones are on their way," Maya said, watching Liv's movements.

"Cool," Liv said. "How're things? Are we sorted for a dress-fitting date?"

"Yep," Maya replied, her voice seeming a little subdued. "I've got the three of us booked for the fitting, and Mum and Tara are tagging along for a fashion show." She shot Elise a concerned look and Liv realized that they must have been talking about her defeat of Dave prior to her arrival.

Elise shifted her chair closer to Liv's. "How are you? After yes-terday. I hope you don't mind that Maya told me."

Liv shook her head. "Of course I don't." She gave Maya a smile. "Or that Sam told you. To be honest, it makes it easier for me that I don't have to do the telling."

Maya took her hand and gave it a squeeze. Just then, the wait-ress arrived with their tea and scones, so they leaned away from each other to let her deposit everything on the table, and said their thanks as she departed.

Elise placed a scone on Liv's plate. "Here. You deserve this."

Maya poured some tea. "Tell us how you're doing."

"Fine, to be honest," Liv said.

"You don't have to pretend, you know," Elise said softly.

She shook her head, giving Elise a smile. "I'm not, but thank you. I really don't give a crap about what happened with Dave. He deserved it, and I'm glad I was the one to give him what he deserved."

The others were silent for a moment. Then Maya nodded. "Can't argue with that."

Unusually for Liv, the desire to tell them everything she'd told Arran surfaced, and she paused to assess it. It was normally something she would suppress, but today felt different. As if Arran had opened the dam gates.

She eyed her best friends, summoning the courage to voice what she'd been avoiding for years. Her instinct to bury it came to the fore, her reluctance to burden those she loved taking hold.

But then she remembered how good it had felt to confide in Arran. She took a deep breath to bolster her nerve, her heart hammering. "However, it did make me face up to my issues." She cleared her throat, trying to ignore the whoosh of blood in her ears. "The ones related to me having been a massive commitment-phobe for most of my adult life."

She paused, unable to believe that admission was finally out there.

It hung in the air between the three of them, as she glanced from Maya to Elise, trying to gauge their reactions, her nausea intensifying at the idea that telling them this was selfish.

Maya was watching her curiously. "Commitment-phobe? You?"

Elise smiled gently. "Tell us more."

Liv swallowed. "It's not something I'd told anyone, until Arran and I discussed it last night. But the whole Dave thing . . . well. To cut a very long, complicated story short, I've always worried that Sam takes after Mum and I'm more like Dad."

Maya frowned, taking Liv's hand. "You are *not*."

Elise lifted a hand to tuck a strand of Liv's hair behind her ear, and Liv absorbed the warmth of her friends' affection and support.

She took a breath. "I know it's dumb. But stuff kind of added up, then snowballed over the years, and all the daddy issues must have twisted it in my heart and mind. Especially with some issues between me and Mum and then when I broke up with Dean in a less-than-constructive way and he told me I was just like my dad."

Maya narrowed her eyes, putting on a Liam Neeson–esque voice. "I will find Dean. And I will kill him."

Liv smiled, squeezing her hand. "That's okay. I'll allow him to live."

"Our minds can play tricks on us," Elise said, giving her a soft smile. "And they're sneaky little buggers, because they make us believe things that couldn't be true in a million years. What you've told us isn't dumb, but we can assure you it is one hundred percent untrue."

A lump formed in Liv's throat, making her eyes prick with tears. She blinked a few times in quick succession.

Maya leaned in to kiss her cheek, making a noisy slobbering sound. Then she did the same to Elise. "You two are the bestest people ever and I love you both."

Liv blinked again, as the tears began to fall. Elise passed her a tissue. "Thank you." She drew a breath to steady her wobbly voice, dabbing at her eyes. "I love you guys too."

"Same," Elise said, smiling, her voice also a little unsteady.

Maya leaned back, giving one of Liv's curls a gentle tug. "You can tell us anything, you know? We wouldn't ever judge you. And for the record, I agree that it doesn't sound dumb. I totally understand where you're coming from because I know how your beautiful mind works."

Liv studied Maya's face. "You do?"

"Yep. You're such an empath that you always take on board and agonize over other people's opinions of you. You validate them even when it's a load of absolute bollocks." She kissed Liv's cheek. "Because you are such a fucking delight."

Liv laughed. "Thank you."

Elise squeezed her shoulder. "I'm really glad you've told us, Liv."

She nodded, her voice catching again. "Me too." Taking a breath, she realized that her whole being felt lighter somehow. As if she were the freest she'd been in years.

The scones on their plates caught her gaze, and she gave Maya some side-eye. "I just remembered that I forgot to tell you guys that Arran discovered some important scone-related intel."

"Oh yeah?" Maya said, raising an eyebrow, as Elise gave them both a wry smile.

Liv nodded, pausing for dramatic effect. "Queen Elizabeth herself used to put the jam on first." She grinned. "I figure Liz was the greatest authority. Hence, I win the great scone debate."

Elise laughed. "I think she's got you there, Maya."

Maya stared at Liv for a couple of seconds, then narrowed her eyes. "Adebayo is going to get it for this."

Liv blinked. He got it, all right. Twice. Or was it three times? The shower probably counted as a separate encounter. Heat rose in her cheeks at the thought, and Elise gave her a curious look.

Lifting her scone, Maya made intense eye contact with Liv as she aggressively slathered it in *cream* first.

Liv hid her smile behind her teacup.

Maya smiled back, then cocked her head. "Something's up with you. You went all pink just now when we mentioned Arran." She took a bite of scone and mumbled through the crumbs, "Spill it."

Liv glanced around the tearoom. "I don't know what you mean."

Elise smiled. "I spotted it too. There was definitely a blush about your cheeks."

Her heart rate picking up, Liv grasped her cup. She kept her voice low. "Okay. Don't overreact, but we had sex today."

Maya squealed a mouthful of crumbs across the table, and a pair of elderly ladies at the next table gave them curious looks.

"Shh," Elise said, glancing behind them at the older ladies and mouthing, *Sorry*.

Liv shot the women an apologetic look. They gave her a knowing smile in return, and Liv felt like the whole café probably knew she'd gotten lucky today. "I told you not to overreact," Liv told Maya through the side of her mouth.

"Oh. My. God," Maya said in a low voice. "This is epic news."

Liv leaned in toward them both, gesturing them to do the same. "And it happened twice. This morning and this afternoon."

Elise raised her eyebrows. "Wow. Twice in one day?"

Liv hesitated. "I suppose it was three times really."

Maya slapped a hand over her mouth, squealing behind it.

Elise's eyes were as wide as saucers and Maya's face was turning blue. Maya leaned farther in, removing her hand from her mouth. "You mean to tell us you've come straight from a sex session?"

Liv nodded, pushing her glasses up her nose.

Maya held her hand out for a low five. Which Liv obliged.

"Nice," Maya said, giving her a nod of approval and lifting her cup to clink against Liv's, then Elise's. She took a sip. "So what does this mean?"

Liv sighed. "Fuck knows."

Elise frowned. "Why?"

She rubbed her forehead. "I feel like there's something major going on between us. Like I've made a bit of a breakthrough with my own emotional baggage. But he's not voiced anything serious, except that he clearly finds the whole thing hot. I don't know what he wants and I'm reluctant to tell him what I want, in case I scare him off."

Elise shook her head. "I'm sure it wouldn't scare him off."

Liv bit her lip. "After all the Jess stuff? I think it might. He's been so sure he didn't want another relationship, and I can't help thinking . . ." She tailed off, staring into her tea.

"Thinking what?" Maya asked, her eyes wide.

Her heart squeezed painfully. "That the reason for that, as much as he denies it, is because deep down it's still her that he wants."

"It can't be," Maya said. "He would've gone after her by now."

Liv shook her head, her mouth dry. "He's too proud. Once she backed off, he wouldn't try to pursue it. Especially when she's with another guy."

Maya blew her fringe out of her eyes. "You were right about this being complicated."

"Yep," Liv muttered. "I don't know what to do about Arran. So I'm going to sit on it for a bit."

Maya snorted. "I bet you are."

Liv let out a laugh and caught the ladies at the next table giving her an amused look. She curtailed the laugh and smiled back at them.

Elise was glancing nervously around the tearoom, so Liv touched her hand. "Sorry for being loud," she told her, aware that her friend always worried what other people thought.

She smiled. "Oh no, that's okay. I just wanted to check none of my patients were in here." Her smile broadened. "Just in case they go around spreading the rumor that Dr. Kowalski runs sex-therapy sessions at the local tearoom."

Liv laughed, and Maya joined in.

Maya's features settled into a more serious expression. "Shall we ask Sam what he thinks you should do?"

Liv pushed her glasses up her nose. "You can tell him what's happened. I'd probably prefer it came from you. It'll be a bit weird if I tell him myself. But as for advice . . . I don't know. I need to mull stuff over. Give Arran time."

Maya nodded. "Whatever you think is best."

One of the older ladies from the neighboring table got out of her chair to approach them, and for a moment Liv panicked that they were no longer amused at the raucous laughter. Elise appeared concerned too.

The lady leaned between Elise and Liv, to address the three of them. "Sorry about this, but see my friend Agnes over there?" She gestured to her companion, who gave them an enthusiastic wave, which they returned. "Well. She's a bit of a brazen one. She tuned her hearing aid in to your conversation and wants to give you some advice, but she's got a bad hip so I've been sent over as messenger."

At that point the lady had to stop talking because Liv burst out laughing, Maya and Elise joining in. Liv pushed her finger under her glasses to wipe her eyes. "That is awesome. Not the bad hip, but the hearing aid thing. I love Agnes already. My middle name is Agnes too, by the way."

"Is it?" Agnes asked loudly from her table, clearly still tuned in to their conversation. She gave Liv a wave. "All the best people are called Agnes!"

Liv managed a nod and a thumbs-up through her laughter.

"Anyhow," Agnes's companion continued. "My name's Nancy, by the way. She told me what you were discussing, and we *both* say—go for it. Tell the laddie how you feel." Nancy leaned in to stage-whisper. "And have plenty of fun along the way." She gave them an exaggerated wink, which set the laughter off again, as Nancy left to rejoin the audacious eavesdropper Agnes.

Maya lifted a napkin to wipe her eyes as she gave them a wave.

"They're awesome." She pointed. "Yes, you, Agnes. I know you're still listening."

Agnes gave them a big smile.

Elise chuckled. "You should definitely keep Agnes and Nancy's advice in mind, while you're mulling over what to do."

"Absolutely," replied Liv, shaking her head as she drank her tea. "I'll keep it in mind."

Chapter
TWENTY-FIVE

THERE MUST BE A GERMAN WORD FOR IT. FOR WHEN SOMETHING you've longed for and built up in your mind eventually happens, and it's *even better* than your wildest dreams. Because that was what being with Liv had been like.

Arran was struggling to concentrate on his painting. Refining Liv's features on canvas was a poor second to stroking her face and kissing her actual lips. It'd only been a few nights since he'd seen her, but the time was passing agonizingly slowly.

They'd formulated a plan to meet at the weekend, among the explicit messages they'd been sending each other. But even the weekend seemed too far away. A number of times he'd picked up his phone with half a mind to ask her if he could come over, there and then, but he'd thought better of it. If she wanted that, then surely she'd ask. He needed to give her space. Let her see that this was going somewhere and she didn't need to be scared of it.

Is it really her who's scared? Or is it me? He was fearful of losing her, that was for sure. Now it was Friday night and only two more days until he'd see her. She had a breakfast with her family the next morning. In the afternoon, he was picking up Jayce from Jess and they were going to his parents' to stay over, so he and Liv had opted to meet on Sunday evening. Now he wished he'd asked his parents if they could postpone.

Arran had called Sam pretty soon after Liv had left the weekend before, feeling that it'd be best to keep him in the loop after Sam had kind of engineered the whole portrait thing to Arran's advantage. It hadn't been as cringe to fess up what'd happened as he'd thought, though he hadn't gone into any detail whatsoever because that would've been weird.

He'd also stopped short of telling Sam he was in love with Liv, because it just didn't feel right to say it to someone else before he'd told her. Partly for romantic reasons, but he was aware pride was also involved. If it transpired that Liv didn't feel the same, then he'd rather no one else know. That way he could hide his humiliation a hell of a lot more easily than he had a year ago, when the whole town had known about him getting dumped a few weeks prior to his wedding. He shuddered thinking about it.

Sam had been supportive, tried to get him to speak to Liv about however he felt and what he wanted. But Arran had shut him down—he didn't want to disclose anything to Sam regarding what Liv had confided; she needed to tell her brother under her own steam. Sam, always the thoughtful, understanding guy, hadn't pushed it. The sound of the doorbell cut into his ruminations, and it occurred to him that it could be Liv. He jumped to his feet and left the studio. Maybe that work thing she had on tonight had been canceled.

His heart full of hope, he opened the door. Then his spirits crashed down around his ears when it revealed Jess standing there.

Jess raised her eyebrows and he realized that he was frowning at her and not saying anything.

"Sorry," he said. "You took me by surprise."

She swayed a little in the doorway. "Can I come in?"

He tried to gather his thoughts. Had Jess said she was bringing Jayce over tonight? He'd thought that he was picking him up tomorrow. A glance behind her confirmed she was alone.

"Arran?"

"Yeah, sorry," he said, stepping aside to let her in. Then he realized something. "Where's your car?"

She stumbled a little on the way past, and he detected the smell of alcohol. "I got a taxi over." She removed her shoes and carved a wobbly path toward the kitchen.

He followed her, frowning and confused. "Are you pissed?"

"Nah," she said, rummaging in his cupboard and getting out a bag of crisps. "Just tipsy."

This was weird.

"Sit down and I'll make you some tea," he said, moving over to the kettle.

"Thanks." She sat and began munching on the crisps.

Arran glanced up as he made the tea. "Where's Jayce?"

"He's at my mum's," she said through her full mouth. "Staying over."

That's good. Seeing as you're as pissed as a fart. He brought over a couple of mugs, handing one over, then sitting across from her with his. She continued to munch on the crisps. When she saw him watching her, she gestured the open end of the packet toward him.

Arran waved his hand. "No, thanks." He watched her for a few more seconds, waiting for her to explain her presence. But she just continued crunching on the crisps. He cleared his throat. "Are you going to tell me why you're here?"

Her eyes welled up, and she hiccuped a couple of times before getting her words out. "Me and Rory had a fight." She sipped her tea, blinking.

Arran felt bad for her but couldn't fathom how any of this was his business. "Sorry to hear that. Why didn't you go to your mum's?"

She hiccuped again. "I didn't want Jayce to see me upset."

"Uh-huh." Kind of fair enough, but still weird. "And . . . why come here?"

Her voice broke. "I didn't know where else to go." Tears began to fall and Arran felt like a dick for being blunt.

"Hey, it's okay," he soothed. Although, she did have any number of friends she could have gone to.

"Thank you," Jess said, giving him a watery smile and reaching over to squeeze his hand. Instantly he felt uncomfortable, and snuck his hand from under hers to grasp his mug.

"Can I stay over?" she asked.

How the hell could he say no to a distraught, tearstained woman? "Yeah." He sighed. "That's fine." She could have his bed and he'd stay on the couch. "I'll drop you at your mum's in the morning and pick Jayce up at the same time."

She swallowed. "Thank you." Taking another sip of her tea, she eyed him. "Aren't you going to ask what the argument was about?"

Arran was so weirded out he felt like departing for the sofa right that instant. "Nope. It's none of my business."

Jess ignored him. "It was about you."

"Me?" he asked, his pulse spiking. "What the hell have I got to do with anything?"

Jess met his gaze. "Rory reckons I'm still hung up on you."

For fuck's sake. This was fast becoming painfully uncomfortable. "Okay," he said, placing his palms on the table. "I'm going to get ready for bed." He scraped his chair back and got to his feet.

Jess stood. "Me too."

She followed him up the stairs and went into the bedroom while he opened the linen cupboard and got out the spare duvet, leaving it at the top of the stairs to take down. He just needed to fetch his favorite pillow. Sleeping without it was an impossibility.

The bedroom door was open, and the sound of water running

came from the en suite. He grabbed the pillow—and Liv's T-shirt—and when he turned, Jess was standing in the doorway of the bathroom, wearing only her underwear.

"Fucking hell," he said, covering his eyes and turning for the door, rushing in his discomfort.

"Wait," she called after him. "Where are you going?"

"To sleep on the sofa," he said, unable to suppress his pissed-off tone. "You didn't think I was going to sleep here with you, did you?"

Her lack of response said it all. He closed the door loudly behind him, then grabbed the linen and took it down to the living room, where he got under the duvet on the sofa, bringing it right over his head in an effort to cocoon himself from the painful awkwardness of the evening.

SATURDAY MORNING BREAKFAST WAS NOT GOING WELL FOR LIV. Sam was talking but she couldn't take anything in.

He paused, eyeing her. "Liv?"

"Mm-hmm?" Her mind was on the series of intimate messages she and Arran had been sending over the past few days.

Sam shot her a knowing look, and she guessed Maya had told him about the Arran-related developments. He glanced toward the kitchen, where Tara and Angus were preparing breakfast in a very lovey-dovey, adorable manner. He leaned in. "I know what you're thinking about. Or should I say, *who* you're thinking about." He shot her a grin.

She rolled her eyes. "I know that you know. Because I told Maya you were allowed to know, you know?"

He shook his head. "Maya didn't tell me. Well, she did. But I already knew because Arran had called."

Her ears pricked up. "And what did he say?"

Sam appeared shifty for a moment. "Don't worry, he didn't give me any details." He screwed up his face. "Because that would be both weird and yuck."

Liv punched his arm. "Plus, it's none of your biz."

"Yeah, I know," he said rubbing his arm and poking his tongue out at her. He settled back in his seat. "How do you feel about him?"

She paused, taken off guard. "Strongly. But I'm not sure he feels the same."

He raised his eyebrows. "Why not?"

Her heart felt heavy in her chest. "He hasn't said anything. Hasn't indicated any clue about whether he's thinking this is casual or something else."

Sam fiddled with his mug. "I think it's the latter."

She gave him a nudge, her hopes rising. "How do you know?"

"I just do. The way he's behaved. How he was pining for you after the Skye trip. The way he spoke about you when he told me."

Pining for her? Her heart warmed at the idea that he could like her enough to pine, but then she was needled with guilt at the thought of his being forlorn. "Did he actually tell you that he *like* likes me? That he wants a relationship?"

He opened his mouth, then closed it again. "Not in so many words, no." Her disappointment must've been obvious, because he grasped her hand and gave it a squeeze. "Trust me, Liv. I know him."

She sighed. "What about all that stuff he's said over the past year? That he doesn't want another serious relationship. Plus, he always gave off the impression that if Jess wanted to rekindle things, he'd jump at the chance."

Sam shook his head. "That was before. It's been different since the New Year. And I reckon that's to do with you."

To do with me? Her heart rose at the thought that he might feel something deeper for her. He'd told her that although he missed being a family with Jess, he didn't miss her as a person. Surely that meant he'd finally moved on. And yet, she was still flooded with panic at the idea that he might want to rekindle with Jess if the opportunity arose. Would things be different if Jess wanted to get back together?

Sam took her hand. "Listen. You were there for me while I was with Cat." He gave a little shudder as he said her name. "Then it was your wisdom that guided me onto the right path with Maya." Liv raised her eyebrows at him when he uttered the word *wisdom*, and he shot her a grin. "Don't give me shit for admitting you're the wise one, or I'll steal all your stuffed animals." That was the kidding-around threat he used to use when they were younger, and unlike back then—when she'd burst into tears and punch his arm—this time it made her smile. "Anyway," he continued. "You need to let *me* help you now. It's your turn to get some support." His voice became a little strained. "You said you wouldn't hold stuff back from me anymore, when we spoke before Christmas. But I know you have been."

Her heart sank to her feet, weighed down by guilt. "Sam—"

He held his hand up. "It's okay. Don't apologize or feel bad. I'm not pressuring you. When you're ready to talk, I'm here."

Tears pricked at her eyes and she glanced over to check that Tara and Angus were still distracted. Letting one family member know about her pain was hard enough; she couldn't contend with the guilt of weighing down two more. "I didn't mean to keep it from you. I just didn't know how to voice it without sounding unhinged."

Sam slid an arm around her shoulder, kissing the top of her head.

"Did Maya mention anything?" she asked.

He gave her a squeeze. "She alluded to something. But she didn't want to give any details because she thought I should hear it directly from you."

Her heart warmed at that sentiment. She lowered her voice. "Can we talk in the other room?"

Sam nodded, getting up and leading the way out of the kitchen, where their mum and Angus seemed oblivious to their departure, dancing to an old disco tune.

They went into the living room and Liv sat on the sofa, Sam taking the chair next to her.

"It's all to do with Dave, really," she told him.

Sam hesitated for a beat. "I thought as much."

Liv took a breath, avoiding her brother's gaze. "Basically, I got paranoid over a number of years that I was like him. Especially because of something Dean said when we broke up."

His voice was tight. "What did he say?"

She gave him a soft smile. "It doesn't matter now. But in any case, I was a little at fault for how I handled breaking up with him, and then it made me become wary. Then that wariness morphed into fear, which became this kind of phobia." She shuddered. "I know it sounds ridiculous. But if I started to get vibes that a guy I was seeing was catching feelings, I'd get these horrible palpitations. I felt physically sick. Then I'd finish with him." She glanced up, worried that she'd see judgment in his eyes. Her shoulders relaxed at the sight of the empathy shining in them.

He gave her a soft smile. "I always thought Dean was the one who finished it. You were so upset about it."

She nodded. "I'm sorry for letting you think that. And I was upset, because of how I'd hurt him and because I believed him when he said I was like Dave."

His voice was firm. "You aren't."

Liv cleared her throat. "I didn't feel anything, Sam. After I practically beat up our own father."

He squeezed her shoulder, studying her face. "Why should you? He sabotaged your relationship from day one. Made you feel belittled and insignificant. He created the void between you. That's why you didn't feel anything." He gave her a meaningful look. "Not because you're a cold monster like him."

Each time she told someone, a little piece of the burden drifted from her soul. "You know something?"

"What?"

"When we were sixteen, and you gave up karate but I carried on, it was because I fantasized that one day, I'd use it on Dave."

Sam tucked a strand of hair behind her ear. "Good for you."

She searched her brother's face. "You don't think that makes me a bad person?"

"Nope." He leaned in. "The very fact that you worry so much about being like him means that you're nothing like him. Do you think Dave gives a shit about how he is? How his actions affect others? That's all you care about, sis."

"I don't think Mum would agree."

Sam was silent for a moment. Then he left his chair to sit next to her on the sofa, pulling her in for a hug. He kissed the top of her head. "I'm sorry."

She shook her head against his shoulder. "It's not your fault."

"Yeah, it is. I should have been there for you. I should have made it easy for you to tell me all this stuff years ago."

She pulled back to look him in the eye. "I mean it, Sam. I didn't tell you this to make you feel bad."

"Yeah, well. I should have noticed it all myself instead of being wrapped up in my own shit."

She raised an eyebrow. "Wrapped up in shit? That sounds pretty stinky."

A smile tugged at his mouth as he nudged her arm. "You know what I mean." He paused to rub his beard. "Do you think that's another reason why you invested in karate? Maybe it was an unconscious tactic to help you get out all this stuff."

She hadn't thought of it that way. "Yeah, maybe. It could have been an outlet for the emotions I didn't feel able to show in any other way."

He reached over to squeeze her hand. "I'm glad you told me. Now I can reassure you that you have no need to worry about being anything like our deadbeat dad, and you can feel free to say whatever's on your mind. Negative or not. I've got your back."

Warm relief soothed her system further, calming her troubled thoughts. "Everything you're saying mirrors what Arran said. I'm so glad I told him."

Sam's face softened. "You confided in Arran?"

She nodded.

"And you hadn't told anyone before?"

She shook her head.

Sam smiled. "He's enabled you to open up, Liv. And he's encouraged you to go on doing that. Don't you see how significant that is?"

She frowned. "Of course I do. He's an amazing friend."

He gave her another squeeze. "It means more than that. Maya is an amazing friend. So is Elise." He pretended to dust his shoulder. "And so am I." She punched his arm lightly and he gave her a mock wince. "But you still didn't confide in any of us. There's something between you and Arran. A special connection." He raised his eyebrows. "And I think you know what it's called."

The frown melted from her face as she processed what Sam was saying. She and Arran were best friends, but she didn't have the same intense connection with her other best friends. And the shift to becoming lovers had brought something unexpected with it. *Love.*

Her jaw dropped.

Sam was smiling softly. "You've just figured it out, haven't you?"

Her mouth was dry. "Yeah," she said, speaking through sandpaper. "I have."

"You have to tell him," Sam said.

Shit. I do.

She stood abruptly. "I have to go now. Before I lose my nerve."

He nodded "Go for it. I'll cover for you with the olds."

"Thanks, bro." She kissed his cheek, then hotfooted it out of the living room, down the hallway, and out the front door, where she hurried into her car and pulled away.

Somebody must have extended the road between her mum's and Arran's, because the journey took *forever*. She checked the time on her car display. It was only ten a.m. He wouldn't have left to collect Jayce yet.

What was she going to say when she got there? "Morning. I love you. Fancy a cup of tea?"

Her heart was racing by the time she arrived, and she sat for a minute, attempting to gather her thoughts and taking a couple of deep breaths. When no helpful thoughts were forthcoming and she felt as if her heart was going to beat out of her chest, she left the car and somehow managed to ring the doorbell without passing out.

It seemed to take a while for the door to be answered, and she wasn't sure if it was just her warped sense of time since she'd decided she needed to come here and declare her feelings for Arran out in the open.

Then the door opened, and she held her breath in anticipation of seeing his beautiful face.

But instead of Arran standing there, it was Jess. Her long sandy hair was tousled and she was wearing a T-shirt that was definitely Arran's . . . and, it appeared, nothing else. Jess shifted in the doorway, the T-shirt riding up a little, and Liv caught sight of a flash of lace.

Phew. She's wearing underwear.

Liv swallowed hard, dragging her eyes up from Jess's very lovely legs to meet her eyes. What the hell was she doing there? Practically naked except for Arran's T-shirt?

The memory of straddling Arran, lifting his T-shirt over her head, flashed into her mind. Nausea swelled in her gut.

Jess frowned. "Are you looking for Arran?"

Clearing her throat, Liv managed a nod.

Jess rubbed her forehead as if she had a headache. "He's not home. He said he had to go out for something."

Her throat felt dry and scratchy. "Will he . . . be back soon?"

Jess shrugged. "He didn't say."

Her brain was screaming, "Retreat, retreat!" So she shuffled backward, muttering something about needing to be somewhere and catching him later.

Jess was still frowning. "Are you okay, Liv?"

"Yep, yep," she said, darting her gaze around like a madwoman, her palms sweating. "Have a great day."

Jess glanced down at herself, then lifted her gaze again, opening her mouth to say something, then appearing to think better of it.

Liv gave an awkward wave, turned on her heel, and hurried to her car, climbed in, and drove off.

Chapter
TWENTY-SIX

"HELLO? EARTH TO ARRAN."

Arran blinked, lifting his gaze from the messages, or lack thereof, on his phone to meet his mum's eyes across the kitchen.

Fiona arched an eyebrow. "I asked you what you want for dinner."

"Oh, sorry." He ran a hand over his hair. "I really don't mind. Whatever you and Dad fancy."

He frowned at his phone again. Why hadn't Liv returned his messages? He'd sent one as soon as he'd gotten back from his impromptu morning walk, being in such a hurry to leave the house that he'd forgotten his phone. Jess had been wandering around for what felt like an eternity wearing nothing but the T-shirt she'd borrowed to sleep in and her underwear, and it had made him painfully uncomfortable. He'd kept telling her to feel welcome to grab a shower and that she could borrow any clothing that she wanted, but it had seemed to fall on deaf ears.

Eventually, when he had been trying to make a drink and she'd kept brushing close beside him, he'd announced that he needed to go out for something. Then he'd bolted out of there, not stopping to grab anything, in case she'd followed him out of the bloody house still in that goddamn T-shirt and knickers.

Liv hadn't answered that first message, sent in the late morning. Nor the one he'd sent that afternoon once he'd dropped off a (finally) clothed Jess, picked up Jayce, and arrived at his parents' house. And both of the texts had been hot, explaining with an impressive amount of detail what he wanted to do to her the next day.

She was probably just busy. She'd had breakfast with her family, then no doubt she would've gone to see Maya, who'd been at her own parents' for lunch. Or maybe she'd popped in to see Elise and Jack. It wasn't like she'd be staring at her phone, waiting for him to message. The way he was doing with her.

"Your dad fancies steak," his mum was saying.

"Great," Arran said absently, wondering what Liv was doing right now.

Fiona came to sit beside him. "What's wrong, love? You've been distracted since you arrived. Everything okay with Jayce?"

He touched her arm, regretful that he'd made her concerned. "He's great. Absolutely brilliant."

"The studio, then?" She crossed her arms. "I know it's something. You've got a face like a skelped arse, boy."

He laughed despite himself. "Sorry, Mum."

She sighed. "Dinnae apologize. Just *explain*."

Arran hesitated. He couldn't very well say "I'm worried that the woman I've been sexting hasn't replied."

"Ugh," Fiona said, huffing out another breath. "You are something else. I'll be more specific. What's happening with Liv?"

He snapped his gaze up to meet her eyes. "What?"

She shook her head. "Och, don't act all surprised. I know there's something going on with you two. Every time I speak to you it's 'Liv this, Liv that.' Today is the first day in months you haven't mentioned her. So that, plus you behaving like you're about to bawl your eyes out, is a giveaway."

Arran rolled his eyes. "Okay, Sherlock. Yeah, something happened. And now she's ghosting me."

Fiona frowned. "Ghosting? You mean she dressed herself up in a white bedsheet and said 'boo'?"

He laughed. "It means ignoring all someone's messages."

"Ah, I see." She leaned in conspiratorially. "What did you do?"

Arran raised his eyebrows. The audacity of Fiona Adebayo knew no bounds. "What do you mean? I did nothing!"

She pressed her lips together, shaking her head. "In my experience, that means a man has done *something* to upset his woman. Whether he realizes it or not."

Arran's dad entered the room, holding Jayce's hand, clearly catching Fiona's words and sending Arran a "just agree with whatever she says" look. He took the wee one to raid the biscuit jar.

Arran's heart rate picked up. "I can't think of anything I might've done."

"Humph. Well, that's typical of you men."

"I like the way you automatically assume I'm in the wrong, even though I'm your bloody son," he muttered.

She gave him a soft tap on the back of the head. "That's because I'm a wise woman."

He shook his head, unable to suppress his smile. "Fine. Counsel me, oh wise one."

Her eyes seemed to sparkle as she leaned in. "Can I give it to you straight, no sugarcoating?"

At that point he laughed solidly for a good few seconds. "You mean, that *isn't* what you've been doing so far in this conversation?" He blew out a breath. "That makes me worry. Okay, fine. Shoot."

His dad sat across from them with Jayce on his knee, seemingly interested in whatever wisdom his wife was about to spout. "Listen to your mother, son. I can tell you, she is always right," Abeo said in his soft Nigerian lilt, opening a chocolate biscuit for Jayce, whose eyes were as wide as saucers as he eyed his bounty. Morning, noon, or night, if Jayce asked his grandfather for a biscuit, the answer was always yes.

Clearly delighted at the prospect of telling her son how it was, the sparkle in Fiona's eyes intensified. "I know Liv, and she's a bloody delight. I can't believe it's taken you this long to figure that out, by the way."

Arran closed his eyes painfully, and she continued. "Anyway. She's also not the sort to play games and mess you around, like this specter thing you mentioned."

He frowned. "*Specter?*"

She waved her hand in a dismissive manner. "The not-answering-the-messages thing."

"It's *ghosted*, Mum," Arran said, eyeing the chocolate smeared all over Jayce's face like the kid was giving himself a facial.

"My point is, if Liv hasn't answered when she normally would have, then it means she's upset with you." She gave him a pointed look. "And she's such a delightful girl, that means *you've* done something wrong."

He opened his mouth to protest, then realized there was truth in his mum's deductions. Liv wouldn't play games, that was for sure. And she did normally answer straightaway. So, either she was upset, or something urgent had happened today to waylay her.

Abeo sucked his breath in through his teeth. "I think she has hit the nail on the head. You've probably been a bit of a Dundee United."

Anxiety stabbed Arran in the gut. What if something was wrong? The worry snowballed into a tidal wave that nearly knocked him off his chair. *What if she's been in an accident?*

He stood abruptly. "Can you guys keep an eye on Jayce while I go call Liv?"

Abeo nodded. "Of course, son. Go."

Fiona got up from the dining table and moved into the open-plan kitchen, muttering, "It's about bloody time."

Arran left the kitchen, heading into the front sitting room, where it was quiet. He dialed her number and it rang and rang. With a sinking heart he thought it was going to voice mail, but at the last minute, she answered. Her voice sounded weird.

"Thank God," he said with a sigh. "I was in a free-fall panic that you'd been hurt or something and that's why you hadn't answered my messages."

She took an audible breath. "I didn't realize you'd be worried. I've just . . . been busy. Sorry."

Something was definitely wrong. "No need to apologize. I don't expect you to be at my beck and call." The fact that she'd answered, and was okay, was a huge relief. But the knowledge that something was bothering her needled him. What if she'd realized how he felt and she didn't feel the same way?

He rubbed at his chest, remembering her story about Dean. How she'd wanted to back out just as he was getting serious.

So, she'd ghosted him.

His breath caught in his throat, the hollow feeling splitting wide open. "Are you still coming over tomorrow? Or I can come to you?" He clamped his mouth shut, worried that he sounded a little desperate.

There was a second's silence. "You still want to meet?"

It was getting harder to ignore the sinking feeling. "Why wouldn't I?"

She was quiet again. As if she was expecting him to say something. But what was he supposed to say? "Liv, if something's up, I wish you'd tell me."

She cleared her throat, a pointed tone to her voice. "Yeah, that's how I feel too."

Arran rubbed his face, his brain a complete mess. His heart too. It sounded as though she was going to say something more, but then there was a noise in the background that sounded like someone calling her name. Maya, perhaps?

"Listen," she said. "I need to go. But I'll still come over tomorrow so we can talk about this. Okay?"

Talk about what? He still didn't know. "Okay," he managed to say.

"I'll be over tomorrow." She ended the call.

"LIV," MAYA CALLED THROUGH THE BATHROOM DOOR. "ARE YOU okay?"

"Yeah," she replied. "Just coming." She unlocked the door and came out, and Maya enveloped her in a hug.

"I take it that was him on the phone?" Maya asked.

Liv nodded against her friend's shoulder.

"Come on. Let's go to my room. Well, my old room. Don't suppose I can call it mine now that I live with Sam."

Maya took her hand and led her to the bedroom, where she made Liv sit back on the pillows, covered her in a fleecy throw, and then put a teddy in her arms.

Liv laughed. "Thank you."

Maya gave her a soft smile, sitting next to her. "Did he mention Jess?"

A lump rose in her throat. "Nope."

"Did you ask about her?" Maya asked, lifting the throw to get under it with her.

Liv screwed her face up.

Maya sighed. "And you tell me *I'm* the conflict-avoidant one."

"It's not that," Liv said, inadvertently cuddling the soft teddy. "I wanted *him* to be the one to bring it up, you know? I didn't want to back him into a corner. I wanted him to be open and honest."

Maya was silent for a moment. "I suppose I can see your point. Are you sure we shouldn't call Sam?"

"No," Liv replied quickly. "I don't want to cause trouble. Let me speak to Arran first. If he doesn't bring it up tomorrow, then I'll ask him about it." She leaned back into the cushions. "Sorry for barging in on you and your parents, by the way. I didn't mean to gate-crash your family time. I needed to tell someone and didn't feel like that should be Sam, or Mum and Angus. Or Elise. Goodness knows that woman has enough to worry about."

Maya eyed her. "Do you really think they slept together?"

"No. Maybe." She took a deep breath, the idea of it making her sick to her stomach. "I really, really hope not."

Maya snuggled in beside her and gathered her up in her arms, stroking her hair. "I don't think Arran would do that."

"Me neither. But it did look very incriminating. Then he didn't even mention it just now. Plus, if he does still have feelings for her, it would explain why he's been giving off this whole holding-back vibe ever since we slept together."

Her eyes stung, so she closed them to hold back the tears. "It really hurt, you know? Seeing her there in his T-shirt when that's what he did with me. Gave me his shirt, and I was still wearing it when we . . ." She stopped talking because the words were like little knives cutting her vocal cords as she uttered them.

Maya gave her a squeeze. "I know," she said softly. "Maybe you should call him back? Ask him now?"

Liv swallowed the painful lump in her throat. "I feel like I need to ask him in person. See the expression on his face. It's an in-person conversation."

Maya nodded. "Okay."

"Maya?" Liv said, her throat pained by her own voice.

"Yeah?"

"I don't know what I'll do if they're getting back together."

Maya rubbed her back. "I know. It'll be okay."

But she couldn't help thinking that she'd blown it. She'd been afraid to tell him how she felt, so he'd have no idea that she didn't just want something casual. Then, when the love of his life came along, wanting to rekindle things, of course he'd jump at the chance.

ARRAN PACED THE HALLWAY, PAUSING EVERY SO OFTEN TO PEEK through the peephole to see whether or not Liv's car had pulled up. He checked his watch. Any minute now and she should be there.

The noise of a car sounded outside and he zipped to the door again. It was her. The phone began to ring, but he ignored it in his hurry to unlock the door, opening it before she'd even reached it. She was wearing her faded jeans and a fur-lined jacket hanging open to reveal a T-shirt that said "Obstinate Headstrong Girl" on it.

She came in, and the pinched, anxious expression on her face made his mind race. She was clearly anxious about whatever she wanted to tell him, and it put him in mind of Dean, how Liv had been anxious about breaking up with him. And connecting those dots made him feel sick. "Tea?" he said, for want of a better greeting.

They went into the kitchen and she helped him make a pot, both sneaking glances at the other but not saying anything beyond functional phrases such as "here're the teabags" and "I've got the milk."

Once they sat down, he looked at her, and she met his eyes. It was like some sort of standoff, each one waiting for the other to speak.

Eventually, she spoke first. "Is there anything you want to tell me?"

He raised his eyebrows. "I should ask you the same thing."

She bit her lip, then pushed her glasses up her nose. "I came to see you yesterday morning."

Arran frowned, trying to remember what day yesterday had been, because the past twenty-four hours had seemed more like two years. What had he been doing yesterday morning? He should've been home. How come he hadn't been? "Oh yeah, I was out for a walk. Sorry I missed you."

Why would she be upset that he hadn't been home when she'd called? He studied the hurt expression on her face.

Then the penny dropped. Only it wasn't so much a penny as a sledgehammer of epic proportions.

Jess.

He smacked his palm to his forehead. "Oh shit."

She raised her eyebrows, as if to say, "Too damn right."

He groaned, closing his eyes and rubbing his forehead, which was actually a bit sore from the slap he'd given it. "She answered the door, didn't she? And she would've been wearing that goddamn T-shirt because she was *still* fucking in it when I got home."

Liv was looking at him as if her heart might break, and he was hit by conflicting emotions—hope that her being upset might mean she felt something for him beyond friends with benefits, and a gut-wrenching pain that she'd been inadvertently hurt by him.

He grabbed her hand across the table. "Liv, nothing happened."

Her eyes were wide and he got the palpable sense that she wanted to believe him. "She didn't tell you I came over?"

That part of the scenario hit home, and he gritted his teeth. "No. She did not."

Liv kind of deflated in her chair, as if a weight had been lifted from her, and she held on to his hand tightly, waiting for him to elaborate.

He took a deep breath. "She turned up pissed the night before. Said her and Rory had had a fight and she didn't want to go to her mum's because Jayce was staying over there and she didn't want to upset him. I thought it was weird that she didn't go to one of her friends' places, but then I felt bad when the waterworks started. So, I gave her a T-shirt and my bed, and I slept on the sofa. *Nothing happened.*"

Liv nodded slowly. "But it sounds like she wanted something to happen."

Arran hesitated, adding up a few points that he'd been trying not to think about. Firstly, Jess had told him the argument with Rory was about him. Secondly, Jess had given him the impression she was expecting him to share a bed with her. And thirdly, all the hanging around bare-legged in his T-shirt brushing against him the next morning. It had been obvious what she'd wanted.

But in the car on the way to her mum's, he'd kept shutting her down every time she tried to talk to him about it. "Yeah." He sighed. "I think she did." A thought occurred to him, one that made his anger snowball. "So when you came over, she didn't say anything to clarify the situation? Just that I wasn't home?"

Liv shook her head. "She said you'd gone out. Then she seemed to take on board that I was kind of . . . shell-shocked." He squeezed her hand, his pulse firing. "Then it seemed as if she was going to say something else, but she didn't."

"Fuck," he said, for want of a better response.

They both sat in silence for a few seconds. Arran's mind cycled quickly through all his questions. Had Jess deliberately made it look like they'd slept together, in order to push a wedge between him and Liv? Did Liv really believe that nothing happened? Did the fact that Liv had been upset about it mean she cared for him the way he did for her?

But the first question to come out of his mouth was, "How come you came over yesterday morning?"

She appeared caught off guard, squeezing his hand tightly and opening her mouth, but staying silent. His heart clenched. *Please don't tell me you were coming over to say you want to end this.*

The doorbell rang, and Arran let out an expletive that would've made Fiona Adebayo slap him around the head.

Liv smiled weakly. "You can answer it."

He looked at her for a moment, tempted to blurt out how he felt. But he just needed to send whatever tosser was on his doorstep packing first.

With a sigh, he reluctantly released Liv's hand and made for the door.

When he opened it to reveal Jess on the other side, he briefly considered running out the door, down the street, and cross-country, Forrest Gump–style.

"For fuck's sake," he muttered.

Jess frowned. "Pardon?"

He stared at her. "Nothing."

"Can I come in?"

He gritted his teeth. "Why?"

She stared at him as if he'd grown two heads. "Please, Arran."

He stayed put, imagining that he possessed Superman laser vision that could zap his ex out of existence. "Liv's here."

She had the decency to appear guilty. "I know. I saw her car. But I want to speak to her too."

Of course she knew what Liv's fucking car looked like. She'd seen it the previous morning when she'd scared her off.

Liv appeared at the other end of the hallway and gave him a reassuring smile, gesturing for him to let Jess in. But her smile didn't light up her eyes like usual.

Resigned to whatever fresh hell this was going to be, he shifted to the side, gesturing for Jess to come in.

He followed her into the kitchen, waiting for her to take a seat across from Liv. Then he sat right next to Liv, hauling his chair up close to hers and putting an arm around her shoulders.

Jess looked as though she wanted the ground to swallow her up.

Liv glanced at him, biting her lip. "Maybe I should leave you guys to it."

She shifted as if to stand, and Arran clamped a hand on her thigh, keeping her in her seat. "Don't."

She snapped her eyes to his, and for a moment, he was transported back to his studio, her naked on the couch and meeting his gaze steadily as he sketched her.

Jess shook her head. "No, don't go, Liv."

Arran dragged his gaze over to Jess, keeping his hand on Liv's leg and wondering what the hell was going on.

Jess cleared her throat. "This concerns both of you." She shifted in her seat, fiddling with her nails. "I wanted to apologize. For yesterday morning. I, er, I think I kind of gave you the wrong idea."

"Kind of?" Arran said, unable to keep the anger out of his voice.

Liv slid her hand on top of his, and it immediately infused him with some calm.

Jess glanced up and back down quickly. "Yeah. I know what it looked like, and I get the feeling that something might be going on with you guys, so I just wanted to say I'm sorry, and that nothing happened with me and Arran."

"Too fucking right it didn't," Arran said, appreciating the manner in which Liv rubbed her thumb over his skin in response.

"If you don't mind me asking," Liv said, shooting him a calming look. "I think you realized at the time how it appeared. So how come you didn't say anything?"

Jess kept her eyes down. "I won't lie. I came over here hoping something would happen, and when it didn't I was angry. Then when you arrived, I was jealous." She took a shaky breath. "I've been jealous of you two hanging out together for a while."

Arran's pulse spiked. "You've no right to feel jealous."

"I know," Jess said, squeezing her eyes shut as if she was in pain. "I'm sorry."

Liv stroked Arran's hand. "Then why did you?"

Jess looked at Liv. "I guess because . . . things aren't going well for me and Rory. And just as that started to happen, and I wondered whether things weren't going to work out with him long term, you two seemed like you were more than friends. It made me confused about whether I'd made a mistake."

Arran ran a hand over his hair. "Jess." He sighed. "Just because things aren't going well for you doesn't give you the right to sabotage me."

The dejected expression on her face sent an icy splash of cold onto the heat of his anger.

They sat in silence for a couple more seconds, Arran glancing at Liv and taking in the soft expression on her face as she studied Jess.

"Can I ask another question?" Liv said.

Jess nodded, blinking quickly.

"And there's no judgment," Liv continued softly, giving Arran a reassuring look. "But had you . . . become interested in Rory while you and Arran were still together?"

Jess nodded again, eyes down. A few months ago, that admission would've cut him like a knife. But now, he didn't even care.

"The grass seemed greener?" Liv asked.

"Yeah. I kind of . . . felt down on myself. Things hadn't been the same between me and Arran for a while, especially since we had Jayce." She glanced up at him. "Don't get me wrong, I love Jayce to bits. But my life changed completely when we had him, whereas sometimes I felt like yours hadn't. Then Rory had this carefree attitude and a party lifestyle."

Liv nodded. "But it wasn't really what it seemed."

"No," Jess said. "It was good at first. Exciting. But the novelty wore off. Especially when I couldn't keep up with all his partying. I do have a small child to care for. I thought I still wanted all that carefree stuff, but I don't." She took a breath. "And I think he's cheating on me. But when I asked him about it, he deflected by accusing me of being hung up on Arran."

Liv reached over to touch Jess's hand. "I'm sorry it didn't work out how you'd hoped," she said quietly.

Jess's expression softened, and she blinked again, her eyes wet. "Thank you."

Arran's heart swelled with love for Liv. *She always understands everyone else's point of view. Always makes everything okay.* He glanced at Jess, begrudgingly acknowledging that his anger had fizzled away, leaving only sympathy and sadness for her.

Liv gave Jess a reassuring smile, then turned to him. "Can I have a quick word in private?"

"Yeah," he replied, unsure where all this was going, but pleased that Liv was there to act as a mediator because it would've gone very differently if she hadn't been present. They got up and he glanced at Jess. "Back in a sec."

He took Liv into the living room and shut the door.

She turned to him, grasping his hands. "Listen. Maybe you should give her a chance."

His heart thudded and sank right to the bottom of his stomach. "What?"

Her eyes were wide and shining. "Just hear her out. She was in a bad place, vulnerable. Sounds like her mood was low. She made a mistake with Rory, when instead she should've spoken to you to see whether you could've worked things out."

He held her hands tightly, trying to combat the feeling that she was slipping away. "It doesn't matter now. It's all in the past."

She ran a hand up his arm and he felt as if the resulting bolt of electricity might stop his heart.

"Remember how devastated you were when she left? You said yourself you wanted her back. What if this is her coming to her senses?"

Arran's head was swimming. She was touching him, making him want to kiss her and undress her and do things to her on the sofa that might very well harm the integrity of the furniture. And yet the words coming out of her mouth were that he should consider getting back with his ex?

"What if you could work it out? Don't you owe it to yourself? Not to mention Jayce."

He shook his head.

She stepped closer. "If you don't try, you might regret it."

She went to release him but he held on to her. "I don't want to give her a chance. I want us to see where this goes."

Something shifted in her gaze, and her eyes shimmered behind the lenses of her cute purple-framed glasses. She blinked, and her voice caught. "We can't, Arran. Not when all this is still playing out."

He searched her face. "It isn't playing out. It's ended. And there's no rewinding; this is a DVD, not a VHS situation."

She smiled weakly. "Just listen to her. For Jayce's sake. Your pride might've stopped you from convincing her to stay last time." She took a breath, her voice cracking. "I can't be the one who gets in the way. I refuse to be the third wheel here. You take some time out to think about things and decide what you really want. Then after a couple of months, if what you really want is me, we can talk again."

He couldn't speak. *Is this what a heart attack feels like?* He rubbed his chest, swallowing the painful lump that was swelling in his throat. Maybe she wouldn't be saying all this if she knew how he felt. Then it dawned on him. The third-wheel complex. This was all down to the way her father had made her feel like a side character in her own story. How she'd been brought up to pipe down and let other people have their way. Just because she'd managed to voice it to him a few days ago didn't suddenly make it all better. It would take much more than that. Much more from him, and then likely his support while she got to the place where she felt comfortable in seeking some therapy. This wasn't the sort of thing that he could kiss better for her. Plus, all he'd done for the past fucking year was voice how he wanted to steer clear of relationships—like one of these Nice Guy™ pricks who got his heart broken once and then swore off women for eternity. He'd sown the seed that he wanted his ex back into the love of his life's head, and then nurtured it, like a fucking dickhead.

He had to give her the time and space she was asking for. Not to reconsider his relationship with Jess—he had no doubts whatsoever that was over. But to help Liv accept that this was for real. That she was it for him.

He reached for her, taking in the way she came to him readily, nestling her face against his chest. He knew in the very core of his being that she loved him back. "Listen. There's a lot I need to say to you, but I know you're not ready to hear it. So this is what we're going to do." He stroked her hair. "I'm going to give you some space. Not a couple of months, but as long as I can hold out. And then I'm going to tell you how I feel about you and that I want us to be together. Okay?"

She let out a little sob against his chest.

"Shh, it's okay. Everything is going to be okay. We're going to get through this."

She pulled back, her face wet with tears, doubt written all over it. "I hope so." Her voice cracked, and he wished that he could make her believe it now. But he'd done this damage, at least in part, and now he had to work to make it better. Words weren't enough. He needed to show her he loved her, to prove his love, before he voiced it.

He kissed her cheek. "I'm going to be there in the background, every day. Showing you how I feel. Just how you've been there for me every day for the past year."

There was a sliver of hope in her eyes, and that was all he needed. That was enough. He rubbed the moisture from her cheeks, then took her to the front door, where he knelt down to put her shoes on for her, the way he'd done on Skye in the aftermath of her attack. She rested her hand on his shoulder, watching him, and he hoped the symbolism of him kneeling before her wasn't lost on her.

Then he rose to kiss her goodbye, determined that this was only a goodbye for now. He brushed his lips to hers, sliding his fingers into the soft curls of her hair and rubbing his thumb tenderly over her cheek. He slid his tongue along the seam of her lips and she opened for him, just like he knew she'd open her heart to him eventually—if he was patient enough. When he pushed his tongue inside, she let out the sweetest little moan. He held the back of her head more firmly in response, letting his fingers massage her scalp, soothing her as he commanded her with his mouth. *You're mine, and I'm yours.*

When he broke off, he held her gaze for a moment. "I'll see you soon. And in the meantime, you'll be hearing from me."

Eyes wide, she swallowed hard, giving him the tiniest of nods, and then she opened the door and stepped out.

He watched her leave before closing the door and leaning on it for a second. Then he returned to the kitchen, where Jess was sitting at the table.

"I'm sorry for barging in," she said quietly. "I didn't mean to make Liv leave."

He took a seat across from her, folding his hands as he looked at her. He'd stepped back and allowed her to move on when she'd left, albeit after an initial discussion during which he'd asked her to come back and work on their relationship. However, once she'd made it clear that wasn't what she wanted, he'd accepted it. It had hurt more than anything in his life before, but he'd done it with the help of his family, Sam, Nico, and Liv.

Getting over his pride and humiliation had been hard. He hated having to ask people for help, and the whole period had been traumatic for him, especially when the timing had been shit. He'd lost his painting and decorating job and had been trying to get the studio off the ground. Sam had forced some financial help on him and Arran had been grateful but uncomfortable with the whole thing. He'd been paying Sam back gradually, a little each month since.

But despite all that, he couldn't fault her. She'd done the right thing when he'd been blind. Their relationship had run its course, but when they might have called time on it earlier, having Jayce had made them carry on—out of habit and convenience rather than love. Jess had done him a favor when she'd left him before they'd made the mistake of going through with the wedding. Plus she'd given him the gift of their son and set him on a path that had led to Liv.

All the resentment and anger he'd felt toward her earlier, when he'd suspected her of attempting to sabotage him and Liv, had fizzled out. Because really, it had been self-sabotage on his part—his attitude over the past year had seeped into Liv's psyche, ready to grow out of control and cast doubts on his feelings for her when the time came. It had been unbeknownst to him, but his fault nonetheless. "What do you want to say to me?" he asked gently.

She sighed. "I'm just . . . so confused. I thought I knew what I wanted. I was so sure we weren't going anywhere and it'd reached a natural end. Now I feel that way about Rory and me." She fiddled with her rings. "I felt like I had to say something to you. We've got Jayce and that binds us together." She trailed off, meeting his eyes, and tears were forming.

He took a deep breath, then reached for her hand. "Listen. I think what's really happening here is a reaction to the loss of your and Rory's relationship. It's not me you're craving; it's familiarity." He sighed. "Don't take this the wrong way. But I think, if the situation were the same and I was completely single, you wouldn't be here asking me to get back together. I think that subconsciously, it's the fact that I was involved with someone else that made the idea of me more attractive to you. But that's not real; it's just an illusion. Created by your sadness over what's happening with you and Rory."

She remained silent, eyes down, but didn't try to argue.

He gave her hand a squeeze. "You've always had trouble with being on your own, Jess. But being single is better than being with the wrong person. I'm not the answer here. *You* are. You need to spend time with yourself and figure out what it is you really want."

From her resigned expression, he could tell that she knew he was right. She stared at where he was holding her hand for a few seconds, blinking. Her voice was strained. "Maybe."

"Listen," he told her, letting go of her hand. "Things weren't right before Rory came along, were they?"

Jess glanced up and shook her head.

"He wasn't the cause of us going wrong, just the consequence. So the fact that you and he aren't going to be a forever thing has no bearing on the fact that you and I weren't a good fit either."

Something seemed to click in her eyes, and she let out a big sigh, rubbing her face. "I guess . . . I know you're right."

He studied her for a moment, guilt washing over him. "I owe you an apology."

Her eyes widened in surprise. "What for?"

He swallowed. "What you said earlier, about your life changing completely when we had Jayce, but mine not doing the same. You hit the nail on the head. I think one of the many things that were not right between us was that I took a lot of what you did for granted. I should've pulled my weight more. With him, and lots of other stuff."

He closed his eyes in discomfort as he remembered the things he'd told Liv a few weeks back. About pretending to load the dishwasher wrong to get out of doing it. About making out he was worse in the kitchen than he really was. "I'm sorry I didn't see it at the time. But I've got a lot of work to do on myself. And I'm going to do it."

She nodded slowly. "Thanks for saying that."

He rubbed the back of his neck. "I'm also sorry for not noticing that you were feeling down. I should have."

She managed a weak smile. "And I'm sorry things ended the way they did. I should have told you sooner about my doubts. Nothing happened with Rory until after, by the way, but my attraction to him did give me the push to leave."

Arran smiled back. "To be honest, I should thank you for that. I clearly couldn't see the forest for the trees where we were concerned, and you speaking up when you did saved us a load of heartache and hassle. Better to do it pre-wedding than post, and have a divorce to navigate."

She raised her eyebrows. "I didn't expect you to see it that way."

He shook his head, trying to keep the emotion from his voice. "Liv helped me to see it that way."

Jess managed a weak smile. "She's a good one. Hold on to her."

Arran smiled back. "I intend to." He took a breath. "I think we should re-evaluate our childcare arrangements, make sure it's fifty-fifty down the line. It's not fair for you to shoulder the lion's share of responsibility, and I should've realized that before."

Jess swallowed. "I'm good with it, by the way. With Liv being involved with Jayce. She'll make a great co-parent."

The idea of Liv co-parenting his son with him made his heart swell to twice its normal size. She was his family and had been for the past year. He'd just been too much of an idiot to see it.

She managed a stronger smile. "Okay. Let's chat more about it soon." She stood. "I think I'd better get back to Mum's."

He eyed her for a moment. "Will you do me a favor?"

Jess nodded. "After barging in here twice in quick succession? I think I owe you more than one."

He smiled. "Can you consider getting some support for your mental well-being? I'm sorry that I didn't see what you were going through after we had Jayce. I think I just normalized it as our transition into parenthood. But I want you to be happy, for Jayce's sake but also your own. I still care about you even though we aren't in love anymore."

She nodded, her voice wobbly. "I will."

They got up and Arran showed her to the door, waving her off and genuinely hoping she was going to be okay.

The phone started to ring again, so he shut the door and moved over to grab the receiver. "Hello?"

"Where have you been? I've been calling you the past twenty-four hours."

"I was at my parents' with Jayce. Why, what's up, Agnes? Did I put the kidney beans in the wrong place again?"

She tutted. "No, it's more important than that. That's why I was calling you earlier on. I saw something yesterday morning. Your lassie Liv looked upset and I think your ex-fiancée was to blame."

"It's okay, Agnes. We worked it all out." He paused. "Kind of."

"What do you mean?"

"Liv thinks I still love Jess, and I need to convince her that's not the case."

There was a moment's silence. "What are you going to do?"

He pressed his fingers to his temple, squeezing his eyes shut. "I'll think of something." He shifted over to look out of the small window next to the door, watching Agnes's net curtain twitch. "By the way, does this mean you're finally admitting to spying on everyone?"

She chuckled. "Well. Maybe this once I *was* being nosy. But only because I'm invested in you two young ones."

He laughed despite himself.

"Right. We need to make a plan for you to win back your sweetheart."

He raised his eyebrows. "We?"

"Yes. I've read all of the romance novels at Glenavie Library. I'm an expert on the situation. We'll have her back with you in no time."

"Well, I'm definitely not going to say no to any help that's on offer. I'm coming over."

"I'll get the biscuits out."

Arran hung up the phone, then departed for next door to get to work on a master plan to win over the woman he loved.

Chapter
TWENTY-SEVEN

ON MONDAY MORNING LIV HAD MORE TROUBLE THAN USUAL dragging herself out of bed. She'd slept in Arran's T-shirt again and was beginning to worry that his scent was fading from it. Just like how she was worried he was fading from her life altogether.

She wanted to believe what he'd said about them being together. But whenever she contemplated it, a sickening doubt would overwhelm her, leaving her breathless and determined not to let herself hope, for fear of being let down.

In the end, after showering and getting ready, she put his shirt back on under her outfit. She felt like a pathetic loser but couldn't help herself. She was so desperate to hold on to a tiny piece of him.

Going through the motions of her morning routine like a lovesick zombie, she managed to complete the required tasks and get to the front door to pull on her shoes and jacket. She lifted her bag and grasped the handle, then realized there was an envelope sticking through the letterbox with her name on it. In Arran's handwriting.

She was paralyzed for a split second, before a spike of adrenaline zapped her into action and she grabbed hold of the envelope, tearing it open and unfolding the piece of paper inside.

Dear Aggie,

I told you I'd give you time and I meant it. But I also stipulated it would only be as long as I could hold out, and I'm afraid to say that will be just under two weeks, because there's no way when I see you again at Sam and Maya's wedding that I'll be able to hold back. So this is a heads-up that I'll be coming for you then, sweetheart. Save that first dance for me.

In the meantime, please find enclosed a little token from our first "date." God, you looked so beautiful that night I felt like I'd been punched in the heart. I wish I'd told you that at the time.

Love, always,

Arran

Her heart pounding, Liv peered inside the envelope. David Tennant's smiling face greeted her, glued onto the badge that Arran had worn on their blind date. David's face went fuzzy as tears misted her eyes. She pinned him onto her jacket, fingering the badge as she left the house and trying to quiet her racing mind and heart.

TUESDAY CAME, AND LIV FELT LIKE SHE MUST HAVE READ ARRAN'S letter a million times, her heart still pounding each time she did. She still hadn't been able to bring herself to take off his T-shirt, as if she might jinx things by removing it.

Her mind was numb from trying to analyze everything he'd said in the letter. Could he and Jess already have decided they weren't going to make another go of it? Wasn't that too quick a decision? She didn't know what to think anymore.

She made her way to the front door and grabbed her bag, a piece of toast hanging from her mouth. Another letter was peeking out from the letterbox. Her mouth dropped open, the toast falling and smacking onto the floor. She stepped over it in her hurry to grab the envelope. Again, her name was written on the front in Arran's handwriting. This time she dashed to the window next to the door, hoping to catch a glimpse of him leaving the area. But there was nobody there.

She ripped it open.

Dear Aggie,

Day two. I feel like I haven't seen you in years. I miss you, sweetheart. There are two confessions I need to make.

1) *I still sleep with and smell your T-shirt every night (see enclosed picture).*
2) *I love the way you look in a wet T-shirt. Yes, I looked.*

Love, always,

Arran

Liv stuck her fingers into the envelope and pulled out a Polaroid, slapping a hand over her mouth as laughter erupted from her lips. It was a photo of Arran, pouting into the camera and wearing her T-shirt. It was so tiny on him that the sleeves were skintight around the tops of his biceps, his muscles bulging from underneath. The top hugged the upper half of his torso tightly, revealing the outline of his pecs, and the hem lay at mid-abdomen, exposing his glorious abs.

She leaned against the door for a moment, a wave of dizziness washing over her. Then she opened the door and left for work, tucking the photo carefully into her bag.

ON WEDNESDAY MORNING SHE ABOUT BOUNDED DOWN THE stairs to the front door before even showering, desperate to see if another envelope awaited her. And there was indeed one present. But again, nobody was visible when she peered out the window.

Dear Aggie,
     Morning, sweetheart. Hope you slept well. Day three, and I
wanted to remind you of our cozy little hiding place and to tell
you that I miss my half and half pizza buddy.
     Love, always,
     Arran

The Polaroid inside was of Arran inside the fort, patting the
area next to him and holding an open pizza box with half a veggie
supreme and half a pepperoni pizza inside.

She ran upstairs to grab her phone, texting a message to Maya.

> **Arran has been posting messages and
> tokens of our friendship through my door
> every morning. What should I do?**

Maya messaged back:

> **They aren't tokens of *friendship* dummy 😊.
> And I'm not allowed to talk to you
> about it. Arran told us all to give you space
> and not hassle you.**

Liv's already-fit-to-burst heart swelled even further. She tucked
the latest Polaroid into her bag alongside the one of him in her T-
shirt.

THURSDAY BROUGHT A SIGNED PHOTO OF RALPH MACCHIO (THE
original Karate Kid himself), and Friday, a Devil's Erection EP—
featuring a sleeve containing all their lyrics on which Arran had
doodled pictorial representations of the words. Liv couldn't help

smiling whenever she looked at them, alongside her Polaroids, all tucked safely in her bag where she could sneak them out and go through everything at intervals during the day.

Nobody made her smile or laugh or feel good the way he did.

ON SATURDAY MORNING SHE WAS UP EARLY, PARTLY BECAUSE IT was dress-fitting day for the wedding but also because she'd been rising earlier and earlier, hoping to get a glimpse of her handsome postman, but every time she ended up disappointed.

This time the envelope was bigger and bulkier.

> Dear Aggie,
>
> Day six. Remember how we danced together at Angela and Sarah's wedding? I wanted to kiss you so badly. Every time I listen to this song, I think of you. Though to be honest, I think of you every second of the day anyway. But the song makes you more tangible and fills me with hope that we'll dance together again very soon. I want to dance with you and only you, sweetheart.
>
> Love, always,
> Arran

The letter had been wrapped around a CD single of Whitney Houston's "I Wanna Dance with Somebody."

Liv ran through the house to drag out an old CD player. Even though she could easily have pulled the song up on her streaming service, she wanted to play the copy that Arran had given her. The one she knew his fingers had touched. She held the case over her heart as she cranked up the volume, swaying in time to the music in her kitchen.

———

THE DRESS STORE WAS LIKE A TREASURE TROVE, BEAUTIFUL GLIT-
tering gowns in every color of the rainbow. Liv was tempted to run
around touching every material in sight but figured that might be
frowned upon in this posh bridal store.

She was intrigued to see what Maya had chosen, having the ut-
most faith that her best friend wouldn't have selected any hideous
meringues for her and Elise to wear. When Maya had asked whether
she and Elise wanted to see them in advance or have it be a surprise, Liv had gone for a surprise. She'd gotten the feeling that Elise
would probably have preferred a sneak peek, being more cautious
in nature. But she'd said that if Liv wasn't getting a preview, then
she didn't want one either.

All they knew was their two best-women dresses were not the
same. Maya had chosen a different one for each of them.

Tara and Maya's mum—Yvonne—were chatting excitedly nearby
as they discussed the outfits they had already purchased for the
wedding. Liv smiled to herself, allowing their pleasure to take her
mind off her obsession with Arran and his sweet and lovely messages and gifts. The only snag to the dress-fitting trip was that Elise
was late, which wasn't like her. Liv checked her watch. The store was
on an industrial estate out of town and she'd offered to give Elise a lift.
But Elise had said she might be late after her first Saturday morning
shift at the GP out-of-hours center and didn't want to hold them up.

Tara came alongside her and gave her a hug. "Okay, love?"

"Fine, thanks," she said quickly. "This place is amazing."

Tara nodded. "I love the fusion of Eastern and Western design.
I wouldn't even have known it was here, so it's great that Maya found
it." She cleared her throat. "Are you sure you're okay? You haven't
seemed yourself since that incident with your father."

She'd hardly thought about Dave over the past week. A caramel-colored dress caught her gaze, and the hue of Arran's eyes came to mind. It wasn't as if the dress was the same color as his eyes, but it was close enough to remind her of him. Not that it took much, because he was always hovering at the forefront of her thoughts. "Honestly, I'm fine, Mum. I'm really not that bothered about Dad."

Tara didn't appear convinced. "I often think about how I should've thrown him out way before he left us. But I'm sorry to say I was blinded by him for years." She sighed.

Liv took her mum's hand. "I know. It wasn't your fault. It was his."

Her mum met her gaze for a second, then gestured over to a couple of chairs outside the fitting area. "Can we sit? I need to speak to you about something."

"Sure," Liv said, puzzled.

Her mum led her over and they sat down together. "I've come to realize that I've done you a disservice."

Liv frowned. "What do you mean?"

Tara blinked. "I want to apologize for what I said after you protected Angus from your father. You did the right thing."

Liv's breath caught in her throat as she attempted to compute what her mother was saying.

"I also acknowledge that I've done the wrong thing by you for a long time now. I didn't mean to, but I've limited you in speaking your mind, prevented you from being your authentic self. And I'm worried that it's damaged you." Her eyes filled with tears.

Liv reached out to take her hand. "Mum," she said quietly.

Tara shook her head. "Don't try to excuse my behavior, love."

Liv gave her a weak smile, not knowing what to say.

"I know that your dad was the big villain in our lives. But that doesn't make me blame-free."

Liv's voice broke. "Oh, Mum."

Tara squeezed her hand. "You are a brilliant person, Liv. And not only when you're being positive and vibrant. You're a good person on your worst days. When you feel down or angry. And you don't have to hide when you are. You let out whatever you need to let out and know that I love you as you are. And you are absolutely nothing like that good-for-nothing father of yours."

Liv threw her arms around her mother, letting her tears flow. "Thank you."

Her mum's voice was broken by tears. "You're welcome. It was long overdue."

Liv pulled back, rubbing at her face. "Did Sam speak to you about this?"

Hesitantly, her mum nodded. "He did. He sat me down and we had a long, honest conversation. I'm ashamed to say that at first, I couldn't see it. But your brother is very persuasive and determined when he's got his heart set on something." She smiled. "And Angus backed him up."

Liv managed a small laugh. "He's a good egg, that bloke of yours."

"I know," Tara said. "But if there's ever a next time, though I hope there isn't, then I want to hear it directly from you. Not the men in our lives. And I promise to listen. Okay?"

Liv nodded. "Okay."

Her mum hugged her close and Liv had to admit that her twin brother was the absolute best.

Tara pulled back. "What has been on your mind, then? Just now you looked a million miles away, but you said it wasn't because of your dad."

Liv bit her lip. "Just a bit of guy trouble."

Tara's expression indicated that the penny had dropped. "Arran?"

Liv glanced at her. "Has Sam said something?"

"No. I just figured you two seemed close. Especially after he drove you over when your father showed up."

"Yeah, we are." Her heart thudded. "Or were. I don't know. I'm trying to work some stuff out."

"What happened?" Tara asked.

Liv let out a dry laugh. "I did."

Her mum appeared puzzled.

Liv rubbed her face. She was going to need the mother of all facials before this wedding, what with all the crying she'd been doing. Her face must look like a big, puffy, blotchy mess. "It's taken me a long time to work out. But I've had this phobia of serious relationships. After witnessing other people's experiences." Her mum squeezed her hand and Liv gave her a reassuring smile. "Plus ignoring my own personal demons. Then, when I finally felt like I was making headway and letting Arran in, I got really paranoid that he wanted to get back together with Jess. But instead of letting him reassure me, I backed off and hid. I told myself—and him—that it was because I didn't want to get in the way of his family getting back together. And although that's true, perhaps it was also for self-preservation because I'm terrified of how big my feelings for him are and what'll happen if I let myself be vulnerable and then he changes his mind."

Tara frowned. "When your father first left, I would've given anything to have him back. But time made me realize the error in that thinking."

"That's not the same, Mum. Jess is basically a good person." Liv pushed her glasses up her nose. "It's not fair on them, or Jayce, for me to stand in their way."

Tara took her hand, her amber eyes shining. "You've always worried about getting in the way. Ever since you were little. And that's your father's fault."

Something clicked in the back of Liv's mind.

"You weren't the one in the way, sweetheart," Tara continued gently. "He was. You, your brother, and I, we were the team. And your father was the spoke in our wheels."

Liv blinked, trying to stop the hot sting of tears. "Arran's been sending me these messages, Mum. And I want to trust in his feelings for me, and mine for him. But I'm terrified, and as much as I try to work it out and rationalize it, I don't really know why. I think I'm just broken."

Her mum shook her head. "You're not broken, love. Just a little dented. But dents can be smoothed out over time." She reached out to tuck Liv's hair behind her ear. "And just because an emotion can't be rationalized doesn't make it invalid. You'll get there; you just need to be kind to yourself, and trust yourself." She smiled. "And for what it's worth, I think you can trust in Arran too. I can tell that boy thinks the world of you. He looks at you like you're the moon and stars rolled into one. Plus, a man who wasn't in it for the long haul wouldn't have been there for you the way Arran was that day your father barged into the house."

Liv was about to say more when she heard her name being called from across the shop. They turned and Elise was hurrying toward them through the clothing racks, Jack on her hip.

"Hey," Liv said, standing and taking in her wild-eyed appearance. "Are you all right?"

"I'm so sorry for holding you up." Her words came quickly, tripping over one another. "Mum's had a bad morning with her joints and she couldn't manage to have Jack into the afternoon as planned, so I had to go and pick him up after work."

Maya approached and gave Elise and Jack a hug. "It's no problem. You've not held us up."

Elise glanced around the group. "I know it's not ideal having him with us, but I couldn't think who to ask."

Tara smiled, also standing and joining them. "Don't worry,

sweetheart. I'd love to look after him while you girls try on your dresses."

"Me too," Yvonne said, emerging from the changing room. "I've not had a cuddle from wee Jack in ages. He can play with us and watch the fashion show after."

"Are you sure?" Elise asked as Tara took Jack from her. "He constantly wants to walk around just now. No wonder poor Mum's back and shoulders are sore."

"Don't you worry," Tara said with a wink. "I had two of these at the same time, remember?"

Elise laughed, her posture relaxing a little.

"Come on," Maya said, taking Elise's and Liv's hands and leading them into the changing room. "You two both need a bit of pampering." She took a couple of glasses of fizz from the store assistant and handed them over. "The changing rooms are back there." She leaned in and spoke out of the corner of her mouth. "Just don't spill the drinks on any of the dresses, capisce?"

"Aye, Captain," Liv replied, carefully sipping from her glass before walking into the back.

"That's your room in there!" Maya called. "And, Elise, you're next door."

Liv placed her drink on a small shelf at the back of the changing room, then unzipped the bag that contained her dress, her excitement peaking.

She quickly stripped off her clothing and pulled it on, stretching one arm over her head with the other behind her back and contorting herself to try to zip it up unaided. "Come here, you slippery little blighter," she muttered to her new archnemesis, aka the zip. She managed it, then turned to the mirror in triumph, sucking in a satisfied breath at her reflection.

The dress was a sleeveless sea-green prom style that came to mid-thigh. A fitted bodice with an A-line skirt, her favorite style. The skirt swished out satisfyingly as she swayed in it.

"Are you ready, Liv?" Elise called from next door.

"Yep," Liv said, putting on the heels she'd brought with her. She stepped out of the changing room in front of a wall-length mirror. "I *love* mine."

Elise emerged behind her and took a sharp breath. "Liv, you look absolutely *gorgeous.*"

Liv turned to say thank you and had to stop herself from gasping. "Oh my God. You look amazing."

Elise hugged her arms. Her dress was a light blue matte satin floor-length number with thin straps and a cowl neck. It clung seductively to her slender figure. "Are you sure? I don't know if it's a bit too sexy."

Liv raised her eyebrows. "No such thing. You're allowed to be sexy, you know."

Elise joined her by the mirror, studying her reflection as she turned from one side to the other. "I don't mean that," she murmured, glancing behind them. "I mean I don't know if I can pull off sexy."

Liv's mouth dropped open. "Please tell me you're kidding. You, Dr. Kowalski, are one sexy mofo."

Elise's cheeks flushed pink. "I don't know about that."

Liv put an arm around her and pointed to the mirror. "That's your evidence right there."

"Oi!" Maya called through from the seating area. "Where's my fashion show?"

They both laughed, and Liv took Elise's hand to lead them both through to where Maya, Yvonne, Tara, and little Jack were waiting. With her killer heels on and Elise wearing kitten heels, the two were nearly the same height.

The others all stilled, mouths open, as the two women rounded the corner.

"Oh my God. I'm a flippin' fashion genius," Maya said, staring at the two of them. "You both look absolutely *amazing*."

Tara was dabbing at her eyes and Yvonne got out a tissue to pass to her.

Maya went over and took Elise's shoulders. "You are one sexy lady." She released Elise to take Liv's hand and twirl her around. "And you are one hot tamale."

Yvonne was smiling. "You both look beautiful. And each dress matches your eye color perfectly."

Liv did a double take down at herself, then across at Elise. She hadn't even clocked that. Maya had picked out styles that suited them perfectly and that matched her green eyes and Elise's blue ones. She began to well up. Again. She was going to have to get a beauty parlor on speed dial.

"Go and put yours on, Maya," Yvonne said.

Maya let out a little squeal, eliciting a laugh from the group, then disappeared around the corner with the store assistant in tow.

Another assistant came out of the changing area, bringing Liv's and Elise's glasses of prosecco with her. Liv took hers and carefully sipped, terrified of spilling any down her lovely dress.

It was a few minutes before Maya rounded the corner, but it was worth the wait. Her dress was a shimmering blue-green, with different hues blending into one another as the eye moved down the gown. A modern sari style, it consisted of a short-sleeved bodice that gave way to material that appeared to wrap itself around Maya's body to her feet, and at her left shoulder it flowed over and down her arm to the ground.

For a moment Liv nearly lost her hold on her glass. She swallowed hard. "Stunning."

Maya grinned and did a twirl. Liv glanced over to look at Elise, who had her hand over her mouth, her eyes welling. She slid an arm around Elise's shoulders and gave her a squeeze.

Yvonne went over to hug Maya. "Sweetheart, it's so beautiful."

"Why, thank you." Maya did a mock bow. "I'm thinking of jacking in my job at the ski resort to go into styling full-time."

Yvonne laughed. "Another career change already?"

Maya shrugged. "If you've got the gift . . ."

Tara bounced Jack on her knee. "All the dresses are perfect for each of you. And I love how they fit together. The green of Liv's dress and the blue of Elise's incorporated into yours, Maya."

Maya looked at Liv and Elise, her voice uncharacteristically devoid of humor. "The three of us complete each other."

Elise let out a little sob and Liv felt as if the lump in her throat might strangle her. She took Elise's hand and led her to Maya, where they had a three-way hug, though somewhat awkwardly with her and Elise holding out their glasses to a safe distance and attempting not to get tears on Maya's dress.

THE NEXT DAY WAS SUNDAY, AND THIS TIME, LIV HAD SET A SUPER-early alarm to see if she could catch Arran in the act of delivering her message. Although what she'd do if she did spot him, she had no idea. Probably veer between the desire to run out and kiss him all over his lovely face and the instinct to hide behind the curtain and spy on him.

However, she had no need to worry about choosing between the two, because on her arrival downstairs, there was nothing in the letterbox. Her disappointment was so palpable she felt it in her bones.

She shuffled into the kitchen in her fluffy slippers, made some tea and toast, and then snuggled into the sofa and loaded up *Pride and Prejudice and Zombies* to try to cheer herself up.

Just as she reached the part where the Bennet sisters were slow-mo striding down the hallway at Meryton, slashing zombies in their wake, she heard a sound at the front door. Without pausing to decide whether she was going for the kissing option or the hiding-behind-the-curtain option, she ran for the front door and flung it open. Standing on the other side with a look of shock frozen on his face was not Arran but her brother.

Her shoulders sagged. "Sam. What're you doing here?"

He raised an eyebrow. "Delighted to see you too, sis."

She dropped her gaze to register a white cardboard box at his feet. "What's that?"

He ran a hand over his hair. "This one wouldn't fit through the letterbox, so I was going to leave it on the doorstep."

"You mean . . . it's been you delivering all the messages? Not Arran?" She felt disappointed to be disabused of the idea that Arran had been on her doorstep every morning at dawn.

Sam nodded. "Yeah. He asked me to be his delivery guy. He didn't trust himself not to ring your doorbell if he did it himself."

That statement warmed her heart. She glanced down at the box again, her interest piquing.

Sam bent down to lift it. "Here. I can see you're dying to know what's inside."

She took the box. "Come on, you might as well come in."

He followed her to the living room, where they sat on the sofa, and she undid the green ribbon tied around the box. It looked like a cake box.

"What the fuck are you watching?" Sam asked, looking at the TV screen, where the image was frozen on Lily James dressed in a dark satin ball gown and brandishing a sword.

"*Pride and Prejudice and Zombies*," she murmured absently as she lifted the cake box lid.

"For fuck's sake," Sam muttered. "I'll bet Maya would love this."

"She does. But not as much as the 2005 adaptation with Keira Knightley." Liv opened the lid fully, and her eyes about came out on stalks. "A selection of scones from the teahouse!"

Sam laughed. "This guy knows the way to your heart."

She glanced up. "Do you want one?"

He shrugged. "Why not?"

Liv fetched a tray with some plates and fresh tea and they each chose a scone. The box even contained some cream and jam, and Liv did her best to avert her eyes when Sam applied his condiments cream first, just like Maya the scone traitor.

"By the way," Sam said, his mouth full of scone. "How did the dress shopping go?"

"None of your biz," she told him.

He swallowed his mouthful of scone and grinned. "How beautiful did my fiancée look?"

Liv had to fight back tears at the memory of how gorgeous Maya had looked. "Put it this way. You'd better keep some tissues in your sporran on the day, because you're going to bawl like a baby when you see her."

His smile faded to give way to a wistful expression. "Can you give me any clues?"

"Get lost, bro. I'm not giving a single detail away." She mimed pulling a zip across her lips.

He sighed. "Should've known there was no way I'd break you."

She smiled. "It'll be worth it when you see her."

He smiled the sappiest smile in the history of the universe. Liv half expected a Celine Dion ballad to start playing in the background at any moment.

"How excited are you for the wedding, on a scale of one to ten?" she asked him, munching on her scone.

"Like, an eleven," he said, chomping the last piece of his scone in one go. "These are awesome, by the way."

"I know," she said with a sigh. She darted her eyes over at him, then back to her creamy, jammy treat. "Has Arran said anything about me?"

Sam shook his head. "I'm not allowed to talk about it. Arran said—"

"You weren't allowed because I need space," she finished for him. "Maya told me."

Sam shrugged, grabbing his mug of tea to take a sip. "Rules is rules."

"Humph."

He shot her a smile. "I think you know in your heart what you want, and need, to do."

If only it were that easy. She cleared her throat. "I don't understand why it's so hard to get past my own emotions, especially since I've now managed to voice them."

He gave her an empathetic look. "A couple of conversations don't wipe out a lifetime of trauma, Liv. Remember what you told me at Christmas—that I needed to face my past and work through it with Maya. Oh, and I believe you also said, 'Get some therapy,'" he added with a smile.

"I know," she said, fiddling with her throw. "But that was different."

"Different as in—do as I say, not as I do?" He raised an eyebrow. She stayed silent.

"Being strong for others doesn't mean neglecting yourself, sis," he said gently. "There's a lot to unpack."

She bit her lip in an effort to hold back the tears. "Thanks for speaking to Mum for me." She nudged his arm. "You're all right, as far as twins go."

He nudged her in return. "Same goes for you." He lifted his wrist to check his watch. "I need to head out. Few more errands to run apart from delivering messages of love from my bestie to my sister." He stood.

Messages of love. Had Arran told Sam he loved her? She thought about his letters, all signed *Love, always, Arran.* Had he meant that literally?

She thought back to the last time she'd seen him, when he'd told her that he was going to tell her how he felt—once she was ready. Or at least once he could no longer hold out. She hoped he meant that his feelings ran as deep as hers, that not only did he want a relationship but that he loved her too.

She got up to follow Sam to the front door, where she waved him off.

"Thanks for sharing your scones with me," he said as he departed. Then he gave her a wink over his shoulder. "And don't worry. I have a feeling that everything's going to come together at the wedding."

Chapter
TWENTY-EIGHT

L IV DIDN'T BOTHER TO GET UP ANY EARLIER THAN HER NORMAL on Monday, now that she knew the person delivering her messages and treats was Sam and not Arran. But she still headed straight for the letterbox before having a shower.

The envelope contained a picture of Arran dressed like Regé-Jean Page's depiction of the Duke of Hastings, and she let out a gasp when she saw it. "That is amazing," she said out loud. He looked hot AF. She unfolded the letter.

Dear Aggie,
I hope you enjoyed the scones and that they reminded you of our afternoon tea. Another confession—that afternoon your outfit had me fantasizing that you were a hot librarian and I had my wicked way with you amongst the stacks. Speaking of which, I've watched the first series of Bridgerton as research after you told me I looked like the dude from the show. I'm thinking of investing in a library ladder . . .
    Love, always,
    Arran

"Holy shit." He'd watched *Bridgerton* for her. And referenced *that* scene. A romance reader's dream. Liv pulled at the collar of her T-shirt as her core temperature rose by a couple of degrees.

Then, all day, images of that very scene kept passing through her mind, except she was the one on the ladder with Arran's face buried between her legs.

THE NEXT MORNING, WHEN THE ENVELOPE CONTAINED HER NUDE charcoal sketch, Liv very nearly got out her phone to call him to come over. But something still stopped her—apart from the desire to see what the rest of the week brought in terms of his messages. It was clear he felt something for her. But was that enough? Was she enough? Did she even deserve him when she was so . . . dented, as her mother had put it? She opened the letter.

Dear Aggie,
This is an image I really, really hope I get to see again. That day was the hottest experience of my life. You are the most beautiful thing I have ever painted or sketched. More so than any spectacular view in Glenavie or the whole of Scotland. The world even. I want to paint you every day. Then get paint all over you and wash it all off in the shower.
Love, always,
Arran

WEDNESDAY BROUGHT A BEAUTIFUL PHOTO OF THE MAY BLOS-soms in Japan.

Dear Aggie,

The last time we spoke about travel, I very nearly asked you if you wanted to get something locked down and book a trip away together. I don't know if you remember, but we were both naked on the sofa in my studio at the time. Which was fucking awesome by the way. I can't look at that couch without getting a hard-on now. I've had to ban anyone from coming into the studio because if they see me staring at the furniture with a boner, then they're going to think I've got some kind of weird IKEA fetish.

Anyway, the enclosed photo is an invitation to come on an adventure with me and Jayce.

Love, always,

Arran

THE NEXT DAY THERE WAS NO ENVELOPE, NOR ANY SIGN OF SAM with a cake box. Liv headed to work, finding that her hopes were still so easily dashed despite the consistency of his messages.

She arrived at the nursery school, hanging her jacket and stowing her bag. Drop-off time arrived, and her kids entered the classroom one by one.

Jayce's adorable face peeked around the corner, the last to arrive. His babysitter was usually the last drop-off. "Psst. Miss Lib."

She smiled. "Yes, Jayce?"

"I need to show you something."

"No worries. Just bring it in here, buddy."

He shook his head. "It's in my bag. On my peg."

Puzzled, she stood. "Okay. I'm coming."

He dashed off around the corner, and she followed him down the corridor to the pegs; he was standing by his bag, looking around furtively.

"What is it?" she asked him, stifling a laugh at how serious he appeared.

He unzipped his bag, which sported a picture of a noble steed. "In here."

She peered inside, and there was a book. Puzzled, she lifted it out, discovering that rather than a book, it was a photo album.

"What's this?" she asked Jayce, then realized she was speaking to his retreating form as he bounded back down the corridor toward the classroom, where her teaching assistant would be gathering the children in the reading corner.

Curiosity got the better of her, and rather than following Jayce back to class, she sat on one of the benches by the pegs and opened the album.

Her hand went to her mouth, tears pricking at her eyes.

Inside were Henry's photos of her, Jayce, and Arran. And they were beautiful. She leafed through, stopping to admire each shot. Some were of her and Jayce on the beanbags, laughing together as they either toppled onto the bags or lay cuddling on them. And then some were of the three of them—Arran falling comedy-style onto the bag as she and Jayce laughed, Arran pulling them both down with him, and then the three of them cuddling. The first of those showed Arran and Liv smiling at Jayce as he giggled. Then the next showed Arran gazing at Liv as if she were the most revered thing in his universe.

Her breath caught, and tears spilled over onto her cheeks. She stayed there for a few more seconds, taking in every detail of the picture. Then she flipped the page over to reveal Arran's writing on the inside of the back cover.

Dear Aggie,

I hope you don't mind, but I intercepted Henry before he could email these to you so I could have them printed and bound in an album. I wanted to save this gift for last because it depicts what I want for our future. Our little family. I really hope you want that too.

I'll see you tomorrow, sweetheart.

Love, always,

Arran

Chapter
TWENTY-NINE

C OME ON, DUDE. CHEER THE FUCK UP. IT'S A WEDDING."

Arran raised an eyebrow at Nico. "I *am* cheery. This is my cheery face." He kept his expression deadpan for comedy value.

Nico laughed. "I'd hate to see you pissed off, then."

Arran smiled and moved away a couple of paces to adjust a chair that didn't need adjusting, trying to distract himself from his nerves. They were at the venue for the ceremony—under a gazebo at Maya and Sam's favorite stargazing spot, where Arran had been on the receiving end of Sam's pep talk a few weeks ago. The top end of the gazebo was open so that the majestic mountains became the backdrop for the ceremony.

His eyes were drawn to the view, his heart aching with the romance of it all. The chairs were all arranged neatly on the flooring under the gazebo, adorned with pretty fabric in hues of blue and green. It gave off the effect of sea waves rolling over the chairs. Immediately his mind settled on Liv's eyes. Not that it took much nowadays, but these sea tones were very evocative of her eye color.

Across the field, he thought he spied his pal Hamish the Highland cow cozying up to a lady cow. "Nice one, Hamish," he murmured. "Hopefully I'll get my girl too, before the day is out."

Nico came over and gave him a pointed look. "Are you talking to yourself now?"

"No. I'm talking to my friend Hamish." He nodded toward the cows.

Nico let out a deep breath. "You've finally lost it."

Arran pursed his lips. "No, I haven't. We're kindred spirits."

A smile played at Nico's mouth as he reached out to straighten Arran's green cravat. Arran tried to bat him away, but Nico was having none of it. "Let me sort it. You need to look your best for when your lady love arrives."

Arran sucked in a breath, letting Nico work his magic on the cravat. "I really hope she wants to be my lady love."

"She will," Nico said, frowning in concentration. "You've put in a fuckton of groundwork. I might marry you myself."

Arran managed a smile, despite his escalating nerves.

"Anyway." Nico stood back to survey his cravat tidying. "You're a handsome artist who's also a single dad. Last I checked, that ticked a lot of romance-hero boxes."

A noise at the front of the gazebo had Arran snapping his gaze up to see whether the bridal party had arrived. But it was just Sam shifting a chair.

Nico was watching him with a frown. "You okay there, champ? I thought it was only Holland I'd have to coach through today, not you too." He brushed his hands down his own navy waistcoat, taking hold of the sides of his jacket. They were all wearing matching navy waistcoats and jackets, with a blue-green tartan kilt, black kilt socks, and sporrans. Nico's cravat was sky blue, and Arran's sea green. *Like Liv's eyes.*

"Yeah," Arran said. "I was just so sure she felt the same as me and convinced that I could show her how good we are together. But now today is here and I'm absolutely shitting myself that I've failed." He rubbed his eyes. "Maybe I should've given in and called her or gone to see her."

Nico shook his head. "You promised her space. And you outlined exactly when you were going to see her to talk about it—today. You made everything clear and safe for her."

"I hope you're right."

Nico shrugged, a wry smile on his face. "I'm always right."

Arran let out a laugh.

Nico shifted closer, lowering his voice. "By the way, I need to tell you how proud I am of you, bro."

Arran raised his eyebrows. "Are you being sarcastic?"

Nico rolled his eyes. "No. I'm not. I'm proud of you for getting over yourself and going for it with Liv. You've laid it all out there, which is the most fucking courageous thing a guy can do." He gave Arran a nudge. "It's good you didn't let your pride get in the way. You're not actually Mr. Darcy, despite those analogies Maya makes about Liv finding him." Nico glanced over his shoulder, as if checking that no one could hear. "I'm glad you didn't make the same mistakes I did."

They both looked up as guests began to arrive along the walkway to the gazebo, where Sam was greeting them with a smile and a handshake.

Arran frowned, searching Nico's face. *What mistakes?* But before he could ask, Nico smiled. "Now, come on. We have duties to perform." He turned and walked down the aisle toward Sam, and Arran hurried after him.

The guests were all seated and the groom's party waited at the top of the aisle. Sam stood with Tara and Angus at either side, and he and Nico behind them. Sam and Maya had opted not to go for the "traditional" giving away of the bride because Maya had said that she wasn't her father's property to give away, nor did she intend to become the property of her husband. So the arrangement was more akin to two families coming together, with Sam's side waiting at the top of the aisle for Maya, her family, and her best women to arrive. Of course Liv had a place on both sides, though she'd be arriving with Maya. But that made it all the more poignant.

Arran's thoughts raced. Liv would be here soon, but he wouldn't get a chance to speak to her until after the ceremony, once they were at the castle. And even then, it would likely be after dinner and once the dancing began. He was due to accompany Liv to join in the first dance, and Nico was going to dance with Elise.

But when she arrived, would he be able to tell how she felt? Would she give anything away to help put him at ease?

He thought back to what Nico had said. Nico didn't give out compliments very easily, and Arran felt a warm glow that his friend felt proud of him. He suspected that, deep down, his pride probably had been a secondary factor in not telling Liv he was in love with her as soon as he'd realized. His main objective had been not to overwhelm her when she was so vulnerable, but self-preservation might have played a part. Maybe he should have just said it in the moment, and then perhaps she would have trusted in his feelings when Jess had put a spanner in the works. Though he suspected the outcome would have been the same—Liv needed extra reassurance, through actions, not just words. And he was more than happy to give it to her. He'd give her anything she wanted.

The piper began to play just outside the other end of the gazebo, standing next to the temporary walkway on the grass and just visible through the sheer curtain of fabric that covered that end. That signaled the imminent arrival of the bridal party, and Arran's heartbeat took on a steady thrum in anticipation of seeing Liv.

Arran glanced at the piper squeezing his bag. He'd never been a huge fan of the instrument's rather shrill tone. Just then the bagpipes let out a squeak as the piper nearly slipped in something on the grass. A glance down confirmed that Hamish had left a little present underfoot for their noisy friend. Arran looked across the field at where Hamish was canoodling with the fluffy-looking lady Highland cow.

He smiled to himself. *When I marry Liv, we'll have a string quartet instead.*

Fuck. That organic thought had come out of nowhere. And it felt so right.

Arran snapped his gaze up to where Omar and Yvonne, Maya's parents, were coming down the walkway at the opposite end. He couldn't see the rest of the bridal party yet.

As they drew closer, he realized he was the only one in the entire congregation who wasn't straining to see the bride. It was Liv he wanted to lay eyes on.

Maya came into view walking behind her parents, flanked by Hana—her heavily pregnant sister—and her soon-to-be sister-in-law, Rosie, Hana's fiancée. Maya was beautiful, wrapped in a gown of sea green and blue. But those tones reminded him of only one woman, who was walking behind Maya and her family, holding Elise's hand.

Elise did look stunning in a floor-length blue gown, but by God it could've been any one of the hottest and most beautiful of celebrities walking next to Liv, and they still would've paled in comparison.

He couldn't take his eyes off her. The long line of her neck and the smooth skin of her bare shoulders. The way her sea-green dress clung to her chest in a fitted bodice, flaring out into a short skirt that swished about her thighs and made him imagine sliding his hand up the outside of her leg, his mouth following suit up the inside of her thigh . . .

He shifted in an attempt to get his sporran into a shielding position, lest his thoughts be betrayed by what was straining underneath. A true Scotsman wears no underwear with a kilt, after all. A fact that would no doubt be proven at the reception when someone would get pissed and give everyone a flash. *Probably Nico.*

Then Liv lifted her gaze to his, and it almost appeared that she lost her stride a little. Arran nearly reached out to hold on to Nico's arm, she made him so weak at the knees.

Liv didn't look away, continuing to meet his eyes as the party arrived and the two sets of parents greeted each other. He prayed to God that was a good sign.

Arran eventually managed to drag his gaze away from Liv and take in Sam's face as he met Maya. There were tears in his eyes as he held her face to kiss her, the two sets of parents hugging and taking seats in the front rows.

Arran's heart swelled as he watched Sam and Maya, knowing with absolute certainty that they were perfect for each other. *Not like Jess and me.* The more hindsight he gained, the clearer it became that it hadn't been right. Arran glanced at Nico and noticed that he was staring across at Elise in her satin gown.

Sam took Maya's hand at the altar and the registrar began the ceremony. Arran sat forward a little, glancing over at the bridal party to sneak another peek at Liv. Her bare legs were crossed as she watched her brother and her best friend.

Nico leaned in. "Check out Ben and Brodie."

Arran turned his gaze farther back into the congregation. Ben and Brodie were holding hands a few rows back. He shot Nico a smile. "Love is in the air."

"Yeah," Nico said in a low voice, smiling back.

Arran had trouble keeping his eyes on the bride and groom, and off the best woman in the green dress. He kept tuning in and out, admiring the way that Liv's eyes lit up when there was a tender moment between her brother and best friend, and smiling broadly when something humorous was said.

Her hair was swept up and piled on top of her head, with a couple of waves coming down to frame her face. Her eyes were huge and luminescent, outlined in a smoky hue and minus her signature glasses. She must have been wearing her contacts; otherwise, she would've stumbled up the aisle. He smiled to himself just as she glanced over and caught his eye, sending a shock wave into his heart.

Sam was saying the vows he'd written. "I promise to always tell you you're a much better skier than I am." There was a chorus of laughter from the congregation. "And I promise to keep you in as many scones as you can eat."

Maya smiled. "I promise to lie to you and say that *you're* the best skier." An even bigger laugh. "And I promise to love and support you, no matter what."

Sam took her hand. "I promise to love and protect you, no matter what."

Arran swallowed hard, his gaze drawn back to Liv, finding that she was watching him too. Unable to take his eyes off her, Arran leaned in to Nico. "Liv wouldn't need me to protect her. She's such a badass."

Nico glanced at him, clearly taking in that he was still staring at Liv. He spoke in a low voice. "Guys labor under the misapprehension that all women need from them is their physical protection, when most of the time, what they really need from us is emotional validation and support." He seemed to dart a quick glance at Elise as he uttered that last sentence.

Arran allowed his eyes to slide back over to Liv's lovely green-clad form. She'd let him in emotionally. Confessed to him her deepest and most private vulnerabilities, things she'd never told anyone else. Sam had told him that it had enabled her to confide in both her brother and her best friends.

He'd helped her to do that.

His pride rose, but this time for positive reasons. He was proud to have supported the woman he loved. Proud of her for being brave enough to trust him with her emotions. That was where his pride should be rooted—in positive experiences. Not in creating barriers in the way of his own happiness.

Chapter
THIRTY

LIV CONCENTRATED HARD ON NOT PEERING DOWN THE TOP table to look at Arran for the hundredth time that evening. He was so goddamn handsome in that blue-green kilt. The black socks hugged his muscular calves and he'd rolled up the sleeves of his white shirt to reveal the hard contours of his forearms. Now he was lifting an arm to loosen the green cravat at the top of his waistcoat, and she was practically drooling in response.

It was true that a kilt made any man appear at least fifty percent more attractive, but a guy who was already as handsome as Arran? It was stratospheric.

The band were setting up across from the top table, and the other tables had been moved to the side of the long, high-ceilinged ballroom to make way for the dance floor in the center. Portraits of stuffy old lairds and ladies lined the wood-paneled room, watching everyone enjoying themselves with condescending expressions. Evening guests were arriving and taking their seats as Sam and Maya made their way around the room to greet people.

Liv had lost count of how many times she'd looked over all Arran's lovely messages and photos, trying to analyze every single word. And the photo album was the icing on the cake. She couldn't get through it without becoming teary. Surely it all meant that Arran, true to his word, wanted to be with her. Something else occurred to her. Over the last several weeks, Arran had started referring to Rory by his actual name, rather than calling him "the boyfriend" in that resentful tone. Perhaps that was another sign that he was finally letting go of his relationship with Jess. And that predated anything that had happened between the two of them, so maybe it all had been completely over in his mind before they'd even kissed. Which would mean that his relationship with Jess would have been over even if Liv weren't on the scene, and she was not a third wheel by any measure.

She was in no doubt that she loved him, and her little seed of hope that he loved her back had been nurtured and grown by Arran's sweet and winsome gestures. So only one barrier remained—was she brave enough to take a chance on a relationship with him? The stakes were high. She could lose her best friend, and Jayce, if it went wrong. And the chances of her making a wrong move must be high given her emotional baggage and inexperience with long-term relationships.

The speeches were over and Liv had been impressed at how Sam had managed to give a coherent and touching address, despite having drunk a considerable amount of wine over dinner. Though it was a good thing he'd gone before Maya, because her speech had brought the house down. Nobody would have wanted to follow that little number.

Something tugged at her arm and she startled out of her reverie. Elise was pulling her in. "Listen to me. The band are getting ready for the first dance, so you need to get yourself sorted out before you and I join them on the dance floor with Arran and Nico."

Liv's heart rose into her throat and she swallowed, bringing her eyes up to meet Elise's. "I'm scared, Elise."

Elise gathered her into a hug. "What are you scared of?"

Her pulse picked up speed. "Of messing up. Of driving him away."

Elise sighed. "I understand. However, I think you need to look at it this way—you'd have nothing to lose by taking a chance, but a lifetime of happiness to lose if you didn't. Take Arran and Jess, for example. They're on good terms, despite a messy breakup, and they have lovely Jayce to show for it." Elise pulled back to meet her eyes. "But if you want my opinion, you and Arran are the real deal. We can all see it."

Liv tried to speak, but the lump in her throat hindered her.

Elise took her hand, looking at their entwined fingers. Her voice was quiet. "What could've gone more wrong with Harry and me than him dying and leaving me alone? Our son won't even remember him."

Liv sucked in a sharp breath, her heart cracking in two. She closed her eyes briefly to squeeze back the hot sting of tears.

Elise swallowed, clearly working hard to keep her voice even. "But I regret nothing. I wouldn't have missed out on a single day with him, and I will *always* cherish the time we had together."

The band announced the first dance, and Sam led Maya onto the dance floor, but Liv couldn't look at them; she was too caught up in the emotion in Elise's shimmering blue eyes.

"You have to do it, Liv. Take a leap of faith and trust that whatever happens, your time together will have been worth it."

The band announced that the best women and men would be joining the bride and groom, and still Liv couldn't tear her eyes from Elise. Until Nico arrived and held out his hand.

Elise gave Liv a smile, then took Nico's hand and followed him to the dance floor, where they joined Maya and Sam.

For a moment, her limbs felt heavy and stuck.

Then Arran was there. Taking her hand and lifting her to her feet, guiding her to the dance floor and moving with her in unison to the music. She gripped his strong shoulder and he held her waist securely, her hand in his as they moved across the dance floor to Louis Armstrong's "We Have All the Time in the World."

She'd been afraid that she'd prevent him from being happy, because she loved him and Jayce too much to mess it up. *Loved him*. She was so in love with him. But that meant gambling on him—on both of them—and finally, she realized she was equipped to meet the challenge. She wasn't going to let the legacy of Douchebag Dave taint her chance at happiness any longer.

The band called the rest of the guests to join the dance, and the floor quickly became packed. Arran pulled her closer, hugging her to him. With her heels on, the top of her head reached just under his chin. They fit together perfectly, in every way. The epiphany that Elise had helped her to reach shone brightly, lighting up her soul and burning away the remnants of her fears. She needed to tell him how she felt.

She lifted her head, intending to ask him if they could go somewhere to talk.

"We need to talk," he told her, before she got the chance.

"Yes," she said, and as the song ended, she tugged his hand to lead them from the dance floor and across the stone floor, exiting the ballroom into the bar area. Liv scanned around for where might be quiet to talk, but there were people everywhere.

"This way," Arran said, leading her toward the spiral staircase that led down to the entrance hall, and sneaking past the "No Entry" sign that blocked the way up. They ascended right to the top, their shoes creating an echo on the stone steps that reverberated ahead of them, as if finding the summit by echolocation.

The stairs gave way to a small room at the top of the turret, containing one small window overlooking the grounds. It was cool up there after the heat of the reception, and Liv wrapped her arms around herself.

Arran pulled her to his chest. "I should've brought my jacket for you."

"It's okay," she said, pressing her cheek to his chest and breathing him in. "I prefer this to a jacket."

He tightened his arms around her in response. Liv lifted her hand to touch his face. "I need to tell you something."

"Wait," he said, softly. "I have to say something first." He took a deep breath. "I'm hoping you've guessed by now that I want us to be a couple. A family, with Jayce." He fingered one of the ringlets that framed her face. "I wish I'd known everything you've been going through sooner, so I could've been there for you. But I'm here now, sweetheart, and I'm not going anywhere. I'll give you as much time as you need to work through whatever you have to. I can wait as long as it takes for you to be ready."

He paused to take another big breath, and she lifted a finger to his lips. They were so soft. "You have exactly zero seconds to wait. Because that's what I wanted to tell you. I want us to make a go of it. Make a go of *us*." She brushed her finger over his lower lip and absorbed the way his eyes darkened in response. "I love you," she whispered. "That's what I was coming to tell you that Saturday morning, when Jess answered the door in her tiny undies."

He laughed softly, closing his eyes. When he opened them again, the moonlight shone on his face, lighting up the gold of his eyes with a silver tone. A smile spread over his features as he brought her closer, resting his forehead against hers the way he'd done that night on Skye. "That is music to my ears. I love you too. I realized after our first time together, but the reality is I've loved you much longer than that." He eased back a little to look into her eyes. "You don't need to worry about taking a back seat ever again, because you will always come first with me. You and Jayce are my whole world, and I've got you. Okay?"

She nodded, tears welling in her eyes as he kissed her softly. But it was mere seconds before the touch of his lips had trails of fire seeping like rivulets down her body, making her breasts tighten and a liquid heat pulse in her core.

Liv buried her fingers in the soft coils of his hair, bringing his mouth down harder onto hers and igniting the tinder that had been gathering inside her all day as she'd watched him in that goddamn sexy kilt.

Arran teased her mouth with his tongue, sliding his hand down her side onto her skirt, his breath hitching as his fingers touched her skin and slid up the outside of her thigh. "I've been thinking about this all day," he murmured. He moved his mouth onto her neck, then lower, kissing and biting the skin of her shoulder. "You look so beautiful. And really fucking hot."

Something electric shocked into Liv's core and she pressed closer to him, a hardness digging into her thigh. His sporran, or something else?

Arran shifted her back against the wall and slid both his hands under her skirt and onto her arse, moving them up to where her flimsy underwear rode low on her hips. He hooked his fingers over the fabric and tugged them slowly down her legs, keeping his gaze locked on hers. "Is this okay?"

"Hell yes," she breathed, and he gave her a wicked smile.

Arran got to his knees, lifting her leg over his shoulder. He brushed his lips slowly up the inside of her thigh, making her shiver uncontrollably. She flattened her palms against the cold wall behind her, willing him to move faster, to reach where she needed his touch. But he kept his movements slow, teasing her until the ache between her legs was agonizingly exquisite.

Arran paused, hovering over her core, the heat of his breath on her skin. Then he buried his face between her legs and she let out a sharp gasp, shuddering in response.

Gripping her backside, he pulled her closer, licking his tongue over the exquisite sensitivity, then driving it inside her. She moaned, hearing the sound echo down the stone stairs and not giving a shit if anybody heard her.

Liv dug her fingers into his hair. Perhaps they'd get caught, but it was too good for her to care. Arran licked his tongue over her, teasing her, kissing her, sucking her. He drove her closer and closer to the edge, until the only word she could remember was his name.

But she needed more. She needed him.

She tangled her fingers into his hair, shifting his head gently away. Then she tugged him to his feet and swung his sporran around to the back, lifting his kilt. "You'd better be a true Scotsman under here."

"Of course," he said, his breathing labored as he lifted her against the wall to straddle him. His hard tip brushed against her core and she shivered with anticipation. Bracing them against the wall, he drove into her, catching her gasp with his mouth.

"I've never had sex wearing a kilt before," he breathed.

"Shame," she said, a smile on her face. "When it's really rather convenient."

He laughed softly, then thrust harder, and her smile gave way to an open-mouthed gasp as she was overwhelmed by sensation. The hardness of him driving into her, his hot mouth on her skin, the thrill of sneaking off to have sex at the top of a tower. But most of all, love. She loved him with every fiber of her being.

"Arran," she cried out, as the ripples of her orgasm tightened around him.

He groaned into her neck, saying her name as he came. He pressed them against the wall, holding her close, her legs still wrapped around him as they both trembled with the intensity of it.

Eventually, he lifted his head to kiss her, before gently untangling them to lower her to the floor. "I could keep those gorgeous legs of yours wrapped around me all the livelong day."

She laughed. "You can carry me around like that if you want. Cuddled against your front like a koala. I'm probably small enough without the heels."

He smiled down at her. "I love how petite you are. Petite, but superstrong. A force to be reckoned with in a small package." He kissed her. "But I have to say, I loved the fact that you kept those heels on."

She smiled against his mouth. "Noted. And I have to say, I love this risqué side of you."

He grinned. "The gloves are off now, baby. I'm all yours."

She nipped his lower lip with her teeth. "Glad to hear it."

Arran gripped her more tightly. "Careful. Or I'll need to have you again, then everyone will wonder where we've gone."

Liv laughed. "Come on. We need to get back." She grabbed her underwear to slide it back on, then tugged him toward the stairs.

He groaned.

"Don't worry," she said. "You're invited to my room tonight."

He grinned, pausing at the top of the stairs and holding out his hand for her to take. "Awesome."

They descended and arrived back behind the "No Entry" sign, which made her chuckle and raise her eyebrows suggestively at Arran. There had been plenty of entry, all right.

He tugged her close as they laughed softly, Liv scanning from the shadows so they could time their exit.

Managing to slip out onto the stone landing toward the bar, holding hands, Arran swung their arms while pretending to whistle nonchalantly. Liv dissolved into laughter. Nobody made her laugh like he did. She eyed him, again admiring how devastating he looked in that kilt. The thought that one day he'd wear one to their wedding popped into her head, bringing with it the most wonderful feeling of serenity and contentment, and not an ounce of fear along with it. The only palpitations she felt were those of excitement.

Glancing up, she spotted Nico watching them across the bar. He flashed them a grin and held up his glass.

"Don't look now, but I think Nico's rumbled us," she whispered to Arran.

"Mm-hmm," Arran replied in a surreptitious tone. "And he's not the only one."

She shifted her gaze over to where he was gesturing and spotted Elise, who was giving them a soft smile. Liv raised her hand in a little wave and gave her a big grin back.

HIS ENTIRE BODY WAS FILLED WITH A DELICIOUS ACHE. LIKE HE'D had a vigorous workout at the gym the previous day. Arran opened his eyes, taking in the old-style opulence of the four-poster bed and the tartan-clad room around them.

Except he hadn't been to the gym, but rather had a personal workout with the lovely Olivia Agnes Holland. All night long.

Smiling, he trailed a finger along her naked thigh and over her waist to where her arm was holding a sheet against her front. He loved this contradiction of a woman. Sweet, empathic, and could probably kill you with her bare hands. Warmth filled his chest, and he realized that the hollow sensation that had plagued him for the past year had disappeared.

She stirred, opening those gorgeous green eyes and pinning him with her gaze. "Morning, you total sex god."

"Well," he said, bending an elbow behind his head with a shrug. "I do try."

Liv shifted over to kiss him, then glanced over his shoulder. "Shit. We're late for breakfast."

Arran looked at the clock. "Fuck."

They both jumped out of bed and had a hurried shower, Arran cursing that they didn't have time to re-create what they'd done the last time they'd showered together.

"Later," Liv had whispered when he'd complained, and that was all he needed to hear.

They left the bedroom in a hurry, holding hands and laughing as they descended the large sweeping staircase that led from the bedrooms to the ground floor of the castle. Despite being late, they still found time to laugh at each other's crap jokes, and it occurred to him, not for the first time, that not only did nobody make him laugh the way that she did, but nobody got his dumb jokes and laughed back like Liv.

The memory of waiting for her to emerge into the wedding gazebo, his heart in his throat, surfaced, along with that random but oh-so-right thought about the piper—*when I marry Liv, we'll have a string quartet instead*. Then something that Jess had told him randomly popped into his head. *"She's a good one. Hold on to her."*

Liv went to lead them around the corner, but he tugged her back, watching her eyes widen and pupils dilate as he brought her into a kiss. He broke off to press her gently against the wall. "I need to ask you something."

Her lips were swollen and her eyes hazy from their kiss. "What is it?"

He took a breath, pulse accelerating. "Just a hypothetical at this point. But what would you say if at some point soon, I asked you to marry me?"

Her breath hitched as she searched his face. "Are you being serious?"

He arched an eyebrow. "Deadly serious."

She let out a soft laugh, then paused for a couple of seconds.

"We only became a couple last night, so that thought should probably terrify me. And yet . . ." Her eyes sparkled.

"And yet what?" he asked, tucking her hair behind her ear.

Liv smiled. "And yet it feels completely right." She touched his face. "I was even thinking the same thing myself."

He gave her his best catalog pout. "Is that because I looked so awesome in my kilt, you couldn't help but want to marry me?"

She grabbed the front of his shirt to pull him into a kiss, taking his breath away. Then she broke off to whisper, "Yeah, pretty much."

Arran smiled against her mouth. "So, the answer to my hypothetical proposal is . . . ?"

"Yes," she whispered, her eyes shining.

"Excellent," he said softly. He took her hand to lead them down the corridor. "You know what this means, don't you?"

She shook her head. "What?"

He grinned. "It means we're engaged to be engaged."

Liv laughed. "Pre-engaged."

They reached the door of the breakfast room, and he gave her hand a squeeze. "Do you want to tell the others?"

"About us being a couple? Yes." She broke into a smile. "But let's keep the pre-engagement our special secret."

"No problem, Aggie," he said, giving her a wink.

The breakfast room was housed in the library, with all the bridal party already in place tucking into full Scottish breakfasts around tables of varying sizes.

Sam eyed the two of them as they took seats next to him at the main table. "Morning."

Arran ran a hand over the top of his hair. "Good morning. How's married life?"

Sam grinned, shifting his hand to hold Maya's. "Awesome."

Maya turned and leaned across Sam to give them each a kiss

on the cheek. "Hello there. You two are looking rather *rosy* this morning."

Arran felt heat rising in his face, and as he glanced at Liv, he saw pink was staining her cheeks. He cleared his throat. "Yeah, well. Being in love suits us."

Maya's mouth dropped open and she squealed. Everyone in the breakfast room turned to look at them. She waved her hand. "Never you mind, people. Back to your business." There was a ripple of laughter and Maya shoved her chair closer to Sam's, sliding an arm around his shoulders to lean over him and address the two of them. "It's pretty clear that my husband and I weren't the only ones getting some action on our wedding night."

Liv laughed, shifting closer to Arran and bringing their entwined hands into her lap. He got the feeling she was reassuring him about the embarrassment of Maya's teasing. But he didn't feel embarrassed, simply happy. He looked at her and she gave him a little wink. The warmth of their special secret shone brightly in his heart.

"Well, *Mrs.* M," Liv said. "As you once told me, I have to grab my Mr. Darcy by the waistcoat."

Maya grinned. "Or perhaps, Miss O, by the kilt?"

"Indeed," Liv replied, smiling up at Arran.

"ARRAN, I SWEAR TO GOD, IF I FALL AND KNOCK OVER A PAINT POT, then it's totally your fault."

"I won't let you fall, Liv."

She felt him guide her into the studio, his hands over her eyes. "Okay . . . here," he said. "Ready?"

Her heart was beating hard with anticipation. "Yes."

He dropped his hands from her eyes to circle her waist, holding her close as she took in the painting.

Her heart nearly stopped. "It's so beautiful," she breathed.

Arran kissed her neck. "That's because it's of you."

"I love it," she said, joy filling her soul to the brim.

Elise called from the hallway. "Can we come and see now?"

"Yep," Arran said. "Come in."

Elise and Nico entered the studio, taking in the painting and exclaiming how talented her boyfriend was.

"I know," Liv said, bringing his head down from behind to kiss him.

"Ugh," Nico said, smiling as he left the studio. "Get a room."

Liv laughed as Arran pretended to aim a kick at Nico's arse, and they all followed him back to the kitchen, where Jayce and Jack were drawing at Jayce's low plastic table.

Elise smiled as she poured them some tea. "What do you think Maya and Sam are doing right now?"

Nico raised his eyebrows. "Right *now*? On their honeymoon? Shame on you for such dirty thoughts, Kowalski."

Elise shot him a look that would have felled a bear. Though Nico was kind of built like one. "That's not what I mean. Get your mind out of the gutter." She sipped her tea, muttering, "Though I'm aware that's where it permanently resides."

A smile tugged at the corner of Nico's mouth, and Liv couldn't help her mind drifting to that enemies-to-lovers suspicion again.

Arran tugged her hand to bring her onto his knee. "I reckon they'll be carving up the slopes in the Alps, then having a bit of après-ski."

"I hope they're having an amazing time," Elise said, staring off wistfully.

"They will be," Nico said, giving her a smile that was decidedly softer than the usual wry one he aimed at her.

Liv hadn't been at all surprised when Maya and Sam had opted to find a resort at enough of an altitude that skiing in June was possible. The pair were ski obsessed.

Elise and Nico started debating the merits of skiing in the French Alps. Well, it was more of an argument than a debate.

Arran leaned in to brush his lips against her ear, sending a tingle down her spine. "I need you to do me a favor later," he said in a low voice.

"What's that?" she murmured.

He gave her a wicked grin. "Pin me to the bed and screw me senseless, karate kid."

Smiling, she kissed him, the tingling sensation firing into every nerve ending in her body. "Your wish is my command."

L IV RUMMAGED AROUND IN THE STORE CUPBOARD, WONDERING why Mrs. MacKay couldn't find her own bloody stationery. The older teacher had come into Liv's class when there were only twenty minutes of the school day left and asked her to go and find some colored card stock. Apparently, the cupboard was too dimly lit for Liv's colleague to see the color she wanted.

After what seemed like half an hour, though a look at her watch confirmed it had only been five minutes, Liv located said card stock buried under some boxes of pens. *Weird that someone moved it under there.*

She lifted the pile of card stock and left the cupboard, turning off the light and closing the door behind her. As she made her way back to the classroom, she gave the teaching assistant in Mrs. MacKay's class a wee wave. The assistant gave her a wave—plus a knowing smile—in return. That was a little odd.

Arran popped into her mind, and her heart lifted at the thought of seeing him in a mere few hours. They had been spending every night at his place over the last couple of months, and it was weird how everything had just fallen into place—as if they'd always been not just a couple, but a little family with wee Jayce right at the center.

Her sense of comfort and grounding had been cemented by her mum and Angus funding her some private therapy, with Arran being there to support her every step of the way. Although her journey where that was concerned wasn't over, it was well underway.

Turning to enter her classroom with a happy sigh, she found the main area unexpectedly empty. Shuffling noises and giggling came from the back room, which housed the painting corner.

Frowning, Liv moved toward the back, hoping that the kids weren't running rings around Mrs. MacKay. Though surely not, because the woman certainly ruled her own class very firmly and was a stickler for the rules.

As she entered the space, the kids all froze, looking at her and then over to Mrs. MacKay with cheeky smiles on their faces.

Liv gave them all a bemused look. "What's going on?" she asked, taking in a row of five easels behind the children, all of which were turned away from her.

Mrs. MacKay shot her a knowing smile, not unlike the one that her assistant had doled out a minute before. "Okay, children. Take it away."

There was a burst of chatter and scrambling as the children assembled around each easel, then scraping noises as they worked together to turn them all around.

Liv stood open-mouthed as the paper side of the easels came into view. Each had a colorful word painted upon it in the children's hands. And together, they read:

Will you marry me Liv?

She blinked, attempting to understand why her class was proposing to her. Then a noise made her turn her head. Her pulse picked up as Arran appeared from behind the bookcase in the reading area, where he must have been crouching the whole time, out of sight. Jayce was with him, holding his dad's hand on one side and carrying a little black box on the other.

A burst of excitement made her drop the pile of card stock, pieces fluttering all over the floor and making a terrible mess that she didn't care about in the slightest.

Arran gave her a soft smile as they reached her.

She swallowed hard, heart hammering. "Arran?"

He looked down at Jayce, giving him a nod.

Jayce stepped forward, a serious expression on his little face. He opened the box, and Arran simultaneously got down on one knee.

Liv's heart rose right into her throat, and the children all burst into excited chatter.

"Shh, children!" Mrs. MacKay said, the smile nearly splitting her face.

Jayce held up the box, where a shiny silver ring set with her birthstone twinkled. Jayce cleared his throat in an exaggerated manner. "Miss Lib, will you marry us?"

Happy tears pricked at her eyes as she took in the handsome man she was hopelessly in love with—down on one knee—with his adorable son, whom she cherished like her own, at his side. She blinked hard, trying to force her voice past the lump in her throat. "Of course I will," she managed to scratch out.

"Yes!" Jayce cried, pulling his plastic sword from out of the back of his jumper, where Liv hadn't even noticed he'd been hiding it. The rest of the class started screaming in delight and Mrs. MacKay had to come over and shush them all before they collapsed from overexcitement.

Arran was blinking hard, his eyes shining, as Jayce handed him the box. He tried to get up, but Jayce stopped him.

"Wait, Daddy."

Arran paused to look at him.

Jayce solemnly lifted his sword and touched it to each of Arran's shoulders in turn. "I now dub you: Miss Lib's husband."

Liv let out a laugh at the same time as Arran, who pulled Jayce into a hug. "Thanks, pal. Now help your old man up."

Jayce took Arran's hand and Arran made a show of getting to his feet, holding on to his back as if he were pained and then giving Jayce a wink.

He stepped over the pieces of card stock fanning at her feet and took out the ring, meeting her gaze steadily as he placed it on her left ring finger. It fit perfectly.

Liv lifted it, lost for words. "How did you know my size?"

He grinned. "Maya and Elise."

She smiled. "Of course."

Arran took her chin gently, lifting her face to his for a soft kiss. It was met with a mixture of cheering and "yuck" noises from the kids.

He pulled back, running his thumb over her bottom lip with a smile. "It's just a temporary ring. Until I can save enough for a big sparkly diamond."

She shook her head, drinking in the liquid honey of his eyes. "No. I like this one."

His jaw worked, and he nodded, giving her another kiss, which he broke off after a few seconds because the "yuck" noises were starting to drown out the cheering.

"Okay, guys," he said, turning to the kids and rubbing his hands together. "Thank you all! Operation Marry Miss Holland is a big success."

Jayce whooped loudly as he galloped round his cheering class-mates, like a victorious knight on horseback.

———

LATER THAT EVENING THE FAIRY LIGHTS TWINKLED AROUND THE edge of the fort, filling the area with a warm glow that matched the one inside Liv's chest. The TV played quietly across the living room, visible through the open end of the fort.

She snuggled closer into Arran's side and he tightened his arm around her, bending his head to kiss the top of hers. Jayce was lying sleeping on Arran's chest, his little fingers curled around Liv's index finger as he snoozed.

"I should really take him up to bed," Arran murmured, the soft rumble of his voice soothing her cheek.

"Just five more minutes," Liv said, letting out a contented sigh and taking a deep breath of both the gorgeous scent of Arran and the adorable smell of Jayce.

Arran's voice was laden with love. "Okay, Aggie."

She shifted her face to nestle into his neck, taking in the way he shivered in response. She eyed Jayce's fist clasped around her finger, and her engagement ring shining on the same hand.

Arran kissed the top of her head. "When do you want to get married?"

She gave him a squeeze. "I really don't mind. As long as I get to have you forever."

He chuckled, rubbing her back. "Done deal. I was thinking about next year, maybe? Or the year after? I want to save up enough dosh to give you everything you want."

She shook her head. "All I want is you and Jayce. But I don't mind waiting if you prefer." She lifted her head to look into his eyes. "Although I thought you said that long engagements were a bad idea."

He smiled. "Not if they're with the right person."

Her heart practically glowing with warmth, she leaned up to kiss him. "I love you guys. Our wee family."

He kissed her back softly. "We love you too."

Jayce stirred, and Arran froze—a "yikes" expression on his face making Liv stifle a laugh.

"Okay. I'm going to take him up and get him settled," Arran said, gathering Jayce close and managing to shift out of the fort and onto his feet like a pro. "You stay here and think about me until I get back."

Liv chuckled. "No problem. Pretty much got you on my mind twenty-four seven anyway."

He gave her a wink over his shoulder. "Good girl."

He left the room to climb the stairs with Jayce in his arms, and Liv shifted onto her back to gaze at the fairy lights, utterly content with her brilliant lot in life. Plans were already afoot for their travel adventure with Jayce next summer, and for the first time ever, she felt she had things to look forward to. Gone was the dread in the pit of her stomach whenever she pictured a future with a man, and instead joy shone in her heart whenever she contemplated what was to come with Arran.

He came back down the stairs and into the fort, lying down next to her and tucking an arm around her middle, rolling her onto her side to look at him as he propped himself up on his elbow. He gave her a coy smile. "Hi."

"Hi," she said, unable to keep the grin off her face.

"Miss me?"

"Yes." She gave him a kiss and then let out a contented sigh. "I can't believe we're finally together. After all that's happened."

"I know," he said, kissing her forehead. "I feel like the luckiest guy in the world. I hate to say it, but at one point I thought this was never going to happen."

Liv chuckled. "At one point? How about for bloody years, on my part."

Arran frowned, cocking his head. "Years?"

"Yeah," she said. "Or is this the wrong moment to confess that I've fancied you since we were, like, twelve years old?"

His mouth dropped open. "You had a crush on me for fifteen years?"

"Yep."

Arran's eyes darkened, and he suddenly flipped them over so that he was lying on top of her, eliciting a little squeal from her lips.

"That's hot," he said, his voice husky.

"Is it?" she asked, the last syllable turning into a gasp as he kissed her neck.

"Fuck yes," he muttered, biting her skin gently. He slid a hand down onto her thigh, then around to squeeze her arse. He lifted his head to meet her eyes. "I wish I'd known you liked me like that. We could have had more time together."

She shook her head. "I think it was meant to be. Because this way, we got to have Jayce."

Arran swallowed hard, lifting a hand to caress her cheek. His voice came out hoarse. "I love you so much. I'd move heaven and earth for you. You know that?"

She smiled, absorbing the adoration in his eyes. "I know you would," she said softly. "And I love you too. Always."

ACKNOWLEDGMENTS

Thank you so much for reading Liv and Arran's story! I hope it brought you a wee bit of joy.

I need to thank my husband, Mark, who is my absolute rock. His unwavering support buoys me through the worst imposter-syndrome-ridden storms. He also bigs me up at every turn and even pitches my books at his workplace! Sorry, Mark's colleagues. Hope you like romance!

Many thanks to my wonderful Berkley editor, Kerry Donovan, who never fails to pin down exactly how to make my books shine. Also thank you to Kerry's fabulous assistant, Genni Eccles, and to Jessica Plummer and Kristin Cipolla in marketing and publicity over at Berkley for their endless patience in answering my daft emails.

Many thanks to Monika Roe and Rita Frangie Batour for the fantastic US cover illustration and design.

Also at Berkley I'd like to thank the following people who worked on this book: Chelsea Pascoe, Elisha Katz, Christine Legon, Joi Walker, Caitlyn Kenny, Eileen Chetti, Alicia Hyman, and Crystal Erickson.

Thank you to my lovely editor Audrey Linton at HQ Digital for all her hard work on the UK editing side, and to all of the Harper-Collins team, including copy editor Helena Newton, proofreader Eldes Tran, cover designer Anna Sikorska, and Hanako Peace and Isabel Williams in marketing and publicity.

At the Madeleine Milburn Literary, TV & Film Agency, I need to thank my amazing agent, Hannah Todd, and also the lovely Elinor Davies. Thank you to Valentina Paulmichl in the foreign rights team and Hannah Ladds and Casey Dexter in the film/TV team.

Thank you to fellow authors Katherine Dyson and Emma Jackson, who beta read an early version of this book for me and provided invaluable feedback.

I am really grateful for the support of all my fellow romance writers, in particular the Romantic Novelists' Association Scottish Chapter, headed up by the fantastic Mairibeth MacMillan, and the RNA Conference Ryanette's WhatsApp group (named after Ryan Reynolds, naturally). I'm also grateful for the support from the Chick Lit and Prosecco Facebook group plus Writers' Dream House, both headed up by fabulous chick in charge Anita Faulkner. The romance writing community is such a supportive place, and I am lucky to be a part of it.

If you missed Maya and Sam's story,

THE EX-MAS HOLIDAYS,

keep reading for an excerpt.

WHERE THE HELL ARE YOU, YOU FOOT-CRIPPLING LITTLE devils?"

Maya rummaged in the passenger-side footwell among various bags in order to find her heels, kicking off her trainers in favor of the more fitting party footwear.

Upon opening the car door to a blast of ice-cold air, she paused to put on her jacket before climbing out. *How is it possible for the temperature to drop about fifty bloody degrees when I've only traveled forty miles north?* Goodness knows how much colder it'd be when she continued on up the road later that evening.

As she strode out along the gentle incline of the driveway, she was distracted by the imposing size of the massive mansions on the cul-de-sac. Her feet went out from under her, and she only just managed to grab hold of a railing, narrowly preventing a fall onto her backside. "Shit!" Looking up, she checked that none of Kirsty's posh neighbors were around to hear her yelling that expletive. A glance back down confirmed the subtle shimmer of ice on the paving. "Bloody hell. Stupid winter weather."

A thought crossed her mind—was it a good idea to leave all her worldly possessions in the boot, outside, in the dark? *It's a nice area. Should be okay.*

There was something sad about the fact that her whole life fit in the back of her car. Sacrificing all the big items of furniture to Rich had seemed sensible when they divided it up—he was going to a new flat after all. *No point wasting money on storage when I'm going to be a sad twentysomething living in my childhood bedroom for the foreseeable future.* It's not as if there had been loads of stuff anyway. Their flat and ultimately their mortgage had been modest with her having chosen to work at a small accountancy firm and Rich opting to take on a finance role for a charity.

Though there had been a couple of items that had sentimental value, and were smaller. Such as the vintage Royal Albert afternoon tea plate that she would have loved to bring home in order for her and Liv to place scones upon it and pretend to take tea with Mr. Darcy and Mr. Bingley. But it had been a gift from Rich's mum, therefore Maya had relinquished it to him. Rich didn't even like afternoon tea, or scones. And he certainly wasn't partial to either Darcy or Bingley. But still, it was the right thing to do and, in any case, she was getting too old to be pretending that she was a character in a Jane Austen novel.

Maya picked her way to the front door, arms outstretched and legs akimbo, like the most inept trapeze artist in existence. There were a couple more slips, and she heartily wished that she'd kept those damned trainers on, but she'd come too far to turn back now.

"Come on, Maya. Grow a pair of ovaries." Fixing her gaze on the doorway, and wondering where this newfound habit of talking to herself had come from, she continued on her mission. Without further incident she managed to complete her quest, and arrived on the sanctity of the doorstep, in order to ring the bell.

Blowing out a relieved breath, she watched it puff into little clouds of condensation, misting up the beautiful stained glass window embedded in the door. The realization that she wouldn't know anybody at the party except for Kirsty hit, and she fiddled with her charm bracelet.

The door opened with a flood of warmth. "You made it." Kirsty grabbed hold of her in a tight hug.

"Hi," Maya said, her voice muffled by Kirsty's sequined shoulder. "You look fab. And your new house is fantastic."

Kirsty released her with a smile, transitioning into a curtsy. "Why, thank you." Straightening up, she winked. "Come in. That's everybody here now. And I do mean *everybody*."

Maya stepped inside to secure less slippery footing. Before she could ask why Kirsty had emphasized the *everybody*, she was ushered down the wide hallway and into a large living room. The surroundings resembled something out of a show home, all clean lines and glass.

Kirsty pointed to each of her friends in turn. "These are my neighbors Donna and Karen. And this is Isabelle and Una from work . . ." She went on, introducing Maya to around ten women.

Fixing a smile on her face, Maya attempted to cover the fact that the names were immediately slipping her mind like water through a sieve.

Kirsty held out her hands. "Let me take your coat."

Maya removed it, adjusting her gold off-the-shoulder top. "Can I help with anything in the kitchen?"

"Absolutely not," Kirsty said, giving her a mock-stern stare. "It's all in hand."

For some reason, that statement raised a raucous cheer from the small crowd of women, which almost made Maya jump. It was nice that everyone was able to relax and not be on kitchen duty, but she wasn't sure why it merited such an energetic response. What were they all on? Snowballs and Christmas cheer, most likely.

The others began chatting among themselves, and Kirsty touched Maya's arm. "What drink order can I put in for you?"

Maya wished she could get a hearty slug of whatever was fueling the rest of these women, but there was driving to be done, and disapproving fathers to be faced. "Just a Diet Coke, please. I'm not staying over."

"You're driving back to Glenavie tonight?" Kirsty asked.

Maya played with her charm bracelet, her stomach tightening. "I figured it was better to face the music sooner rather than later."

Kirsty embraced her, giving her a squeeze. "Hopefully you'll settle in quickly. But are you sure you can't stay? The roads are icy."

Maya shook her head, plastering a smile on her face. "I'm in the mindset to get there now."

Kirsty nodded. "You can backtrack at any time if you have a change of heart. Maybe you'll fancy joining in the fun a bit more once you see what I've got in store."

Maya raised her eyebrows. Kirsty certainly seemed rather cloak-and-dagger this evening.

"Have a seat," Kirsty said, with a wink. "I'll be back in a sec."

Maya sat on the massive, soft gray sofa next to a couple of the other guests. The room was so stylishly decorated that it was difficult to keep her envious eyes off all the furnishings. It was clearly a new build, and Kirsty had the place done out to the nines.

A smiling woman wearing a black jumpsuit shifted over to take Maya's hand in a shake. "I'm Isabelle."

Maya returned her smile. "Maya. Nice to meet you."

Isabelle sipped her wine as she nodded toward the large living room window. "I can't believe how cold it's getting."

"I know," the woman next to Isabelle piped up. "*I* can't believe that it's so soon until Christmas." She leaned across Isabelle to address Maya, her black tasseled top nearly dangling into Isabelle's drink. "Hi, I'm Una."

Maya shook Una's hand across Isabelle's front, nearly clotheslining poor Isabelle in the process. "Great to meet you."

Una let out a loud sigh. "I haven't gotten *nearly* enough Christmas shopping done yet."

"Tell me about it," Isabelle replied, rolling her eyes. "I'm never going to get it done in time."

Maya's shoulders relaxed a little. Typical Scottish winter conversation made talking to new people easier. "Same. I've not even bought one present yet, because I'm in the middle of moving home. Literally. All my stuff is outside in the car." She stopped talking, aware that her mouth was running away with her.

"Really?" Isabelle asked, raising her eyebrows. "You're moving house tonight?"

"Yeah," Maya replied. She wished she had a drink in order to soothe her feelings of inadequacy—something stronger than the Diet Coke that Kirsty was fetching. She cleared her throat. "I'm moving home because I lost my job."

"Aw," Una said, reaching across Isabelle to take Maya's hand and nearly falling into Isabelle's lap. "Sorry to hear that. Especially at Christmas."

"Ah, it's fine," Maya said, waving her other hand and plastering on a grin. "Worse things happen at sea."

Why she was comparing her plight to a maritime incident, she had no idea. Since when did sailors lose their jobs, boyfriends, and flats, plus have to go home with their tails between their legs to face their disappointed fathers? Though, granted, Moby Dick probably *would* be worse. Or Jaws. Or Godzilla.

Isabelle leaned back, shooting Maya a sympathetic look. "But still. That must be very stressful. Where's home?"

"Glenavie," Maya replied, coming out of her sea monster ruminations. "Not too far from Glencoe."

"Ski country," Una said, a dreamy expression on her face. "Lovely.
At least it'll be nice and Christmassy."

The image of her Highland hometown entered Maya's mind,
adorned in twinkly Christmas lights and dusted with snow. Christmas in Glenavie was her favorite time of year. The idea of that infused a little comfort into her veins.

Kirsty reappeared with a couple of plates of nibbles, passing
them around the room. "There's more stuff in the oven, so help
yourselves. Oh, and, Maya, your drink's coming."

"No rush." Maya sat back to listen to her new acquaintances. It
occurred to her that Kirsty had said her drink was "coming," so
who was fetching it if not Kirsty?

She heard the door open behind her. The other women's voices
rose by a number of decibels, plus an octave or two. Turning her
head to find out what the kerfuffle was about, Maya was greeted by
the sight of a firm and perfectly shaped naked male bottom across
the huge floor space. A well-toned man had his back to her as he
handed out drinks, not wearing a stitch of clothing except for a tiny
apron around his waist, the strings of which were entwined with
tinsel.

Maya laughed, finally realizing why Kirsty had been behaving
in that "nudge-nudge, wink-wink" manner. Plus, why the women
seemed drunk on more than just alcohol. They were also high on
the sight of a hot naked man. She raised her eyebrows, turning
back to Isabelle and Una. "Kirsty's hired one of those naked wait-
ers, I see."

"Yes," said Isabelle, smiling. "He's been preparing and serving
our drinks. What a treat."

Maya shook her head. "That's what she meant when I arrived.
She was being all cryptic and like 'everybody' is here."

Isabelle laughed. "She *is* rather pleased with herself."

"*I'm* rather pleased too," Una said, eyeing the man's back. "He's bloody gorgeous."

"I wouldn't know," Maya replied with a shrug and a smile. "I've not seen his face yet."

Una sighed. "The back of him is as appealing as the front." She placed her hand onto her forehead in a mock swoon. "Sandy-brown hair, ravishing amber eyes, and a sexy closely trimmed beard. My favorite."

Isabelle snorted. "Don't pretend that you've been looking at his face, Una. Not with that perfectly chiseled torso."

Una laughed.

Sandy-brown hair and ravishing amber eyes. Maya had known a man of that description before, minus the beard. Though she'd been eager to forget him, and that task had taken her a little while. The realization hit that, very soon, she might see him on a more regular basis. *Another reason to dread going back.*

Kirsty was gesturing to the naked waiter. "The Diet Coke is for the lady over there, on the sofa." Kirsty pointed toward Maya.

"Here you go," Una whispered. "Brace yourself."

Maya smiled, shaking her head. Who was this guy? Chris Hemsworth? She was sure he couldn't be *that* devastating.

The man turned. Maya's smile froze on her face, her jaw dropping as she took in his familiar, handsome features with a sinking heart. "*Sam?*"

His face fell, the creaminess of his cheeks staining pink. "Maya."

ZOE ALLISON was brought up in a mixed-race family in Yorkshire, but now lives in Scotland with her husband, two children, and a massive notebook collection. Her favorite pastimes include reading, movies, music, and pop culture, and walking into rooms and then forgetting what she went in there for.

Growing up, she always enjoyed stories about falling in love. But rather than daydreaming of being rescued by a knight in shining armor, she would imagine fighting dragons alongside him.

As an adult, she went to medical school and became a doctor. However, as time passed, she began to crave a creative outlet to counter the burnout that her career inflicted upon her, and also to achieve the happy endings that were so often lacking in the real world. And so, she began to write romance.

VISIT ZOE ALLISON ONLINE

ZoeAllison.co.uk

ZoeAllisonAuth1

Zoe.Allison.9279

ZoeAllisonAuthor

ZoeAllisonAuthor

Ready to find
your next great read?

Let us help.

Visit prh.com/nextread

Penguin
Random
House